SHALAKO
&
CATLOW

Bantam Books by Louis L'Amour

ASK YOUR BOOKSELLER FOR THE BOOKS YOU HAVE MISSED.

NOVELS
Bendigo Shafter
Borden Chantry
Brionne
The Broken Gun
The Burning Hills
The Californios
Callaghen
Catlow
Chancy
The Cherokee Trail
Comstock Lode
Conagher
Crossfire Trail
Dark Canyon
Down the Long Hills
The Empty Land
Fair Blows the Wind
Fallon
The Ferguson Rifle
The First Fast Draw
Flint
Guns of the Timberlands
Hanging Woman Creek
The Haunted Mesa
Heller with a Gun
The High Graders
High Lonesome
Hondo
How the West Was Won
The Iron Marshal
The Key-Lock Man
Kid Rodelo
Kilkenny
Killoe
Kilrone
Kiowa Trail
Last of the Breed
Last Stand at Papago Wells
The Lonesome Gods
The Man Called Noon
The Man from Skibbereen
The Man from the Broken
   Hills
Matagorda
Milo Talon
The Mountain Valley War
North to the Rails
Over on the Dry Side
Passin' Through

The Proving Trail
The Quick and the Dead
Radigan
Reilly's Luck
The Rider of Lost Creek
Rivers West
The Shadow Riders
Shalako
Showdown at Yellow
   Butte
Silver Canyon
Son of a Wanted Man
Taggart
The Tall Stranger
To Tame a Land
Tucker
Under the Sweetwater Rim
Utah Blaine
The Walking Drum
Westward the Tide
Where the Long Grass
   Blows

SHORT STORY
COLLECTIONS
Beyond the Great Snow
   Mountains
Bowdrie
Bowdrie's Law
Buckskin Run
The Collected Short Stories
   of Louis L'Amour
   (vols. 1–7)
Dutchman's Flat
End of the Drive
From the Listening Hills
The Hills of Homicide
Law of the Desert Born
Long Ride Home
Lonigan
May There Be a Road
Monument Rock
Night over the Solomons
Off the Mangrove Coast
The Outlaws of Mesquite
The Rider of the Ruby
   Hills
Riding for the Brand
The Strong Shall Live
The Trail to Crazy Man

Valley of the Sun
War Party
West from Singapore
West of Dodge
With These Hands
Yondering

SACKETT TITLES
Sackett's Land
To the Far Blue
   Mountains
The Warrior's Path
Jubal Sackett
Ride the River
The Daybreakers
Sackett
Lando
Mojave Crossing
Mustang Man
The Lonely Men
Galloway
Treasure Mountain
Lonely on the Mountain
Ride the Dark Trail
The Sackett Brand
The Sky-Liners

THE HOPALONG CASSIDY
NOVELS
The Riders of High Rock
The Rustlers of West Fork
The Trail to Seven Pines
Trouble Shooter

NONFICTION
Education of a
   Wandering Man
Frontier
THE SACKETT COMPANION:
   A Personal Guide to the
   Sackett Novels
A TRAIL OF MEMORIES:
   The Quotations of
   Louis L'Amour,
   compiled by
   Angelique L'Amour

POETRY
Smoke from This Altar

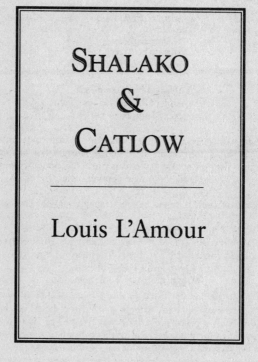

SHALAKO
&
CATLOW

Louis L'Amour

BANTAM BOOKS

SHALAKO / CATLOW
A Bantam Book / March 2008

Published by Bantam Dell
A Division of Random House, Inc.
New York, New York

Photograph of Louis L'Amour by John Hamilton—Globe Photos, Inc.

Bantam Books and the rooster colophon are registered trademarks
of Random House, Inc.

ISBN 978-0-553-59181-1

Printed in the United States of America
Published simultaneously in Canada

www.bantamdell.com

OPM   10 9 8 7 6 5 4 3

SHALAKO

To Casey

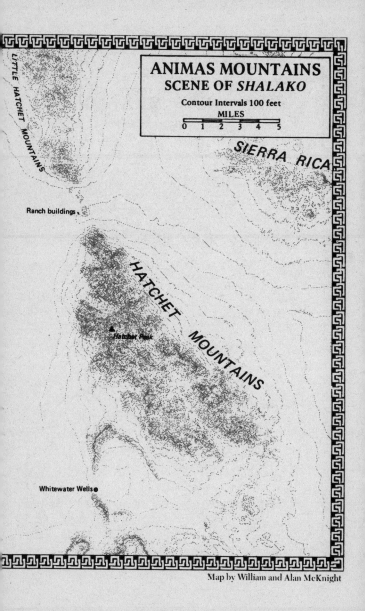

ANIMAS MOUNTAINS
SCENE OF *SHALAKO*

Contour Intervals 100 feet

MILES

0 1 2 3 4 5

LITTLE HATCHET MOUNTAINS

SIERRA RICA

Ranch buildings

HATCHET MOUNTAINS

Hatchet Peak

Whitewater Wells

Map by William and Alan McKnight

CHAPTER 1

FOR SEVEN DAYS in the spring of 1882 the man called Shalako heard no sound but the wind . . .

No sound but the wind, the creak of his saddle, the hoofbeats of his horse.

Seven days riding the ghost trails up out of Sonora, down from the Sierra Madre, through Apache country, keeping off the skylines, and watching the beckoning fingers of the talking smoke.

Lean as a famine wolf but wide and thick in the shoulder, the man called Shalako was a brooding man, a wary man, a man who trusted to no fate, no predicted destiny, nor to any luck. He trusted to nothing but his weapons, his horse, and the caution with which he rode.

His hard-boned face was tanned to saddle leather under the beat-up, black, flat-crowned hat. He wore fringed shotgun chaps, a faded red shirt, a black handkerchief knotted about his throat, and a dozen scars of knife and bullet.

It was a baked and brutal land, this Sonora, sun-blistered and arid, yet as he sifted his way through the stands of organ-pipe cactus, prickly pear and cat's claw, he knew the desert throbbed with its own strange life, and he knew those slim fingers of lifting smoke beckoned death.

He was a lone-riding man in a lonesome country,

riding toward a destiny of which he knew nothing, a man who for ten long years had known no other life than this, nor wished for any other.

What else there was he had known before, but now he lived from day to day, watching the lonely sunsets flame and die, bleeding their crimson shadows against the long, serrated ridges. Watching the dawns come, seeing the mornings stir with their first life . . . and the land he rode was a land where each living thing lived by the death of some other thing.

The desert was a school, a school where each day, each hour, a final examination was offered, where failure meant death and the buzzards landed to correct the papers.

For the desert holds no easy deaths . . . hard, bitter, and ugly are the desert deaths . . . and long drawn out.

Merciless were the raw-backed mountains, dreadfully desolate the canyons, the white-faced ancient lakes were dust . . . traps where a man might die, choking horribly upon alkali or the ashen powder of ancient rocks.

For seven days Shalako heard no sound but that of his own passage, and then a gunshot bought space in the silence, a harsh whiplash of sound, followed after an instant by the shattering volley of at least four rifles.

The rifles spoke again from the sounding board of the rocks, racketing away down the canyons to fade at the desert's rim.

Motionless upon a sun-baked slope, he waited while the sweat found thin furrows through the dust on his cheeks, but there was no further sound, no further shot, nor was there movement within the range of his vision . . . merely the lazy circle of a buzzard against the heat-blurred sky.

If they had not seen him already they would not see him if he remained still, and Shalako had learned his patience in a hard school.

Movement attracts the eye, draws the attention, renders visible. A motionless object that blends with the surroundings can long remain invisible even when close by, and Shalako was not moving.

About him lay vast, immeasurable distances, pastel shadings of salmon, pink, and lemon broken by the deeper reds of rock or the darkness of cliff shadow. Overhead the sun was lost in a copper sky above the heat-waved reaches where all sharpness of outline melted in the shimmering movement of the air.

The innocent distance that lay before him was broken by hollows, canyons, folded hills, but it seemed an even, unbroken expanse from where he sat. There were *cholla* forests out there, scatterings of lava . . . a land where anything might be and something obviously was.

The notch in the hills toward which he was pointing held a pass through the mountains, and within the pass lay a water hole.

His canteen was half-full and if necessity demanded it could be made to last another three days . . . it had done so before. In the desert a man learns to use water sparingly and to make a little cover a lot of distance.

The roan gelding was a mountain-bred horse and could survive on *cholla* or prickly pear if the spines were burned away, but water and grass lay within that opening in the hills, and Shalako had no intention of skirting the mountain unless circumstances insisted. Yet the sound of shots had come from that direction.

After a while he made, with sparing movements, a cigarette, his eyes holding on the far, blue mountains briefly, then surveying the country while he worked with the small, essential movements. He considered the possibilities, knowing that a desert offers less freedom of movement than at first seems likely. All travel in the desert, of man or animal, is governed by the need for water. Some animals learned to survive for days without water, but man was not one of these.

Four rifles . . . at least four rifles had fired that volley, and four rifles are not fired simultaneously unless fired at another man or men.

Sunset was scarcely an hour away, and the water hole was at least that far distant.

It was unlikely that whoever fired those shots would, at this hour, ride farther than the nearest water. Therefore the chances were that the water toward which he was riding would be occupied by whoever had done that shooting.

On the slope where he had drawn up neither the roan gelding nor himself would be visible at any distance, so he waited a little longer, inhaling deeply of the sharp, strong tobacco.

Four men do not fire in unison unless from ambush, and Shalako had no illusions about the sort of men who attack from concealment, nor what their attitude would be toward a drifting stranger who might have seen too much.

Whatever of gentleness lay within the man called Shalako was hidden behind the cold green eyes. There was no visible softness, no discernible shadow left by illusion. He was a man who looked upon life with a dispassionate, wry realism.

He knew he lived by care and by chance, knowing the next man he met might be the man who would kill him, or the next mile might see his horse down with a broken leg . . . and a man without a horse in this country was two-thirds a dead man.

To his thinking those men who thought their hour was predestined were fools. Whatever else nature was, it was impersonal, inexorable. He had seen too much of death to believe it was important, too much of life to believe that the destiny of any creature was important to any but itself or those dependent upon it.

There was always life. Humans and animals and plants were born and died, they lived their brief hour and went their way, their places filled so quickly they were scarcely missed.

Only the mountains lasted, and even they changed. Their lasting was only an idea in the minds of men because they lasted a little longer than men. Shalako knew he would live as long as he moved with care, considered the possibilities, and kept out of line of any stray bullet. Yet he was without illusions; for all his care, death could come and suddenly.

The margin for error was slight. A dry water hole, a chance fall, a stray bullet . . . or an Apache he missed seeing first.

Those who talked of a bullet with their name on it were fools . . . to a bullet all targets were anonymous.

Behind him to the east lay Mexico, but what trail he left back there only an Apache or a wolf might follow. Deliberately, he had avoided all known water holes, keeping to the roughest country, seeking out the rarely used seeps or *tinajas*, and avoiding the places an Apache might go in search of food.

He had seen nobody in those seven days, and nobody had seen him. He was quite sure of that for, had he been seen, he would be dead. Yet he knew that the Apaches had come down out of the Sierra Madre and were riding north.

He read the story in those weird hieroglyphics of the desert, the trails of unshod ponies, deserted rancherias, faint dust trails hanging above the desert, and always of course, the talking smoke.

Holding to the seeps and the natural tanks as he had, he had been fairly safe. Such places were rarely used except when the year was far along or it was a dry season. Early in the spring the desert water holes were full and there was no need to stray from them.

Removing his hat, he wiped the sweatband. No further sounds had reached him, nor was there any dust. Around him the desert lay still as on the day the earth was born. Yet he did not move.

Big Hatchet Peak towered more than eight thousand feet just to the south and west. He had crossed the border from Mexico into the States at a point in the foothills of the Sierra Rica, knowing the approximate location of the water hole toward which he was riding.

It lay about two miles up a canyon and two trails led from it. One started south and east, then swung westward toward Whitewater Wells, every inch of it Apache country.

The second trail was dim, scarcely used even by Indians, an ancient trail that dated back to the

Mimbres people, long vanished from their old haunts, if not from the face of the earth.

This trail led almost due west from the water hole, was much shorter and less likely to be watched. The mind of the man called Shalako, as of most Western men, was a storehouse of such information. Where guidebooks and maps are not available, every camp-fire, chuck wagon, and saloon bar becomes a clearing-house for information.

It was hot, and the roan was streaked with sweat and dust. The border country can be cool in April. It can also be an oven, the way it was now.

He started his horse, walking it to keep the dust down. From the shade of a nearby boulder an irrita-ble rattler buzzed unpleasantly, and then for a time a chaparral cock raced ahead of him, enjoying the company.

He paused again by a clump of ironwood, enjoying the fragrance from the yellow blossoms of some nearby cat's claw. Sometimes called "wait-a-minute," it was a low, spreading shrub with peculiar hooklike thorns that had crippled many a horse or other animal.

His eyes studied the desert. The tracks of a small lizard were visible in the sand . . . bees hummed around the cat's-claw blossoms. Shadows were begin-ning to thicken in some of the far-off canyons, al-though the sun was still high.

Shalako continued to walk his horse forward, and each time he mounted a slope, he came up easily at the crest until only his head showed above the hill, and there, holding very still to simulate a rock, he al-lowed only his eyes to move until he had scanned the area within view.

After almost an hour of slow progress, he rode down a draw toward a small playa, or dry lake. It was unlikely the killers had remained in the area but Shalako was not a trusting man.

Within the mouth of the draw he drew rein again. With his first glance he recognized the body for what it was, but only when he was quite sure that he was alone did he approach it. He circled it as warily as a wolf, studying it from all angles, and when finally he stopped within a dozen feet of the dead man he knew much of what had happened at this place.

The dead man had ridden a freshly shod horse into the playa from the north, and when shot he had tumbled from the saddle and the horse had galloped away. Several riders on unshod ponies had then approached the body and one had dismounted to collect the weapons.

The clothing had not been stripped off, nor was the body mutilated. Only when he could learn no more by observation did he dismount and turn the body over. He was already sure of the dead man's identity.

Pete Wells . . .

An occasional scout for the Army, a sometime driver of freight wagons, a former buffalo hunter and lately a hanger-on around Fort Bowie, Fort Grant, or Tucson. A man of no particular quality, honest enough, and not a man likely to make enemies. Yet now he was dead, shot from ambush.

Circling, Shalako discovered where the ambushers had lain in wait.

Four men . . . four Apaches.

He studied the droppings of the horses, kicking

them apart with a boot toe. He recognized in those droppings seeds from a plant found in the foothills of the Sierra Madre, but not farther north.

These were not reservation Indians from San Carlos then, they were some of Chato's outfit, just up from below the border.

Their trail when they left Wells's body lay in the direction he himself was taking, and that meant the water hole was off-limits for Shalako unless he wished to fight them for it, and no man in his right mind started a fight with Apaches.

When the time came for fighting, the man Shalako fought with a cold fury that had an utterly impersonal quality about it. He fought to win, fought with deadly efficiency, with no nonsense about him, yet he did not fight needlessly.

Despite his weariness and that of his horse he began backtracking the dead man.

Pete Wells was not likely to be alone, so his presence indicated a camp nearby, and a camp meant water. Yet Shalako puzzled over his presence here at such a time.

The Hatchet Mountains were in a corner of New Mexico that projected somewhat south of the rest of the state line. It was a desert and mountain region, off the main trails and offering no inducements to travel except several routes into Mexico. These were routes used by the Apaches in making their raids, but by no one else.

Unless Wells had been with the Army.

Within a few minutes Shalako knew that was highly unlikely, for Wells had been following another rider or looking for someone whom he did not fear.

Wells had mounted every ridge and knoll to survey the surrounding country, and Wells knew better than to take such risks.

Obviously, he knew nothing of the movement of the Apaches, and that implied that nobody else knew as yet. Wells was close to the Army and would be among the first to hear.

Shalako had backtrailed Wells for less than two miles when he came upon the trail Wells had lost.

Pausing briefly, Shalako tried to form a picture of the situation, for to follow a trail successfully it is first necessary to know something of the motives of the person followed.

Both horses were freshly shod, and both moved with an eagerness that implied they had come but a short distance.

Wells was no such tracker as Shalako, a fact Wells would have been the first to admit and, swinging a wide circle, Shalako picked up the lost trail in a matter of minutes.

What he found was merely a white scratch . . . the scar of an iron shoe upon a rock. Farther along a bit of stepped-on sage, then a partial hoof track almost hidden by a creosote bush. The trail led toward the Hatchet Mountains and, judging by the crushed sage, it was no more than two hours old.

By the time, some thirty minutes later, that he was riding up the slope that led to the base of the Hatchets, he knew a good deal more about the person he was following. He also knew why Wells had been following and that there was a fairly large camp in the vicinity.

In the first place, the rider was in no hurry, and was

unfamiliar with the country. As there were no inhab-
ited ranches or mines in the area, this implied a camp
close enough for the rider to return before dark.

Here and there the rider had paused to look more
closely at things, interesting enough in themselves,
but too familiar for a Western man to notice.

At one point the rider had attempted to pick the
blossom from a prickly pear. The blossom lay where
it had been hastily dropped. Shalako's face broke into
a sudden grin that brought a surprising warmth to his
bleak features.

Whoever plucked that blossom had a bunch of
stickers in her fingers.

Her?

Yes, he was sure the rider was a girl or woman.
The tracks of the horse, for example . . . it was a
horse of medium build with a good stride . . . the
tracks were but lightly pressed upon the sand, which
implied a rider of no great weight.

Moreover, Pete Wells had been extremely anxious
to find the rider, which also implied a woman about
whom he was worried. He might have followed any
tenderfoot, but a man like Wells, almost any Western
man in fact, would have the feeling that whatever a
man did was his own problem.

If a man was big enough to make his own tracks
and carry a gun, he was a responsible person, responsible for himself and his actions, and not to be
pampered.

A man in the Western lands was as big as he wanted
to be, and as good or as bad as he wished. What law
existed was local law and it felt no responsibility for
the actions of any man when they took place out of its

immediate jurisdiction. There were very few border-line cases. Men were good and bad . . . simply that . . . the restrictions were few, the chances of concealment almost nonexistent. A man who was bad was boldly bad, and nobody sheltered or protected any man.

But this rider was a woman, of that Shalako was now sure.

The horse the woman rode was a mare . . . back there a short way the rider had drawn up to look over the country and the mare took the occasion to respond to a call of nature . . . from the position of her feet it was obvious she was a mare.

Men in the West rarely rode mares or stallions. There might be exceptions, but they were so scarce as to attract a good deal of attention. They rode geldings because they were less trouble among other horses.

Suddenly, almost in the shadow of the mountains, he saw where a trail of unshod ponies had crossed ahead of him. The rider he followed had noticed them also.

"One up for her," he said aloud. "At least she has her eyes open."

The rider had drawn up, the mare dancing nervously, eager to be moving.

Now he scored another mark for the rider . . . a tenderfoot and a woman, but no damned fool . . . she had turned abruptly north and, skirting a nest of boulders, had entered a canyon. That last was not a good move but, obviously alarmed, she was seeking the quickest route back to camp.

The roan stumbled often now and Shalako drew rein beside the boulders and got down. Pouring a little water into his bandanna, he squeezed the last drop into the roan's mouth. He did this several times, and was about to step back into the saddle when he heard a horse's hoof click on stone.

He swung his leg over the saddle, then stood in the stirrups to look over the top of the boulder.

Evidently the canyon had proved impassable or a dead end, for the rider was returning. And the rider was a woman.

Not only a woman, but a young woman, and a beautiful woman.

How long since he had seen a girl like that? Shalako watched her ride toward him, noting the ease with which she rode, the grace of manner, the immaculate clothing.

A lady, this one. She was from a world that he had almost forgotten . . . bit by bit his memories had faded behind the blazing suns, the hot, still valleys, the raw-backed hills.

She rode a sorrel, and she rode sidesaddle, her gray riding skirt draped gracefully over the side of the mare, and she rode with the ease of long practice. Yet he was grimly pleased to see the businesslike way her rifle came up when he appeared from around the rock. He had no doubt that she would shoot if need be. Moreover, he suspected she would be a very good shot.

She drew up a dozen yards away, but if she was frightened there was no visible evidence of it.

"None of my business, but this here is Apache country."

"So?"

"You know a man named Pete Wells?"

"Yes. He's our wagon master."

"Pete never did have much sense." He gathered his reins. "Lady, you'd better get back to your camp wherever it is and tell them to pack up and hightail it out of here."

"Why should I do a thing like that?"

"I think you've guessed," he said, "I think you had an idea when you saw those tracks back yonder." He gestured to indicate the mountains far behind him. Their near flank was shadowed now, but the crest carried a crown of gold from the sun's bright setting. "Over there in the Sierra Rica there's an Apache named Chato. He just rode up out of Mexico with a handful of warriors, and here and there some others are riding to meet him. He will soon be meeting with some more who have jumped their reservation, and within forty-eight hours there won't be a man or woman alive in this corner of New Mexico."

"We have been looking forward to meeting some Indians," she replied coolly. "Frederick has been hoping for a little brush with them."

"Your Frederick is a damned fool."

"I should advise you not to say that to him."

Shalako handed her his field glass. "Over east there. See that smoke? Over by the peak?"

"I see nothing."

"Keep looking."

She moved the glass, searching against the far-off, purpling mountains. Suddenly, the glass ceased to move. "Oh? You mean that thin column of smoke?"

"It's a talking smoke . . . the telegraph of the Apache. You and your outfit better light out fast. You already got one man killed."

"I . . . *what*?"

"Pete was always a damn fool, but even he should have known better than to bring a party of green-horns into this country at a time like this."

Her cheeks paled. "Are you telling me that Pete Wells is dead?"

"We've sat here too long. Let's get out of here."

"Why should I be responsible? I mean, if he is dead?"

"He's dead, all right. If he hadn't been skylining himself on every hill while hunting for you he might not have been seen."

He led off along the base of the Hatchets, heading north. The gaunt land was softening with shadows, but was somehow increasingly lonely. The girl turned in her saddle to look toward the distant finger of smoke, and suddenly she shivered.

"We're at a ranch north of the range," she told him. "Mr. Wells took us there. The place is deserted."

"How'd you get in here past the troops?"

"Frederick did not want an official escort. He wished to see the Apache in battle."

"Any man who hunts Apache trouble is a child."

Her tone was cool. "You do not understand. Frederick is a soldier. He was a general in the Franco-Prussian War when he was twenty-five. He was a national hero."

"We had one of those up north a few years back. His name was Custer."

Irritated by his amused contempt, she made no reply for several minutes yet, despite her anger with him, she was observant enough to note that he rode with caution, never ceased to listen, and his eyes were always busy. She had hunted before this, and her father had hunted, and she had seen the Masai hunt in Africa . . . they were like this man now.

"It is silly to think that naked savages could oppose modern weapons. Frederick is amused by all the trouble your Army seems to have."

He looked uneasily into the evening. There was a warning in the stillness. Like a wild thing he felt strange premonitions, haunting feelings of danger. He felt it now. Unknowingly he looked eastward toward the mountains, unknowingly because upon a ridge of those mountains an Apache looked westward . . . miles lay between them.

Tats-ah-das-ay-go, the Quick Killer, Apache warrior feared even by his own people . . . master of all the wiles, the deceits, the skills. He looked westward now, wondering.

At the no longer deserted ranch where the hunting party of Baron Frederick von Hallstatt built its cooking fires, a man beside one of the fires suddenly stood up and looked away from the fire.

He was a lean and savage man with a boy's soft beard along his jaws, high cheekbones, and a lantern jaw. His thin neck lifted from a greasy shirt collar, and he looked into the distance as if he had heard a sound out there. The .44 Colt on his thigh was a deadly thing.

Bosky Fulton was a gunman who had never heard of either *Tats-ah-das-ay-go* or Shalako Carlin. He did not know that his life was already bound inextricably to those two and to the girl Irina, whom he did know. Yet the night made him restless.

Back upon the desert, Shalako had drawn up in a

cluster of ocotillo clumps and under their slight cover he studied the country around, choosing a way.

"Every Apache," he said conversationally, "knows all your Frederick knows about tactics before he is twelve, and they learn it the hard way. The desert is their field of operations and they know its every phase and condition. Every operation your Frederick learned in a book or on a blackboard they learned in battle. And they have no base to protect, no supply line to worry about."

"How do they eat?"

He swept a gesture at the surrounding desert. "You can't see them but there are a dozen food plants within sight, and a half dozen that are good for medicine."

The sun brushed the sky with reflected rose and with arrows of brightest gold. The serrated ridges caught belated glory . . . out upon the desert a quail called inquiringly.

She felt obliged to defend their attitude. "There are eight of us, and we are accompanied by four scouts or hunters, eight teamsters, two cooks, and two skinners. We have eight wagons."

"That explains something that's been bothering me. The Apaches started eating their horses two days ago."

"*Eating* them?"

"Only thing an Apache likes better than horse meat is mule meat. He will ride a horse until it's half dead and, when they find a place where they can get more horses, they will eat those they have."

"You are implying they expect to have our horses?"

The desert was too still, and it worried him. He got down from the saddle and rinsed his bandanna once more in the roan's mouth. As she watched him the girl's anger went out of her.

She looked at him again, surprised at the softness in his eyes and the gentleness with which he handled the horse.

"You love your horse."

"Horse is like a woman. Keep a strong hand on the bridle and pet 'em a mite and they'll stand up to most anything. Just let 'em get the bit in their teeth and they'll make themselves miserable and a man, too."

"Women are not animals."

"Matter of viewpoint."

"Some women don't want a master."

"Those are the miserable ones. Carry their heads high and talk about independence. Seems to me an independent woman is a lonely woman."

"You are independent, are you not?"

"Different sort of thing. The sooner women realize that men are different, the better off they'll be. The more independent a woman becomes the less of a woman she is, and the less of a woman she is the less she is of anything worthwhile."

"I don't agree."

"Didn't figure on it. A woman shouldn't try to be like a man. Best she can be is a poor imitation and nobody wants anything but the genuine article.

"Nature intended woman to keep a home and a hearth. Man is a hunter, a rover . . . sometimes he has to go far afield to make a living, so it becomes his nature."

He kept his voice low and without thinking of it she had done the same.

"And where is your woman?"

"Don't have one."

The sun was gone when they reached the last rocky point of the Hatchets. About a mile away a tall peak thrust up from the desert and beyond were a couple of lesser peaks, and still farther the distant bulk of the Little Hatchets. West of the nearest peak was a dark blotch of ranch buildings, and among them some spots of white that could be wagon covers. And in their midst blazed a fire, too large a fire.

Smelling water, the roan tugged at the bit, but there was a feeling in the air that Shalako did not like.

They sat still, while he listened into the night, feeling its uneasiness. It was not quite dark, although the stars were out. The desert was visible, the dark spots of brush and cacti plainly seen.

Into the silence she said, "I am Irina Carnarvon."

She said it as one says a name that should be known, but he did not for the time place the name, for he was a man to whom names had ceased to matter.

"My name is Carlin . . . they call me Shalako."

He started the roan down the gentle slope. The roan was too good a horse to lose and in no shape to run, but the ranch was safety and the ranch was two miles off. He slid his rifle from its scabbard.

"Get ready to run. We'll walk our horses as far as we can, but once we start running, pay me no mind. You just ride the hell out of here."

"Your horse is in no shape to run."

"My problem."

The roan quickened his pace. There was a lot of stuff in that roan, a lot of stuff.

"You *actually* believe we are in danger?"

"You people are a pack of idiots. Right now you and that tin-braided general of yours are in more trouble than you ever saw before."

"You are not polite."

"I've no time for fools."

Anger kept her silent, yet she sensed the uneasiness of her horse and it made her wary. A fine horse-woman, she knew the feeling at once and it frightened her far more than the warnings of the stranger.

Silence, and the distant fire . . . the hoof falls of the horses . . . the stars against the soft darkness of the sky, the loom of mountains . . . a coolness in the air, balm after the day's fierce heat. The quickening pace of the horses, the faint gleam along the rifle barrel. A slight breeze touched her cheek.

"Shalako . . . it is a strange name."

"Name of the Zuni rain god. Seemed like every time I showed up in their country it rained, so they called me that for a joke."

"I did not realize Indians had a sense of humor."

"The greatest. Nobody has more humor than an Indian, and I know. I've lived among them."

"I heard they were so stoical."

"Indians act that way around white men they don't know because they don't want to answer a lot of fool questions."

They were out of the flat now, at least a quarter of a mile gained.

The Apache, in distinction from many other Indians, preferred not to fight at night, believing the soul of a warrior killed at such a time must wander forever in darkness. That did not mean that on occasion an Apache would not take a chance.

When the camp was less than a mile away and they could hear faint sounds, an Apache suddenly raised up from behind a greasewood bush with a bowstring drawn back . . . but he had stood up directly in front of the muzzle of Shalako's rifle and less than thirty feet off.

He heard the *thud* of the bullet into flesh in the instant the arrow whizzed past his ear.

Startled by the explosion of the gunshot, both horses leaped into a run. Behind them there was another shot and Shalako felt the bullet when it struck the cantle of his saddle and caromed off into the night.

The roan ran proudly, desperately, determined not to lose the race to the fresher horse. A wave of fierce pride swept over Shalako and he realized again the unconquerable spirit of the roan mustang.

Neck and neck they raced for the ranch, and Shalako let go with a wild Texas yell to warn those ahead that he was not a charging Indian.

On a dead run they swept into the ranch yard and drew up in a cloud of swirling dust. Several people started toward them, and Shalako glanced sharply around, taking in the camp and those who peopled it with that one sweeping glance.

The man who walked up to them first was tall. He was lean and strong, with blond hair and handsome, if somewhat cold, features. His eyes were white gray, his boots polished and immaculate, his white shirt crisp and clean.

"What happened? Did you see a coyote?" His eyes went from Irina to Shalako, taking in his dusty, travel-worn clothing, his battered hat, and unshaved face.

"Better circle your wagons into the gaps between the buildings," Shalako suggested. "Get your stock inside the circle. That was an Apache, not a coyote."

The gray eyes turned again to Shalako, cool, attentive. "There are no Indians off the reservations," the blond man said. "Our man Wells told us—"

"Your man Wells is dead. If you want him you'll find him all spraddled out in a dry lake southeast of here, as full of holes as a prairie dog town . . . and it wasn't any reservation Indian who shot him."

"Who is this man, Irina?"

"Mr. Carlin, the Baron Frederick von Hallstatt."

"If you want to live," Shalako said, "forget the formalities."

Von Hallstatt ignored the remark. "Thank you for bringing Lady Carnarvon back to camp, Carlin. Now if you want something to eat, just go to the cook and tell him I sent you."

"Thanks, but I'm not staying that long. This outfit doesn't have a prayer and I'm not going down the chute with it. I'm riding out."

"Your pleasure," von Hallstatt replied coolly, and lifted a hand to help Irina from the saddle.

Two of the men who had come forward were standing by, and one of them said, "Forget it, General. This fellow was scared by a shadow."

The roan gelding swung as of its own volition and faced the speaker. Shalako's face was half-hidden by the pulled-down brim of his hat, but what the man could see he did not like. "Mister"—Shalako's voice was utterly cold—"I saw Apaches out there. What I shot was an Apache. Do you want to call me a liar?"

The man backed off a step. Desperately, he wanted to call the name and draw his gun, but something about the man on the roan horse made him hesitate.

"None of that!" Von Hallstatt's voice rang with the harshness of command. "Carlin, we thank you for escorting Lady Carnarvon back to camp. Eat if you wish. Sleep here if you wish, but I suggest you be gone by daybreak."

"By daybreak you'll be fighting for your lives. I'll be gone within the hour."

Turning away from them he rode the roan to the water tank. An ambitious settler had built this tank before the Apaches canceled out his faith in humanity by putting a half-dozen arrows in his belly.

He had been a sincere man, a good man. He believed that he who planted a tree or dug a well was closest to God, and would be blessed by all who needed water, or needed shade.

He also believed, good trusting man, that if he was himself peaceful others would be peaceful toward him.

He did not realize that others operate by a different philosophy and to those peace is unrealistic. Nor did he know that to an Apache all who are not of his tribe are enemies, that kindness was to them a sign of weakness.

He was, nevertheless, a man of stamina as well as faith, and he lasted for three days, the arrows in his belly, tied head down to a wagon wheel, close to water but unable to reach it . . . and all this under a blazing summer sun.

He left no record of his philosophy at the end of that time.

Shalako allowed the roan to drink sparingly, then drew him back from the water and, stripping off the saddle, rubbed the horse down with a handful of dry grass, and as he worked his eyes took in the disposition of the camp.

He had never seen anything like it. The wagons were scattered haphazardly about, the teamsters loafing around a smaller fire, von Hallstatt's companions dressed as if for a hunt in England or Virginia, served by a chef in a white apron and chef's hat.

No effort had been made to prepare for attack, all was elaborately casual, with much conversation and laughter.

The stable was the sturdiest-looking building, close to the water tank, and with a lower story of adobe, an upper story of hewn logs. There were several narrow ports for firing. The stable was built much like an old-fashioned blockhouse.

The house had been built at a much later date and by the peace-loving settler, and offered no practical defenses. Nor did the sheds and outbuildings. Yet they did form a rough rectangle with the house at the east end and the stable on the south. By drawing wagons into the gaps between the buildings the area could be made a fortress against any ordinary attack, with a final retreat to the stable in a last emergency.

Suddenly a sound of approaching steps made him look up. "*Shalako!* I'll be damned! Where'd you blow in from?"

Shalako straightened wearily, dropping the grass. "Buffalo? This is a long way from Fort Griffin." He dusted fragments of dry grass from his fingers. "Me? From the Sierra Madre, riding neck and neck with Chato and about forty Apaches. At least, there'll be forty of them by now."

"You ain't foolin'?"

"I'm riding out tonight."

Buffalo Harris swore bitterly. "An' the Army doesn't even know we're in the Territory! Was that you who shot out there awhile back?"

Shalako indicated the cantle of his saddle. "Feel of that . . . fired from off at the side or it might have taken me right out of the saddle."

Buffalo laid a finger in the groove and whistled softly. "They don't come much closer."

"How'd you ever tie up with a haywire outfit like this?"

"Haywire? Are you crazy? This here is the most fixed-up outfit I ever seen! They got champagne, crab, oysters . . . everything. She's a mighty plush setup, Shalako, an' don't you forget it . . . and the best grub I ever eat."

"So you lose your hair. Saddle up and come with me."

"Can't do it. I told them I stay the route."

Von Hallstatt strode up and, seeing Buffalo, stopped. "Harris, do you know this man?"

Buffalo spat. "I know him. He was scoutin' for the Army when he was sixteen. Knows more about this country than the Apaches do."

"Then you should go to work for me, Carlin. I can use a good man."

"If you don't pull those wagons into position you won't be in shape to hire anybody. Chato started eating his spare horses two, three days ago, which means they planned to steal yours before they crossed the border."

"That's impossible. They could not have known we were here."

"They knew . . . they knew you have four women with you, how many horses and mules you have, and how many men. No, I'm riding out of here."

Yet, even as he said it, he knew the roan was in no shape for an all-night ride . . . or a ride anywhere, for that matter. The mustang needed rest, food, and water.

Nevertheless, he was getting out. These people had come there under their own power, they could get out the same way.

Von Hallstatt measured Shalako with cool eyes. He disliked the man, this he admitted. On the other hand, someone who knew the country as well as Buffalo said he did might be useful. Especially with Wells dead, if, of course, he was dead.

"If you would name your price, Carlin, we would like to have you with us." He took his pipe from between his teeth. "You might at least stay and see the fun."

"You're not going to be having any fun." Shalako was brusque. "Unless you're shot with luck every man jack of you will be dead within forty-eight hours."

Von Hallstatt laughed. "Oh, come now! Naked savages against modern weapons?"

On a beat-up horse his chances of survival were slight, but this camp had the mark of death upon it, and realization that he had no choice but to make a run for it made Shalako increasingly irritable.

"Mister, let me tell you a little story about a West Pointer we had named Fetterman. He used to make his brag that given eighty men he could ride through the whole Sioux nation. Fetterman was well trained, he was efficient, and he was bulging at the seams with all those fancy European tactics, and he was confident.

"One day they sent him out with eighty men to rescue some wagons that were under attack, and they warned him if the Indians ran, not to chase them.

"He had his eighty men and his chance, and he chased them. His eighty men lasted less than twenty minutes, less time than you'd take to drink a cup of hot coffee, actually."

Shalako began to build a smoke. "Do you know how they did it? Like Hannibal at the Battle of Cannae . . . the center fell back and, when Fetterman followed them in, the flanks closed around him and wiped him out."

"You would have me believe these savages understand tactics?"

"Unless I miss the breed, you'll be from one of the old Junker families of Prussia. War has been a way of life to you for centuries, yet I doubt if you have seen more than ten battles, or that your oldest general has seen more than thirty."

Shalako folded the paper over his cigarette. "Mister, out there in the dark there are forty or fifty Apaches and the chances are there isn't one of them who isn't a veteran of fifty to a hundred battles. They fight Americans, Mexicans, other Indians. War is a way of life for the Apache, too, and every child learns his tactics by listening to the warriors talk of their battles.

"There isn't a thing in Vegetius, Saxe, or Jomini an Indian doesn't know, and more besides. He is the greatest guerrilla fighter the world has ever known.

"He doesn't know a thing about all that military balderdash of close-order drill, military courtesy, or parade-ground soldiering. Everything he learns is by applying it that way. He's taught, sure, but he's taught to fight and to win and he wastes time on none of the fixings.

"You boys say close-order drill is good for discipline. That's nonsense. The only kind of discipline that counts is the discipline of training to function in battle. How to keep in touch with the men on either side of you, how to advance and retreat under fire, how to give covering fire and supporting fire, how to select routes of travel under risk of attack. You don't learn any of that training for a lot of parade-ground nonsense.

"There isn't a thing to learn about fighting in this country—and this is the worst country in the world to fight in—that every Apache out there doesn't know."

"I am surprised," von Hallstatt said contemptuously, "that your Army is able to defeat these supermen of yours. These super-Indians."

"I'll tell you why. Only one out of three or four has a rifle, and he may not have a dozen rounds of ammunition. Unless they can find a crooked trader to supply them they have to kill to get weapons, so they are always in short supply.

"And the Army outnumbers them fifty-to-one. And that Army is the best bunch of fighting men the sun ever shone on. They use Indian tactics part of the time themselves, and General Crook, who knew more about fighting Indians than any of them, he used Indians to fight them."

Shalako turned toward the fire. "And let me tell you something else: Any rattle-headed fool who would bring a bunch of women into a country like this at a time like this deserves to be shot."

Deliberately, he turned his back and walked away toward the fire where he glanced at the coffeepot, then walked on to the stable where he filled a feed bag and carried it back to the roan. The feed bag was alien but the oats were not. After a little hesitation and backing away the roan decided to accept the situation.

Von Hallstatt had walked away, but Harris was still there.

"That was medicine talk, but the general was sure sore." Harris watched while Shalako picked up his rifle. "What happened to Pete?"

Shalako explained, then jerked his head toward von Hallstatt. "Is he carrying money?"

"You ain't just a-woofin'! And diamonds? These women are wearin' diamonds like they were candy! And you should see their rifles and shotguns! Inlaid with gold, ivory and mother-of-pearl. I d'clare, Shalako, these folks must have a fortune in guns."

"Then I know why Rio Hockett is here."

"Where'd you know him?"

"The Rangers chased him out of the brush down on the Nueces a few years ago. He's been a horse thief, a cow rustler, and a scalp hunter. If you folks get out of here alive, you talk von Hallstatt into getting rid of him. He's trouble."

Buffalo was silent for several minutes, and then he said, "You don't think we've got a chance, do you?"

"With Chato and forty Apaches out there? What do you think?"

Irina Carnarvon came suddenly from the darkness with a plate of food and a cup of coffee. "You must be starved, Mr. Carlin."

Buffalo Harris faded discreetly into the shadows and Shalako reached for the food gratefully. The very smell of it made him faint, he was that hungry. He had run out of jerked meat—the last food he had—the day before yesterday and had not dared chance a shot, although he had seen a couple of deer.

Irina stood beside him, and the faint smell of her perfume stirred old memories. He glanced at her over his coffee cup. She was tall for a woman, slender but rounded . . . quite a woman.

His eyes went beyond her to the tables that were being spread with white linen and set with silver and sparkling glassware. He shook his head in amazement to see such a thing in New Mexico, with Apaches around the camp.

There was a low murmur of conversation from a group of people who sat in camp chairs near the fire. It was the polite conversation of well-bred people everywhere, idle, interesting talk, but strangely incongruous here.

"What are you doing with this outfit?" he asked bluntly. "You're real."

She turned to look at him. "They are real, too, Mr. Carlin. It is merely another sort of life."

"But unreal here, and unrealistic. That sort of thing is fine in England, or New England. Out here, at a time like this it reminds me of Nero's fiddle."

"You asked me what I was doing here. These are my friends, Mr. Carlin . . . and I may marry Frederick."

It irritated her that she hesitated before saying it, almost as if she were ashamed, which she certainly was not. In the East and in Europe, almost everywhere in fact, Frederick von Hallstatt was considered quite a catch. His was an ancient family, he had won many honors in the Prussian Army, he had a title, position, and wealth.

He put down the plate. "Men must be mighty scarce where you come from."

"Most people believe that I am fortunate."

He glanced at her. "You are warm, friendly, and I think sentimental," Shalako said. "He is cold, calculating, and ruthless. Furthermore," he added, "he's a fool, or he would never have brought you here."

"You make up your mind very quickly," she spoke stiffly. "I am not sure you are qualified to render an opinion."

"Out here we don't have time to consider folks. We have to make up our minds fast, and we judge a man by his looks and his actions. We pay no attention to titles or honors or whatever because we have found they don't measure a man. Yes, I made a fast judgment on him, and I may be wrong."

"I think you are very wrong."

"I don't believe you," he said. "You're too smart a girl to make a mistake like that."

This man was a total stranger, a big, unshaved, and rugged man out of the desert. Very likely he had not bathed in a week . . . where he would get the water she could not imagine . . . and she was discussing her friends with him. It was preposterous.

His thoughts had moved into the darkness, thinking beyond this place, thinking of the trail westward. The roan was in no shape, but if he could get over into the Animas Mountains he might hole up and rest for a while, then move out and keep to low ground.

"Come with me," he said suddenly, "and I'll get you out of this."

"And leave my friends? You must be mad." She paused. "I scarcely know you, Mr. Carlin, and I could never leave my friends if they are in as much danger as you assume."

He was scarcely listening, his mind was out upon the desert, thinking of the way that lay before him. He owed these people nothing, and this was a country where a man saddled his own broncs and fought his own battles. They had come into the country recklessly, foolishly, hoping for a "brush with the Apaches" . . . well, they would get it.

"You must take one of my horses, Mr. Carlin. I have three, very fine horses, and your horse is half-dead."

"You'd swap?"

"Certainly not. But I will loan him to you, and when you can, return him and pick up your own horse. If you are correct and we do not get out of here, you may keep him."

"You needn't do this, you know. You owe me nothing."

She looked up at him. "I wasn't thinking of you, Mr. Carlin. I was remembering what you said about them eating their horses. I couldn't bear them eating Mohammet."

He chuckled suddenly. "Now I like that. You're honest, anyway. All right, I'll take care of your horse."

She turned abruptly and walked away, and he stared after her, aware of a feeling of guilt. In a few minutes Harris returned, leading a stallion.

Black as midnight, he knew at once that he had never seen a horse to compare with it. Clean-limbed and strong, it was built both for speed and staying power. When he reached for the stallion it thrust a velvety nose into his palm.

He talked to the horse, rubbing its neck and making friends.

"You must have put the sign on that girl, Shalako. This is her best horse, and she treats it like a child. Pure Arab, right out of the desert."

He threw his saddle on the stallion and cinched it up, and the stallion took the bit eagerly, as if he was eager to go. Shalako had known such horses, as excited about a trail as a man would be.

Buffalo Harris left, and when he returned he had a small packet of food. Shalako took his time, reluctant to leave now that a way was open.

Von Hallstatt had given the order and the wagons had been pulled into the spaces between the buildings, making a fairly tight circle. It was too large to defend well, yet it could be defended, and there were quite a few men, all well-armed.

As Shalako put his blanket roll behind the saddle, someone behind him spoke.

"What you all figure to do with that horse?"

Shalako turned slowly.

The man facing him was lean and narrow-shouldered, a sparse beard on his jaws. Bosky Fulton was a trouble-hunting man, and Shalako read him at a glance, nor was he inclined to sidestep it. Shalako knew all too well that any sign of hesitation would be accepted as a sign of fear.

"None of your damned business," he said coldly, and as he spoke he stepped closer to Fulton.

Few gunmen could stand up to a close fight. Most of them fancied their shooting ability, but at close range there was too much chance of both men being killed . . . and no man wants to die.

Fulton backed off a step, to keep the distance between them, but Shalako followed. "None of your business," Shalako said coldly.

Fulton stared hard at Shalako, thinking to intimidate him, but the eyes that looked back into his showed only contempt, and something else that Fulton liked even less.

Before Fulton could speak, Harris interrupted. "Lady Carnarvon loaned him the horse, Bosky. It's all right."

"*Loaned* him?" Fulton was incredulous. "She won't even let anybody touch him."

Frederick von Hallstatt walked up; he ignored Fulton, but glanced from the horse to Shalako. "Lady Carnarvon loaned you that horse?" he asked doubtfully. "I can't believe it."

Laura Davis and Irina had also come up. "Yes, I loaned Mohammet to him, Frederick. I believe if we are attacked he will be safer with Mr. Carlin than with us."

"Attacked? You believe that story, then?"

"You forget, Frederick. I was out there with him. Those shots were very real."

"If you can get out of here," Shalako suggested, "make a run for it to Fort Cummings. Lieutenant Colonel Forsyth is in command there."

He lingered, reluctant to leave. "You get your grub and ammunition inside the stable. They'll be all around you, come daylight, and you won't see any of them.

"The way I read the smokes, Indians have left the reservation to join Chato, and that means the Army will have been notified and Forsyth will be out. If you burn your wagons the Army will be likely to see the smoke."

"I doubt if it will come to that," von Hallstatt replied. "We have a good-sized force and we are well-armed. And several of us have had military experience."

"No matter what experience you've had, in this kind of war you're a tenderfoot." Shalako gathered the reins. "Thanks, ma'am, and good luck. You're quite a woman."

He walked the Arab into the darkness near the stable and drew up to listen, shutting out the sounds of the camp to hear only the desert.

There was an eagerness in the stallion. The Arab liked the feel of the night and the desert, and no doubt some forgotten or atavistic memory stirred his Arab blood on such desert nights as this.

Ears pricked, dainty as a dancer, the black Arab moved down into the wash, holding close to the near bank and the deepest shadow.

His hoofs made no sound in the soft sand, and for

several minutes they went cautiously forward, but soon Shalako sensed that something lay to the north that the Arab did not like. Shalako let the horse pull away to the south a little, trusting the horse had caught the scent of an Apache.

Westward, eight or nine miles away, lay the Animas Mountains, an area he knew better than the Hatchets, and a place where he knew of a hideout where with luck he might hole up. Yet the farther he rode the more irritable he became.

The wind was in his face . . . he smelled dust.

Quickly he drew the Arab into the deepest shadow, whispering to him to quiet his excitement.

And then he heard a sound . . . the soft scuffle of hoofs in the sand.

A party of riders coming from the northwest, and they would be coming down into the wash somewhere close to him.

Shalako drew his Colt and rested the barrel on the saddle horn. The night was still and cool, the sound of hoofs was closer now, like surf upon a sandy shore. His mouth was dry, and he kept his thumb on the gun hammer, ready to fire.

CHAPTER 2

WHEN HE HAD gone she stood listening, oblivious of the camp sounds and conversation, but she heard nothing. There was no shot, no shout . . . nothing.

He had ridden into the shadow beside the stable and paused there, but when he moved from that shadow into the outer darkness she had no idea.

He was gone.

Irina Carnarvon felt a curious sense of loss . . . a ridiculous thought, for the man was not her sort, anyway. Yet the feeling remained, and she asked herself, What was her sort?

What sort of man did she want? What sort of life? It was an odd question, for she had believed that was settled in her mind. She had thought to marry Frederick, and it was unreasonable that a ride of a few miles with a strange, unshaved, unwashed man of the desert could change that.

Nor had it been changed. Only there was a subtle sort of difference in her feelings now. What had moved her to let him ride Mohammet? She had never allowed Frederick to ride the horse, and actually, aside from one groom on their estate in Wales, nobody had ridden him but her father and herself.

What was her sort? What kind of man did she want? And what sort of man was this man called Shalako?

Certainly, she did not want him. She did not know him, and then he was only a wanderer, a hunter, big, uncouth . . . but was that fair? What made her say he was uncouth? Actually, there was a strangely gentle quality in the man . . . it was in nothing he had said, rather his handling of his horse, and aside from his brusque way of speaking, his manner toward her.

Yet it was he who caused her to think of herself and of Frederick. Not for a long time had she thought as she was thinking now.

This man had come up from the desert, and now he had returned to it.

Who was he? What was he?

Above all, who was *she*? She had scarcely known her mother, living much in a world of men. Her father had never been content with the hunting of Wales or of Scotland. He had hunted wild boar in France as a boy, and then had gone to Africa. She herself had been to Africa and to India with him.

Her father held an ancient title, possessed ancient wealth, but he had been a hunter. Never so much at home as when he was far from home and in the deep woods, the far veldt, the desert, the mountains.

THE TABLE HAD been set up on a stretch of hard-packed adobe clay, swept clean of dust. Now it was spread with white linen, set with silver and glass. It seemed strangely incongruous in the midst of this desert, yet it had never seemed so before.

Charles and Edna Dagget were already seated at the table, with Julia Paige and Laura Davis opposite them. They looked up as she approached.

"I never knew anyone like her, Julia," Laura said, with a teasing smile. "She rides out into an empty desert and comes back with a man."

"And what a man! Where is he, Irina? Don't tell me you let him get away?"

"Yes, he's gone."

She looked around with wonderment. All this, these pleasant people at the table, the others that would soon join them, this was her world . . . but what was it doing here? Suddenly, with a kind of embarrassment, she realized how foolish all this must have seemed to Shalako.

Like a group of children they had come running into this country to play, this country where everything was the utmost in reality. For there was something positive about the desert . . . it was stark, strong, definite. There were few shadings here, and many points of no return. The margin between life and death was infinitely narrow.

Pete Wells . . . in the morning she had talked with him, a quiet, rather colorless man, yet a man, filled with life, enjoying his small pleasures. And a few hours later he was dead, shot down by men he had not even seen.

Count Henri came up to the table and joined them. He was a tall, well set-up man with a shading of silver at the temples. He had been a soldier in the French Army, serving somewhere in the Far East, and he had written a book on China, a scholarly work which she had not read.

"I am sorry he went away," he said, "I liked the look of the man, and if there is trouble, he would have been a good man to have around."

Von Hallstatt overheard the comment. "There won't be trouble, Henri. I was just talking with Hockett and he assures me the Apaches are all south of the border or on reservations."

"Mightn't it be a good idea to pull out in the morning, Fred?" Henri watched the food being placed on the table. "I don't like the look of things."

Von Hallstatt glanced at him. "Don't tell me you've got the wind up? Hockett says that the Apaches rarely move in groups larger than twenty or thirty, and no party that small would be likely to attack us. We're too many for them."

He paused. "No, Henri, I came down here to get a desert bighorn, and I shall. And if we have a bit of a skirmish, so much the better."

Henri glanced across the table at von Hallstatt, a cool, measuring glance. "It is not as if we were all men," he said. "I doubt if we have the right to subject the ladies to such risk."

"There is no risk." Von Hallstatt glanced up at him. "Forget it, Henri. This man frightened Irina with some talk of Indians. I have no idea what he hoped to gain. Or perhaps I do. At least he rode away on our finest horse."

"I believed him," Irina said quietly, "and I still believe him."

Von Hallstatt smiled at her. "I am afraid he impressed you too much. Did you not tell me you had read the novels of Fenimore Cooper? I am afraid you see your man from the desert as another Leatherstocking."

Irina smiled. "And he may be. I think we could use one now."

The conversation took a turn away from the moment, but Irina was silent, scarcely hearing the talk that went around and across the table. She was thinking again of the man who had ridden into the night on her favorite horse . . . Would she see him again?

Von Hallstatt talked easily. He was a good conversationalist, if somewhat opinionated, and not quite so easy with words as Count Henri. An inordinately proud man, he was undoubtedly brilliant. Long ago, when she first met him in London, she had been told that had he not gone into the military he might have become a brilliant mathematician.

She looked up, feeling eyes upon her. Across the table and back at the edge of the firelight was the man called Bosky Fulton. He looked at her without smiling, but there was a boldness in his eyes that irritated her. She looked away, taking up a comment of Henri's but her thoughts remained with Fulton.

He made her uneasy . . . there was something unclean about the man that had little to do with his physical dirtiness, something that warned and repelled her. For that matter, aside from Buffalo and that other young man, the one who drove the wagon—Harding, his name was—she found little to like in any of the men Frederick hired.

When they were outfitting none of the men recommended to them had cared to join up. These men were fiercely independent and they resented Frederick's manner. He was accustomed to Germanic subservience to authority, and persisted in regarding the men he hired as servants or peasants, and no one could call these men either. Work for you they might, but they remained themselves, proud, independent, and prepared to fight to preserve their independence.

The result had been that the men he could get were the worst, the scum, the hangers-on. Even Pete Wells had objected to the hiring of Rio Hockett . . . but when Fulton appeared Wells simply turned away and would say nothing. Like the others, Wells had been afraid of Fulton.

She looked down at her plate, appetite suddenly gone. For the first time in days she thought of her father, and wished he was here. He had been a calm, sure man who always seemed to know what to do, and who had an unerring judgment of men.

She looked up. "Frederick, why don't we go back?"

He took his wineglass in his fingers and turned it slowly, watching the reflection of the firelight in the wine.

"We came for a hunt. You knew when we came how long we would be gone, and we had planned this hunt in detail. I do not wish to leave."

"We might do better in the mountains near Silver City," Henri suggested. "There is a plenty of timber there."

"You, too, Henri? Don't tell me you are afraid? I thought the French were a bold, dashing lot? Reckless, and all that?"

Henri's eyes chilled, but he smiled. "Dashing? Yes. But cautious also, and lovers of comfort. I believe a move to the north would offer more of both."

"And I do not."

Julia Paige lifted her large, dark eyes and looked down the table at Frederick. Irina felt a little tightening inside, knowing what Julia was going to say. Julia had made no secret of her interest in Frederick.

"After coming all this way it would be foolish to go back emptyhanded. I think we should stay. At least we should stay long enough to see if Irina's desert man will come back again."

"I am perfectly prepared to stay," Charles Dagget said. "We have only just come, and there seems no reason to be frightened. If there are Indians, I have no doubt the Army can cope with them."

"Yes," Irina said as she arose. "I believe they could cope with them . . . if they knew where they were, and where we were." She smiled sweetly. "You will remember, Charles, that the Army has no idea we are here."

She walked away, going toward the stable. She had never been inside the building, but this was the one Shalako had suggested they could defend.

Harding was seated near the door, but when she approached he got quickly to his feet. "Howdy, ma'am. Something I can do for you?"

"Would you show me the stable, Mr. Harding? Mr. Carlin was saying it would make a fort."

"Sure would! I been looking it over, ma'am, and whoever built this knew a thing or two. Old, mighty old, but strong. And the portholes are placed just right to cover everything."

Within the barn Harding held up a lantern. It was a long room, and there had been stalls for eight horses, a storeroom for harness, and a big area where hay had been kept. There was a steep stair that led to the loft.

"There's a bigger room upstairs," Harding explained. "They must have lived there for a time." He led the way up the steps and showed her the room up there.

The floors were solid, the planks well fitted. There were loopholes here also, and, from a large window, Irina could look out over the entire camp, lighted as it was by campfires.

The wagons had been drawn into the gaps between the buildings, but there was no evidence of alertness among the men, to say nothing of those who lingered about the table.

The sky was scattered with stars, the black serrated ridge of the mountains rimmed the sky, and there was a velvety coolness in the night.

"Mr. Harding, have you lived long in the West?"

"Yes, ma'am. Since I was eleven. Before that my home was Ohio. Raised on a farm, ma'am, and done a sight of hunting back there.

"We came West and my family was wiped out by Kiowas while I was from home, visitin'. I've been freighting and buffalo hunting since then. Done a mite of rough carpentering here and there."

"What do you think? Are we in danger of attack?"

"Yes, ma'am. Where there's Apaches there's danger. Or most any Indians, for that matter. War is a way of life to them. They count wealth in horses, and a man who can steal horses better than somebody else is a big man, a mighty big man."

"Mr. Harding, that man . . . Shalako . . . he suggested we think of defending this place if it becomes so bad we cannot defend the circle. He thought we should have food and ammunition here, prepared ahead of time."

"That's good thinking."

"He also suggested that we keep someone we can trust inside here, or close by. I want you to be that man, Mr. Harding."

"Yes, ma'am. Begging your pardon, ma'am, as long as we're on the subject. This is a mighty poor lot of men you have here. I wouldn't place much dependence on them, and that Fulton, ma'am, he's a bad lot, a bad lot."

She turned away from the window and walked to the steps. At the head of the steps she paused again. "Mr. Harding? What do you know about Shalako?"

Roy Harding was a lean, raw-boned young man, not tall, but muscular and fit. He paused near her. "I never saw him before, but I'd heard tell of him, ma'am. Buffalo, he knew him a long time back. Shalako grew up out here, ma'am. Someplace in California, I think, and then lived in Texas awhile. When he was eighteen or so he pulled out and it was six or eight years before he showed up around again, and then it was up in Montana.

"Nobody knows much about him except that he's said to be one of the best shots on the frontier. He can track better than most Indians, and can ride anything that wears hair.

"Buffalo Harris says he's hell-on-wheels in any kind of a fight." Harding paused. "I sure wish he'd stayed with us."

VON HALLSTATT GLANCED around as Irina returned to the table, but offered no comment. A servant was filling their glasses again. "You must try this, Henri. It is one of our finest German wines."

"A good wine, a very good wine."

"Ah? I was not aware that the French ever conceded there was any good wine but French wine."

"On the contrary, Baron, if it has quality, no matter what it is, we French have it. We have learned how to be content with the best of everything."

"There is a story behind this *Bernkasteler Doktor*. It is said there was a certain bishop who had fallen ill of some confusing illness, and no matter what the doctors did for him, he continued to lose strength.

"Finally, or so the story goes, an old soldier who was a friend of the bishop filled a keg with *Bernkasteler* and, in spite of the protests, wheeled it into the bishop's room and filled a glass with it, and then another.

"The following morning the bishop was much better, and he declared, 'This wine, this fine doctor, has cured me!' Hence, the name of the wine."

"It is growing cold," Edna Dagget said. "I believe I will go in."

Charles arose and walked with her toward the wagon where they slept.

"She is not fitted for this life," von Hallstatt said. "Charles would have done well to leave her behind."

Irina glanced at him, and said, "Wives are not so easily left behind. A wife's place is with her husband."

"Not at war," von Hallstatt replied, "nor the hunt. Still, hers was a good idea. It grows late and tomorrow I want to try for a bighorn." He got to his feet. "Good night, my friends."

He turned from the table and walked away, and for a moment there was silence. Then Count Henri said, "And how about you, Julia? Are you going with us tomorrow?"

Julia Paige smiled quickly. "Of course, I cannot leave all the hunting to Irina."

Laura Davis had been quiet. "You know," she said, "I agree with you, Henri, and with Irina. I think we should leave, as quickly as possible."

When Julia started to object, she continued. "My father entertained General Crook one evening while I was at home, and they discussed the Apache. Some of the stories were horrible, utterly horrible! They did not know I was listening," she added.

Hans Kreuger shrugged. "I trust the baron," he said. "He is a man of great judgment and discretion."

"It is different here," Laura said. "I think we should go."

"You heard what he said," Irina replied, "and we are his guests."

Count Henri slowly filled his pipe. "I think we should go, Hans. There is no game here that we cannot find farther north, and under pleasanter circumstances."

"Except Apaches." Hans glanced over at Henri. "I know the baron seriously wishes for a bit of fighting. I have heard him express his contempt for this American Army that chases Indians but cannot catch them."

"Has he had experience with guerrilla warfare, Hans?" Henri asked gently. "I have . . . much like this, I think, for I fought in the mountains and desert against the Arabs in North Africa.

"Luckily, I had read Washington's comments on Braddock's defeat by Indians and was cautious.

Believe me, the circumstances are much different, and no tactics so far taught in Europe can prepare an army for that kind of fighting."

"Speaking of tactics," Kreuger commented, "I wonder what school the man Shalako attended?"

"School?" Henri glanced around at the young German. "I understood he had lived here all his life."

"Perhaps . . . but he mentioned Jomini, Saxe, and Vegetius. I should not expect to hear them mentioned by a buffalo hunter, or whatever he is."

Henri walked off toward her wagon with Julia, and Hans followed. There was a slight stir of wind that ruffled the flames. Buffalo came from the shadows and added fuel to the fire, yet he did not build the big flames.

The bed of coals glowed a deep red, here and there a yellow tendril of flame lifting with the smoke toward the stars.

"You liked him, didn't you?" Laura said.

"Him?" Irina looked up, startled. Then she laughed, knowing evasion was impossible and slightly ridiculous. "I don't know. I never knew anyone quite like him."

"Except your father."

"Oh . . . not very much. They both like wild country. I don't think that makes any difference, anyway."

"And both of them are those big, self-contained men who do everything well. And Shalako is a handsome man, Irina."

"I never really looked at him . . . not that way. Somehow it did not seem to matter. It was something else that impressed me. I cannot remember ever feeling so safe as I was with him."

There was silence between them, and she looked out over the desert, wondering. Where was he now? Was he still riding? Westward, perhaps?

"It's very silly," she said suddenly, "talking this way about, well, a man like that. There's no telling what he really is, and, after all, a girl just doesn't go running off with any man who rides in out of the desert."

Irina remained watching the stars over the mountains long after Laura had gone to bed. The general, Baron Frederick von Hallstatt, was a man of strength and courage, an interesting man in every sense, but hard in a way that she did not like. Occasionally, and rarely to be sure, he had shown an utter disregard for the feelings of others, even including herself, that was disturbing.

He was ruthless, that she accepted. So for that matter was this stranger, this man Shalako who had suddenly occupied so much of their thinking by merely appearing on the scene. Shalako was ruthless, she knew this at once, but his ruthlessness would be applied to enemies, not to those close to him.

A lonely man, traveling alone and living alone, he was nevertheless far from selfish. That he had ridden off into the desert to leave them was, seeing it as he did, simply good sense.

Their party had not been invited into this area, and what had begun as a sort of lark when the excitement of hunting buffalo had palled, had suddenly turned into something foolhardy and dangerous.

When she had first accepted the baron's invitation to hunt on the prairies and in the mountains it had seemed tremendously exciting. Many Europeans had come west to hunt on the plains. Hunters talked as much of hunting buffalo in America as they talked of hunting lions in Africa or tigers in India.

The element of danger from possibly hostile tribes added spice to the idea, and yet seemed very remote. It was one thing to talk of hostile Indians in the fashionable restaurants of New York or Saratoga, and quite another thing to face the danger of attack in a remote desert.

What had seemed exciting in a conversation at Delmonico's in New York was frightful here, and she was not calmed by Frederick von Hallstatt's attitude.

The fact remained that Pete Wells was dead, and his death was in part her own fault.

In part it was all their faults for coming out here in the first place. How many more would die before this venture ended? If there was no attack, they should leave. Suddenly, she resolved. Regardless of what the others did, she was going to Fort Cummings as Shalako had advised and then back home.

The crunch of a boot on the gravel behind her was her only warning. And then the smell of stale, unwashed clothing before the voice spoke.

"Waitin' for somebody, ma'am?" It was Bosky Fulton. "If you are, you just don't have to wait no longer."

She turned and measured him coolly. "I am waiting for no one. Will you step aside?"

Fulton made no effort to move. "You're goin' to need a friend, so don't come it so high and mighty over me, ma'am. You better make up your mind that you're goin' to be nice to me, or else you'll find yourself in the hands of some Apache . . . and that could be worse. Could be." He chuckled.

"Will you step aside?"

Fulton hesitated, grinning insultingly, and then he stepped aside and as she walked toward her wagon, he said, "And if you want to get that general of yours killed, you just tell him what I said."

She was trembling when she reached the wagon and she stopped, her knees shaking. She remembered then some of the talk around the camp, that Bosky Fulton was a gunman who had killed several men in gun battles.

Suddenly there was no safety anywhere, and the night seemed filled with crowding menace.

She started to get into the wagon, then hesitated again. Would they not be safer in the upper room at the stable?

If she and Laura, and some of the others . . . ?

_____

SHALAKO HEARD THE whisper of the approaching riders' coming through the sand, and he eased his position in the saddle, holding the Colt ready to fire.

The horsemen, riding single file, came like ghosts out of the night, and for an instant each Indian was starkly outlined against the sky as he reached the edge of the wash, then dipping into it he dipped into shadow and was gone, like the targets in a shooting gallery. There were six.

Only those brief, momentary shadows, a whisper of hoofs in the sand, the rattle of a stone as they left the wash, and they were gone.

He walked the Arab steadily into the night, holding his pace down, wanting no Apache to smell dust as he had smelled it, for others might be coming.

There was a canyon of which he knew, a canyon that reached back into the mountains south of Gillespie Peak, and there was a place there he might hole up. Farther up the canyon there was a trickle of water that occasionally flowed in the early months of the year.

He walked the stallion for approximately three miles, then touched him lightly with a spur and let the Arab run. The horse ran tirelessly until the black wall of the mountain loomed over them. He knew when he had reached the mouth of the canyon by the sudden coolness of the air, and turned the Arab.

Twice he rode past the place he sought, but finally he located the small hollow, shielded from the rest of the canyon by brush and boulders. There was an acre or so of sparse grass where water from the spring kept it fresh. There he unsaddled and picketed the horse on the grass.

Spreading his groundsheet and blankets, he stretched out with a sigh, easing his tired muscles and closing his lids over eyes that ached from the strain of watching a far land under a blazing sun. Once more he opened his eyes to look up at the pinnacle of the mountain, and the last sound he heard was the placid munching of the horse, close beside him.

LIEUTENANT COLONEL GEORGE A. Forsyth, in command at Fort Cummings, replaced the letter on his desk and was for a moment swept by a wave of helpless fury. His lips tightened and he sat very still, fighting down his anger before he looked up at Lieutenant McDonald.

The colonel pushed the letter across his desk. "Look at this! Of all the damned fools!"

McDonald took the letter and read it through twice before realizing all it implied.

> Fort Concho, Texas
> April 3, 1882

> Officer Commanding,
> Fort Cummings,
> New Mexico Territory

> Sir:
> The Baron (General) Frederick von Hallstatt and party, believed in your area. Last seen, vicinity of Lost Horse Lake, buffalo hunting. Eight wagons, twenty-odd persons, including four white women. One of the latter is Lady Irina Carnarvon, another is the daughter of U.S. Senator Y. F. Davis. Locate, and escort out of the area.

> Sincerely,
> John A. Russell,
> General Commanding

Lieutenant McDonald was shocked. "My God! Four *women*! At a time like this!"

Colonel Forsyth tapped his pencil on the edge of the desk and studied the map before him. If von Hallstatt's party had been in the vicinity of Lost Horse Lake on or before the third it was just possible they had reached this area. But why would they come *here*?

Antelope were the only game, and there were more of those in the country from which they had just come. In the mountains there were bighorn sheep, but they also could be found farther north. The desert mountains to the south were bleak and inhospitable to an outsider, offering little, promising less.

A veteran Indian fighter, dangerously wounded in the Beecher Island fight in which Roman Nose was killed, he respected the Indian as a fighting man, and knew few warriors more cunning than Chato existed.

The barrel-chested, flat-nosed Apache had the torso of a two-hundred-pound man on his stocky body, and enough battle lust for a dozen men of his size. Not an hour before had come word that Chato was over the border and moving north.

Moreover, Nachita and Loco had fled the San Carlos reservation with a party of young braves who were spoiling for a fight, and undoubtedly the two groups would meet somewhere to the south. And right in the middle of the country where the meeting was likely to take place was a party of casual tourists, ignorant of the desert and the Apache. If anything happened to any one of them he would be replying by endorsement to the War Department for the next two years.

Colonel Forsyth's force was too small and the area he was expected to patrol too large. Military forces much larger than his had failed to pin down the will-o'-the-wisp of an Apache band. Chato would be sure to raid north and east, trying meanwhile to augment his forces still further by drawing upon discontented elements at San Carlos.

For months Forsyth's scouts at the reservation had warned that trouble was stirring.

"Lieutenant," Forsyth said at last, "I want you to take your scouts and ride west toward Stein's Peak, then swing back a little south of east and come up toward the Hatchets. If you cut the trail of those wagons go in and bring them out of there. Understand?"

"Yes, sir . . . I have heard, sir, that von Hallstatt can be difficult."

"You are a soldier, McDonald. Bring him out of there."

"Yes, sir."

"Lieutenant Hall will make a scout toward the Hatchets, so be on the lookout for him. I shall follow with six troops of the Fourth Cavalry."

When McDonald had gone, Sandy Forsyth sat back in his chair and considered the situation. He was a handsome, square-jawed man with the scars of his wounds to prove what Indians could do. Trust an Indian to know of any movement in the area . . . there was not the slightest possibility that Chato did not know of the von Hallstatt group.

Hall would swing south and west, McDonald south and east, so if von Hallstatt was in the area they would be sure to cut his trail. At the same time their pincers movement might catch Chato in between. Meanwhile he would come down from the north with the Fourth Cavalry.

The colonel scowled as he studied the map. That was the way he had planned it and that was how it was supposed to work. The difficulty was that things almost never worked as planned, for Chato and his band would break up and proceed as individual members to a predetermined rendezvous. He had seen such groups fragment before, leaving nothing but a confusion of tracks almost impossible to follow.

Von Hallstatt had horses, and by the time the Apaches came up with his party, the Apache would need horses.

So few men, so much territory. Forsyth walked to the window and looked out. Somewhere in all that dusty, brown vastness was a party of dusty, brown bodies, bodies with hard faces and narrow eyes, scanning the desert as he was scanning it. And those bodies were those of forty or fifty of the most dangerous fighting men on earth.

The moves had been made, and it remained to see what happened. His task was to reach von Hallstatt before the Apaches did and, if possible, to capture or defeat the Apaches.

He swore bitterly. A party of casual hunters had gone in boldly, carelessly, where companies of soldiers rode with caution.

———

LYING ON HER pallet in the upper room at the stable, Irina could not sleep. It had taken all her arguments and persuasive powers to convince the others that they should move from their comfortable beds in the wagons to the stable, but even now she was not satisfied.

Only Laura Davis had listened and agreed, but Laura's mind had been made up beforehand. Edna Dagget had complained of the trouble, Julia Paige had scoffed mildly, but with a bit of a bite to her scoffing, too.

Julia had long had her cap set for Baron von Hallstatt, a fact of which only von Hallstatt seemed unaware, and it irked Julia to see Irina walking off so easily with the man she wanted.

Lying in the darkness, Irina stared up at the ceiling overhead, and considered the people with whom she faced this emergency, if such it would prove to be.

With the exception of Count Henri, none of these people had ever faced any kind of a difficulty, or were less prepared to deal with an emergency.

Frederick had been a highly successful officer in a highly organized army, accustomed to issuing orders and seeing them obeyed, yet the organization of that army was such that it left little initiative to any of its officers.

He had won victories over a disorganized, retreating foe, one whose generals had grown old and tired in their positions and who thought in terms of wars long completed and over. Frederick had received orders and given them, but there had been little chance for improvisation.

How would he react against an enemy when he would receive no orders himself, and where he must fight in person against an elusive enemy?

Count Henri, somewhat older than Frederick, was in many ways much younger. Henri had fought against Frederick in the Franco-Prussian War, but what was more important, Henri had served in the African desert against a foe much like the present one. Yet he was a man who talked little.

Frederick was brave . . . of that she had no doubt, yet more and more she was beginning to be aware that he was not only terribly self-centered, but that he was also without imagination.

Charles Dagget was not a fighting man. He was a diplomat, shrewd enough, congenial, and pleasant company always. This was his first venture into any wilderness greater than the environs of Paris or London. Furthermore, he was not suited to a rugged life.

Edna Dagget was a pretty woman, too thin, and apt to become somewhat hysterical . . . yet a lovely and gracious person under normal circumstances.

Laura Davis was the only American among them, a pleasant, charming girl, just short of being really beautiful, and a fine horsewoman. She had traveled in Europe, lived in Washington and New York, and had hunted in Virginia and Kentucky.

Hans Kreuger had been Frederick's aide during a brief period at the Franco-Prussian War's end. A serious, capable young man from a poor but honorable family. Like Frederick and Henri, he was an excellent rifle shot.

Edna loathed guns, and Charles had never fired any kind of a gun until this trip, and was notably poor as a rifle shot. Julia was an excellent horsewoman but uninterested in guns . . . as for herself, she had hunted with her father from childhood, killing her first wild boar at fourteen with her father standing by, and her first lion at seventeen.

Hours after she finally dropped off to sleep she awakened with a start, staring wide-eyed at the roof above. For a moment she could not recall where she was. The faint glow from the dying fire reflected on the underside of the roof, coming through the wide open door at the side of the building, which they had opened to get fresh air.

Otherwise, it was quite dark and she could hear no sound from the outside. Careful to make no sound so as not to disturb the others, she got to her feet and tiptoed to the door.

The fire was a bed of glowing red coals with only a few tendrils of flame doing their weird ballet above them. Beside the fire, his chin on his chest and evidently asleep, was the sentry.

The area within the circle of buildings was perhaps thirty yards long by twenty wide, and the firelight flickered on the canvas wagon tops and made weird, dancing shadows around their spokes. A few men slept under the wagons.

Nothing stirred in the space below, yet she stood for an instant, enjoying the stillness of the night and the red glow of the coals. Then from the corner of her eye she seemed to detect movement near the fire.

The guard was slumped forward, the black log near the fire was . . . *there had been no log*!

She reached quickly for her rifle, but even as her hand grasped it, the log came suddenly erect, a knife flashed in the firelight, and the guard toppled forward, falling at the edge of the fire.

She fired . . . too quickly. The Indian turned as if stunned and looked up at her. She saw the wide, hard-boned face and the dark holes where deep-sunk eyes would be, and then a second shot merged with the echo of her own. The Indian took two staggering steps and fell on his face.

From outside the circle there was a sudden chorus of yells and then a rush of hoofs that turned into a thunder of racing horses and mules . . . and then the sound died and there was only the dead guard and the naked dusty, brown figure sprawled face down on the hardpacked earth to indicate that anything had happened.

Men came from all over the yard, rushing out, then ducking for cover as there was an outburst of firing. She had never seen men take cover so quickly.

Edna Dagget sat up, clutching the blankets to her breast. "What is it? What has happened?"

"We've been attacked." Irina was surprised at her own calm. "A man has been killed."

Irina dressed quickly, and beside her Laura was dressing also. Irina took up her rifle and started toward the steps. Edna Dagget stared at her, frightened. "Where are you going? Why is everybody dressing? It isn't even daylight."

"We should all dress and be ready to help. A man has been killed."

"*Killed?*" Edna Dagget's shrill cry faded into a gasp of horror, and she started to dress also.

For the moment there was no further shooting. After the outburst of sound the silence was frightening. Stars held still in the sky, and the night was velvet soft. It was unreasonable that a man was dead . . . two men.

She went to the guard and, taking his sleeve, pulled him away from the edge of the fire that was already smoldering in his coat.

Buffalo called softly. "Ma'am! Get out of the light! *Quick!*"

She turned quickly and sprang away from the fire

just as a bullet kicked sparks near where she had been standing.

She knelt beside Buffalo, at the rear wheel of a wagon. There was something reassuring about his stalwart body. He was unshaved, and probably un-bathed, but he possessed an air of competence that gave her confidence.

Buffalo had drawn up the old chopping block and a couple of loose rocks for added protection.

"If I had been a moment sooner I could have saved that guard. I did not recognize that Indian until just before he moved."

"Figured that was you shooting. You set him right up for me. That was good thinking, ma'am."

Inordinately pleased at the compliment, she crouched lower, looking out into the darkness. Here and there she could make out clumps of creosote bush, but nothing more.

For the first time she thought of what had hap-pened and its meaning to them. The Apaches had stampeded their wagon stock and now they were im-mobilized unless they wished to abandon all their belongings. The saddle stock had all been held inside the circle . . . a small concession to Shalako's warning.

"Were there no guards outside the circle?"

"Two. Look close and you can see one of them ly-ing out there. He's the lucky one, he's dead."

Vague recollections returned to mind of stories she had heard, and only half-listened to, about what Indians did to prisoners. Suddenly the night was filled with menace, and with horror.

The castle in Wales where she had lived, London,

Paris, New York ... they seemed to be in another world.

"How much chance do we have?"

With other women he might have lied, but he respected the coolness and intelligence of this girl and she seemed somehow one of them. In part it was her own attitude and quickness with the rifle, in part it was the fact that she had loaned a horse to Shalako.

"Less'n fifty-fifty, I'd say. Ma'am, I ain't a-lyin' to you, you keep one bullet for yourself, d' you hear?"

She had never thought of death as something that could happen to her ... older people died, or lives were lost in accidents, and she heard of them or read of them in newspapers and was rarely stirred. The facility with which people bore the hardships of others was amazing.

She had always known that someday she would die. We are born with this knowledge or acquire it soon after birth, but death always seems remote and far-off. To realize there was no special protection for her ... that she, Lady Irina Carnarvon, could die a bloody and cruel death out here in these sand hills filled her with horror and distaste.

"He was right to leave us," she said.

"Mighty independent man. Wish he was here, though."

Buffalo Harris was doing some thinking of his own. How did a man get himself into a fix like this? How long had he been learning about Indians, anyway? Since he was six, crouched in a cornfield with his sister, listening to the awful, dying screams of his father and mother. He had fought Sioux, Kiowa, and

Comanche, and certainly knew better than to latch onto a greenhorn outfit like this.

It didn't make any kind of sense, the things a man would do. He was loafing around and not even broke when the offer came, and the others were taking it up, so he did, too. It sounded like a few months of mighty easy living and good grub . . . now he would be lucky to get out with his hair.

"Have you known him long?"

Buffalo shifted the tobacco to his other cheek. Odd, how good tobacco tasted when time was a-wasting.

"Awhile. He's a man minds his own affairs, and doesn't wait around much. I mean he rides in and if something isn't taking on to interest him, first thing you know, he's gone.

"He prospects a mite, rides herd once in a while. Been over the trail to Kansas with cowherds a couple of times, and one way or another, he keeps busy."

With faint gray where night's darkness had been, the Apaches came out of the desert like ghosts, running silently in a staggered skirmish line. Buffalo, whose eyes had never stopped searching, nailed the first one off the ground.

He saw the warrior's knee buckle at his shot, and then the girl beside him was shooting, and she put a bullet into the chest of the man he had wounded. And then they vanished like puffs of smoke . . . only they were closer now.

Buffalo turned his shaggy head to grin at her. "Two for us. Ma'am, you must have done a sight of shootin'."

Von Hallstatt ran up and dropped to the earth

beside them. His eyes were hot with excitement. "They move quickly." He pointed with the muzzle of his rifle. "One dropped to the ground out there, and when he rises, I shall kill him."

"He shifted position soon as he hit dirt," Buffalo advised. "They always do."

Von Hallstatt glanced at him irritably, then turned his eyes back to the desert. The light was growing now . . . he would not have believed that thirty or forty men lay within rifle shot.

As if speaking only to Irina, Buffalo began to discuss the Apache. "Start figurin' 'em like other folks an' you'll get yourself killed. You never get more than a split-second shot at an Apache, and in a setup like this they attack on foot, all scattered out. An' they can wait . . . time means nothin' to an Indian."

"Why don't they attack?" von Hallstatt demanded impatiently.

"Eatin' your wagon stock, most likely. They don't figure we'll be goin' anyplace."

Irina felt a chill of apprehension. Lying on the cold ground, her eyes searched the desert, but she saw nothing.

She heard movement behind them and glanced around to see a teamster hurrying toward the tank with a bucket. Yet even as she looked he seemed to stumble, his knees crumpled and the sound of a shot battered against the hills as he toppled face downward upon the sand.

Von Hallstatt's rifle had come up sharply, expectantly, but there was nothing at which to shoot, simply nothing at all.

"Three men killed, one missing," Buffalo spat into the sand, "an' we killed maybe two of them."

The hours dragged. Irina slipped from her position and careful to keep under cover, returned to the stable.

Laura had a fire going and coffee on. Mako was breaking eggs into a frying pan. Over at the house where most of the teamsters had slept, another fire was going. There was an occasional shot.

Charles Dagget was breaking down the partition between two stalls for fuel, and making an awkward job of it.

It was early, but already the sun was hot.

Suddenly, the morning air was rent by a shocking scream of pure agony, the scream of an animal in mortal anguish. Irina came up, her eyes wide with horror, and Edna clapped both hands over her ears. It came again, that same hoarse, choking scream . . . the scream of something in pain beyond belief.

Von Hallstatt cried out, "What in God's name is *that*?"

"Now"—Buffalo rolled his tobacco in his cheek and spat—"now we know where that other horse guard is."

———

THE SOUND OF gunfire awakened him. He lay on his back staring up at the last of the stars, listening.

He picked up the cigarette he had carefully rolled the night before and put it between his lips. As he struck his match, there were other shots. At least they had not been caught sleeping. They would make a fight of it then.

His mouth tasted bad and the stubble on his jaw itched. He should have been twenty miles along the Tucson trail.

He threw off his blanket and sat up, careful to check the cliffs around with cool, dispassionate eyes. He was a man without illusions, and there was no reason to believe that all the Apaches were over yonder at the point of the Hatchets. He might have picked up a few himself.

The Arab nickered softly and came up to be petted and scratched, making a show of pulling away from his hand, but not doing it.

He saddled the horse first, ready to ride out in a hurry if need be. Then he took up his rifle and led the horse to the trickle of water. His rifle would not change what was happening back there, and he saw no reason to get himself killed because of another man's mistakes. He made enough mistakes of his own without paying for another man's.

Nor was he opposed to boy generals. The younger ones were the best, as time and history had proved again and again. Napoleon had completed his Italian campaign by the time he was twenty-five, Hannibal was thirty-three at the Battle of Cannae, Alexander the Great had been twenty-five at the Battle of Arbela, and Wolfe had been thirty-two at the Battle of Quebec . . . he could think of fifty others.

The older ones were slower to change their ways, always wishing to fight new battles the way they had won old ones.

From time to time there were solitary shots . . . more than likely fired by the defenders who probably were seeing Indians where there were none.

He broke some branches from an antelope bush and fed them to the Arab. The stallion nosed doubtfully at the strange stuff, curling his lips around the leaves, hesitant, but aware that for some reason the man wanted him to eat them. Trying them, he liked the taste, and accepted more.

"You'd better learn, boy. You won't have oats very often, traveling with me."

He left his night camp then, and concealed the horse high up in the rocks where there was more antelope bush and another forage plant called wool fat. Then seated against the rock that offered the best position, he studied the situation.

The problem was not one to be solved by a lot of dashing about and shooting. If solved at all it would be by thinking, thinking first and carefully.

It was reasonable to suppose that only a small part of the Apaches were involved at the ranch. As the smoke signals told him, Chato was seeking reinforcements from San Carlos, and some of the Indians had left the reservation to join him.

Moreover, owing to the necessity of living off the country, the Apaches coming up from Mexico were traveling in more than one group, hence one could never be sure of where to expect an enemy.

Colonel Forsyth was in command at Fort Cummings, and would be out in force to round up the Indians.

If some trick could draw off the attackers at the ranch, then the group there might be gotten away to Fort Cummings or into a better defensive position in the mountains. At the ranch, the defenders would be driven to the buildings eventually, and cut off from water.

Putting himself in Forsyth's position, Shalako tried to guess the moves that would be made. Both the Animas and Playas valleys offered highroads into Mexico for the fleeing Apaches. Hence troops would surely be sent south along the Hatchets and along the Pelonchillos.

As always at these heights in the southwestern deserts, the air was unbelievably clear. From where he sat the ranch buildings were quite visible, as were the white tops of the wagons. He could distinguish no features of either, but the place itself was clear and sharp.

What was the old rule for judging distance? At one mile the trunks of large trees could be distinguished, at something over two miles—say two miles and a half—one could distinguish chimneys and windows, at six miles windmills and towers could be seen, and at nine miles a church steeple could be recognized.

The rules were for average atmosphere, much thicker than the clear desert air. In the desert there was no smoke, dust, or moisture as a rule, and only one-fourth the atmosphere of the eastern states, consequently one could see much farther.

Seated on a rock in the morning sun, Shalako watched the ranch and considered the problem in all its aspects. There was just a chance that a smoke signal might work, and he was going to try.

Heat waves shimmered above a desert where nothing moved. Lying on his stomach at one corner of the ranch house, Frederick von Hallstatt, baron and general, tasted the flavor of bitterness.

Sweat trickled down his forehead and into his eyes. From time to time he dried his palms on his shirt, and licked the sweat from his upper lip with his tongue. Heat waves shimmered, and he squinted into the unreality of the desert with a knot of cold fear clutching at his belly.

On his left, some forty yards away, lay an Apache warrior, one arm thrown wide. To von Hallstatt's knowledge this was the only Indian he had killed and he had fired at least thirty rounds.

He swore bitterly, in German. This was not the kind of fighting he was used to, nor the kind he expected. He glanced around at the others.

Henri faced south from the stable. Buffalo Harris, his skull wrapped in a bloody bandage, was facing west. On the north Charles Dagget held a rifle in unfamiliar hands, and beside him was Roy Harding, late of Ohio, and Bosky Fulton, that ill-smelling, hatchet-faced gunman. Rio Hockett was inside the house.

Early that morning one of the mule skinners had slipped a hand through a wagon flap and stolen a bottle of cognac, and when he stole that bottle he stole death.

The bottle lay out there now, only a third empty, reflecting the morning sun in a bright arrow of light. It had taken only a couple of swallows to make the mule skinner careless, and bottle in hand he started across the open ground toward the stable. The bullet had gone in over his ear, mushroomed, and tore away half his skull when it emerged on the other side.

Inside the stable in the coolest spot on the ground floor lay Hans Kreuger. A handsome young man who danced well in the ballrooms of Berlin, Vienna, and

Innsbruck, he lay dying on a pallet against the wall. He had made up his mind to die well, for it was the last thing left to a man, and he had a pride in such matters.

He was a sincere young man who had tried all his life to do things with dignity and manner. He was a proud, but not a vain man, convinced there were certain ways in which a man should conduct himself, and he had lived according to his principles.

It was incredible to him, as it was to von Hallstatt, that their losses had been greater than the attacker's, for it went against all military reason.

Hans Kreuger lay on his back staring up at the ceiling. Whenever anyone on the upper floor of the barn took a step a little puff of dust came through the cracks. Cobwebs trailed their gray nets to catch stray sunbeams . . . perspiration beaded his face but he held himself tight against the pain that was in him and thought of how little a man knows of what destiny has in store.

How proud he had been when he became aide to General von Hallstatt! How proud his parents had been when he was asked to accompany the general on his hunting trip to America, partly as aide to the general, and partly as a guest.

The others of the party would be people a young man of poor family rarely met. It would be a unique opportunity. He had no idea when accepting the offer that he was accepting an invitation to die.

To remain a man and a gentleman to the end, this was all that remained.

Removed from active combat by the bullets that ripped into his body, he could still observe. Laura

Davis had grown somehow. She was no longer the friendly, pretty girl, although she was that, also. She was more quiet, more sure of herself. She worked at whatever she did with quick but capable hands. Laura Davis . . . young, beautiful, and exciting. And he lay dying.

Edna Dagget he had once thought frail but lovely, now she was frail and haggard, her loveliness scarcely a memory. Her lips worked with wordless movement, and at every shot, she cringed. A few days ago he had admired her rather biting wit, and her coolness, yet when the emergency developed she proved a hollow shell with nothing inside.

Her husband, whom Edna had always spoken of in disparaging terms, had shown surprising strength. He almost seemed to welcome the fighting. He was entirely ignorant of warfare, yet he was observant, quick to learn, and careful to take no chances.

Hans Kreuger closed his eyes against the ache and the tiredness and tried to remember how the apple trees had looked when they bloomed across the countryside around his home in Hofheim, near Frankfurt. He felt Laura wipe the perspiration from his face, and he opened his eyes to look up at her, proud that he could conceal his pain.

How excited his family had been when he became aide to the baron! He was a powerful man of ancient family and much influence, and Hans's family assured him his fortune was made. How little had any of them known!

How can a man know? How can he guess which decision it is, often an inconsequential one, that sets him irrevocably upon the highway to failure, success, or sudden death? How can a man guess that from one particular instant he is committed, where the cogs will fit, one into the other, and each one turning the wheel inevitably closer and closer? How can he know as he laughs over a glass of wine, as he marches proudly, as he talks softly to a girl on the terrace . . . How can he know that each is a move that brings him closer to the end?

And had he taken another turn, met another girl, drunk his wine in another café, he might have lived a decade longer . . . or three decades even?

In the loft over the stable, Irina yielded her place at the window to Bosky Fulton.

She had been looking out over the desert when she heard faint movement behind her and smelled the stale odor of unwashed clothing. She turned and he leered at her, his shirt collar edged with grime, the grime showing in the skin of his neck.

He grasped her arm and pulled her toward him and she jerked free, astonished and angry.

"Aw, don't look at me that way! Before this is over you'll be glad to ride out of here with somebody who can take care of you."

"I can take care of myself."

"Can you now?" He gestured toward the ladder. "Go ahead an' fix the grub. Meanwhile you better think on this: you cotton up to me or you stay here as bait for those 'Paches. I can get you out of this, and that fancy Fritz Baron of yours, he can't get himself out."

She was trembling with shock and anger when she came down the steps. Yet she was frightened, too, deeply, seriously frightened. And she could not remember being frightened in the same way before this.

One by one the men came for their food, crawling around the rim of the circle, keeping to the small shadow and what protection the buildings and wagons offered.

There was little talk. The men ate quickly, seriously, then returned the way they had come. Only Charles Dagget was excited. "I think I hit one," he said. "Scared him, anyway."

Irina scarcely heard what he said. Should she say anything about what Fulton had told her? And did he really believe what he said? Or was that merely something to use as an argument to her?

He believed it. She suddenly knew that he believed it. Bosky Fulton did not think they were going to get out alive.

Coming after what Shalako had said, she was convinced of their situation. Yet it had not been that which frightened her, but Fulton's own attitude. His cocksureness, his disregard of what would happen to the others, and the sudden sharp awareness that nobody here could protect her. Von Hallstatt was a man of undoubted courage, so was Count Henri, but she had heard enough talk around camp to know that something else was demanded, and she had seen some very tough men walk softly around Bosky Fulton.

Buffalo Harris came in while von Hallstatt and Count Henri were still there. "Smoke over the Animas," Buffalo said. "Wished I knew what they meant. Shalako now, he could read them. He—"

Buffalo broke off sharply, the idea startling him with its possibilities. "No . . . couldn't be that."

"What?"

"By this time he's clean t'other side of the Stein's Peak range, but I was just thinkin', Shalako knowin' the smokes, and all . . . if he sent up a smoke . . . no, it ain't reasonable. Only he savvies that smoke talk as well as any Indian."

"You mean he might send up a signal that would draw them off? But they would come back."

Bosky Fulton descended the ladder. "How's for some coffee?" He grinned insolently at Irina, then glanced at von Hallstatt as if to challenge a reprimand.

"You've left your post." Von Hallstatt eyed him coldly. "Get back up there until you're relieved."

"You want somebody up there," Fulton replied, "you go yourself."

Never had Irina seen such a shocked expression on any man's face as crossed the baron's at that moment. He probably never had had an order refused before.

An instant only . . . then his face was swept by cold fury. His rifle stood near the door. He started for it.

Bosky Fulton's gun slid into his hand, and the cocking of the gun was loud in the sudden silence.

"You pick that up," Fulton drawled, "an' you better walk right outside with it. You turn on me, I'll kill you."

Von Hallstatt stopped. Always before the might of the Prussian Army had stood behind him. Now there was only himself. Never had he been threatened with a pistol, and terrible fury choked him. Yet at the same instant there swept through him the icy realization that he could die. That the man behind him would surely kill.

The baron had been given a choice. Could he lift the rifle, turn and cock and fire before the man behind him could fire?

"Put up your gun, Fulton!" The voice rang with the harshness of command. "Put up your gun and get back to your post."

Of them all, von Hallstatt was the most surprised, for Hans Kreuger had lifted himself to one elbow and in his hands he held the twin barrels of a shotgun, the muzzles pointed at Fulton.

The distance was scarcely twenty feet, the shotgun a short-barreled express gun. Kreuger's face was pale and perspiring, but there was no doubt that he meant what he said.

"I have enough buckshot to cut you in two, Fulton," Kreuger said, "and nothing to lose."

The gunman's eyes seemed to change color. Or was it the light in the room? Irina, who was watching him, saw an ugly hatred come into those yellow eyes, but he eased the hammer back in place with elaborate care, and then he turned and started for the ladder. There he hesitated, stealing a glance over his shoulder, but the twin muzzles followed him relentlessly.

When Fulton had disappeared up the ladder, Kreuger lay back on his pallet, gasping hoarsely, his brow beaded with sweat.

Von Hallstatt remained standing by the door, staring out across the desert, his back to the room. The sun was going down. The day would soon be gone.

He stared blindly, conscious of it all but seeing

nothing. He had been afraid. He, Frederick von Hallstatt, had been afraid.

He had known that surely as he stood there that unwashed hireling would kill him. No command of his mattered here, no authority of position or personality stood between him and these men.

He hated them, he hated the wild, irresponsible freedom and independence there was in them all. He was used to subservience, to acceptance of his authority, his position. That independence was in Shalako, Harris, Fulton . . . all of them.

Buffalo Harris's frank, matter-of-fact, man-to-man talk had always offended him, yet it had taken a cocked gun in the hand of Bosky Fulton to make him aware of how little he mattered here. He, Frederick von Hallstatt, baron and general, could be shot down and killed as simply as any peasant.

Turning slowly, he threw a glance at his wounded aide. "Thank you, Hans," he said.

Taking up his rifle he went outside and returned to his position, and not until he was there, watching the desert once more, did he realize that for the first time he had called Kreuger by his given name.

And well he might, for Hans Kreuger had saved him from more than he knew. Possibly he had saved him from death, possibly from an exhibition of cowardice.

Had Kreuger not intervened, what would he have done? Would he have attempted to turn? Or would he meekly have submitted?

Blindly, Frederick von Hallstatt stared out across the desert. For the first time in his entire life he did not know. For the first time, he was unsure.

CHAPTER 3

W HEN VON HALLSTATT had gone, nobody
spoke for several minutes, then Buffalo
Harris finished his coffee, and went to the door. He
hesitated there, turned as if to speak, then ducked outside and was gone.

Count Henri's handsome features were expres-
sionless. He glanced at her. "I am sorry you are here,
Irina."

Then he went outside also.

Her decision, when it was made, was deliberate.
And in the moment of deciding she knew it was a de-
cision that should have been made before this.
Gathering her skirts, she started for the door.

"Irina!" Laura caught at her arm. "Stay away
from the door! What can you be thinking of?"

"I am going to the wagon," she said calmly, "for
some food and ammunition."

"You will be killed!"

"I do not think so," she replied calmly, "I think
they will want the women alive."

Laura's eyes were without expression. "Yes, yes, of
course. But be careful."

It was a silly thing to say at such a time, but what
could be said? She took a deep breath and, stepping
outside, she walked coolly and deliberately to the
nearest wagon.

Climbing into the wagon, she gathered up a parcel of food, a medicine kit with additional medicines, and a box of ammunition. Putting them all in a burlap sack, she swung it over her shoulder and walked back to the stable.

Returning, she climbed into the wagon again. The heat was stifling under the canvas wagon top and the interior smelled of the sun-hot canvas, a smell like no other, yet not unpleasant.

From a box of her own things she took a .44-caliber derringer with two barrels, one over the other. Checking to be sure it was loaded, she tucked it into her clothing. Loading another box of ammunition and more food into her sack, she returned again to the stable.

She had concealed the sack when Bosky Fulton suddenly came down the ladder and, without glancing at her, went outside and worked his way around to the house.

She recalled hearing a low mutter of conversation from the loft, and remembered that one of the other teamsters was up there.

Fulton remained in the house but, after a few minutes, Rio Hockett came to the door and motioned to one of the other men. The man crawled, then suddenly darted for the door and ducked inside, a bullet tapping the doorjamb with a disgusted finger.

Aided by Laura, Irina returned to the wagons and removed more of the food and ammunition. No shot was fired at them.

Buffalo returned to the stable. "They're pullin' out," he said. "Those smokes are drawin' them off. I'd say we'd better light out of here."

"Do you suppose it is a trick? Something to draw us out of this position?"

"Don't think so. Their dust shows up too far off for that. They've sure enough taken out."

Roy Harding strolled up to the door. "What do you think, Buff? Could we make Fort Cummings? My guess would be the troops are out by this time."

The rest of their party slowly congregated. "Please," Edna Dagget said, "let us go now."

Bosky Fulton spoke from the stable door. "Too late for you folks. You're goin' to stay here. We're takin' out."

Their heads turned as one, and Bosky Fulton stood in the stable door behind them, and beside him were four men with rifles, hip high, ready to fire.

"We decided we don't like it here no more," Fulton said. "Rio, you shuck their guns and shake them down for money or whatever."

"If you wish to leave," Count Henri said coolly, "you must realize you are not alone. We were discussing such a move when you came in. I suggest you harness the teams and be ready to move out."

"We go," Fulton repeated, "you stay."

Von Hallstatt clutched his rifle by the upper barrel, but he stood among the women and there was no chance of bringing it into use without endangering them all. And he had seen how quickly Fulton could go into action.

"If you appear with our belongings," Dagget warned, "questions will be asked. It must be obvious to you that many of our weapons and other belongings will be recognized or easily identified."

Fulton grinned at Dagget. "Not in Mexico. Not in

the border towns. And when the Apaches get through with you folks nobody will be asking any questions at all."

He glanced over at Harding. "You're in the wrong crowd, Roy. You belong with us."

"I like it where I am," Harding replied bluntly. "I never did cotton to thieves. Nor do I want to get my neck stretched."

Fulton shrugged. "Suit yourself. Soon as they see what those smokes meant the Apaches will be back. They'll take care of whatever we leave."

When they had been disarmed, their guns were emptied and handed back. "Look funny if you had no guns. It would make the Apaches talk and we might have to answer to the Army if we were caught. So you just keep those fancy guns."

Irina thought of her derringer. If she could get it out . . . but that would only lead to shooting and her friends would be wounded or killed.

Hockett took their rings from their fingers and what valuables they had on their persons. Cold with anger, Irina watched, knowing the men were as helpless to act as she herself.

The heaviest of the riding stock were hitched to the wagon into which they loaded all that remained of food, ammunition, and valuables that could be disposed of below the border. The horses were not broken to drive, but to men accustomed to the handling of broncos it made no difference. Her own horses were led out and for a moment she felt a savage pleasure. Neither of her horses had ever been ridden by a man, and while these men were horsemen, nonetheless she knew the mares would be watching for an opportunity to throw their riders and escape.

"Leave the roan," Fulton said, "he's all stove up."

"They'll take that horse and hunt for help," Hockett objected.

"Rio, you know that horse is in bad shape. Where would they go for help? The nearest would be seventy or eighty rough miles, maybe twice that far, and Apaches all over the country."

Suddenly Fulton's eyes switched to Irina. "You," he said, "you and that Davis gal. You're a-coming with us."

"I think not."

There was an odd, snakelike quality in the way in which Fulton turned his head.

Count Henri had spoken, and now he met Fulton's gaze calmly. Only a fool could look at the Frenchman and doubt that he would fight.

Roy Harding took a step wide of the group, but in a position that made his intentions obvious. Von Hallstatt gathered himself, giving all his attention to Fulton.

"Ride out with what you have," Henri said coolly, "otherwise you must kill us all, and you'll not do it without our leaving a mark on you.

"I suspect this Colonel Forsyth of whom we have heard will be curious as to why we were all shot at close range and why a wagon is gone. Also," he added, "the Apaches may not be so far away as to wonder why there is shooting when they are not attacking. They might be curious enough to return to find out."

"Forget 'em, Bosky," Hockett said. "We'll find plenty of women in Mexico."

Fulton turned abruptly. "All right, let's go!"

They left in a swirl of dust, and when they were gone, only Roy Harding, Buffalo Harris, and Mako, the cook they had brought from Europe, remained with them.

Irina uncovered the ammunition hidden under a pile of blankets in a corner, and ammunition was passed out among them. The sun was setting.

"We cannot defend this place," von Hallstatt said. "We are too few."

"We'd do better to run for the hills," Harding suggested. "We might find a better place to hole up."

"We'll need water," Buffalo said doubtfully.

———

SHALAKO RODE UP out of the wash and walked the Arab stallion into the circle. "Get whatever grub you've got, blankets and whatever you can carry. If you want to live you've got to get out of here."

"There's water here!" Dagget protested. "And that stable is built like a fort!"

Shalako wasted no words. "How will you get water with Indians shooting into the door?"

"A trip across the desert will kill my wife!" Dagget protested.

"What will happen if she stays here?"

Irina wasted no time listening. Mustering the help of Julia and Laura, they began getting what blankets and food there was. Von Hallstatt and Henri made a stretcher of two long coats by slipping a pole through the arms of the two coats on one side, then another pole on the other. Then they buttoned the coats.

It was quite dark when they finally moved out.

Edna Dagget went first, walking beside her husband. The roan followed, led by Julia, and packed with food and medical supplies. The Arab was also loaded down, and led by Laura.

Henri and von Hallstatt carried the stretcher on which Hans lay, protesting the necessity for taking him. Harding and Harris brought up the rear, and Mako walked behind the Arab.

Shalako had removed his boots and donned moccasins for the walk. They were Apache moccasins that came well up the leg and had stiffer soles for desert walking.

The stars were out, the night very still. Once, three years before, he had camped at the place where he planned to take them. He had no idea of attempting to make Fort Cummings. With the wounded man and Edna Dagget they could not hope to make the distance, and Apaches had been known to kill right under the walls of a fort. Nor would Julia Paige stand up to such a walk . . . the others might.

The journey before them was serious enough without thinking of the much, much longer trek to Fort Cummings.

All he could expect to do was to hide them in the hills and hope the backwash of retreating Apaches did not find them.

Harris had told him briefly about the robbery and flight of the group under Fulton, but that was none of his affair.

Shalako walked to the head of the small column, Irina falling in beside him. Von Hallstatt glanced at them as they went by, but made no comment.

"Why did you come back?" she asked suddenly.

If there was an answer to that he did not know what it was, nor was he a man given to self-analysis or worry about his motives. If they were caught out in the open there was no chance for them, simply none at all.

Knowing no logical answer, he did not attempt to make one, but walked beside her in silence. He walked well ahead of the others so the sounds from the desert would not be merged with their own sounds.

When they halted he fell back and squatted on his heels beside the stretcher, rolling a smoke in the darkness. Carefully shielding the flame, he lighted it, then handed it to Kreuger.

The German inhaled deeply, gratefully. "It is the little things," Kreuger said.

"Yes."

"It is far?"

This man was beyond truth or lies, and he had shown himself a brave man. "It is farther than I told them. You will understand."

"A good place?"

"At the last it will be bad for you, Hans. There will be climbing and turning, but it is a good place."

"Do not think of me."

The bulk of Gillespie Mountain lifted against the sky, still several miles away. The notch toward which he directed their steps was just to the south of it. The cliffs at that place reared up more than a thousand feet and, atop that cliff, between it and Elephant Butte Canyon, there was a place to hide. There was water at the head of Park Canyon and the corner where the two canyons headed up was a difficult place to attack.

"I do not think you have long been a Western man," Kreuger said. "The general was surprised when you mentioned Vegetius and Saxe."

"A Western man is a man from elsewhere," Shalako said. "The West was an empty land and men were drawn to it from the East, from Europe, even from China. An officer killed with Custer at Little Bighorn had been a Papal Guard at the Vatican. I know a rancher in New Mexico who was an officer in Queen Victoria's Coldstream Guards. There is a marshal in the Indian Territory who served in the French Army. Western men were poor men, rich men, beggar men, thieves. Only whatever they were, they were strong men or they did not come West, and of those who came, only the strongest survived."

"And you?"

Faintly, on the soft wind, was a smell of woodsmoke. Shalako swore. "There are Indians south of us."

"And you?" Kreuger persisted.

"A man who wanders, that is what I am. It is a wide land, and much of it I have not seen, and much I wish to see again. A man is what he is, and what he is shows in his actions. I do not ask where a man came from or what he was . . . none of that is important.

"It is what a man does, how he conducts himself that matters, not who his family were." He got up. "I know it is otherwise in Europe."

"Not entirely," Krueger said, "but it is important." He paused, then added defensively, "Breeding is important."

"Breeding can breed weakness as well as strength, cowardice as well as bravery. I do not think much thought was given to virtue or courage when the bloodlines were laid down. They did not breed for quality, they bred for money. Estates were married, not people."

"There is something in what you say," Kreuger confessed reluctantly.

Walking forward again, he spoke to each of them. "Not a whisper," he said, "not a sneeze. If you drop anything you may drop our lives with it. No matches, no cigarettes . . . there are Indians south of us."

The woodsmoke might come from Cowboy Spring or even that other spring beyond the buttes. Not far enough away for comfort. When they moved out again, Buffalo took the lead and Harding shared the stretcher with Shalako.

Edna Dagget was already dragging her feet. Julia, although she walked well, was showing discomfort.

They walked and rested, they walked again . . . without the stretcher they might have made it by daybreak, as it was a rising wind tuned the violins of the desert shrubs, the Animas Mountains lifted a black wall before them, but a tinge of crimson touched the ridge. Reluctantly the darkness retreated into the narrow-mouthed canyons.

No smoke against the sky. They halted again where mountain run-off had cut a gash in the accumulated debris at the mountains' base. Charles and Edna Dagget huddled together, holding their faces tight against disaster. Laura's eyes seemed larger this morning, and there were hollows in her cheeks.

Only Hans Kreuger seemed unchanged.

Mako, a thin, wiry man who looked more like a doctor of philosophy than a cook, glanced up as

Shalako approached him. "I could make some coffee, sir," he suggested.

"No."

Shalako allowed nearly an hour of rest, for the Daggets had little reserve remaining.

It was cold in the shadow of the mountains. The desert lay pale beige before them, dotted with cloud shadow and desert shrubs. Julia Paige looked at the desert and held her shoulders pinched against the chill. Von Hallstatt had a stubble of beard on his jaws, and he stared sullenly at the sand. Count Henri leaned back against the bank, breathing easily.

Shalako squatted on his heels and studied them from under the brim of his hat, assaying the reserves of each.

Von Hallstatt was like iron. Whatever else he was, there was strength in the man, strength of body and strength of will. The breeding had told there, all right. This was one who had been bred for the Prussian Army officer corps . . . yet the breeding had lost something, too.

Henri . . . a member of the nobility who still possessed nobility. His physical strength might be less, but his morale was greater, he had stamina of the spirit, which outweighs all physical strength.

Shalako was rising to start them moving again when he heard a sound that was more than the wind. Hat off, he lifted his head slowly until his eyes cleared the bank. Not fifty yards away were four Apaches, riding single file.

Naked but for breechclouts, rifles in their hands, they were walking their horses toward the wash in which Shalako stood. Only their line of travel would take them into the wash some fifty or sixty yards ahead of their party. It was Shalako's good luck that their eyes had been averted as his head cleared the edge of the wash.

Von Hallstatt was beside him, and there was no mistaking the look in his eyes as the rifle started to come up. Shalako shoved the rifle barrel down, and the German jerked it from under his hand and started to lift it again. At that instant an Apache looked toward them.

"Let go, you fool!" von Hallstatt whispered. "I am going to kill him."

"What about the women? Do you want to get them killed as well as yourself?"

Their eyes locked and meanwhile the Apaches dipped into the wash ahead of them. They crossed the wash around a slight bend from the waiting party, and neither group could see the other, but they heard the scramble of the horses as they left the wash.

"You put a hand on me again," von Hallstatt said, "and I shall kill you."

"I seen it tried," Buffalo commented.

"You would have killed one Indian," Shalako said, "and then we would have been pinned down without water. Right where we stand it will be more than a hundred degrees within two hours, and maybe ten degrees hotter before the day is out."

"We could have killed them all."

"As long as I am with this party you will be guided by me. If you want to kill Apaches you can go out on your own."

"Take your horse, then," von Hallstatt replied, "and get out of here. We don't need you."

"Frederick!" Irina was appalled.

"If he hadn't interfered we could have killed all four of them," von Hallstatt said angrily.

Shalako gestured toward the mountains. "And what about *them*?"

The German's head snapped around. Along the wall of the mountain, a good half mile away, moved a party of at least eight Indians.

The German's jaw set sullenly, but he said nothing.

"All right," Shalako said, "if you want me to leave, I'll leave. I'll take my horse and ride out of here."

"No, Mr. Carlin," Irina interrupted. "I loaned Mohammet to you. I want you to stay, but if you must go, by all means take him."

"If he goes," Buffalo said, "I go."

"Go, then. And be damned to you!" Von Hallstatt's face was pale with fury.

He could not have said why he was angry. For the first time in his life he was faced with a situation which he could not command. Common sense warned him that Shalako knew far more of what it was necessary to know to save them, but from the first there had been a conflict of personalities coupled with what was undoubtedly jealousy at Irina's seeming interest.

Yet through his anger these threads of reason showed, irritating him all the more.

"I suggest we talk this over," Henri said. "We have much to consider, Frederick."

Roy Harding had been watching von Hallstatt with a curious, unbelieving expression on his face.

"Meaning no disrespect, General von Hallstatt," Kreuger spoke weakly from his stretcher, "but where would we go? What would we do?"

Count Henri arose and walked to the rear end of the stretcher, Harding picked up the front end, and Shalako walked off to the head of the small column. Without further discussion the others fell into place and followed after.

Von Hallstatt looked at them with mingled exasperation and relief. "I have no reasonable alternative," he said, after a minute.

Buffalo Harris had stopped beside him, and together they walked off, bringing up the rear of the column.

They were climbing now, every step an effort, nor did Shalako hold down the pace. He stepped out swiftly, knowing the sooner they got among the rocks or in some kind of cover the better off they would be. The nakedness of the desert was appalling, and he had seen a detachment of troops surrounded and picked off one by one in such a position as theirs.

Irina kept pace with him but only with an effort, and it was only the lure of the shade offered by the canyons that kept her going.

Edna Dagget fell down. She was helped up by her husband, who half-carried her as they continued. Julia was lagging, and she had torn her skirt on a cactus thorn.

Several times they made brief stops, and then when Gillespie Mountain loomed to their north, Shalako stopped in the shade of a cliff. To the south the wall of the mountain reared up a thousand feet, not sheer, but incredibly steep.

"We will go up there," Shalako said.

Von Hallstatt glanced at the cliff, then looked over

at Shalako, completely incredulous. Irina was appalled.

"It will be pretty rough going," Shalako admitted, "but there's a makeshift of a trail. I'll take Count Henri and go up first. We will need a man with a rifle up there to cover our climb."

"Why not me?" Irina suggested. "I can't help with Hans, but I can use a rifle."

It was a logical suggestion, and he had thought of it. "You will be up there alone," he said. "I've got to come back down."

"I've been alone before."

"As you wish."

Hitching his pack into position, he took up his Winchester and started for the trail, and Irina fell in behind him. Von Hallstatt threw his pack on the ground and spat.

Buffalo glanced at him and, catching Harding's eyes, he shrugged.

Walking into the maze of rocks, Shalako ducked under a slab, entering a narrow space between boulders. They emerged in a narrow watercourse and beside it a trail.

"Sheep trail," Shalako commented. "Bighorns."

Once he started to climb, he walked slowly, for he had climbed often and knew that only a fool hurries. The narrow trail switched and doubled. The sheep had used it single file, and it was incredibly narrow. The sun was blazing hot, and when her hand accidentally touched a rock, she jerked it away with a gasp. It was hot enough to fry eggs.

Here and there Shalako paused to move rocks from the trail or to widen it for those who would follow. Then the trail jogged a little and briefly they would be in the shade of the cliff.

Shalako stopped and removed his hat, peering at the trail ahead, and wiping the sweatband. Irina was flushed and panting, glad of the momentary respite.

"Will they find our trail?"

"They'll find it."

"Have you lived in the West all your life?"

He glanced at her, faint humor lurking in his eyes. "It's a good country," he said, "and a beautiful country. It's an easy country to get lost in."

"If one has reason to get lost."

He smiled. "Yes, if one has reason. Or if one doesn't." He gestured, "It's a big country, and a lot of men have come West their folks never heard of again. Some were killed, some died, some made new lives for themselves and wanted no part of what they left behind. Some men find out here the answer to all they need."

"And you?"

"It's a big country, and I like it. A man has room to think out there, and room to move. I'm a man who doesn't like to be crowded."

"And what of the future?"

"Ah . . . the future? Yes, there's always that. Someday I must sit down and think it all out, but perhaps I shall take up some land, build the kind of house I want, and raise some cattle, breed a few horses." He got up. "You took a risk coming into this country with a stallion like Mohammet. To say nothing of those mares."

He took up his rifle. "It is a thing I've noticed, Miss Carnarvon, the first generation out here want horses that will stand the gaff, stand up to brutal work and hard riding, the second generation are already thinking of horses that look like something, and the next generation will only want fancy horses and all the elaborate leather and silver they can get on them."

He started off, and she followed. A moment later she paused, and he stopped. She eased her foot inside her boot, then started on. "You have no silver on your saddle," she said.

"I'm from the first generation," he said, "and silver reflects sunlight. Nobody but a fool wants flashing metal on his gear or a white horse in this country. Too many folks can know when you're coming."

They skirted the edge of a cliff that fell away for several hundred feet, wedged themselves between boulders, and then suddenly emerged on top.

"You will never get the horses up that trail," she said. "No kind of a horse could get between those rocks."

"I'm going to ride around . . . and it is a long way around."

The air was surprisingly cool. A faint breeze smelled of pines and cedars. Facing south she overlooked the deep gash of Elephant Butte Canyon. Park Canyon, starting almost at her feet, pointed away toward the southwest. The point of land on which they stood was but a few acres in extent, and there were scattered pines, some cedar, and a few shrubs of which she knew nothing. They were the dry, harsh-looking shrubs of the desert mountains. There was also a little grass.

"Wait at the top of the trail," he told her, "but do not be distracted by what is happening on the trail itself. They will get up somehow and that is not your problem.

"Watch the desert, watch all the approaches to the trail below. Do not fire unless necessary, but if they start toward the foot of the trail, stop them."

"Is there danger behind us? From the south?"

"You never know, so you had better keep a careful lookout."

He discarded his pack, leaving it beside her. "I will be going down."

"Why are you doing this? You were clear of it, you were away, you were free. And sometimes I think you do not even like us."

"Shooting downhill that way . . . it can throw you off your target."

"You didn't answer me."

"Does a man have to have a reason? Maybe it is because you loaned me a horse." He paused at the trail's head and pointed off through the trees to the southwest. "You watch for me there. I'll come up west of that small canyon. But don't take it for granted that whoever comes will be me, and I won't come in the night.

"I'll identify myself, so be careful."

"It is good of you to help us, Mr. Carlin. Especially when Frederick has been so difficult."

He threw a quizzical glance at her. "I don't blame him. If I had a girl as lovely as you, I'd be careful, too. I wouldn't want her traipsing around the country with a strange man."

"Maybe he trusts me."

"Doesn't look like it. Anyway, it isn't a matter of

trusting. Maybe he's afraid I'll just take you and run, leave them all to the desert."

"I'd have something to say about that." She looked at him boldly. "Are you trying to frighten me?" She paused. "After all, I am practically engaged to Frederick."

"Doesn't mean a thing."

He started to walk away, and she looked after him. "Frederick has been difficult," she added.

When he said nothing, but started down the trail, she called after him, "And you're difficult, Mr. Carlin!"

She had no idea whether he heard her or not. She heard his footsteps on the trail, and then they faded, and she was alone. Wind stirred in the cedars, and there was no other sound for a long time.

The air was very clear. She looked north up the wide valley toward the ranch they had left. Dancing heat waves cut off the view in the distance along the foot of the mountains.

Shalako . . . it was a strange name, an exciting name. And he was an exciting man. Exciting, yet strangely calming at such times as this, for he seemed so completely in command of the situation . . . not that any person could be sure of coming out alive from such an ordeal, but she had the feeling that if they failed, if Shalako ever failed in such a situation as this, it would only be after everything possible had been done.

What there was to do, he would do; what there was to consider, he would have considered.

She had told him she was almost engaged to Frederick. Now why had she said *that*? It was not true. There was a sort of understanding between them, but nothing had been said, not really. She knew that Frederick wanted to marry her, and she knew she had been considering it.

And now Shalako.

But how could she consider him at all? How would he look among her friends in London? His weather-beaten features, his big, strong hands, that shaggy, powerful look he had about him.

No, he would not fit.

Or would he? Some of the soldiers from the Northwest Frontier of India were like that . . . not shaggy, however. But a haircut would take care of that.

But why consider his coming into her life? And what made her believe he would be happy there?

No, this was his country, this was his land, and it was a strong, beautiful land. She inhaled deeply. There was something about the mountain air that made one want to inhale deeply . . . it was like fresh, clear, cold water in the throat.

BUFFALO HARRIS WAS the last man up the trail. At the last, when Harris waited to follow the others, he stood for a minute or two finishing a cigarette with Shalako.

"Along the east side of the mountains they rise up steep and high for several miles, so I'm going on up this canyon we're in and strike the head of Wolf Canyon. There's an old Indian trail running back toward the southeast from there, and a fork in that will take me right into the park."

"You take care. I don't cotton to that general."

"He's a good man, Buff. Just out of his element, that's all. Don't worry about him."

He watched Buffalo start up the cliff, then picked up the roan's lead rope and mounted the stallion. It was very hot, and weariness suddenly flooded over him. Just as the long, hot ride had taken its toll from the roan, it was now getting to him. It had been a long time since he had been this tired.

Squinting his eyes under the pulled-down hatbrim, he studied the terrain with care. Nothing must happen to him, for he carried nearly all the food and ammunition for the party.

Behind him was the Playas Valley, before him, beyond the mountains, was the Animas Valley. He started Mohammet, walking the stallion out of the copse where they had assembled for the climb, and he turned the Arab westward.

The sun burned on his back, and his eyelids were heavy. His eyes ached and the lids burned with staring over the wide, hot spaces. There was no sound but the hoof-falls of his horses, the creak of the saddle. He touched his tongue to his dry lips and mopped his forehead with the sleeve of his shirt.

He topped out on the rise, and Wolf Canyon lay before him. He came down off the ridge and in the brief shadow of the boulders, he studied the terrain again. It was hard to focus his eyes, but he took his time, measuring the sunlit vastness before him, the great shoulders of raw, red rock, the splashes of green, the great, broken, shattered land.

A lizard darted out on a rock near him, and stopped, its side panting with the heat. Overhead a buzzard circled, but the blue sky of morning was gone, and in its place was a sky of heat-misted brass from which the sun blazed. He rubbed the stubble on his jaws, and started the Arab forward, feeling his way down the slope, watching for the trail he knew was there.

———

UPON A SHOULDER of Gillespie Mountain, *Tats-ah-das-ay-go* turned his cold eyes toward the southwest . . . movement! Something stirred among the sunlit hills.

Squatted in the shadow of a rock, the Quick-Killer's eyes held upon the far distant hill. The movement had been there, and then it was gone . . . it had been no sheep, and nothing else would be large enough.

Again!

He squinted his eyes against the glare. A man. A rider with two horses. Swiftly, he turned and went down off the mountain to his horse.

Let Chato go his way . . . let Loco and the others go . . . he would find his own kills, and leave them where he found them.

———

FAR AND AWAY to the south and east, along the foot of the Big Hatchet Mountains, Rio Hockett led the stolen wagon and its cargo. Bob Marker rode beside him.

Flanking the wagon were two riders, and two men rode the seat of the wagon. Two more brought up the rear, riding wide of the wagon to be free of its dust.

Two more rode inside, armed and ready. Bosky Fulton brought up the rear, nor was it by accident that he chose the position.

They had seen no Apaches, nor any Indian sign at all. Rio Hockett was walking his horse and well out in the lead with Marker when he smelled dust. Drawing up sharply, he turned in his saddle. No wind was blowing.

Uneasily, he looked around him. Nothing stirred. The smell of dust was gone. He looked across toward the Animas Mountains, but saw nothing. Nearby were several drowned peaks, almost buried in the sand that would eventually cover them.

Hockett mopped his brow and looked around him again. Bob Marker, a mean-looking Missourian, shot him a sharp glance. "What's the matter?"

"I don't like the feel of things. I thought I smelled dust."

"Our own, prob'ly. Let's go. There's water south of them peaks, and Mexico not far beyond it."

"Bosky wants us to go east toward Juarez . . . not a bad idea. Say! I know a little Mex gal in Juarez, who—"

And then he saw the tracks.

Hockett turned swiftly, slapping spurs to his horse, and started for the wagon. He saw it swing broadside, saw a man fall from the wagon seat into the sand, and then he heard the report of a gun . . . seconds later there were other shots.

He glanced around for Marker and saw his horse running riderless, stirrups flapping. He felt his own horse go under him and kicked his feet free of the stirrups, dropping like an acrobat even as his horse went head over heels. He turned in his tracks, firing his rifle from the hip.

Hockett was a big man, and tough. He had been a buffalo hunter, a cow thief, and a scalp hunter, and he had nerve. Levering the Winchester, he fired again and again. He got one, saw another stagger. He hosed bullets at them . . . too fast.

The Winchester clicked on an empty chamber and he dropped it, drawing both guns. Something jerked at his sleeve, sand kicked against his boots. He saw a horse fall, heard a shrill scream of pain from behind him, and he thumbed back the hammer of the .44, firing coolly.

There was no doubt in his mind. With shocking clarity, he realized this was the end.

A bullet smashed into his shoulder, turning him half around. He dropped his gun, but with a border shift tossed the gun from hand to hand, then fired again. He stood, spraddle-legged atop a hummock of sand, his long hair blowing wild, a splash of blood across his face from a split scalp.

A bullet knocked a leg from under him, and on one knee he calmly fed shells into the gun. His shoulder was hurting, but he could still use it, so no bone was broken. Behind him there were yells, screams of anguish, and the crackle of flames.

Now a dozen Indians surrounded him, baiting him as they might have baited a wounded bear. He mopped the blood from his face, holding his fire.

His horse was down not far away and his canteen was on the saddle. The distance to the rocks was no more than thirty yards. Straightening to his feet, he limped and staggered to the horse for the canteen and slung it over his shoulder.

Glancing around, he saw the wagon top ablaze, and the bodies of the others scattered around, festooned with arrows. Indians were looting the wagon before the burning canvas fell in upon it.

Taking up his rifle, he merely glanced at the Indians, who watched him curiously. Then he started toward the rocks.

He understood them, he thought bitterly, and he knew they would wait, just as he in their place might have waited. They would allow him to get close to the rocks, almost to safety, before they opened fire.

So he must judge. He walked on, his back muscles held tight against the expected bullets. One step . . . two . . . three.

He broke into a plunging run, staggering and falling, dragging his injured leg.

He managed at least three steps before every rifle smashed lead at him, every arrow sought him.

Yet he made it to the rocks, pierced through and through with bullets and arrows, and then fell into a crevice among the rocks. In the last moment before he toppled into the rocks he turned on them and opened fire, emptying his pistols. And then he fell.

An Apache, riding close, thrust a spear into his side.

And then they left him alone, for they knew he would not move again and they would return for his weapons when they had looted his wagon.

He coughed blood, lying jammed among the rocks, and once he opened his eyes to look up at the wide sky. Like Bob Marker, Rio Hockett had been a

Missourian, and when only a youngster he had ridden on a couple of raids with Bloody Bill Anderson, riding with a young horse thief with red-rimmed eyes who kept batting his lids named Dingus James. Jesse James, they called him later.

The sky looked the same as in the days when he had plowed a straight furrow back on the farm . . . he had never plowed one since.

He coughed again, and closed his eyes. There was so much pain that he hardly felt any of it at all, but he could hear the Indians shouting and laughing as they pulled the rest of the supplies from the wagon.

Suddenly he felt a tug at his belt, and opening his eyes he looked up at Bosky Fulton.

Fulton was holding a finger to his lips, but seemed unharmed. Swiftly and roughly, Fulton pulled Hockett's gun belt loose, then took his gun and what remained of his belongings. With no thought for the pain he might cause by the rough handling, he turned the wounded man roughly this way and that, going through his pockets.

Hockett grasped at Fulton's sleeve with fingers that no longer had the strength to grasp, but Fulton brushed them aside, and then he was gone. Hockett tried to call after him, but no sound came, and then he died.

Fulton had been hanging back when the wagon was attacked, and in the first flurry of movement, he took to the rocks and fired no shot that would attract attention to him. He abandoned his friends without hesitation, and remained in the rocks until the shooting was over, then crawled out to get Hockett's weapons and ammunition.

Returning to his horse he led the animal farther away, then waited. In his pockets he had most of the money and the best of the jewels taken from the hunting party, which he had held pending a division in Mexico. It was not, he decided, a bad deal. The rest of them were dead, and instead of going to Juarez, he would go west to Tucson and San Francisco.

At approximately the same time that Shalako took leave of Buffalo Harris, Bosky Fulton was searching for a trail through the same mountains from the east, and shortly after sundown he turned his horse into the same trail as that on which Shalako rode.

Ten miles or more divided them, and each made dry camp, each went to sleep without food. Bosky Fulton in a small clump of brush, Shalako behind the ruined adobe.

BEYOND THE HATCHET Mountains, Lieutenant Hall, with a small detachment of troops from Fort Cummings, made a fireless bivouac. West of the Animas Mountains, bound for Stein's Pass, Lieutenant McDonald camped with his Indian scouts and one corporal. To the north, not yet in the arena of action, Lieutenant Colonel "Sandy" Forsyth camped with some four hundred men of the Fourth Cavalry.

There had been a big fight at San Carlos, and now the scattered bands of the Apache were gathering under their three leaders, Chato, Loco, and Nachita. They were perfectly aware of McDonald's presence and that he had with him a number of Yuma and Mohave scouts, including Yuma Bill.

The Apaches had fled south from San Carlos,

while Forsyth had come west from Fort Cummings. The Apaches, who usually know everything in the desert, did not know this. Their scouts had seen McDonald's small force, and they knew of Hall . . . of Forsyth they knew nothing.

———

IN THE SMALL area at the head of the canyons, Buffalo Harris argued for small fires, carefully shielded, and he kept them together in the most defensible position he could find.

Von Hallstatt spread his blankets and stretched out, dead beat. He had expected nothing like this. When attacked, he had believed they would be mass attacks of running, easily killed savages, and instead there had been few targets, those few fleeting and gone. Deserted by his teamsters, he was here, where he had never expected to be, moving at the whim of a man he scarcely knew and profoundly disliked.

Thinking of the Indians irritated him, for it brought to mind an almost forgotten lecture heard while still a cadet, when they were told that all warfare would be revised, influenced by the fighting on the American frontier.

The warfare of the future, they were told, meant aimed rifle fire, mobility, infiltration, and individual enterprise. The idea had been unpalatable to the students, and they had rejected it en masse, for it meant initiative by the individual soldier, and seemed to imply less control from the top.

Von Hallstatt lay with his hands clasped behind his head and coldly appraised the situation as it had taken place at the ranch. Despite superior fire power, superior weapons, and perhaps superior marksmanship, they had been immobilized and rendered incapable of counterattack.

For the first time he had faced an enemy who was virtually invisible, an enemy who knew and utilized the terrain.

Despite his unfamiliarity with the country and Indian warfare in general, he was beginning to see how a small, well-trained force, virtually living off the country, could defeat or at least nullify the efforts of a much larger and better equipped command. It was his first experience with guerrilla warfare, and the very idea of war conducted on such principles made his gorge rise.

War under such conditions was no longer a gentleman's game. It became harsh, practical, and utterly realistic business. Firing in volleys as at a massed enemy front was absurd, for there was no enemy front, the enemy was a shadow, a will-o'-the-wisp.

Frederick von Hallstatt was nothing if not a realist. Lying stretched on his back, staring up at the stars, he considered the situation. Encumbered by the women there was nothing they could do but hope for the arrival of the Army . . . the very Army he had often ridiculed for being unable to dispose of a pack of naked savages.

The chances of getting out were small indeed. The food supply was low. There was ammunition enough for a good long fight, and small chance of worry on that score, but the food they carried could last them only three days, four at the most.

Despite his resentment of Shalako, it was obvious they could not survive without him. Even Buffalo admitted that Shalako was much more familiar with the country and the Indians than anyone else.

This very trip to America had been less for the purpose of hunting big game than for an opportunity to fight Indians. He admitted to himself what he had not admitted to anyone else, although he had jestingly commented on hoping for a brush with the Apaches. Well, he was having it. And so far he had acquitted himself very poorly indeed.

He was a superb rifle shot, yet he had killed but one Indian in all the rounds he had fired. Moreover, he had a feeling the Apaches were shooting more effectively than he, for there had been at least twenty extremely narrow misses back at the ranch; at least twenty times when bullets had come within fractions of an inch of hitting him.

Firelight flickered on the under branches of the surrounding pines, reflected from the smooth faces of the rocks. The air was scented with pine and cedar, and the fire crackled and sparked as it burned pine and needles.

A quail called, and far off, a lone coyote cried his immeasurable woe to the starlit sky. Buffalo Harris knelt by the fire, feeding its hungry flames with sticks gathered from under the trees. Irina placed the coffeepot on a flat stone, close to the flames.

"I've set some snares," Buffalo commented. "In the morning we may have a rabbit or two."

"Where is he now?"

Buffalo stretched his big hands toward the warmth of the flames in a timeless gesture of devotion to the gods of fire. He waited while the flames seared the few drops of spilled water from the outside of the coffeepot.

"Sleepin', most likely. He's a man sets store by sleep, although I never knew a man to get less of it."

"What's he like? I mean, beyond what you see?"

"He's an uncommon hard man to read. Leaves mighty little sign, no matter how you study his trail."

"Has he been married?"

"Now as to that I couldn't say. Kind of doubt it. Womenfolks take to him. I've seen that aplenty. And he's uncommon gentle with them, although I doubt he'd be that way if they crossed him.

"You'd look long to find a man who knows wild country better, and he tracks like any Apache. He can live off less and travel farther than anybody except maybe an Indian.

"One time I saw a book of this here poetry in his saddlebag. Near wore out from reading. Of course, that doesn't spell, because out here a man gets so hungry for reading he'll read anything in print. I've lived in bunkhouses where the cowhands used to see who had memorized the most labels off tin cans . . . and any book or paper is read until it's wore out."

"Where's he from?"

Buffalo glanced at her. "Question we never ask out here. We count a man as one who stands up when trouble shows, and we never look to see how much of a shadow a man cast back home. You can't wash gold with water that's run off down the hill."

Von Hallstatt had come up to the fire. "Tradition is important," he said quietly, "and a man has a right to be proud of what he has been and what his family have been."

"Maybe so," Buffalo acknowledged, "but out here we feel we're starting tradition and not living on it. One time you folks in Europe founded families and shaped a tradition, and I've no doubt they were strong men who did it." He got to his feet. "We're making our own traditions now, founding families, building a country.

"We don't figure a man's past is important. We want to know what he is now. The fact that his great-granddaddy was a fightin' man won't kill any Indians today.

"A man starting into wild country wants a man riding beside him that he can depend on. We're a sight more interested in red blood out here than in blue blood, and believe me, General, the two don't always run together."

Buffalo added fuel to the fire. The wood was very dry and burned with a hot, eager flame and little smoke. He accepted a cup of coffee from Irina, tasted it, and said, "Ma'am, you make a man's cup of coffee. Never figured it of you . . . you so stylish and all."

"I learned to cook over a campfire when I was twelve. My father often took me hunting with him."

"That there's the way it should be. A woman should know how to cook and do for a man."

"Does Shalako think that?"

"He's a puzzlin' man, like I said. Who knows what he thinks? But he's a man to have on your side in a difficulty, and addicted to sudden violence when wrongfully opposed." He sipped coffee. "He favors desert and mountains more than towns."

"Is he running from something?" Von Hallstatt

was irritated that the conversation should have turned to Carlin.

"Whatever else may have happened, I strongly doubt Shalako ever ran from anything. He's a most stubborn man when it comes to troublesome times."

"Whatever he is," von Hallstatt said stiffly, "he will be well paid for whatever he does for us."

"Meanin' no offense, General, but if it wasn't for the ladies I reckon you'd all be dead by now. He's of the opinion that every man should fight his own battles and saddle his own broncs. You can lay a bet he's never given a thought to payment."

Buffalo wiped off his mustache with the back of his hand. "Obliged for the coffee, ma'am. I'll be getting out where I can smell Indian."

When he had gone, Irina glanced at von Hallstatt. "Frederick, be careful about offering money. These men have a pride every bit as stiff-necked as your own. You must not offer money to Shalako."

"Perhaps not." He took the coffee she offered. "The man gets my back up. I have no idea why, but it is so. I went to school in England as you know, and always got along fine with the British, but these Americans . . . I cannot like them."

"You are not accustomed to independence in men you think your inferiors, Frederick. I think, perhaps, that is the reason."

"No . . . no, it is something else. I confess that disturbs me in some of the others, but somehow"—he was surprised to realize this was true—"somehow I never thought of him as an inferior."

He tasted the coffee. "It *is* good coffee, Irina. You

continue to surprise me." Then he added, "The man has education, undoubtedly a military education."

It was her turn to be surprised. "I was not aware of that."

"The names of Vegetius, Saxe, and Jomini are not as familiar to you as to me, nor are they familiar to the average educated man. They speak of specialization."

"Hans said something to that effect, but he may merely have read the books."

"Possibly. As Harris has said, he is a puzzling man." He glanced at Irina. "And one not to underestimate in any respect."

Irina kept her eyes on the fire, a little startled by the implication. A few days ago she would have been merely amused at the implication that she might be interested in such a man as Shalako Carlin. Now she was no longer sure.

"If we are fortunate, Frederick, we will be far away from here in a few days. Then I doubt if we shall ever see him again . . . or any of these people not of our own group."

"Perhaps." He sounded doubtful, and he was not a man to be uncertain of anything, especially of himself or any situation in which he was involved.

She pushed some sticks farther into the fire and watched the sparks fly upward. How much their lives had changed! Hans was dying . . . Frederick was less arrogant than at any time since she had known him . . . and she herself? Had she changed?

Von Hallstatt got his rifle and moved out to the perimeter of the camp, and Laura came to the fire from Kreuger's bedside.

"He's asleep, I think. Sometimes it is hard to tell . . . he makes believe so we will not feel it necessary to remain at his side."

"Strange, that it should be him. Frederick said two of the wounds were enough to kill him, each in itself. I don't know how he has lived so long."

Laura was silent, and then she said, "Irina . . . I like this . . . the desert, the fire, the stars. If the situation was different, I could love it."

"So could I. Once when I was in Africa with Father, we were camped away out on the veldt, just a small group of us. It was a lovely night. I remember him saying that he would like never to go back."

"It all seems far away." Laura looked thoughtfully at her friend. "You've changed, Irina. It seems so impossible that it was just the day before yesterday that all this started."

"Your father will be worried."

"I hope we'll be safe before he hears about it. He didn't want me to come." She glanced at Irina again. "Father didn't take to Frederick. Thought he was too stiff-necked."

"He isn't, really. And he's lost a lot of what he did have, these past few days."

"Are you going to marry him?"

Irina seated herself on the log near the fire and carefully spread her skirt over her knees. "I don't know, Laura. I really don't know."

"Shalako?"

"That's silly, isn't it? We come from different worlds, we live in different ways, we think differently. The whole idea is absurd."

"With a man like that? Not to me, it isn't. Anyway,

I've heard you say many times that you had no desire to live in London or Paris . . . that you wanted an estate in the country. So why not a cattle ranch in New Mexico or Arizona?"

"That's foolish, and you know it."

The night was cool and, above all, singularly still. Beyond the light of the fire the night was a curtain of darkness.

Count Henri came in from the edge of camp and poured a cup of coffee. "It is too quiet," he said, "I don't like it. It reminds me too much of Africa."

He sipped his coffee. "They are out there, I think. I think they are very close to us."

"I wish Shalako would come back," Laura said.

He glanced at her. "So do I, Laura. So do I."

Shalako Carlin bedded down on a patch of sparse, coarse grass well hidden by brush back of the ruined adobe cabin.

Originally built of rock, the cabin had evidently fallen to ruin, and then had been rebuilt with adobe bricks, and had now fallen to ruin again. But despite the shelter offered, he had no intention of being caught within the walls, preferring freedom of movement.

Mohammet, stripped of saddle and bridle, was picketed on the rank grass of a slope just behind him. The night was still, and Shalako was dead tired . . . he fell asleep at once.

An owl hooted from a nearby tree, and a pack rat cowered at the sound, then sniffed curiously in the direction of the sleeping man.

Out in the forest a pinecone fell and the owl took off on lazy wings through the dark aisles of the scattered trees. The pack rat, relieved, moved hesitantly from the shelter of the catclaw, circled the small clearing and disappeared on some nocturnal business of his own. A bat poised, fluttering dark wings in the air above the ruin, then swooped off, pursuing insects, and there was no other sound but the horse cropping grass. The stars hung their bright lanterns in a dark, still sky and the slight breeze carried a scent of pines along the high ridges.

A long time later, and far out among the trees, sound suddenly seemed to hesitate, and then for a moment there was silence. The stallion's head came up alertly, ears pricked, and the man Shalako opened his eyes, and lay still, listening.

His guns were at hand, but he ignored them, reaching for his knife. He held the blade ready, cutting edge turned up . . . only a fool stabs down with a knife. There is too much bone structure in the upper part of the body . . . unless a man can find that particular vital spot. Holding the knife low, edge upward, one strikes at the soft parts of the body where no bones deflect the blow.

No sound . . . time went by, but he did not relax. Suddenly, the stallion drew back sharply and snorted, and Shalako smelled the Apache. It was a smell of wood-smoke, buckskin, and something acrid, strange . . . a shadow moved . . . lunged.

Shalako rolled to his knees. Unable to judge the position of the Indian in the darkness, he risked everything and slashed across in front of him, and felt the tip of the blade catch flesh. There was a muffled gasp and an iron grip seized his wrist.

Using the powerful muscles of his bent legs,

Shalako straightened sharply, jerking the arm up and tearing it free. Instantly he smashed down with a closed fist and felt it thud against flesh.

The Indian lunged at him, his knife point tearing Shalako's shirt. Shalako lunged in turn, missed, and the Indian seized his knife arm and tried to throw him over his shoulder. Instantly Shalako threw himself in the direction the Indian was throwing him, bunching his knees under him.

The sudden moving weight threw the Indian forward off balance and he fell on his face with Shalako's knees riding his shoulders. Slippery as greased flesh can be, the Apache slid from under Shalako and came to his feet. Shalako rose with him and thrust home with the knife.

The blade took the Indian under the arm and went all the way in, and Shalako felt the warm gush of blood over his hand as he drew back on the knife. The Indian uttered a low cry and fell backward.

Shalako stepped back, catching his breath, and talking softly to quiet the frightened stallion. He stood perfectly still, watching the dark blotch where the Apache had fallen. He could hear the rasping gasps of the dying man, but he was not trusting the sound, and he waited.

Apparently the lone Apache had been left without a horse by some action of which Shalako knew nothing, and had hoped to get both horse and weapons from him. Yet it worried him that the Indian should be here. Had he been followed? Or had the Indian come upon his trail by accident?

After several minutes had passed and he heard no

further sounds, he dropped to his haunches and struck a shielded match.

The Apache was short, powerfully built—and dead.

That first, blind blow with the knife had caught the Indian's shoulder, then cut across his throat, tearing a razor-like gash that covered the Apache with blood.

A relatively new breech-loading Springfield lay on the ground nearby, an Army rifle. The Apache wore an Army belt and an ammunition pouch. The rifle stock was hand-buffed and could not have been out of the soldier's hands for more than a few days, perhaps only a few hours. That stock had been given loving care by a man who appreciated fine wood, something with which no Apache would have bothered.

So the Army was in the field, and probably not far away. If so the possibilities were that Chato was in full flight toward the border, but avid for rapine and murder, hungry for horses and loot.

Untying the stallion, he saddled up, and, sliding the extra rifle into the boot, he checked the loads on his own Winchester '76. The first gray was lightening the eastern sky when he crossed the saddle into Wolf Canyon.

———

TEN MILES TO the south and east, Bosky Fulton turned on his side and opened his eyes. He got up, absentmindedly brushing needles and grass from his clothing, while listening for what the predawn had to offer. It was time to be moving.

He was irritable and worried. The country would be alive with Indians, and he decided his best route would be toward Stein's Pass. Yet he was uneasy, and even after he had saddled up, he did not at once move out.

For the first time he had something to lose, and it worried him. He had money and jewels enough to make him a moderately rich man, and he intended a wild time in San Francisco.

He was somewhere southeast and mostly east of Animas Peak, and the thought of crossing Animas Valley worried him. The valley was a wide-open route south into Sonora and Chihuahua, and a logical route for the Apaches to take. The trail near which he had bedded down led right into the Animas Valley.

He waited a long time, then led his horse forward and waited again. After a while he stepped into the saddle and rode out into the narrow trail. He was somewhere near Walnut Creek, and there was still some distance to go before reaching the valley.

Bosky Fulton scratched warily under his arm and looked cautiously around. He had a way of turning his head without moving his shoulders, dropping his head forward and looking around over his shoulder from the corners of his eyes. He was worried and wary. He recalled all too well a time when he had found two teamsters tied head down to the rear wheels of their wagon. Low fires had been built under their heads. It was an old Apache trick.

Scared? He was scared all right. No man in his right mind rode through Apache country and was not scared. He was scared, all right, but he was ready, too.

That Carnarvon woman . . . he thought of her suddenly. By the Lord Harry he'd like to—

There would be plenty of women in San Francisco

and with the money he had, he could pick and choose.

He walked his horse slowly forward, touching his dry lips with his tongue.

Some miles ahead of him, the Apache known as *Tats-ah-das-ay-go* slid down from the rocks to a point behind the ruined cabin. He found where the stallion had been tied, and he found the dead Apache.

He stared down at him with contempt. He had attacked a sleeping man and had been killed!

Tats-ah-das-ay-go squatted on his heels against the cabin wall and smoked, and as he smoked he read the signs left by Shalako and the Apache with the ease of a man reading print.

The white-eyes had awakened, or had been lying awake. He could see where his knees had been and where his feet had pushed off as he lunged, and the fighting had taken place a few feet away from where the white-eyes had slept.

He left small trail, this white-eyes, and he slept lightly. He was a warrior, and he wore moccasins, Apache moccasins . . . perhaps he had lived among them? To kill such a man would be a great feat. *Tats-ah-das-ay-go* got to his feet and returned among the rocks to his horse.

Yes, a great feat . . .

CHAPTER 4

I T WAS NOON of April 22, two days after the San Carlos fight, that Lieutenant Hall cut the trail of the von Hallstatt party.

Trailing the wagons, the lieutenant came upon the deserted ranch where the remains of the fight lay all about. His scouts worked out a puzzling story that to some extent coincided with his own observations.

There had been a fight with the Apaches; one dead Apache was found within the wagon circle. Apparently the defense had been successful for the wagons had not been looted by Apaches . . . that was obvious from things left behind.

Whoever looted them had made a systematic search for valuables, passing up many things any Apache would have taken. And the Apaches would have carried away the body of their dead warrior.

"Two parties left here, Lieutenant. The first party with most of the horses and one wagon headed south toward the border. The other bunch with two horses and one man carried in a stretcher—wounded man, most likely—cut off southwest."

He indicated the broken boards of an ammunition box. "I count enough shells for one used-up box. They made a fight of it, then there must have been trouble among them.

"The wagon had four horses hitched to it, and, by

their hoofs, small stock. Riding stock, more'n likely. Four of the men with that wagon had flat-heeled boots . . . teamsters, I take it."

"Well, what do you think?"

The scout squatted on his heels, considered a minute, then spat into the sand. "Thievery, that's what I think. That damn' fool Fritz come a high-tailing it into this country with a pack of no-account thieves.

"Rio Hockett never did have no brains. Nervy man, but bullheaded and no-account. I take it he and his crowd helped fight off the Indians, then looted the wagons and pulled out for Mexico."

Lieutenant Hall considered the situation, then mounted his troop and rode off on the trail of the wagon.

By midafternoon they had come up to the wagon. It had been looted and burned, and all about lay the mutilated bodies of the slain men. The lieutenant or the trackers knew most of them by name, and the last one to be found was Hockett.

"Good riddance," Lieutenant Hall said briefly, "the man was a thief and a troublemaker."

"He made a fight of it," the scout said, indicating the brass shells lying about. "Now here's an odd thing . . . his gun belt is gone. Taken by somebody who came up behind the rocks." The scout pointed to the heelprint of a boot. "I'd say that was Fulton. Didn't see his body down there, and if anybody would get out of a mess-up like this here, it would be Bosky."

"He got away?" Lieutenant Hall was incredulous.

"Sure as shootin'. Man had small feet, and so had

Fulton. Seen his track many a time. Him an' Hockett run together, an' bad as Hockett was, he was tame stuff to Fulton."

"He will have to get on as best he can," the lieutenant said briefly. "We must find the hunting party."

Turning north, they skirted the Hatchets. With luck they would cut the trail of the party with the wounded man and the women. Such a group had small chance of survival, and the mystery remained. Why had they turned south?

"They've got a man with them who didn't start with them," the scout said. "Counting the bodies back there and what we found at the ranch, I figure Harding and Harris stayed with the Eastern party, but there's another man."

"Wells, what about Wells?"

"Could be. Don't act like him though."

Miles away, beyond two valleys and the Animas Range, another situation was developing.

Lieutenant McDonald halted his command. It was very hot. Dust arose from every step the horses took and when the troop halted the dust cloud drifted over them and settled upon their clothing, their faces, and in their nostrils. Aside from himself, all were Yuma or Mohave Indians except for the corporal, a stocky man with a beet-red face, and a veteran soldier.

The lieutenant's mission: to find Indian trails recently made, to locate raiding Apaches and report to the main body under Colonel Forsyth. No man was better qualified for the job, nor was any man more conscientious in performance of his duty.

At this moment, Lieutenant McDonald was worried. So far he had found no tracks, but three days had transpired since the San Carlos attack, and the air smelled of trouble. The fact that he had seen no Apaches was no consolation, for he lived by the old rule: When you see Apaches, be afraid; and when you can see no Apaches, be twice as afraid.

Fear was not a thing of which to be ashamed unless a man let fear conquer him. Fear could be a spur to action and a safeguard against carelessness. McDonald had helped to bury a good many soldiers who were reckless or took unnecessary risks.

Yuma Bill, who rode beside him, pointed toward the Pelonchillo Mountains, his face as dark and craggy as the mountains he indicated. "I think," he suggested, as he pointed.

"We'll have a look, Bill."

McDonald lighted his pipe. Why he wanted it at all he did not know, for the smoke was dry and hot, and his uniform smelled of stale tobacco, stale sweat, stale dust, and stale horse. He wished longingly for a cold drink, a drink with ice in it, and he grinned at the thought. How long had it been since he had such a drink? Two years? Nearly three.

Yet this was a brand of warfare at which he felt at home. He had never been a spit-and-polish soldier, and never cared for the brass-bound posts back East. When he arrived on the southwest frontier he knew he had found a home . . . this was for him.

Lieutenant McDonald knew his Indians and they knew him, and every day he learned from them. He was a fighting man with no taste for formal drill, dress uniforms, or parade formations. Most drill was a waste of time, based on the demands of an outmoded idea of warfare, and their practical utility had ceased long since.

The only sensible training for troops was to teach them to fight and survive fighting, and every moment such training was not being given was a moment wasted.

It was battle that paid off, battle was the beginning and the end of a soldier's life. The Apache, the greatest guerrilla fighter the world ever knew, had never heard of close-order drill or any kind of training except in fighting and surviving.

Now, with four scouts ranging out ahead of them to cut any possible trail, they started on.

Yuma Bill rode ahead to join them, and before they had gone fifty yards, he turned in the saddle and waved.

The trail was there. A small party of Apaches, their trail not twelve hours old, moving toward the Gila. At once he sent a scout to inform Colonel Forsyth, then proceeded at a more cautious pace.

Within the mile another party of Indians had joined the first, making a band considerably larger than McDonald's detachment.

McDonald rode warily. He could sense the worry among the members of his command, and he did not blame them. He paused frequently to study the terrain, and changed his direction of travel several times to make ambush difficult.

He could *feel* Indians. Even Yuma Bill, ordinarily a tough, unresponsive sort, seemed nervous. Nobody but a fool would want to ride into an ambush of twice their number of Apaches, and it was their very wariness that saved them.

At this time McDonald was sixteen miles from the main body under Forsyth.

Somewhere in this vast sweep of desert and mountains was a small party of men and women with no experience at Indian fighting, and that party, if not already destroyed, was undoubtedly being stalked by the Apaches.

Heat waves lifted with the stifling dust. McDonald mopped sweat and dust from his gaunt features and swore. His uniform felt stiff and heavy in the burning heat and his suspenders chafed his shoulders. The heat that rose from the sand and rocks was like that from the top of a stove.

Nothing moved . . . before them Horseshoe Canyon opened a way into the mountains. McDonald looked with misgiving at the towering cliffs, at the opening before them.

Yuma Bill, now riding point, was well out in front. He walked his horse into the rocky maw of the canyon. A moment later, McDonald saw him lift a hand.

When they came up to where he had stopped he was standing over the remains of a hastily smothered fire from which a thin tendril of smoke still lifted.

McDonald mopped the sweat from his face, squinting his eyes against the glare to survey the cliffs and the rocks. Deep within him he knew he was in serious trouble, for this fire could have been smothered only moments before . . . perhaps even as they approached.

Had the Apaches fled? Or did they lurk back in the rocks? And how many were there?

"How many would you guess?"

Yuma Bill shrugged. "Maybe five, maybe six here"—he gestured toward the rocks—"but who knows how many there?"

Should he now await Forsyth's arrival? Or should he advance into the canyon?

It was the problem of command, and no one could share his decision or his responsibility. If he sent another man for Forsyth and there were only a few Indians who had fled at his approach, Forsyth and the Fourth Cavalry would have ridden sixteen miles in the hot sun to no purpose. On the other hand, if he went ahead on his own, if he explored the situation a little further . . . ?

"We will move along," he said, but as he turned in his saddle to give the command there was a shadow of movement among the rocks. His shout was lost in a smashing volley, and two of his men tumbled from their saddles. One of them started up, lifting his rifle, only to fall again.

McDonald fired his pistol at a fleeting brown body and saw the Apache catch in midstride, then half-lunge, half-fall into the rocks and out of sight.

The roar of guns and the wild, shrill yells of the Indians were all about him. Coolly, he directed the movement of his small detachment to the crest of a low hill. Even as he shouted his orders he was aiming and firing, trying to make every shot count. This was the virtue of training, of conditioning, that in an emergency one always knew what to do. Panic only entered the empty mind.

Grabbing the shoulder of a scout, he swung the man toward his own horse. "Get Forsyth," he yelled hoarsely, amid the bark of guns.

The Indian leaped to the back of the horse and was gone in a long leap. That was the battalion racehorse and, if he had speed, now was the time to use it.

McDonald returned to directing the fight. He had but six unwounded men. Another had just fallen, and Yuma Bill, that invaluable man, had gone down after apparently getting off scot-free.

The Apaches were coming down among the rocks, closing in. The red-faced corporal, one of the best shots in the battalion, had dropped to one knee and was firing methodically as if on a rifle range.

Quickly as the attack began, it broke off. Four of his men gone, he awaited the next attack. They were in a nest of boulders atop the hill, and without any word from him the men went about making their position more secure.

Piling loose stones into gaps among the rocks, digging out the sand here, making a better firing position elsewhere. They had a little water, ammunition enough for a good fight, and a fair field of fire.

"Take your time," the lieutenant said. "Let's make them buy it."

An arm showed and a scout fired. Lieutenant McDonald believed it was a hit.

Two of the fleeing scouts had caught up ammunition pouches from the fallen men, and another had recovered a rifle. They had two extra weapons, which increased their immediate firepower.

Sixteen miles to go and sixteen to return, a brutal ride in horse-killing heat. Squatted on his heels behind a boulder, Lieutenant McDonald was glad it was Colonel Forsyth out there, for the colonel's memory of the Beecher Island fight would be fresh in his mind and he would understand the situation as only one can who has lived through it.

Riding with him would be four hundred veteran Indian fighters who would understand it, too.

The hilltop was an oven. McDonald shifted his grip on the gun long enough to dry his palm on his pants. "They'll be coming soon," he said. "Let's leave a couple of them on the sand."

Somewhere out upon the hot, dusty desert to the north and east a rider was killing a good horse getting to Colonel Forsyth and the Fourth Cavalry.

The Apaches came again, and again the Cavalry detachment broke the attack, with no casualties on either side. The Yuma scout beside Lieutenant McDonald was gasping from the heat as he fumbled cartridges into his pistol.

It was going to be a long afternoon.

THE SOUND OF distant firing came to the ears of Shalako Carlin. He drew up, listening.

That would be the Army and Chato. He sat his horse near the crest of the divide where Wolf Canyon started down the mountain to meet the Double Adobe Trail, considering the situation and weighing it against their own chances.

Chato had gone north with roughly forty Indians, some of whom had turned off for the attack on the hunting party. The rest had continued on to meet with the restless young warriors at San Carlos, but by now all the bodies should have joined forces, which would add up to nearly eighty Indians. It must be that force or a part of it now in battle off somewhere toward Stein's Peak.

The Apaches would make a fight of it, but if the Army was out in force they would pull out of the fight and run for the border. Whenever possible they would travel the high routes, and that meant they might easily take the Double Adobe Trail down which he now rode. They would be striking at anything they could hit and they would want horses.

The Army would be behind them. Hence, what remained for the hunting party was a fierce and desperate fight until the Army caught up with the Indians.

How much chance would the hunting party have against eighty Indians?

Seated astride his horse in the shade of a boulder, the roan close behind him, Shalako tried to view the situation as it would appear to one of the high-circling buzzards. That buzzard would see a wide skein of trails that were slowly being drawn tighter and tighter, and the center of the skein was held by the hunting party.

Four women, seven men active, and an eighth wounded. Well-armed, however, with ammunition enough for a reasonably long fight. Water, and a fairly good position to defend, but short of food.

There was a chance the Apaches might retreat down the valley, bypassing the mountains and the hunting party.

However, two of the men, Dagget and Mako, the cook, knew nothing of fighting, and the two who were good fighting men had never fought Indians. If they lasted thirty minutes against an all-out Apache attack they would be playing in luck.

"We don't have a chance," Shalako said aloud, "not a Chinaman's chance."

A bee buzzed idly in the brush alongside the trail, and the stallion stamped impatiently, wondering at the delay, but Shalako waited, building a smoke while he studied the terrain.

Off on his right lay Animas Valley, and a considerable plume of dust that indicated a fast-traveling party of horsemen, riding southwest by west and away from him. The Army, more than likely, for Apaches did not like to raise dust and usually scattered out to keep down the dust and so give less indication of their direction of travel.

The trail he followed was rarely used. It had been first used, perhaps, when the mysterious Mimbres people lived in the area, perhaps even earlier. A white man traveling usually keeps to low ground, but an Indian or other primitive man keeps to the high country.

Shalako rode cautiously along the dim trail. The peaks around him rose eight to fifteen hundred feet above him. It was a rugged, lonely country where gnarled cedars clung to the raw lips of canyons and each cliff was banked by the shattered rock remaining from the ruin of itself.

A roadrunner poised on a rock beside the trail, flicking his long tail in a challenge to race, despite the heat. The roadrunner took off, gliding a few yards, then running on swift feet along the trail.

When Shalako had nearly reached the turnoff for the Park hideout, he went off the trail and into the rocks. Taking his Winchester, he left the horses in the shade and mounted the rocks, careful to give himself a background where he would not be outlined against the sky.

He could see almost two miles along the trail ahead from the vantage point he had chosen, and he was no more than two miles from the hideout itself. He had paused here for two reasons. He wanted to approach the camp at sundown, and he wanted to see if he was followed, and if anyone came along the trail.

He had seen no tracks. From all appearances that trail had not been used in months, perhaps not for years.

Moreover, the trail from here toward the hideout was, for the first mile, relatively exposed. He did not want to enter that trail until he was quite sure he would not be seen.

It was very hot. Overhead the inevitable buzzard soared with that timeless patience that comes from knowing that sooner or later all things that live in the desert become food for buzzards, and they had only to wait.

A tiny lizard raced on tiptoe across a hot rock and paused in the shade, tail up, its little throat pulsing as it gasped for air. After a moment the tail relaxed, the lizard quieted, and Shalako made no move.

He was tired and the sun was warm. Slowly, because a sudden move attracts attention, he turned his head and looked down at the horses. Both were browsing absently at the brush.

A dust devil danced in the trail below, then lost itself among the rocks. The lizard's lower lids crept drowsily over its eyes. Just a minute or two more, Shalako decided, and he would move along. The mountains were still, and they might be empty. His head lowered, and he settled to a more comfortable position. His head lowered again, bobbed, as he half-awakened, and then his eyes came all the way open.

There was a rider in the trail below, a rider wearing a wide hat and riding a sorrel horse. And he recognized the mount. It was Damper, one of Irina Carnarvon's mares.

He studied the rider, trying to place him, and then he remembered the black vest. It was Bosky Fulton, the man who had accompanied Rio Hockett. Shalako knew him.

The Arab's head was up, and he was scenting the wind.

"It's all right, Mohammet," Shalako said softly. "Everything is all right."

Shalako watched the rider. When he reached the fork of the trail, what would he do? And where were the others? Where was Hockett and the stolen wagon?

Suddenly the rider below drew up sharply, and seemed to be listening. Shalako listened also, and distinctly heard the sound of pounding hoofs. Fulton crossed the trail swiftly and went into the rocks, shucking his rifle as he did so.

Suddenly, around the bend of the trail came a riderless horse, a saddled horse with stirrups flapping.

It was Tally, Irina Carnarvon's other mare. The mare slowed, sniffed at the dust like a hound, and then came on. Many times Shalako had seen wild horses follow a trail like that, and follow it as skillfully as any wolf, and Tally was obviously following the trail of Damper.

Shalako's expression changed. Suppose the Apaches

had had the mare? Suppose they were following her now?

It would be like an Apache to let the mare loose and follow her back to the other horses.

Tally paused in the trail and Shalako could see from his position how Fulton watched the mare, suspicious of her arrival, unaware that the horse he now rode and Tally had grown up together.

Suddenly Tally turned her head and lifted her nose to the wind. Despite the distance he could almost see her nostrils flare and, with a shock, Shalako realized the mare had caught the scent of the stallion! Even as he realized it, Tally turned from the trail and started up through the rocks toward him.

Fulton half-rose from his position, surprised by the mare's action. Undoubtedly Tally assumed that Damper would be where the stallion was, and was finding a way up through the maze of boulders.

Hurriedly, Shalako left his observation post and, returning to the stallion, he stepped into the saddle. Leading the roan, he started away, keeping the pyramid of rocks between himself and Fulton, and keeping to soft ground wherever possible. Behind him he could hear the mare, and he swore softly.

There was nothing for it now but to ride on to camp and hope that no Apache was trailing the mare.

Would Fulton add things up and come looking? It was doubtful. This was no time to be wasting around in the mountains, and Fulton undoubtedly had places he wanted to go . . . and judging by the direction he was headed he was going no farther than the nearest lot of Apaches.

When he had ridden a couple of hundred yards he

concealed himself in the brush and waited for the mare to catch up. Mohammet could see her coming and started to whinny, but Shalako talked him out of it.

Watching beyond her, he saw she was not followed. Unless Fulton was a complete fool he would hole up somewhere and wait out the raid.

After a while, he continued on, and had gone scarcely half a mile when he saw Indian sign. It was a portion of the track of an unshod pony, and made that very morning. He waited, studying the terrain again. To a man who had seen an Apache wrapped in a dusty blanket appear as another boulder among the many lying about, there was no question of taking anything for granted.

Once, Shalako recalled, he had seen an Apache stand upright among a scattering of yucca trees, a few clusters of yucca blades stuck to his blanket, while an entire Army command rode past without seeing him.

Now, scouting the area with care, he found where two horses had been tied to a clump of brush. He found where the horses had cropped leaves from the brush, and, studying the branch ends to determine their freshness, he decided that the Apaches, riding unshod ponies and not captured stock, had been drawn to the hideout, probably by the smell of smoke, sometime during the previous night.

Studying the droppings left by the two horses to see what they had been eating, he saw the remains of plants that only grew well below the border. These two then were not part of the main band, but had probably followed Chato up from Mexico, leaving well after he had, and coming to this point by a long, hard ride.

They might have gone on to join Chato, perhaps to lead him back to this place. Nevertheless, they might still be lurking in the vicinity.

For some time, he scouted on foot, always keeping his horses in sight, for he well knew what an Indian could do when it came to stealing horses. More than once he had seen them stolen right from under a watcher's eyes. Yet he wished to know if they still remained nearby, and if others had been here.

Evening was near. Shadows grew longer at this hour, and the world became more quiet. The slightest sound traveled easily in the clear air of the desert and the mountains. This was the land of the sky . . . to know the sky, to feel the sky, to appreciate the sky one must be alone with it, somewhere along the hard-boned ridges or peaks at any time during the hours of light.

With darkness a change comes and distance is lost. The night brings all things near, although the desert by night is haunted by specters, with the silent standing columns of the cacti, the close-to-the-earth desert shrubs, or the black mystery of the mountains.

The desert and the sky both demand aloneness . . . to know them completely one must be alone with them in the midst of their emptiness.

At such a time the body grows still, the mind becomes empty, a vast reservoir for the receiving of impressions. The slightest sound is heard or felt. Around one at such a time the desert spreads in all its mystery and strangeness, its timelessness, and overhead the sky is enormous.

The desert, too, seems to be listening, expecting.

Shalako waited and listened. And after a while he made his way back to the horses. The moccasins made moving with stillness a simple thing. No wild animal will break a twig or branch, nor will an Indian. Even in darkness he can sense the branch under his foot before his weight comes upon it, and places it elsewhere. This is one of the advantages of the moccasin.

Mounting up, he started along a bald ridge, keeping off the skyline, working his way toward the hideout. He had tied Tally's reins to the roan, so the horses could follow close behind him.

After a moment he saw the thin column of blue smoke mounting like an offering to the still evening sky. He was very wary now, not wanting to be shot by some trigger-happy member of the hunting party. When he had located the position guarded by Buffalo Harris, he called to him, knowing he would never fire a blind shot.

"All right," Harris replied conversationally, "come on in."

Shalako walked his horse along a cedar-clad slope and into the corner where Buffalo waited.

"Man, am I glad to see you!" Buffalo said. "I feel like a lone shepherd dog with a flock of sheep and the wolves closin' in."

"You got some coffee?"

"Coffee's all we do have. You got most of the grub."

"The Army's out." Shalako indicated the Springfield in the saddle boot. "Some good soldier died before he gave that up."

"Injun?"

"Uh-huh. Sneaked up on me last night. He was making a try for my horses."

"Kreuger's still alive. I don't see how he does it."

Irina was standing by the fire and her whole face lit up when she saw the mare. "Oh! You found Tally!"

"She found me." He did not tell her about Damper. There was time enough for that.

While Buffalo stripped the packs from the roan, Irina got him a blackened cup with coffee, and he brought them briefly up to date. He could tell them nothing except that the Army was in the field, that there was fighting to the northwest, which they already knew, and that within a matter of hours they might be in the path of the fleeing Apaches.

At the end he mentioned Bosky Fulton.

"He was alone?" Buffalo asked quickly.

"Are you making the guess I did?"

"That the rest of them were wiped out? I'd say that's a mighty good guess, unless he had trouble and cut loose from them, and Fulton wouldn't be likely to do that unless they came up with more than his share of the loot."

As he talked and drank coffee, he surveyed the situation. They had done pretty well, yet the area they were trying to defend was too large, there was too much chance of infiltration.

"If the Army is to the northwest"—von Hallstatt had come up to the fire—"why don't we move out and join them? After all, we have three horses now, and we should be able to move faster."

"The Army has its own troubles. You got in here on your own and you'd better figure to get out that way. Anyway, if you start for the Army you'll run head-on into Chato. He'll be coming this way on the run."

"That's supposition."

"Right. And if you want to figure it any other way, you go ahead."

"You would come with us if we started, would you not?" Julia asked.

"I would not."

"You are not very gallant."

"No, ma'am, I'm not. Neither is a bullet." He got to his feet. "You folks do what you want. If you want to make a stand here, I'm with you, but if you pull out you pull out on your own."

"You'd stay here alone?"

"Why not? To track a man even an Apache has to find tracks. I'd just stay right still and make no tracks at all. I'd go hungry four or five days if necessary, but I'd stay right here and sit it out."

He threw the dregs of his coffee into the fire and placed the cup on a rock, then he walked away to see to the horses.

Buffalo returned to his post and, after a little while, von Hallstatt did also.

The feed within the circle was almost gone, yet the horses could survive for a couple of days longer. And there was water.

Little enough had been done to strengthen the position, but it was just as well. What they must do now was pull back. The fire stood on low ground, in a sort of shallow basin, and no flames would be visible away from the circle of cedars, boulders, and brush that rimmed it.

The perimeter of defense was outside that circle, and should be drawn back. The cliff trail could be held by one man, and otherwise they seemed to have a good field of fire, and the best thing might be to make the first defense from the outer line, then fall back to the inner circle, for their force was too small.

He rubbed Mohammet down with a handful of sage, cleaned a few burrs from his tail, then did the same for Tally. He checked their shoes with care, then went to work on the roan. The mustang was in fine shape again, and nipped at his sleeve to prove it.

Irina joined him.

He was very conscious of her presence, but said nothing, working swiftly and silently. A little light remained in the sky, although the first stars had appeared.

"Mohammet likes you," she said, watching the Arab nuzzling him, "and he does not like many people."

"He's a good horse. He takes to this country like he was born to it."

"What are they like? The Apaches, I mean. Are they terribly savage?"

"Depends on how you look at it. Folks back East try to attribute Christian virtues and principles to the noble red man. They're wrong as can be. The red man is noble enough but his principles and way of life are completely different from ours.

"You can't say a man is good or bad because he thinks or doesn't think like you. They respect members of the tribe for altogether different reasons. The best thief among them is the one they admire most, and a killing from ambush is more to be desired than one in open combat.

"The best thief is the one who will be able to give most to his family, so all the Indian girls want a good thief for a husband. Stealing horses and fighting are not only their means to live, but their greatest pleasure. And they have none of our feeling about torture. Theirs is a hard, cruel life and men are valued for their courage, so they torture a man to see if he is brave, and also for fun.

"When they mutilate a body, sometimes it is from hatred or contempt, but just as often it is to cripple him so he won't be able to attack them if they meet in the afterlife."

"I had never thought much about such things, but I remember Father telling me about some of the customs of the people in Africa."

"Each tribe is different, but the Apaches were always fighters. But that's true of their kind everywhere. All the predatory peoples came from lands of sparse, unfertile soil, and their only wealth came from raiding and looting. The Vikings, the Prussians, the Mongols, the corsairs of Brittany . . . all of them made piracy and warfare a way of life, and it is the same with the Apache.

"You can't buy his friendship. If you are friendly he will believe it is because you are weak, and afraid of him. He may watch you for many days before he decides to attack, and he will never attack a party stronger than his own. He has none of our feeling about attacking a weaker or helpless enemy, and he respects only strength and courage."

"You are a puzzling man, Mr. Carlin. I wonder

who you really are?" She searched his face, but his features showed nothing, nothing at all. "Who were you before you became Shalako?"

He straightened up, arching his back against the kink from bending. "Don't get any foolish notions. I am not a cashiered Army officer, nor a foreign nobleman, nor a man escaping from a busted heart. The fact is, I'm a saddle tramp."

"I do not believe that."

"Your privilege."

"What do you want to *do,* Mr. Carlin? What do you want to *be*?"

"What I am. Did you ever top out on a ridge in wild country and look off across miles where nobody had ever been before? Did you ever ride for a month across country without ever seeing another human being? Or even the track of one? I have . . . and I want to again."

"And women? Have you never been in love, Mr. Carlin?"

"Sure, who hasn't? Matter of fact, I'm in love right now."

"Now?" She was startled . . . and dismayed.

"Sure . . . I'm in love with the smell of woodsmoke from that campfire over there, with the wind in the far-off pines, even with those Apaches out there."

"The Apaches? In love with *them*?"

"Sure . . . because they make me know I'm alive and if I slack off one second in their country they'll lift my hair. Say what you want about them, they are first-class fighting men."

The firelight flickered on the flanks of the horses. Somewhere in the outer darkness a pinecone dropped, but nothing else moved. She was very conscious of his nearness, but there was something exasperatingly elusive about him. He was beside her, and yet somehow he would fit into no category, no easy explanation, and he worried her, disturbed her deeply.

Her own exasperation led her on. "And have you no desire for a home? A family of your own?"

He listened into the darkness for a moment before replying. It was too quiet.

"Maybe . . . with the right woman. Or women."

"*Women?*"

"Sure," he said, straight-faced, "there's no reason why a good provider shouldn't have two, three, maybe even four women. Seems almost indecent, a man shutting other women out of his life like that. You never saw a rooster with only one hen, did you?"

"That's different!" She glanced at him quickly. "You're joking, of course."

"Now why would I joke? I've known several Indians who had more than one squaw, and they all seemed perfectly content. Makes it easier on them. They share the work, and there's always somebody to talk to."

He took up his rifle. "Better get some sleep. There may not be another chance."

Shalako strolled away, and she stared after him for a moment, then laughed. As he walked away, he smiled a little. She was quite a woman, too good a woman to be wasted on von Hallstatt.

He scouted from post to post, checking the positions of the defenders. When he reached von Hallstatt the German commented, "It is quiet out there."

"Too quiet. We will get an attack about day-break."

"I hear nothing. I think there is nothing out there."

"Just watch yourself. If you slack off you will never live to see morning."

Shalako was distinctly uneasy, and he shifted his position, squatting on his heels beside von Hallstatt. "It's too damned quiet," he said after a moment, "I don't like the feel of it."

"Yes," von Hallstatt admitted, "there is something in the air. I feel it, too."

Shalako returned to the fire and his blankets. He spread them back at one edge, out of the firelight, and was asleep almost instantly.

Long since he had learned to sleep in snatches, and to catch a bit of sleep whenever possible. He had been asleep a little over two hours when he suddenly awakened. It was still dark, yet day could not be far away. He went to the trickle of water that ran away from the spring and dipped his fingers into the clear, cold water, splashing his face with it and combing his hair with his fingers. Then he put on his hat and walked to the fire.

Henri was there, his face drawn with weariness, nursing a cup of black coffee.

Shalako filled his own cup and squatted on his heels. "They'll be coming just before sunup . . . with the first light."

Henri nodded. "How many do you think?"

"Anybody's guess. Six or seven can be as danger-ous as twice that many. They have more cover here than they had down below."

One by one the men who had slept moved into

position. Mako returned to watch the cliff trail, Dagget took a position where he could look down into and along both sides of Elephant Butte Canyon. Roy Harding was to cover the area between Park Canyon and the edge of the cliff they had mounted. Henri covered the head of Park Canyon itself.

"Buffalo," Shalako said, "you, von Hallstatt, and I will cover the trail and the area between the two canyons."

Von Hallstatt had returned to the fire for the planning. Now he put his pipe between his teeth and glanced quizzically at Shalako. He indicated the peak that reared up nearly four hundred feet behind them, Elephant Butte itself.

"What about that? A good rifleman up there could make our position untenable."

"We've got to gamble. Their only way up there is from the canyon side, a much steeper cliff than here, and we don't have a man to put up there."

It was still dark, but as they moved into position the isolated trees and boulders were beginning to stand out. High in the heavens overhead there was a faint tinge of pink on a cloud, nothing more.

The coolness of night lay upon the land. Nothing stirred. Shalako settled into position, studying the terrain before him. He swept it with a quick, searching glance, then starting far out at the limit of his range of vision, he searched the ground methodically in side-to-side sweeps until close in to his position.

Each rock, each tree, each shrub he studied with particular care, making allowances for the growing light, studying the contours, the length of the shadows.

The first shot was unexpected and it came from Harding's position. A second shot followed the first, and then a shadow stirred in front of his position, but before he could bring his rifle to bear, it was gone.

He waited, his rifle ready, but there was no further movement, and no sound.

Now the Apaches knew they were prepared. Was this an actual attack? Or was it merely a few exploratory advances?

There was a stir of movement beside him, and Irina moved up into position, rifle in hand.

"This is no place for you," he whispered.

She settled into position. "Why not? I can shoot, can't I?"

It was full light, but the sun was not yet above the horizon. There was no movement, no shooting from anywhere. The very silence worried him, for the Apaches must know their weakness . . . and they also knew about the women.

Several times he thought he heard distant rifle fire, but he could not be sure.

Shalako shifted his rifle in his hands and started to speak, then broke off sharply.

From off on their right there was a faint cry, then a shot.

Henri leaped up and suddenly dashed forward and, dropping into a new position, he fired almost as he touched the ground.

And then the cry came again. It was from Roy Harding, and he was hurt.

Shalako left the ground running. A bullet spat gravel just ahead of him as he made a rolling dive for shelter behind some rocks, another bullet splintering rock fragments as he landed safely.

Rolling over, he came up running, then dove for shelter again just within sight of Harding.

The teamster was crawling back, dragging a bloody leg behind him, but even as Shalako sighted him, an Apache lunged from the brush, knife in hand.

Rolling to a sitting position, Shalako fired without bringing the rifle to his shoulder, and the bullet stopped the leaping Indian in midair. A hoarse scream tore the Apache's throat, but he fell near Harding, slapping and stabbing wildly with his knife.

Harding kicked out with his good leg and his heel caught the Indian full in the face. Blood splattered from a broken nose, but despite the bullet and the kick the Apache reared up to his knees and threw himself at Harding.

Harding caught the Indian's knife wrist and wrenched the arm back, falling atop the Indian. There was a moment of brief, fierce struggle on the bloody gravel, and then Harding fell away as Shalako reached his side.

Harding's leg had been torn wickedly by a ricocheting bullet, and he had lost a lot of blood.

Swiftly, Shalako gathered him up, crouched, then left the ground in a plunging, staggering run. A bullet *whapped* the air close to his ear, and then he was out of range and down in the hollow where the fire was.

Gently, he put the young teamster down. "Take care of him, Laura," he said, and ducked back to the firing line.

Picking his rifle from the ground where he had left

it in going after Harding, he dropped flat and peered out between the rocks.

He was gasping from his exertions and when he glimpsed an Apache he fired . . . and missed.

Desperately he tried to steady his breathing, but nothing showed except for dancing heat waves. The coolness of the morning had fled. Suddenly he heard the sound of horses' hoofs. They were coming, the rest of the Indians were coming.

Far below on the trail, a good five hundred yards off, he saw a rider pass, an Apache.

He sighted at the gap between the rocks. Maybe . . . just maybe. He took a careful sight, gathered some slack on the trigger, and waited. Carefully, he took in a breath and let it slowly out, and then a horse's head came into sight and he squeezed off his shot.

Even as the rifle leaped in his hands, the rider came into his sights, then vanished. The report of the shot racketed among the rocks.

He drew back and mopped the sweat from his brow to keep the salt from blinding him. He fed another shell into his Winchester, and waited.

It was time to draw back. They were too spread out and if the Apaches ever got behind them they would have no chance, none whatever.

A slight whisper of sound reached him, and listening he heard it no more, yet he knew that sound. It was the rubbing of coarse cloth on rock.

The canyon . . .

With infinite care he inched along on his belly to a position where he could look into the canyon. It was no more than sixty feet deep at that point, and he could see three Apaches working their way up the steep side.

He was starting to lift the rifle when he noticed the wedge of rock. It was a huge, piano-sized rock poised on the lip of the canyon.

Working his way over to it, he put his back against another rock, doubled his knees back almost to his chest, and put his moccasined feet against the wedge of rock. The rock teetered, but did not fall.

Carefully, he teetered it once again, and when it started to teeter forward, he shoved with all his strength. The stone leaned far out, and then toppled over. From below there came a hoarse scream, ending in the tremendous crash of the falling boulder, then the rattle of pursuing rocks.

Taking up his rifle he worked his way along the line of defense, calling them all back. Henri had a cut over his eye caused by a flying rock splinter, but there were no other injuries.

Once more they took up their positions, but this time at the edge of the circle that surrounded the campfire and backed up against the cliff wall and the tower of Elephant Butte.

Hans Kreuger was still alive, still silent, rarely asking for attention, offering no evidence of the pain he was feeling. Harding was weak from loss of blood, but his leg had been bandaged.

"If we only knew what was happening!" Laura exclaimed. "If we only knew whether the Army was coming or not."

"They may not even know we exist," Dagget said.

"They will know," Buffalo replied. "By now they

know. They may have cut our trail somewhere, and they will know."

He returned to his new position, and settled down for a long wait. He could hear the murmur of voices around the fire, occasionally see them moving there, although he was well back among the rocks and trees. One thing he knew: When this was over he was quitting. He was going to get a stake and a ranch somewhere away from Indians . . . in some safe, sane, reasonable country.

He had been there for some time when he began to feel uneasy. He shifted his position, studied all the terrain about him, but nothing had changed.

Far off, softened by distance, he heard the hammer of gunfire. Somebody was having one hell of a fight. Maybe if the Army gave Chato a whipping he would be running so fast there would be no time to stop.

He yawned and shifted his position. Suddenly his breath stilled. That rock out there, no larger than a man's fist . . . was turned over.

Now the heavy side of a rock is always down in a place where wind and water can reach it, so something had passed that way, moving very fast, and had inadvertently overturned the rock. Something coming toward *him*!

And there was nothing . . .

Really worried now, he got to his feet and checked the area again. Could he have overlooked that rock when he took the position first? He was a man who always noticed such things for such things were his life. But could he, this time at least, have made a mistake?

It was very quiet.

He should move away. This place had good cover and he was well hidden, but nevertheless, he should move. If something was that close to him . . . ?

But nothing was there.

He listened, and heard no sound. He studied again every tree, every rock. He dropped back to his knees finally, and put his Winchester on the ground. He reached back to shift his knife into a better position, and when he did a rock that was not a rock moved behind him, a muscular forearm slid around his neck and across his throat. He was jerked cruelly back, his breath shut off, and he was fighting with his hands to tear the enclosing arm free when the knife went into his ribs.

His big body heaved powerfully, and he almost broke free, and then the knife slid between his ribs again, and then again. Slowly his muscles relaxed and the idea of the ranch was gone from his mind, the idea of survival was gone, and then life was gone. In that big body, so filled with strength and energy and that mind with plans . . . there was nothing, nothing at all.

A brown hand reached over and took up his rifle, unbuckled his cartridge belt, took his tobacco and pistol.

Tats-ah-das-ay-go slid back among the rocks, crossed a narrow space and crouched in the brush where his brown body merged easily with the sandstone and lava.

When he moved again he was well back in the rocks on the rim of Elephant Butte Canyon where he could watch the camp. *Tats-ah-das-ay-go* was a patient man. He had killed once and safely, soon he would kill again, but he was in no hurry. These people weren't going anywhere.

He had already chosen his next victim.

On that hot afternoon of April 23, Lieutenant Colonel Sandy Forsyth was seated on a low knoll studying the terrain about him. There had been no word from Lieutenant Hall, but that worried him less than the fact that he had not heard from Lieutenant McDonald, who had a mere handful of scouts.

His glasses swept the country, caught a flicker of movement, and reversed their field.

A rider . . . coming like hell after him.

His glasses brought the rider closer. An Indian by the way he rode . . . *Jumping Jack!*

That horse was Jumping Jack, McDonald's mount, and the company racehorse, the fastest horse in the regiment.

Trouble . . .

The colonel moved the command down the slope on a course to intercept the rider, and then drew up to await the man as he came nearer.

The Mohave scout leaped to the ground as the horse broke under him and rolled over on the hot sand. The message was quick, concise, definite. McDonald was under heavy attack by a large force. Three or four of his men had been killed.

It was sixteen miles of riding in blistering hot country. It might kill every horse in the command but there was no choice. There had been another time, away back, when Sandy Forsyth had waited, stretched out on his back in the grass of Beecher's Island, suffering from an ugly wound, and praying for relief.

ATOP THE KNOLL where Lieutenant McDonald
was making his fight, his canteen gave off only an
empty sound. Two of his men were down, wounded
and gasping under the broiling sun, for there was no
shade.

Checking the loads on the three rifles he was now
using, he glanced around at his small command. The
red-faced corporal, redder of face now, was still willing and able. One of the Mohaves had a livid gash
across his cheek from a bullet, and one of the
wounded men was delirious and raving of mountain
lakes, of shadows, and of fish splashing in the cool
water. Occasionally he whimpered with an almost animal sound. The other wounded man had dragged
himself to the rocks and was ready with his rifle.

The Apaches were confident. They moved forward
in a short, quick dash. McDonald, a dead shot with a
rifle, picked up the first weapon. An Apache moved
and the lieutenant fired, then fired again, taking the
Apache in midstride. The Indian fell, then scrambled
to safety among the rocks.

Miles away, riding under the blazing sun, Forsyth
heard the shots. He might be in time then . . . he
might still be in time.

There were seventy-five Indians along the cliffs of
Horseshoe Canyon who had taken no part in the attack on the patrol. They awaited bigger game. The
trouble was, they did not expect the number that
came.

Loco, who directed the fighting, put up a stubborn
battle against superior forces and superior arms,

fighting a wary rearguard action, and retreated slowly into the depths of the canyon.

It was not the sort of fighting to be relished by either side. Targets were few and elusive despite the number of men engaged, and there were not many bodies falling. Despite the number of deaths in combat there are never so many as one would expect from the amount of shooting done.

The Apache was always cautious in his fighting, and the soldiers had fought Apaches before and learned from them things no War Department manual could teach, so it was a careful, relentless struggle where every shot was meant to kill but targets were few. There were no amateurs in the battle of Horseshoe Canyon.

The battle lasted until darkness before the soldiers withdrew. They had driven the Indians into the rocks and into the night, and from there on no commander with an ounce of sense would risk his men.

Nor did Forsyth have any doubts that the Apaches were on the run. Detaching Captain Gordon and Lieutenant Gatewood to the pursuit, Forsyth turned to interrogating the prisoners. They had taken but two, one a wounded warrior, the other an ancient squaw. Neither admitted knowing of the hunting party, yet one of the dead Apaches carried a rifle on which was carved the name of Pete Wells.

"It doesn't mean they've been wiped out," McDonald decided, "only that they got Wells, or got his rifle somehow."

"Chato wasn't with this bunch. He must have found them. The rifle could have been carried by a messenger."

Night was upon them and they had no choice but to remain where they were. The brutal charge across the desert in the blazing sun had left the horses in no shape for further travel, so whatever was to be done must be done the following day.

"I wish," Forsyth said, "that we could hear from Hall."

———

HANS KREUGER DIED as the sun went down, going quietly. He asked for a drink of water and Laura brought it to him, and when he thanked her he put his head back on the doubled-up coat that was his pillow and looked up at the sky where the first stars had appeared. He did not move again, nor did he speak.

His passing brought deep depression to the group. Pete Wells had been killed, but he had not been well-known to any of them but Buffalo Harris, and he had been killed far from them. Kreuger was of their own group, and he had been a well-liked, quiet, and sincere young man.

Roy Harding lay wounded, their food supply was dwindling, and then Shalako Carlin found the body of Buffalo Harris.

The big hunter had been dead but a few minutes, and the manner of his death was apparent, even in the gathering dusk. The slight smudges of toes digging into the sand, the indications of a brief, hopeless struggle were there. One thing was immediately apparent to Shalako—Buffalo Harris had been killed by no ordinary Apache.

The buffalo hunter had been familiar with all the

tricks and devices of the Indian, and was a veteran of many a skirmish. Yet there had been slight struggle, and no sound. No wolf or mountain lion could have killed more swiftly, silently, and efficiently.

The killer could have taken the weapons and slipped back among his own people, but Shalako had an uneasy feeling this was not so. He might still be among them, waiting for the chance to kill again.

The world of the Apache was not a large one. From the Tucson area to somewhat east of El Paso, from deep in Sonora and the Sierra Madre to central New Mexico—they raided beyond that area, and the White Mountain Apaches were farther north—this land was theirs.

Within that area among the Apaches and those aware of them, there were names that worked magic. Names of men alive today, names of a few but recently dead. Mangas Colorado, Cochise, Nana, Geronimo, Victorio, Chato . . . and a dozen others. These were their warriors and their chieftains.

Among them also there were tales of other warriors, warriors who were not leaders. It was the name of one of these that came to Shalako's mind now.

The manner of the kill, the silence, the skill . . . it had all the earmarks.

The present area of their camp was no more than an acre. Except for that space immediately surrounding the fire, it consisted of brush, broken rock, deep gashes into the base rock along the lips of the canyons, scattered trees, and behind them, Elephant Butte.

Kreuger was dead, Harris was dead, and Harding was wounded. Only five men remained on their feet and able to fight, and there were the four women. Von Hallstatt and Henri were both good men, Dagget and Mako untried and inexperienced. He walked back to the fire.

"What is it, Shalako?" Irina was on her feet looking at him.

"Stay close to the fire," he said, "and stay together through the night. There's an Indian inside the circle."

"How could there be?" Julia demanded. "We've been watching."

"He killed Buffalo." Shalako turned back to Irina. "Let Julia take over the cooking. From now on I want you and Laura to stand guard with rifles. If you see an Indian, kill him."

"Suppose we hunt him down?" Henri suggested. "He hasn't much room in which to maneuver."

"It would be like going out in the night to feel around in the grass for a rattlesnake. You'd find him, all right."

Henri relieved Mako at the cliff's edge, and the cook returned to the fire.

Shalako prowled restlessly, then he, too, returned to the fire.

"That's *Tats-ah-das-ay-go* out there," he said. "I am sure of it."

"How can you be sure?" Mako asked.

"The way he killed, and the fact that he came into the camp area instead of leaving it."

"How can you be sure he did?"

"Call it a feeling. He's here, all right, and I'm sure that's who he is. He's a great warrior, perhaps the greatest in the Apache nation, and he's a lone wolf. Even the other Apaches are afraid of him. Stays to himself, usually travels alone. I'd say he was down-right unsocial."

He had stalked bighorn sheep in the mountains and deer and antelope upon the low ground. He would understand the use of every shadow, every crevice, every bush. He would know how to hide where it seemed impossible anything could hide, and he would be more deadly than any rattler for he would offer no warning.

It was the waiting that worried them. It worried him, too, but Shalako was a patient man. These others were not patient. All of them, even von Hallstatt, were undisciplined. They wanted what they wanted without waiting. They had never learned to cope with time.

The West taught one how to cope with time, for time measured all things. One did not say it was so many miles from here to yonder, but it was so many days ride. Everything was measured by time and time measured everything.

"Why have you stayed?" Irina said.

"A lady loaned me a horse. Let's just say I was grateful."

"You needn't have been. To be perfectly honest I was worried about my horse. I couldn't bear the thought of his being eaten."

"It adds up to the same thing. Anyway, you could have come with me."

"And leave the others? You knew I would not do that."

He was following the conversation with only half his attention, the rest of it was out there in the rocks, trying to understand the thinking of an Indian who was planning to kill one or all of them.

She had been silent for several minutes, evidently thinking along the same lines, for she said, "How could you know who he is? The Indian, I mean."

"Every person identifies himself by his habits, his mannerisms. Sometimes you know them by the tracks they leave, sometimes by the tracks they do not leave. Little things add up to make a picture. . . ."

"Will knowing who he is help?"

"It might. It makes him easier to understand, and sometimes you can outguess a man you know."

Roy Harding overheard them. "Who did you say?"

"*Tats-ah-das-ay-go,* the Quick Killer."

"I've heard of him."

Among the rocks the Apache heard his name spoken and was frightened. An Apache's name is a closely guarded secret in most cases, and to possess a man's name is to possess a power over him.

His eyes fixed apprehensively on the big man who had spoken his name. By what medicine had this man learned who he was?

This was the one he heard called Shalako. He was the man with whom the rains came.

Tats-ah-das-ay-go watched the big man closely. He was a man to be avoided . . . a great warrior . . . a man with whom the Apache would have risked anything to meet in battle. But Shalako knew his name . . . there was big medicine in this. Nobody had seen him, but Shalako spoke of him.

He remained where he was. The man on the cliff, he was to be the next one.

Shalako glanced around at those whom he could

see, and the tension was obvious. Edna Dagget looked drawn and haggard, starting at the least sound, on the ragged edge of hysteria.

Julia Paige seemed all eyes. The dark circles beneath them indicating lack of sleep and worry. Count Henri had lost weight, but he was cool, competent, and ready.

"You'll have to watch, Roy," Shalako said. "Don't rely on the girls. They aren't up to it. Keep your gun handy . . . they may try to finish you off."

"I'm wondering what became of Bosky Fulton. You said you saw him out there, and there's been no shooting."

"Holed up. That's if he's smart. If he tried to run for it now he'd be sure to be killed."

Shalako knew that Forsyth would have his own problems. By the sound of the firing they had heard, a battle had taken place between two considerable forces. He could only surmise the results, but he imagined the Army would have won. On the other hand they might have suffered, might have lost horses, and either might slow them up.

He glanced around the circle. Their small supply of food would not go much further. The food would give out before the ammunition, and how disciplined were these people?

Could they hold out two days? Three?

Forsyth might be within a dozen miles of them now, but Forsyth could not know where they were. Tomorrow, if an attack was made, he might hear the gunfire. If he were in battle himself, he would not.

Yet by this time Forsyth's scouts would certainly have told him the hunting party had headed south . . .

if they didn't leap to the conclusion that it had been wiped out or taken prisoner.

Laura Davis was the daughter of a United States Senator and by now the wire from Washington would be hot with demands that something be done.

Say three days longer. They must hold out three days longer.

There would surely be an attack tomorrow, which would mean that superstition or not, *Tats-ah-das-ay-go* would kill tonight. He was a lone warrior, and he would want to count coup again before the final attack.

Getting to his feet he circled the line of defense. By day each man could be seen from the central point where the fire was, but by night the positions of several of the men on guard were lost in darkness. It was these about whom he worried.

Von Hallstatt looked up as Shalako squatted beside him. "Don't remain in any position very long," Shalako warned. "Keep moving, watch the shadows. I think he will try to kill at least one more tonight."

Dagget was eager, rather than frightened. For the first time in his life he was actually in the field. He looked around at Shalako. "I'm a fool," he said. "But do you want to know something? I like this."

"It puts a man on edge, all right."

"It's living! Really living! I always wanted to be a soldier, but Father advised diplomacy and, of course, Edna would hear of nothing else. I never had a chance to even try it."

"You'll have to get some sleep. After a bit we will manage to sleep, two at a time."

"I don't mind. I'll stay here."

Henri was settled down with his back against a towering boulder. He had chosen a good, concealed and relatively protected position that offered a good field of fire. The position was so good that it was unlikely he would be attacked.

Shalako went back to the fire, which had been allowed to die down. The fuel they had close by must now be sufficient, for there was no possibility of leaving the circle for more.

Irina was near the fire, and Laura also. Julia Paige was lighting a cigarette for Harding, who lay stretched on a pallet just back from the edge of the firelight.

"It's getting cooler," Laura said. "I can never get used to how cool the nights become after such hot days."

"When I was a little girl in India," Irina commented, "I used to lie awake at night . . . the heat was stifling . . . and listen to the tigers out in the jungle. I could lie there and imagine them slinking through the jungle, their great black and gold bodies moving as soundlessly as a snake."

"We're all going to be killed," Edna Dagget said. "We're all going to be killed, and you just sit there, talking."

"Ain't much else to do," Harding said mildly. "Nobody's going out in that jungle after no Apache. Nobody in his right mind."

He glanced at Irina. "I'd sure admire to hear more about that tiger country, ma'am. I heard somebody say you'd hunted them with your pa."

"Yes, I did."

"Hunted mountain lions a few times," Harding said. "No fun to that, once you get the hang of it.

Lion's a mighty mean animal, but they sure ain't got any brains. I've trapped two lions in the same trap on the same day day . . . with the smell of lion and blood all over the place. You'd never do that with a wolf, nor most any other animal."

IRINA'S HANDS LAY in her lap. They were beautiful hands, but capable hands, too, the hands a woman should have.

It had been a long time since Shalako had thought of himself in connection with any woman as beautiful as Irina, and he was a fool to begin now. He had nothing to offer, and no doubt she would be astonished and then amused if she realized he had even thought of such a thing.

He was a saddle tramp, a drifter with a pistol and a Winchester, a man who rode wild country with wilder men, and to that he had best keep himself. He was Shalako, the man who brought the rains with him . . . and she was Lady Irina Carnarvon, daughter of an ancient Welsh-Irish family. Two people could not be farther apart . . . and the fact that for a few brief years he had known a life not unlike hers was of no importance, and all that was forgotten now. Or was it?

At best, those years had been an interlude, for he was a Western man, and only a Western man . . . nor did he wish to be anything else.

Shalako threw the dregs of his coffee into the fire. "I'm going out there," he said, "and find that Indian."

They looked at him as if he were mad, and perhaps

he was, but, after all, this was the thing he did best, and why should he shrink from trying? He knew enough about that Apache out there to know that hunting a rattlesnake in the grass with your hands might be far safer than hunting that Indian at night among the rocks.

"If I don't find him," he said, "somebody will die before daylight."

"And what if something happens to you?" Irina asked. "What shall we do then?"

He looked at her with sudden bitterness. "You know how much of a hole a man leaves when he dies? The same hole you leave in the water when you pull your finger out. I'll leave no more than that, nor be missed more than an hour or two . . . If anybody here can find that Indian without having him find them first, it's me. I've got a chance."

"Don't go," Irina said.

"We could all come in close to the fire," Laura suggested, "and each could watch the others."

"And by daylight you'd be surrounded and helpless. No, I've got to try." He paused a moment, thinking of what lay out there.

Laura added a stick to the fire and the firelight that blazed up caught Harding's face. "Better wait," he said, "somebody's coming."

He was lying on the ground, and caught the sound before any of them. And then they could all hear it, the pounding of hoofs . . . a wild, shrill cry in the night, and the racing hoofs coming closer and closer.

Shalako sprang back from the fire and lifted his gun. They heard the sharp challenge from von Hallstatt, then a more distant shot, and then they heard a voice say, "Hold your fire, Fritz. I'm coming in."

And the rider came on into the circle and into the firelight. It was Bosky Fulton.

He slid from the saddle, grinning. It was a taunting grin, yet Shalako could see the wariness in it, the animal-like watchfulness.

"There's a passel of Indians out there an' come morning I figured you'd need help. And I ain't sayin' I wouldn't be glad of it my ownself."

Von Hallstatt came into the circle. "You damned thief," he said. "You damned, cheap, murdering thief."

Fulton turned on the German, but he kept smiling. "Now most any other time, Fritz, I'd kill you for that. Right now I figure we got plenty of killin' to do without us shootin' each other."

He squatted on his heels by the fire and picked up a cup. Coolly, he poured himself a cup of coffee. Then he looked up. "If there's one Indian out there, there's fifty. They done give the Army the slip, and that there Forsyth is chasing off toward the border after six or eight Apaches who are making tracks enough for fifty. The rest of them are bunched out here to take this outfit."

"But you came in to help us?" Laura said skeptically. "It doesn't sound like you."

"I came in to he'p myself," Fulton said, grinning insolently. "I'd no chance to catch the Army, and it was gettin' mighty lonesome out there by myself. I figured I better take a chance with you folks."

"You're a cheap coward," von Hallstatt said. "You ran like a rabbit once, and you'll do it again."

Bosky Fulton's lips tightened a little. The smile remained but it was stiff. "Now you'll die for that," he said. "If the Apaches don't kill you, I will."

"You have your nerve," Irina said.

"Sure." He looked at her with a flickering glance that did not quite remove his attention from von Hallstatt. "And if you want to keep General Fritz alive, ma'am, you better quiet him down. If he figures to talk to me like that, he should have that rifle in firing position before he opens his yap."

Fulton had not noticed Shalako, and now Shalako stepped down from the shadows near a tree where he had stepped at the rush of hoofs. "This is fool talk, Fulton, so if you want to stay here with us, cut it out."

Fulton's shoulders hunched as if from a blow. His yellow eyes clung to von Hallstatt. He desperately wished to turn, but he feared to turn his back on the German, and von Hallstatt, seeing his quandary, smiled at him.

"Now that takes a lot of guts," Fulton said. "Coming up behind a man like that. Suppose you meet me face to face."

Deliberately, Shalako stepped up behind him and took him by the shoulder and turned him sharply around. "All right, Fulton"—he stood within two feet of him—"I'm ready. Want to make something of it?"

Fulton stared at Shalako, and Shalako's cold eyes did not waver. "You can stay, Fulton, as long as you carry your weight. When you stop carrying it, or start trouble, out you go."

"And who'll make me?" Fulton was shaking with

fury, but there was something in Shalako that worried him. Shalako was not worried, he was not afraid, he was even contemptuous.

"I'll make you, Fulton. You make trouble here and I'll run you out of camp, like a whipped dog. And when you decide to try gunning me, just go right ahead. I won't be drunk and I won't be scared, and even if you get a bullet into me, *I'll kill you*. Make up your mind to that, Fulton. *I'll kill you*."

Harding had lifted himself on an elbow. For the first time Fulton saw that Harding held a Colt in his hand.

"Bosky, you're a nervy man. *Tats-ah-das-ay-go* is out there in the rocks. Somebody's got to go after him. Why don't you show us just how tough you are and go get him?"

Fulton's anger and frustration mounted within him, yet through it all stabbed a clear, hard grain of sense. *Tats-ah-das-ay-go . . . good God!*

"He killed Buffalo a few hours ago, but he's inside the circle somewhere. He's in the rocks out there, not more than fifty yards away right now. Why don't you go get him?"

Bosky Fulton drew back, then shrugged. "Let him come to me. I ain't lost anything out there in those rocks."

He had taken a gamble, coming back here, but less of a gamble than it would have been out there among the Apaches.

Nor was he worried. If he could last out the Indian raids with this outfit, he would cut and run when it was over, and before they would ask too many questions about their jewelry and money. The thing to do was to get out before the Army found them.

As for von Hallstatt, that German needed killing and he was going to personally take care of that.

He remembered Shalako and was faintly uneasy. The feeling angered him, for there was nothing about Shalako that he should be worried about. Who was he, after all, but a drifting cowhand and prospector . . . although he had the look of a tough man.

A couple of .44 slugs would make him look a lot less tough.

———

WITH THE FIRST coming of day the defenders drew back so they could offer mutual support.

"Why did he have to come here?" Laura asked, indicating Fulton. "I hate that man. And he's absolutely filthy."

"He can shoot," Shalako replied. "We can use him."

"Nevertheless, I don't like him. He's mean, vicious, and cruel." For the first time Shalako learned that Fulton had planned to take the two girls with him when they left.

"A fool thing," he said. "In this country a man can get away with murder sometimes, and with stealing often enough, but a man who bothers a woman will get his neck stretched."

Shalako took up his Winchester and went over to where von Hallstatt had dug out the sand to make a better firing position. Shalako dropped down beside him and, squinting through the rocks, studied the field of fire. It was a good one.

"Watch yourself around Fulton," he said. "He means to kill you."

Von Hallstatt glanced sharply at him but, without returning the glance, Shalako continued. "He's a killer. He's killed a half-dozen men in gun battles, and likes to have the name of being a fast man with a gun. He's proud, and he's touchy. He needs us right now, and we can use him, but when this tapers off, you be ready. Never be without a gun, and never let him have an even break. He'll kill you."

"Can he shoot that fast and with accuracy?"

"You just bet he can."

"We will see. I do not like Herr Fulton."

Shalako got up to move. "Neither do I, but he's no fool, so be careful."

"Why do you warn me? I am not your friend."

Shalako grinned suddenly. "Nor am I yours, but this is a matter of tactics, and his are different than yours. I figured you'd better know what to expect."

"You seem to think a good deal in terms of tactics."

"I want to live."

"Perhaps," von Hallstatt mused, "he will fight according to my tactics. He is a proud man, you say."

Shalako took up a position among the rocks. He glanced slowly around. Their circle was drawn back now, and was scarcely thirty yards from side to side. Close behind them loomed Elephant Butte, on their right, and right beside them, the lip of the canyon, and on the other side, just a short distance away, the cliffs.

"Irina"—Shalako motioned to her—"fill the canteens. You gather all our gear and take it to the edge of the canyon near the butte."

He paused . . . it was very still out there. The last of the stars were gone. There was a faint gray over the distant mountains to the east. "And get Harding back there."

Von Hallstatt was on his right, Dagget close on his left. Bosky Fulton was just beyond.

"Henri," he said, "you relieve Mako. Let him get something to eat."

The Frenchman left the fire and moved away toward the cliff's edge.

He was back almost at once. "Mako's dead," Henri said. "He's been stabbed."

There was a silence. Irina felt herself cold with horror. Another of them gone . . . how many more would go?

"He made a good omelet," Laura said. "He made the best omelet I ever ate."

"He would like nothing better than to hear you say that," Henri said. "He was proud of his work."

"You're not just a-foolin'?" Bosky asked, looking from one to the other. "That damn' Apache killer is really here?"

"You watch yourself, Fulton," Harding taunted, "or he'll take your hair. That tangled mop of yours would make a pretty sight hanging from his bridle. I can close my eyes and just see it there."

"Shut up!" Bosky snarled over his shoulder.

They lapsed into silence. Another gone, and an attack was coming. It was coming and they all knew it was, but when it came it was not as they expected. It was a mounted attack and it came with a rush—

about a dozen horsemen coming through the trees, fleeting, indefinite targets.

Von Hallstatt and Fulton fired as one man, and an Indian pony reared, throwing its rider. Dagget fired, killing the Indian as he started to mount.

"Did you see that?" Dagget yelled excitedly. "I got him!"

He had come halfway to his feet with excitement when a bullet burned his neck, and he dropped flat, clasping a hand to his bloody flesh, an expression of startled horror on his face.

The attack broke as suddenly as it had begun, with riderless horses disappearing among the trees. The Apaches had dropped to the ground close up, and now the small fort was ringed with enemies, all within an easy bowshot of their meager defenses.

From the edge of the cliff behind them they heard Henri fire, then fire again. The sound of his heavy rifle was easily distinguished from the others.

Dagget sat, his legs spread wide, dabbing at his bloody neck. "They damned near killed me!" he said, in a shocked tone.

"But they didn't. You're only scratched." Roy Harding was crawling toward them. "Let me up there."

"You had better return," von Hallstatt told the teamster. "Soon we retreat, and there is no time for carrying you back."

"He's right," Shalako agreed.

An Indian started up and Bosky Fulton fired. The Indian fell, and Bosky shot into him before he could more than make a move to rise.

An angry yell from the trees drew another shot from Fulton.

Count Henri fired again from the cliff, and from the rocks on the side of the Butte, Irina fired. She was shooting over their heads into the trees.

There was a lull. The sun mounted, the heat grew intense. Nothing stirred.

From time to time a bullet nipped at the rocks. The brilliant blue of the sky was gone and it seemed misted over . . . but there could be no mist in such a place. Von Hallstatt glanced at it inquiringly. "It is peculiar," he said. He started to fill his pipe and glanced at it again. "I think it is dust!"

The air grew suddenly cooler. Irina called to them from the rocks, and pointed. They turned to look and saw the horizon obscured with a far-off cloud.

Shalako turned quickly to von Hallstatt. "We've got to fall back and bunch up," he said. "That's a dust storm. Maybe a norther. I've seen the temperature drop thirty degrees in less than an hour in such a storm."

"Thirty degrees? It is too much!"

"Did you ever spend a spring in the Texas Panhandle? Or country adjoining it? My friend, you've seen nothing until you have!"

Quickly, they fell back. Bosky Fulton had already gone for the horses and, with Shalako's help, bunched them in a sheltered corner on the west side of the butte. A shoulder of the butte offered partial protection from the north, with the butte itself rising sheer above them.

Dagget held a bloody handkerchief to his neck, and seemed awed by the fact that he had been wounded. He glanced up at Shalako. "They might have killed me," he said. "I had just moved."

"A bullet doesn't care who it hits," Shalako said carelessly. "Count yourself lucky."

An Indian suddenly left his shelter and darted forward, and, from his vantage point, von Hallstatt saw him clearly. He tracked him a brief instant, then fired. The Indian stumbled and fell.

A gust of wind whipped across the clearing, scattering the remnants of their fire, driving leaves before it, the dried dead leaves of a bygone year.

Another gust, and then with a roar the storm was upon them, blinding, choking sand that blew down out of the north, obscuring all their surroundings, causing them to gasp for breath.

Shalako grabbed Irina. Quickly he tied a handkerchief over her mouth. He had already pulled his own up to cover his lips, and Fulton had done the same. Von Hallstatt was quick to follow suit, and Count Henri, the last man to scramble up to their hollow among the rocks, had already done so.

Crouching together, they waited. Only Shalako and Fulton held to the rim of the hollow in which they had taken shelter, watching below.

Suddenly, almost drowned in the roar of the wind, Fulton's rifle roared, and Shalako followed.

Von Hallstatt, stumbling against the force of the wind to get into a firing position, felt a sharp tug at his clothing. Roy Harding scrambled to the rim of the cusp, lifted his six-shooter and then as if struck by a gust of wind he was whirled around and fell, tumbling over and over into the bottom of the hollow.

He had been shot through the skull.

Edna Dagget screamed, and threw herself against the rocks, clinging there, far from the fallen man. She screamed and screamed again, but her screams were lost in the wildness of the storm.

The wind mounted to an awful roar, battering at the mountain. Sand bit at their faces like tiny teeth and the wind blew down their throats if they opened their mouths until they were almost strangled by the force of it.

Hunched in their tiny hollow, they waited. And under cover of the storm, the Apaches darted closer and closer.

Twice Shalako fired, and each time he missed, his shooting thrown off by the force of the wind and the dimness of his vision.

The sun was blotted out, and the hollow and all the desert around it were gripped by a curious yellow twilight.

Count Henri struggled to hold the horses, which were plunging and frightened, and Irina went to help him, crooning comfortingly to the horses. Her mares steadied under her hands and held close to her, as if for protection.

Under the howling of the wind, sand rattled against the rock and their clothing, driving with force enough to draw flecks of blood on Edna Dagget's cheeks. Hovering against a wall of the mountain, Shalako tried to shield the action of his Winchester from the sand while he stared with straining eyes into the outer darkness.

Suddenly, during a lull in the wind, he heard the ugly thud of a bullet into flesh and an instant later, the report.

Turning swiftly, Shalako stared up at the mountain, but there was no movement up there but the wind. It was a towering butte, the side broken by weathering, offering ledges and footholds clear to the top. And someone was up there.

Tats-ah-das-ay-go . . . of course.

Someone was crying and Edna was screaming hysterically. Glancing into the hollow, Shalako saw Irina tugging at the body of Count Henri. The Frenchman was down and hurt.

Crossing to her, he bent over the man. It needed only a glance to see that Count Henri was finished. The blood was pumping from a wound in his chest, and all of Irina's efforts could not stop its flow.

He opened his eyes and looked up at them, trying to speak and the roar of the wind drowned out his voice. He collapsed suddenly, and behind him Shalako heard a scream, and a roar of guns.

Wheeling, he saw a dozen Apaches scrambling into the hollow. Fulton had fallen back against the rock wall and was firing both pistols, using fearful execution.

Von Hallstatt, cornered, was clubbing his rifle, and Dagget was rolling on the ground, fighting desperately with an Apache who had leaped upon him. Another had seized Laura and was dragging her toward the edge of the hollow.

Lifting his Winchester, Shalako steadied. An instant he held his aim, then fired.

One of the Indians attacking von Hallstatt dropped in his tracks. Wheeling, Shalako swung his rifle and shot another man on the rim of the hollow, and then something dropped off the mountain and struck him between the shoulders.

Rolling over, he came up fast and, as the Indian arose, Shalako swung a wicked fist that knocked the Apache sprawling under the plunging hoofs of the horses.

Drawing a Colt, he fired, killing the Indian who had Laura by the hair. At the same instant a gun roared beside him, deafening him with the blast, and he saw another Indian leap back. Irina was on her knees with his rifle in her hands.

Fulton turned suddenly and ducked into the rocks just as a second wave of Indians swarmed into the hollow. Von Hallstatt rushed at them, clubbing his rifle, and when the stock broke, he drew his revolver and fired. He emptied the gun and threw it aside, grabbing up Henri's rifle.

Shalako, berserk with fury, rushed at the Indians, stopped, and opened fire. And then suddenly, they were gone.

They were gone as if they had never been. Except for the dead lying about, the awful howling of the wind, and the three men who remained.

Edna Dagget was dead, struck by a ricocheting bullet. Count Henri was dead. Laura was dazed and shocked, and Bosky Fulton was gone.

"Yellow!" von Hallstatt said. "The man's a coward!"

"No, he's not a coward. He's just a damned selfish brute." Shalako fed shells into his gun, then began gathering the other weapons. "He's looking out for himself, that's all."

There was no escape. The Apaches would still be

out there, waiting for them. And somewhere in the rocks above was *Tats-ah-das-ay-go*, awaiting his opportunity.

The wind roared over and past them, and the sand whipped into their hollow and rattled against the rocks. Irina stood with her horses and the roan, quieting them. Charles Dagget lifted the body of his wife and carried her into a sheltered place behind a boulder where there was some protection from the wind.

Von Hallstatt put down his rifle and crossed to carry Henri to a place beside her.

Shalako picked up the bodies of the three dead Apaches and dropped them down the slope. Only one of them had been armed with a rifle, but that was loaded and put to one side.

Von Hallstatt's coat was ripped from his shoulders, his shirt torn, his face bloody. He had been struck over the head or creased by a bullet that left a nasty scratch on his skull.

Irina left the horses and knelt beside Laura, holding her close. Julia Paige stared at them, dazed and numb with horror at what she had seen.

Shalako walked to the horses and took a canteen from one of them and rinsed his mouth, swallowed a bit, and carried the canteen to von Hallstatt, then to the girls.

Daggett was sitting beside his wife, his head in his hands.

"Get up!" Shalako said roughly. "Get a rifle. They'll be coming back."

Dagget stared up at him. "I don't care," he mumbled. "I don't care at all."

Shalako took him by the shoulder and lifted him to

his feet. "I care, I care one hell of a lot, and grief is a luxury you can't afford. There are other women here, man. Now stand ready."

"There should be more dead," von Hallstatt said. "I could have sworn—"

"They carry them off. After dark they'll come for the rest."

"We can't last through another night," Dagget protested. "It is impossible!"

"We'll last," Shalako said. He glanced over at von Hallstatt. "How are you, General?"

"I am well," Hallstatt said, "I am well indeed."

The vast roar of the wind did not cease, nor the wild flurries and gusts that blotted out all about them, obscuring even their own faces from one another. Outside the dust was a veil beyond which they could not see.

Nor did the waiting cease. Eyes red-rimmed and bloodshot, they huddled over their guns at the rim of the hollow with the vast bulk of the butte towering above them, and they waited, squinting into the blasting wind, throats parched, lips dried and cracked until blood came, their skins begrimed and gray.

Peering into the dust and the gathering dark, they waited for the Apaches to come again.

About midnight their water gave out, although they had used little for hours. The night wind roared with awful howls, a mighty wall of wind that threw itself against the mountain and swept brush, leaves and branches before it. Loose rock tumbled from the mountain, and then at last, with dawn, the storm spent itself and the wind died away, and they lay like dead men, staring with glazed and empty eyes upon the scene before them.

————

LIEUTENANT HALL HEARD the firing atop the mountain before the storm broke, but could not place the direction of the sound. Several times earlier he had seemed to hear shots but the sounding board of the mountain was rolling the sound away from him.

When the storm struck, he was in the lee of Gillespie Mountain. On his left was the cliff up which the hunting party had climbed. Not knowing of the dim trail, he did not suspect they might have mounted here.

All tracks in the open were obliterated by the storm, and he supposed all other tracks would be gone. In the desert there are places where tracks may outlive the years, but this he did not know. Unaware of the cliff trail, he could only believe the party had gone on through the pass that led across the range and into Animas Valley.

The storm's arrival demanded they take what shelter they could find, and the bulk of Gillespie proved enough to break the force of the wind and sand. Huddled among the boulders, they made a dry camp.

Hall had been asleep but a short time when he was awakened by Jim Hunt, a half-breed Delaware scout.

"There is fighting on the mountain," Hunt said. "I have heard shooting."

Hall listened, but heard no sound save the roaring of the wind.

"In this storm? Impossible!"

"There was shooting," Hunt insisted.

Hall got up and shook the sand from his boots, then pulled them on. He hesitated, then scratched a brief note on a page of his notebook.

"Could you get to Forsyth?" A couple of frightened prospectors, hurrying out of the area, had told them of the fight near Horseshoe Canyon, and that Forsyth had remained there.

"I go," Hunt said.

When he had gone, Hall did not return to sleep. He got up and walked to the horses. They were restless, and kept tugging toward the north.

Brannigan, who was standing horse guard, came up to him. "I think there's water over there, sir," he said. "Want me to have a look?"

"Yes, but be careful."

The lieutenant stood guard while Brannigan made his search, and he was thinking of Laura Davis. He had danced with her once when she had been touring Army posts with her father. It seemed impossible that she could be here, in such a place.

It was nearly light and the wind was dying when Brannigan returned.

"There's water, Lieutenant. About a half a mile from here, right over at the foot of the mountain." He scratched his jaw, which itched from the stubble of whiskers and the dust. "Good water, too."

When the troop had watered their horses and filled their canteens, they made coffee while Hall swept the cliffs with his field glass.

"Something up there," he said finally. "Looks like a body hanging among the rocks well up toward the top."

He stared through the glass, genuinely puzzled, for

there was a spot of brightness there, brighter than any reflection from a rifle barrel.

Brannigan walked over to him, holding a cup of coffee. "Lieutenant . . . this is for you." He squinted at the cliff. "Want I should go up there? I'm a right curious man, Lieutenant."

"Let somebody else go. You've done your bit for the day."

"If the lieutenant pleases, I'd take it as a favor. I've a thought we'll find there's been a fight up there."

"All right, Brannigan. If you wish."

WHEN FORSYTH FOLLOWED Jim Hunt back to the foot of Gillespie Mountain, the troop awaited him beside the body of Bosky Fulton.

The body was horribly mutilated.

"One of the men said it was Bosky Fulton, a gunman," Hall commented. "His pockets were stuffed with money and jewels, sir. Must be fifty thousand dollars' worth or more."

Forsyth looked down at the body. He had known Fulton by sight, and had a sharp dislike for the man, but he could feel nothing but pity now. Fulton had died very slowly, and he had died hard.

"He was jammed among the rocks, sir. Brannigan says he must have been winged, and when he fell, he fell with his gun arm under him, caught between the rocks so he couldn't get himself out.

"His right arm was pinned, and the bullet had gone through his left arm so that he couldn't use it. The Indian must have followed him down and slowly cut him into slices like that."

Literally, the body was covered with blood, blood that had flowed from a thousand small cuts, cuts made deliberately and with care.

"I would wish that on no man, although judging by his pockets, the man was a thief as well as a murderer."

"There's others up there, Colonel. Brannigan heard voices, but after what he'd seen he wasn't sure he wanted to investigate. He couldn't make out what they were talking, but it sounded like English."

"There's a trail up there," McDonald suggested. "We passed it back down the canyon."

"All right," Forsyth said, "we'll take a look. Mount your men, Lieutenant."

S HALAKO SHOOK VON HALLSTATT'S shoulder. "Better wake up, General," he said. "I think we're alone. I think the Indians have pulled out."

Sunrise was two hours gone, and the sky was blue and clear, only a few scattered puffballs of cloud hung against the still blue. The air after the storm was startlingly clear.

No smoke could be seen, nor anything else. Down where the camp had been before the final retreat, birds were scattered about the clearing, picking at crumbs left from their previous meals.

"We've got to have water," Shalako added.

He took the reins of Irina's horses and told Dagget to lead the roan. Then he led the way out of the hollow and down onto the flat where the camp had been.

A few spots of blood were visible, but there were no bodies at all now. The three Apaches they had thrown out of the hollow had been carried away during the night. Carrying his Winchester ready in his hands, and wary of every movement, Shalako led the way.

There was no trouble. All was still. The last of the dust had settled, and the warm sun brought out the smell of pine and cedar. When they reached the spring they dismounted and filled their canteens.

"There's no coffee left, not even the old grounds, but there's tea." Irina looked up at him. "Shall I make tea?"

"Sure . . . at a time like this tea beats anything. Strong black tea, hot as you can drink it. The best thing for shock of any kind, and the best stimulant there is for what we've been through."

He glanced around at the small group. The others were as unlike themselves as von Hallstatt. Julia Paige looked haggard and drawn, ten years older than she probably was. Laura Davis was tired, and only Irina seemed fresh, although her eyes were unnaturally large, and the hollows were deep around them.

"Are they gone?" von Hallstatt asked.

Shalako stood up, his eyes ranging the brush and rocks. "I think so. The Army's coming . . . they would know that before we would, and they would move out. Anyway, they probably decided what we had to take wasn't worth the price."

Except for *Tats-ah-das-ay-go*. He had paid no price at all. He was detached, a thing apart. He was like the wind or the rain, he came and he went and one did not make rules for him.

He might remain behind. It would be like him.

"We'll take no chances," Shalako said. "The one who killed Harris might still be here."

The heat seemed to have blown away with the wind, and the slight warmth from the early sun was only enough to dispel the chill. The birds continued to chirp and call in the brush and trees, and Shalako moved out to one side and sat down, his rifle across his knees.

Von Hallstatt came over and crouched beside him, stoking his pipe.

From where they sat they could look westward over a wild and broken land, the raw-backed mountains, devoid of vegetation for the most part, or scattered with the grays and faint greens of desert growth. The nearer pines and cedars covered only a limited area, and some of those had died and fallen into ruin over the broken red rocks.

"Without you," von Hallstatt said, "we should have been killed . . . all of us."

"The land is hard. A man cannot fight this country, he lives *with* it, or he dies. A man learns to become a part of it, to live like the desert plants do, almost without water, and to use every bit of available cover, like the desert animals do. And to fight an Indian, as Washington tried to tell Braddock, a man has to become like an Indian."

"You spoke once of Saxe, of Vegetius. They are writers on tactics, the knowledge of command. Were you a soldier?"

"I read them." He built a cigarette with careful fingers, his eyes restless in searching the rocks. "When I was sixteen I pulled out from home and fought the last two years of the Civil War with the Union forces, a cavalry outfit. I came out a lieutenant. Didn't figure I knew enough, so I started reading tactics. When the war was over I went to Africa and fought with the Boers in the Basuto War . . . maybe six months. After that I served as a colonel under Shir Ali in Afghanistan in the fighting after the death of Dost Mohammed."

"Henri thought he knew you."

"He saw me twice, I think. Once during the Franco-Prussian War when MacMahon sent me to Metz. I was to take a message through to Bazaine."

"But that was impossible! Metz was surrounded."

Shalako glanced at him. "I went back and forth three times . . . no trouble. Your German sentries should serve on the Indian frontier for a while, General. Any Apache or Kiowa could steal the buttons off their coats."

"And then?"

"The French lost. I shucked my uniform, produced my American papers and went to Paris. Stayed awhile, and went to London. . . ."

Julia Paige suddenly rushed up to them. "Are you mad? Are you going to sit there all day drinking tea and smoking? Or are we going to get out of here?" Her voice rose stridently.

"There is time, Julia," von Hallstatt replied. "We are as safe here as we would be moving, and the Army will come. And then, we must arrange burial for our friends."

She started to protest, then turned away, dragging her feet. "We will be killed," she said dully. "We will all be killed."

Shalako tried to hold his eyes open. He was desperately, brutally tired. There had been too little sleep for him in too long a time. The short rest behind the ruined cabin, the other sleep he had after leaving the hunting party at the ranch amounted to very little, and in between there had been riding, fighting, dust, sun, and struggle. And before that, a long stretch of living on ragged nerve in the mountains of Mexico.

Yet he was uneasy. He scanned the shattered shoulders of Elephant Butte and the edges of the canyon with careful attention. The Apaches had gone . . . his every sense told him that, told him also that the Army was coming. The trouble was that *Tats-ah-das-ay-go* had been out there, and no rule applied to him. The others might go, but he would stay . . . or he might seem to leave and then return.

He lived with the others, but always alone and near them. He sat in their councils, but rarely spoke, and when he fought, it was always alone. Even the Apaches feared him, feared his skill as a fighting man and his uncertain temper.

"Pile on some brush," he said to Dagget. "If we raise a big smoke the Army will find us sooner."

"Couldn't one of us ride to meet them?" Laura suggested. "They might pass us by."

"We'll chance it. We must stay together. There is danger yet."

Irina brought them each a cup of tea. She sat down beside Shalako. "Did I hear you telling Frederick you had been in Paris? What did you do there?"

"Whatever one does in Paris. When I came there it was a few months before the war broke out, and I had a little money. I used to go to a small café in the Avenue Clichy called the Guerbois."

He glanced at her. "I hadn't much education, you

know. There were no schools where I grew up, at least none to speak of. But I'd learned to read, and could write a little, and I started reading stories."

"In *French*?"

"Yes. I read French better than English, and German almost as well. Spoke both of them a sight better than I could read, though."

"But . . . I do not understand. You said there were no schools?"

"No schools to speak of. Only I was raised in Texas, not in California, like some folks say. I was born in California, but went with my folks to Texas. Have you ever been to San Antonio? Well, outside of San Antonio there's a place called Castroville, and a town called D'Hanis, too.

"Castroville and D'Hanis . . . they were founded by a group of colonists brought over from Alsace, only some of them were Swiss, German, Dutch, and just about everything, by a man named Count Henri de Castro in 1844.

"Old buildings stand there yet, and some of the houses are just like in the old country. Folks around there mostly spoke French and German, and about the time I was learning to talk, we moved into that area.

"D'Hanis was the last town . . . nothing between there and the Rio Grande except wild country, wild cattle, and wilder Indians. Well, I started talking down there, and I could speak French and German before I could speak proper English. Comes of playing with youngsters talking those languages.

"Sometimes I sat alongside when their folks taught them from books. Like I said, there was no proper school, but I learned to read some French before I did English."

"You were telling me about Paris."

"Yes. I went to that café on the Avenue Clichy, and I met some fellows there . . . they were painters. One of them they thought so much of they used to save him a couple of tables. His name was Manet."

"Oh, yes! I have heard of him. A friend of mine bought a painting of his in Paris. This friend was an old friend of the family of Degas. Did you know him?"

"The aristocrat? I knew him. And that other fellow who came there sometimes. I read some of his books . . . Zola, his name was, Émile Zola."

She glanced at von Hallstatt, who had gone to the fire. "Do not mention that name to Frederick. He detests him. Calls him a Socialist and a wild man . . . but I like his books."

"He told me some books to read, gave me a few in fact, just after a party we had to celebrate my joining up. It was only a few weeks that I knew them. They were a wild lot, always arguing. I am no painter or writer and understood none of it."

Lethargy settled heavily upon him. Several times he nodded, blinking his eyes open quickly, afraid that she might see . . . and she had.

"Why don't you sleep, Shalako? Frederick can keep watch . . . and I want to brush my hair."

She left him and returned to the fire. Shalako hitched himself into a more comfortable position and slowly searched the rocks again. He could not remember ever being so tired . . . there was a low murmur of voices from the group at the fire.

The Army would be coming soon.

Irina went to the saddlebags that held all that remained of her personal belongings, and found her comb and brush. These, at least, she had salvaged. Von Hallstatt was helping Dagget build up the fire. Laura was brushing her clothing, trying to make herself presentable. Von Hallstatt paused from time to time to look at the rocks, and Julia merely sat and waited, her cup of tea untouched.

TATS-AH-DAS-AY-GO LAY UPON a bare rocky slope within less than seventy yards of the fire. His entire body was in plain sight, its length broken only by an outcropping of sandstone that partly obscured his legs, and a small bit of prickly pear near his shoulder.

He had been lying there for nearly an hour, absolutely immovable. Several times during that period both von Hallstatt and Shalako had looked directly at him without seeing him.

The bare slope was innocent of cover. It was not a place one examined, and the Apache knew that. Several times he could have fired . . . he could have killed one, perhaps more. But he waited.

Now, at last . . . he moved.

He made no sound, but when he stopped moving he was farther to the left and nearer the canyon. His eyes had found their target, for one of the girls was picking up a towel . . . he had watched women and girls brush their hair and wash their faces around the forts too many times not to know what she planned.

The fire was but a short distance from the spring,

which was concealed around a cluster of rock. He watched her walk around the rocks and disappear, and for several minutes he remained where he was, watching the others.

And most of all he watched the man who sat asleep against the rocks.

Was he actually asleep? Or was he only seeming to be asleep? This was the man who brought the rain . . . all the Indians had heard the story. He was also the man who had known the name of *Tats-ah-das-ay-go*, which was a kind of magic.

Finally, he moved from his position, went back into the rocks and circled around to watch the girl at the spring. She was bathing her hands and face, then she began combing out her hair. It was very long hair, and very beautiful. The Apache moved closer, making no sound.

He would kill her now, and when someone came to find her, he would kill another with his bow.

Yet *Tats-ah-das-ay-go* was uneasy. He wished he could see the man sleeping near the rocks. He waited an instant and moved nearer.

He had killed the big man with the beard. He had killed the man on guard on the cliff edge, and he had killed the man with the guns, the one who had fallen into the rocks.

Following the man down he had found him trapped there, and he had spent hours with him, gagging him with a handful of rough grass torn from a tiny ledge among the rocks. The man had died very hard, and very long. In the end all his courage was gone and he was whimpering as a child would whimper.

Now he would kill the girl, and then one other. After that he would go, for the pony soldiers were coming. He had been watching from the rocks when they sent a man up to get the one he had just killed.

It had been a temptation to kill the man climbing the rocks right before the eyes of the soldiers. Only they had rifles which shot very far, and the red-faced man was there, the one who rode with McDonald. That man was a very good shot, and the risk was too great. It was not worth it.

He crept nearer. The girl was close now, and she was brushing her hair over and over again and was engrossed in that. She looked like a girl who thought of a man.

———

SHALAKO OPENED HIS eyes suddenly and from long training he did not move until his eyes had searched the terrain about him, and then he turned his head to look toward the fire.

Von Hallstatt was drinking tea. Dagget was searching for brush and sticks to add to the signal fire. Julia sat very still, hunched over and face down on her arms, while Laura was still painstakingly brushing her clothes. He could have been asleep only a few minutes.

Irina was nowhere in sight.

He got to his feet and walked to the fire, and he was frightened. He looked carefully around before he spoke, not wishing to alarm them needlessly. "Where's Irina?" he asked, after a minute.

"Combing her hair," Laura said, "at the spring."

He glanced toward the pile of rocks that concealed

the spring from their eyes. Would these people never learn that for one to be out of sight of the others was dangerous, that danger was ever-present? Yet he had himself relaxed, so the fault was his as well. He started around the rock, then halted and circled in the other direction. No one at the fire seemed to be paying any attention to him, or to notice anything odd about his actions.

He climbed among the rocks, then lay still, straining his ears to hear.

Water falling . . . the click of something placed upon a rock . . . perhaps a hair brush. Ahead of him lay several large loose stones on top of the rock over which he was crawling. Using them as partial cover, he lifted his head slowly.

At first he saw only the spring, a trickle of water from among the rocks into a basin, after which it ran off down a shallow watercourse toward Park Canyon, some distance off.

Irina was seated on a flat rock near the spring, and she was brushing her hair. Her reflection could be seen in the small pool where the water fell . . . a more peaceful scene could not be imagined.

He started to speak, but something held him back. And then he saw the Indian.

He was taller than most Apaches, yet broad in the shoulders and amazingly thick through the chest. His arms and legs were powerfully muscled, and he moved now like a cat, his eyes riveted on the unsuspecting girl.

He was directly opposite the girl, and there was no way to get a good shot at him.

Tats-ah-das-ay-go was intent only upon the girl by

the spring. Knife in hand he moved down over the rocks and poised for an instant, and in that instant, two things happened.

Warned by some instinct, Irina turned suddenly, and a flicker of movement from Shalako caught the Indian's eye.

Tats-ah-das-ay-go's eyes switched to Shalako, and in that moment the latter dove from the top of his rock. The Indian tried to turn, but his feet were among the rocks and, in turning, he lost balance.

Shalako landed before him even as Irina sprang back. She did not scream. Her eyes went quickly around and she saw men, circling warily.

"Tats-ah-das-ay-go!" Shalako said softly. He held his knife low, cutting edge up. "I shall kill you now!"

The Apache moved in suddenly, his blade darting with a stabbing thrust like the strike of a rattler, and the point ripped a gash in the buckskin of Shalako's breeches at the hip. A little low, a little wide.

They closed suddenly, and rolled over on the sand, stabbing and thrusting; then they came up, facing each other. There was a fleck of blood on Shalako's shirtfront. He sprang suddenly, and the Indian leaped back to escape his thrust, and they fell into the brush and cacti, then were out on the rocks.

Irina, her face white and strained, could not cry out, she could not scream, she could only stare as if hypnotized by the men before her.

Circling, thrusting . . . another fleck of blood showed on Shalako, on his arm. The Apache was incredibly swift, incredibly agile. His flat, hard face, with its thick cheekbones and flat black eyes, was like a mask, showing no emotion.

Shalako moved, seemed to slip, and the Indian sprang in. Instantly Shalako turned and swung with his left fist, catching the Indian on the side of the neck and knocking him sprawling.

Yet the Apache came up swiftly, lunged low for the soft parts of the body, and Shalako slapped the blade aside and lunged. His blade went into the Indian's side, but *Tats-ah-das-ay-go* swung around, striking swiftly with his blade.

The blade went into Shalako, but Shalako struck again with his fist and they both fell. Shalako lost his grip on the knife when his fist slammed against a rock with brutal force. The Indian sprang at him and Shalako rolled over and came to his feet, empty-handed. The Indian lunged to get close and Shalako sidestepped, caught the Indian's wrist, and threw him into a heap of brush.

From beyond the rocks there was a sudden shout of alarm, and Dagget cried out, "Irina! What's the matter? What's happening!"

There was a flurry of feet, and, for an instant, the Apache hesitated, then wheeled and ran into the rocks, and vanished.

Shalako went after him.

From somewhere down the valley came the sound of a bugle. Dagget, von Hallstatt, and the women came around the boulder.

In that instant, the Quick-Killer came suddenly into view, racing over the rocks like a goat, heading for Elephant Butte Canyon. And then he stopped, for suddenly Shalako appeared, almost in front of him.

The Indian wheeled and raced up the side of the butte itself, with Shalako behind him. The Indian turned, toppled a rock toward Shalako, then went on up.

Down below, von Hallstatt stood, rifle in hand, so engrossed in the scene before him that he forgot the rifle and did not think to fire.

The two men vanished, appeared again, and suddenly they were facing each other atop the butte.

The sun was hot, and there was no wind. Atop the butte the rock was flat, here and there the thin sheet of surface rock had broken down and the fragments had been blown away by wind. There were no plants here, no growth of any kind except one gnarled dwarf cedar that clung to the far lip, a few feet below the edge.

Behind Shalako, who had circled somewhat in climbing, the cliff fell steeply away for more than a thousand feet. His shirt, torn before, ripped more in scrambling up the rocks, was now in shreds. Shalako ripped the rags from his back so as not to impede his arms in their movements.

The Indian stood, legs apart, one foot forward, staring at him.

Around them was the vast bowl of the sun-hot sky, below them the awful jumble of broken, jagged rock and desert, mountain, and canyon. They were alone, under the sky, a buzzard the only spectator.

Each understood what was to happen now, each knew that a man would die . . . perhaps two men. Each knew it would be settled here.

The Indian was supremely confident. He had fought many times with members of his tribe or other Apache tribes, and with Mexicans and Yaquis. Yet he was wary of the American, for the man had thrown him into the rocks. He had proved a puzzling, dangerous fighter.

Tats-ah-das-ay-go gripped his knife tighter and moved toward Shalako.

Remote sounds could be heard from below. But on the butte it was very still. Shalako's mouth was dry and he gripped and ungripped his fists, watching every move of the Apache.

The man had a knife, which he was skilled at using. Shalako circled to the right, causing the Indian to turn to keep in front of him. He feinted a move, but the Indian merely watched him and was not fooled.

The heat was frightful. Sweat began to trickle down Shalako's chest. His lips tasted salt from the sweat of his face.

Shalako moved his left foot forward, gaining a few inches, crouching a little. The Apache feinted, then came in fast. Unable to knock the knife blow aside, Shalako struck it down, catching the Apache's elbow in the grip of his hand.

Closing his powerful grip on the man's elbow, he dug his fingers, seeking the funny bone, to find it and paralyze the Indian's arm. For a moment then they fought, straining every muscle, and then Shalako, retaining his grip on the arm, suddenly yielded and stepped back, throwing the Apache off balance.

Shalako hooked a short, vicious blow to the face as the Indian fell into him, and then another. The Indian fought to bring the knife up, but then Shalako's seeking fingers found the nerve he wanted and began to grind upon it.

The Apache cried out and tried to break free, but Shalako crowded upon him, forcing the Indian to move back to keep from falling, and no matter how desperately the Indian struggled, he stayed with him.

Suddenly the Indian cried out and, opening his hand, let go of the knife.

It fell, rattling upon the rocks. Wheeling, the Apache sprang for it, but Shalako was first and kicked the knife, sending it spinning off into space. It caught the sunlight, winked brightly, then fell down among the rocks far below.

Shalako slugged the Indian as they closed and he felt the clawlike hands creeping toward his eyes. Wildly, bitterly, desperately they fought, their bodies greasy with sweat and blood, their faces straining only inches apart.

Again Shalako yielded suddenly, falling back and throwing the Indian over him to the rock. Swiftly, he came up as the Indian sprang on him. The powerful hands grasped his throat, his head was pushed back, he felt the brutal thumbs sinking into the flesh of his throat, and then he jerked his two arms up inside the Indian's arms smashing them apart and away from his throat. The Indian fell forward, and Shalako rolled over and came to his knees as the Indian leaped at him, swinging a vicious kick at Shalako's head.

Throwing himself against the Indian's anchor leg, he threw the Quick-Killer violently to the rock, and Shalako staggered to his feet.

Under the blazing sun, he waited for the Indian to get up. His lungs heaved at the thin air, gasping for breath. The advantage was momentarily his, but he lacked the breath to go forward, and the Apache got to his feet.

For an instant, they stood staring at each other across the rock of the small butte. Lungs heaving, they began to circle. The Quick-Killer sprang, and Shalako grabbed his wrist, swinging the arm back and under, then forcing it up the Apache's back in a hammerlock.

Shalako pushed the Apache's wrist higher across his back, then began with all his strength to force the Indian's right wrist over to his right shoulder. Once the Indian grunted, his face went bloodless and he tried to turn to relieve the pressure, but Shalako blocked the turning and, bending suddenly at the knees, he heaved upward with all his strength and both felt and heard the bone crack.

The Indian cried out, his face white with pain, and he swung free, staggered, and tried to grasp Shalako with his left hand. Shalako swung and hit him, and the Indian lost his footing and fell back. He hit the edge of the cliff above the desert in a sitting position, his broken arm still grotesquely behind him, and then he toppled back, his black eyes still upon those of Shalako, and then he fell slowly over backward into space.

The last thing Shalako saw was the eyes of the Indian, the eyes of *Tats-ah-das-ay-go*, the Quick-Killer, fastened upon his.

As the Apache fell, Shalako cried out suddenly, almost in anguish, in admiration: "Warrior! Brother!"

And he spoke in Apache.

Shalako heard *Tats-ah-das-ay-go*'s wild cry as he

struck, somewhere far below, before the body bounded out again, to fall sheer for hundreds of feet.

And then he was alone upon the mountaintop, and there was only the heat, the sweat, and his lungs gasping, crying for air.

Shalako stood alone there, looking off across the hills, then he lifted his eyes toward the sun-blazing sky, almost as if in prayer.

They were waiting below, he could see them standing there, staring up at him, shading their eyes against the sun's glare.

He could see Irina, von Hallstatt, Dagget, Laura, and Julia. The Army was there, too, the sun glinting on the glossy shoulders of their horses, reflecting from their rifles. They stood there in a long, winding column, several hundred of them, and he was glad to see them.

He climbed down slowly, the sweat streaming into his eyes and causing them to smart from the salt, and when he reached the bottom he walked to where his guns were and picked them up.

They stood watching him, none of them coming up to him, and he walked toward them.

He looked up at Colonel Forsyth. "Howdy," he said. "I guess we can go now."

The colonel started to speak . . . desperately he wanted to know what had happened up there atop the butte, but that this man lived was evidence enough.

"All right, then. We shall go."

Von Hallstatt started to speak, but Shalako walked past him and held Tally's stirrup for Irina. She hesitated an instant, then allowed him to help her into the saddle. Her eyes searched his face and, as the rest of them mounted, he swung his leg over Mohammet and pulled up beside her.

"This is my country," he said. "This and California."

She did not speak, but listened, looking down at her nails. They were broken, no longer perfectly manicured, but they were a woman's hands, strong hands, capable hands. They were hands of beauty, but hands of more than beauty, they were hands with which to do.

"It will be different for you."

"I know."

They rode on, and when they reached the road that turned eastward toward Fort Cummings, they drew up.

Colonel Forsyth rode back to them, von Hallstatt beside him. The colonel's eyes went from Shalako's to Irina's.

"You are stopping?" Forsyth asked.

"Our way lies westward."

Forsyth started to speak, then was silent. Von Hallstatt hesitated, his face stiff and cold. Then he said, "It is a good way, my friend, a good way." He held out his hand, and Shalako took it.

"Irina"—his eyes held upon hers for a moment—"Irina . . . good-bye."

"Good-bye, Frederick."

Von Hallstatt turned his eyes again upon Shalako. Then the Prussian saluted, snapping the salute in the approved military fashion, and Shalako returned it.

As they rode off, Forsyth said, "I did not know he was a soldier."

"He was," von Hallstatt said dryly. "And he is!"

When they had gone a few miles Irina said, "I do not look like a bride."

Shalako shifted his grip on the lead ropes of Damper and the roan. "You will," he said. "You will!"

CATLOW

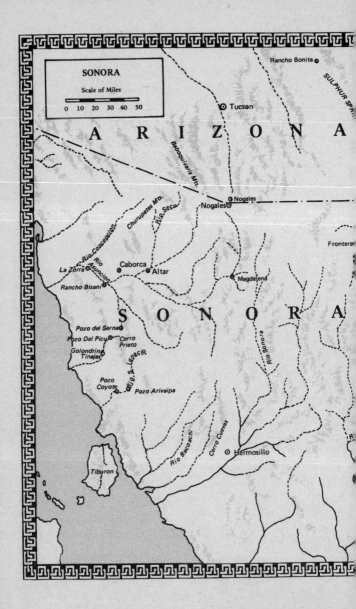

S. W. UNITED STATES
& NORTHERN MEXICO

Scale of Miles

0   100   200   300

Map by William and Alan McKnight

CHAPTER 1

WHEREVER BUFFALO GRAZED, cattle were rounded up, or mustangs tossed their tails in flight, men talked of Bijah Catlow.

He was a brush-buster from the *brazada* country down along the Nueces, and he could ride anything that wore hair. He made his brag that he could outfight, outride, outtalk, and outlove any man in the world, and he was prepared to accept challenges, any time or place.

Around chuck-wagon fires or line camps from the Brazos to the Musselshell, men talked of Bijah Catlow. They talked of his riding, his shooting, or the wild brawls in which, no matter how angry others became, Bijah never lost his temper—or the fight.

Abijah was his name, shortened in the manner of the frontier to Bijah. He was a broad-shouldered, deep-chested, hell-for-leather Irishman who emerged from the War Between the States with three decorations for bravery, three courts-martial, and a reputation for being a man to have on your side in any kind of a shindig, brannigan, or plain old alley fight.

A shock-headed man with a disposition as open as a Panhandle prairie, he was as ready to fight as an Irishman at a Dutchman's picnic; and where the wishes of Bijah Catlow were crossed he recognized the laws of neither God nor man. But the law had occasion to recognize Bijah Catlow; and the law knew him best in the person of Marshal Ben Cowan.

By the time Bijah and Ben were fifteen years old, each had saved the other's life no less than three times; and Bijah had whipped Ben four times and had himself been whipped four times. Ben was tough, good-humored, and serious; Bijah was tough, good-humored, and wild as any unbroken mustang.

At nineteen, Ben Cowan was a deputy sheriff, and at twenty-three a Deputy United States Marshal. By the time Bijah had reached the age of twenty-three he was a known cattle rustler, and an outlaw with three killings behind him.

But it was no criminal instinct, inherited or acquired, that turned Bijah from the paths of righteousness to the shadowy trails of crime. It was a simple matter of frontier economics.

Bijah Catlow was a top-hand in any man's outfit, so when he signed on with the Tumbling SS's it was no reflection on his riding. He hired out at the going wage of thirty dollars per month and found, but the sudden demand for beef at the Kansas railheads turned Texas longhorns from unwanted, unsought wild creatures into a means to wealth and affluence.

From occasional drives to Missouri, Louisiana, or even Illinois, or the casual slaughter of cattle for their hides, the demand for beef in the eastern cities lifted the price per head to ten or more times its former value.

Immediately the big ranchers offered a bonus of two dollars per head for every maverick branded, and Bijah Catlow, who worked with all the whole-hearted enthusiasm with which he played, plunged into the business of branding cattle to get rich.

He was a brush-popper and a good one, and he knew where the wild cattle lurked. He was a good hand with a rope and he owned some fast horses that knew cattle as well as he did, and nobody knew them better. The first month after the bonus was initiated, Bijah Catlow roped and slapped an iron on eighty-seven head of wild cattle.

During the months that followed, Bijah was busier than a man with a dollar watch and the seven-year itch (when he isn't winding, he's scratching) and he averaged two hundred to two hundred fifty dollars a month. In those days nobody made that kind of money on the range, or much of anywhere else. And then the bottom dropped out.

The owners of the big brands got together and agreed that the bonus was foolish and unnecessary, for it was the hands' job to brand cattle anyhow. So the bonus came to an end.

From comparative affluence, Bijah Catlow once again became a thirty-a-month cowhand, and he led the contingent that quit abruptly.

His argument was a good one. Why brand cattle for the ranchers? Why not for themselves? Why not make up their own herd and drive through to Kansas?

After all, most of the mavericks running loose on the plains of Texas came from Lord knew where, for cattle had been breeding like jackrabbits on those plains ever since the days when the first Spanish came there. Nobody could claim or had claimed ownership of those cattle until suddenly they became valuable. Moreover, throughout the War Between the States most of the riders had been away at war and the cattle that might have been branded had gone maverick, and many of their owners had never returned from the War.

The cattle were there for whoever claimed them—so Bijah Catlow banded together a group of riders like himself and they went to work, inspired by Bijah's wholehearted zeal and unflagging energy.

He threw himself into the work with the same enthusiasm with which he did everything else, and it was his zest that fired the ambition of the others. Morning, noon, and night they worked, and at the end of two months they had a herd of nearly three thousand head ready for the trail.

Wild cattle were plentiful in those early years, and the smoke of their branding fires was forever in the air. The riders plunged into the deepest brush and rousted out old mossyhorns and branded them for the Kansas trail, but their work did not go untroubled. Twice they drove off raiding Comanches, and Nigger Jim was gored by an angry bull. They found his ruined body sprawled in the grass near a tiny seep, the earth around torn by the furious battle. A swarthy man, part Indian rather than Negro, he had been a top-hand and a good companion. They buried him on the prairie where they found him.

A few days later Johnny Caxton lost an arm. He was snubbing a rope to a tree, and how it happened he never knew. The plunging steer wheeled suddenly and Caxton's arm was caught in a loop of the rope. The steer lunged back on the rope and it snapped tight around Johnny Caxton's arm.

Two days before he had lost his holster in the

brush when it was torn from his belt, and although he had found his pistol, he had been carrying it in his saddlebag since then. His horse was some distance off, and he had been stalking the big steer afoot when he got his chance to make the throw.

It was hours before they found him, the tough old mossyhorn still backed to the end of the rope, full of fight and glaring wild-eyed, and Johnny sagging against the tree, his arm a black and ugly sight.

There was no doctor within a hundred miles, so Bijah Catlow amputated the arm in camp, cauterizing the stump with a hot branding iron.

It was a week later, with four of their number a quarter of a mile away riding herd on the cattle, that Bijah awakened to find their camp surrounded.

The first man he saw was Sheriff Jack Mercer, formerly on the payroll of Parkman of the OP Bar, and now, as sheriff, reputed to be still on his payroll. Then he saw Parkman himself, Barney Staples of the Tumbling SS, and Osgood of the Three Links. With them were twenty-odd tough cowhands who rode for their brands.

Neither Sheriff Mercer or Parkman had ever liked Bijah Catlow. A year before, when Mercer was still a cowhand, Catlow had whipped him unmercifully in a brawl, and Parkman hated Catlow because the cowhand could get a girl that Parkman could not.

Bijah, who was no fool, knew he was in trouble. Glancing around as he sat up and tugged on his boots, he saw no friendly faces. He had worked for Staples and always turned in a good job, but Staples was a cattleman and would stand with the rest.

Mercer leaned his big hands on the pommel of his

saddle. Deep within him the fire of triumph burned with a hard, evil flame. "Bijah," he said, "I've got a bronc I say you can't ride. Not if you meet the conditions."

Bijah Catlow was not sure how much they wanted the others, but he knew they wanted him. "What's the matter, boys?" he said. "Why the visit?"

"You're a damned, no-good cow rustler," Parkman said. "We hang rustlers."

"Turn the rest of these boys loose," Bijah said, "and I'll ride your bronc—whatever the conditions."

"You ain't heard the conditions," Mercer said. "You ride him with your hands tied behind your back and your neck in a noose...under that cottonwood over there."

Bijah Catlow got easily to his feet and stamped into his boots. He was wearing his gun...it was always the first thing he put on after his hat...and he had already put both hat and gun on when he got up to stir the fire, half an hour before. Nobody had told him to drop his belt. After all, three of them had guns on them.

On his own side, Rio Bray was there, and Bob Keleher—and Johnny Caxton, of course. Since his arm had been lost Johnny had taken over the job of camp roustabout, rustling firewood and water for whoever was cooking for the day. They were good men, but Caxton had lost his right arm and still hadn't won much use of his left, although he had been working on it every day.

"You let them go," Bijah said, "and I'll ride your damned horse."

Mercer's smile was one of contempt. "You'll do

what we tell you . . . and all of you will get a chance at that same bronc."

Bijah thought for a moment that Staples was going to object, but he did not. After all, it was Parkman who was top man here. Bijah knew that when he went for his gun.

Nobody expected it, although they all should have, knowing Bijah Catlow.

Rio Bray probably guessed it first, for as Bijah's gun came up shooting, Rio dove for the shotgun that lay across his saddle. Rio hit the ground, rolled over, and came up on his belly with the shotgun in his hands, and the first thing he saw was Parkman pulling leather on a plunging horse, blood on his shirt front, and Jack Mercer falling.

Rio fired one barrel, then another, and two saddles emptied.

The shooting and the plunging of Parkman's horse destroyed any chance they had at the small targets that faced them in the Catlow camp. And about that time Old Man Merridew, who had been out with the cattle, cut loose with a Sharps fifty.

The cattlemen's posse stampeded and left Jack Mercer dead on the ground. Parkman managed to cling to his saddle and his horse fled with the others.

They were not scared. They were a hard-bitten lot of old Indian fighters, that posse. But they also knew that Old Man Merridew was behind that Sharps buffalo gun, and Merridew was a man who seldom missed what he shot at. It was wide-open prairie where they were, and Merridew was in a tiny hollow of rocks and brush on top of a knoll.

Besides, Bijah Catlow had a gun in his hand, and nobody was buying that if there was a way out.

There was a way, and they took it. After all, they could always get Bijah Catlow. He wasn't going any place.

The law in that section of Texas was whatever the big cattle outfits said it was, and the law said Bijah Catlow was a rustler and a killer. He had killed an officer in performance of his duty, and he became a wanted man.

WHEN PARKMAN BECAME conscious in the big four-poster in his own ranch house he issued the order: "Get Bijah Catlow."

There was a good deal of sympathy in the room for Catlow, but nobody spoke up. To do so was to invite ruin.

Ben Cowan was not present. He was not even in the state at the time. Had he been, he might have told them not to count their hangings until they had a neck in the noose. Somebody had said that Catlow was not going any place...Cowan would have looked his disgust at that. He would have known that Bijah Catlow was already gone.

Within the hour the herd was moving over the river, three miles to the north. They drove on through the night and finally bedded the herd down two hours after daybreak on a small branch far west of the Kansas trail.

By noon they were moving again, following the trail north that had been made by a herd of buffalo, losing their own tracks in the wider trail of the big herd.

Bijah glanced to the south. "Hope there's another herd coming along to wipe out whatever sign we leave," he commented, "because Parkman will be along."

Old Man Merridew lifted a skinny arm and pointed it the way his hawk-beak nose was already pointing. "They's a-comin'," he said. "There's the dust!"

"Maybe that's the posse," Bray suggested.

Merridew spat. "Them's buffler," he said. "Maybe eight, ten thousand of them . . . maybe more."

Nobody argued with Old Man. He had eyes better than any eagle, and a nose to smell buffalo as far as a man could see. The Old Man was older than anybody knew, and looked old enough in the face to have worn out three bodies . . . but he was wiry, strong, and tough as any old Cheyenne or Comanche.

North they drove, with the Drinking Gourd hanging in the sky before them.

North they rode, and Bijah Catlow, the flamboyant, good-natured, hell-for-leather Bijah had become an outlaw.

It would be another week before Ben Cowan heard the news.

CHAPTER 2

DEPUTY UNITED STATES Marshal Ben Cowan was having troubles of his own. He was deep into the Cross Timbers, trailing a bad Indian.

The Tonkawa Kid was no blanket Indian, but an occasional cowhand, farm laborer, and horse trader who had turned renegade. Exactly a month before he had killed and robbed a farmer in the Cherokee Nation, attacked and murdered the farmer's wife, and killed a neighbor attracted by the shooting. Unfortunately for the Tonkawa Kid, the neighbor lived long enough to identify him.

This was the fourth such crime in the vicinity within the year, and then somebody remembered that Tonkawa had been spending more money than he had earned. A sorrel mare he traded in Fort Smith had been stolen from the scene of one of the earlier murders.

Ben Cowan's canteen was dry, and he was working his way toward the Cimarron, hoping to find some branch flowing into the river where he could get water. The river itself was a last resort, for at this season of the year, in this area it was too thick to drink, too thin to plow.

The Cross Timbers country was hell's borderland. It was a stubby forest of blackjack and post-oak mixed with occasional patches of prickly pear. Along the few small streams, most of them intermittent, were redbud, persimmon, and dogwood. Here and there were open meadows, varying in extent. In places the forest was practically impenetrable.

Blackjack, a kind of scrub oak, had a way of sending roots out just under the surface, and at various distances new trees would spring up from these roots. The result was a series of dense thickets, the earth beneath them matted with roots, their stiff branches intermingled.

There were trails made by wild horses and occasional small herds of buffalo or deer, and these usually led from meadow to meadow across the vast stretch of country covered by the Cross Timbers.

It was the spring of the year and the blackjack still held many of the past season's leaves, brown and stiff. Only along the occasional streams was there beauty, this provided by the redbud which grew in thick clumps, its dark, beautiful branches covered with tiny magenta-colored blossoms.

Except in the meadows, grass was scarce. Under the blackjacks there were thick carpets of matted leaves that seemed to crackle at the slightest touch.

It was hot and still. On a branch not far ahead a cardinal peered at something in the grass, and Ben Cowan drew up.

The bright crimson of the bird was a brilliant touch of color in the drab surroundings, but Ben Cowan had reason to be wary. A man in the wilderness soon learns to pay strict attention to the information that birds and animals can give him, and this bird was watching something he did not like.

The last officer out of Fort Smith who had trailed

an Indian outlaw into the Cross Timbers had been found with a bullet through his skull, which for added effect had been bashed in after he had fallen.

Ben Cowan snaked his Winchester from the scabbard, and waited uneasily. Bees droned nearby in the still air. Sweat trickled down his face, prickly with dust. He listened, squinting his eyes against the salt sting of the sweat.

It was dreadfully hot where he sat his horse, and he desperately wished to move. The situation was not at all good, for there was only one direction in which he could go without turning back, and that was straight ahead. Off to the left beyond a thick patch of blackjack there seemed to be a clearing or meadow.

A fly buzzed annoyingly around his face, and he inadvertently lifted a hand to brush it away. Instantly a bullet thudded into the trunk of a tree near his face, spattering him with a hail of tiny fragments. Momentarily blinded by them, he fell from the saddle.

He did it without thinking. It was one of those instinctively right reactions that come to a fighting man who is constantly aware and alert. The position of his horse was such that quick escape was impossible, but there was space to fall in, so he fell.

He hit the ground and rolled over, then lay still. Fortunately, he had retained his grip on his Winchester. Now he put it on the ground and pawed at his eyes, frightened by the thought of being blinded with an enemy so close by.

That enemy had to be close. There was nowhere around where a man could see over thirty or forty yards at most, and even at that distance a shot was a chancy thing, with all the intermingled branches that might deflect the bullet.

Still feeling a few tiny particles in his eyes, Ben Cowan took up his Winchester and turned his eyes this way and that to locate himself.

He had fallen into a shallow depression, only inches below the level of the forest floor. Where he lay there was a small patch of dead brown grass. Right before his head rose the trunk of the tree, not over eight inches in diameter, from which he had received the shower of bark. To his left there was a deadfall and the stark white skeleton of a lightning-shattered tree.

He lay very still. His head was in the shade, but the sun was hot upon his back. In a low-growing black-jack close by, he saw a blacksnake writhing in sinuous coils among the branches. The snake stopped moving and was still.

The Tonkawa Kid, he recalled, had several renegade cousins, and was reputed to travel with them on occasion. It might be there was more than one man lying in wait for a shot at him.

Ben Cowan was a patient man. Tall, lean, and handsome in a rugged way, he was inclined to be methodical. He was a painstaking man, without making any great issue of it. Bijah Catlow had often said that nobody, anywhere, could track better than Ben Cowan, and he might well have added that he never had met anybody who could punch harder. There was a thickening in Bijah's left ear that had resulted from one of Cowan's blows; and the faintly discernible hump in Cowan's nose marked where Bijah had broken it.

But Ben Cowan was not thinking of Bijah Catlow now. He was thinking of the Tonkawa Kid.

That Indian, wily as any fox and slippery as any snake, was somewhere close by, and even now might be working his way into position to kill him, yet Cowan could do nothing. To move silently with those stiff, crackling blackjack leaves lying about was virtually impossible—or was it?

Off to his right a blue jay started raising a fuss... something was worrying it. The sounds the jay made were not unlike those it made when it saw a snake, but different, too. Ben Cowan slid his rifle forward a bit and, easing over on his left shoulder, he looked up into the tree above him.

The tree was actually one of two twin trees of about equal size, and the limbs grew low. There was a fair-sized branch, a relatively wide space, then another branch, and more above; the other twin leaned close up higher, the branches interwoven. It was a risk, but if he could pull himself up there... His clothing was non-descript as to color and it might blend well with the tree and the scattered leaves that remained.

He studied the branches. A grasp there, a quick pull-up, a foot there, then another pull-up, avoiding those leaves.

Carefully, he lifted himself to his knees, cringing against the half-expected impact of a bullet, then he straightened to his feet, grasped the branch and pulled himself up. He got his boot on a lower branch, and then moved up again.

Not the brush of a leaf or the scrape of a boot, and he was there. His eyes searched the trees, the grass, the brush. What he saw was brown grass springing back into position only a few yards away. He looked into the brush...a faint stir of movement and he glimpsed the Tonkawa. Instantly, he fired.

And in the same instant he knew he had been suckered into a trap.

Another bullet spattered bark in his face and something struck his leg a wicked blow and knocked it from its perch. He fell, with the sound of other bullets echoing in his ears. A branch broke as his body hit it, and then he struck the ground with a thud. His horse leaped away, blowing with fear, and Ben Cowan heard the rush of feet in the grass.

He had lost his grip on his rifle and he clawed wildly for his six-shooter, coming up with it just as an Indian broke through the brush, gun in hand, eyes distended with excitement.

Ben Cowan triggered the .45...he fired upward, firing quickly and aiming, he thought, for the Indian's broad chest. The bullet was high, striking the man's chin and smashing upward, driving a bloody furrow along his chin, tearing his nose away, and entering the skull at the top of the eye socket.

Cowan whirled, felt a bullet burn his cheek, and fired blindly at a leaping shadow. The shadow broke stride and fell, the Indian dead before he hit the ground.

Two down...how many were there? Neither of them was the Tonkawa Kid.

Ben Cowan twisted around, found his rifle, and pulled himself to it. His leg felt numb, and when he put his hand up to his cheek it came away bloody... a bullet had grazed the cheekbone.

He eased himself back into a better defensive position and, reaching out with his rifle, tried to draw the rifle of one of the Tonks a bit closer.

The forest was silent again. He gripped the other rifle, put it close at hand, and then with care ejected the empty shells from his pistol and reloaded.

Nothing happened. The slow minutes passed and Ben Cowan suddenly felt sick and weak. His leg was throbbing. Gingerly, he reached down and felt of the leg. The bullet had cut through the muscle of the calf, and his pants leg and sock were soaked with blood. He must get that boot off and get his leg bandaged ... but somewhere around was the Tonkawa ... perhaps more than one.

Delicately, he began to work at the boot to get it off, trying to make no sound. After a few minutes he did get it off, and removed the blood-soaked sock.

His horse, frightened by the shooting, had disappeared, and with it whatever he had, which was little enough, to treat his wound. So he packed grass around it and tied it with his handkerchief, then struggled into his boot. At intervals, he paused to listen.

By this time the Kid undoubtedly knew his friends had run into trouble, if he had not actually seen what happened. Hence, he was either going to run or wait and try again; and if Ben Cowan was any judge, the Kid would wait and take his chance.

His eyes seemed to mist over, and when he tried to move he felt a sudden weakness.

Suppose he passed out? It was possible, for he had lost a lot of blood. If he did pass out, he would be killed.

He must hide.

Somehow, in some way, he must hide. Carefully, he looked about him, but there was nowhere to hide. Only the clumped blackjack, the black trunks of the trees.

But he had to move. He could no longer remain here—if he passed out where he was he would get his throat cut while unconscious. Far better to take his chances in trying to do something.

The nearest Indian had been carrying a Winchester also, so he stripped the man's cartridge belt from him, and his knife. Then he eased from behind the tree and began inching his way through the grass.

He succeeded in moving without making any noise but the slightest dragging sound...that was inevitable. But, it was less than he had expected, and at times he even made no noise at all. His eyes continually searched the ground, the trees, the shrubs. He had gone at least thirty yards when he heard a chuckle.

It was the faintest of sounds, but he froze in place, listening. After a minute, he started on.

"Go ahead," a voice said, "you ain't goin' no place."

The voice was harsh and ugly. It was the Tonkawa Kid. Ben Cowan could not see him, but he knew the Kid must be where he could watch Cowan. Where was that?

He pulled himself a little farther along, sorting the places in his mind. When the Kid spoke again, Cowan threw his rifle around and fired at the sound.

From a few feet away, the Kid laughed again, and fired. A bullet tore a furrow in the grass just ahead of Ben Cowan, almost burning his finger. And then he saw the gully that lay only a few feet ahead and to his right. That gully was only inches deep, but it was enough to offer shelter. Moreover, it deepened farther along.

Using his rifle, Ben Cowan suddenly pushed himself up and dove forward. A rifle bellowed behind him even as he fell into the gully. Instantly, despite the tearing pain in his leg, he threw himself farther along and began to scramble to get farther away.

He heard a rush of feet in the grass and wheeled around, throwing his gun up. As the Indian sprang into sight, swinging the gun muzzle down on him, Cowan fired.

At the same instant, from off to the left, there was another gunshot.

The Tonkawa's body was caught in midair by the bullets; it was smashed back and around. Still he tried to bring his gun down on Cowan, but two more bullets ripped into him from the left and he fell into the bottom of the gully, landing only inches from Ben Cowan.

Cowan heard horses walking in the grass, and then a voice singing: "*As I walked out in the streets of Laredo, as I walked out in Laredo one day...*"

A horse appeared on the edge of the gully, and a grinning face looked down at him.

It was Bijah Catlow.

CHAPTER 3

BEN COWAN OPENED his eyes and looked up into an evening sky where a few scattered clouds were touched with a faint brushing of rose, and along the horizon a dark fringe of trees shouldered against the coming night.

Something stirred near him, and he turned his head to see Old Man Merridew standing by the fire holding a coffee cup.

"Come out of it, did you? You lost a sight of blood, boy."

"I guess I did."

"You done all right," Merridew acknowledged. "You nailed two of them, and your bullet would have killed the Kid even without ours ... only maybe not soon enough."

"Where'd you come from?"

"Pushin' a herd to Dodge. Bijah seen your horse, so four, five of us, we left the herd and back-trailed the horse. Figured you to be in some kind of trouble, losin' your mount that way, and your rifle gone.

"Then we heard the shootin', so we closed in kind of careful-like. We found them Tonks you salted down, and one of our boys who used to hang out up in the Nation, he figured it was the Kid you were after. He knowed those Tonks for his kin."

"You came along at the right time."

Merridew shrugged, and filled another cup, then added a dollop of whiskey. He brought it to Cowan. "I dunno . . . you might have made it."

Cowan drank the whiskey and coffee and felt better. "Who are you driving for?"

Merridew glanced up; his hard old eyes were level. "Ourselves . . . who else? When the big outfits dropped the bonus we struck off for ourselves." He looked suspiciously at Cowan. "You mean you ain't heard?"

"That Bijah's wanted for rustling? I heard, but I never believe all I hear. Before I'd believe a thing like that I'd have to hear it from Bijah." He finished the bit of coffee in the bottom of the cup. "As far as I'm concerned, Bijah has as much right to brand mavericks for himself as for the big outfits."

Johnny Caxton rode up to the fire and stepped down from the saddle. Ben Cowan noted the sleeve folded over the stub of the arm, but he offered no comment. When he had last seen Johnny he'd had two good arms, but as far as he was concerned Johnny would be a top-hand under any circumstances.

Johnny glanced his way. "Hi, Ben. Anybody feed you?"

"Just woke up. The Old Man here gave me some special coffee."

Ben Cowan eased his wounded leg out from under the blankets. A thought struck him and he looked quickly around the camp. "You boys missed a day on account of me, didn't you?"

All the signs were there, the question needless. He knew what a camp looked like after a day, and after two days. He also knew how important it was to all of them to get this drive through on time—before Parkman or the law could interfere.

Johnny brought the pot over and refilled his cup. Ben stared bitterly at the coffee. Bijah was a wild one, but he was no thief . . . at least, he never had been. Yet it was a time when many a man was being called an outlaw for slapping brands on cattle. To get away with that, you had to have a big outfit and breeding stock.

"We missed two days," Johnny commented, "one findin' you, one while you're restin' up."

Bijah came in when the guards changed. "Hiya, Shorthorn!" he said. "Surprised somebody hasn't shot that badge off you by now."

He squatted on his heels and studied Ben Cowan with a hard grin. "You packin' a warrant for me?"

"No. If I was, I'd serve it."

Bijah chuckled, and rolled a cigarette. "You ain't changed none." He touched his tongue to the paper. "We goin' to have trouble in Kansas?"

"You know Parkman."

Bijah lighted the cigarette with a stick from the fire. "Nine of us teamed to make this drive, and we rounded up the stock and did the branding. Johnny there, he lost his arm on the job, an' Nigger Jim was killed. Well, Jim left no kin that anybody knows of, but he thought a sight of that girl he was seeing down on the Leon River. Seemed to me we would take his share to her."

Ben Cowan accepted the plate he was handed, and then he said, "Bijah, you drive on to Abilene. When you're a few miles out, I'll ride in and see how things stand."

"I know Bear River Tom Smith," Merridew commented. "He's a reasonable man."

Cowan glanced at him. "Smith's dead. They've brought Wild Bill Hickok in as marshal."

Catlow looked up quickly. "The gunfighter? I've heard of him."

"He's the real thing, and don't forget it," Ben said. "A lot of the boys from down our way underrate him, but don't you make that mistake."

"I'm in too much trouble now," Bijah said. "I'm not riding into Kansas for anything but a chance to sell this herd."

NIGHT THREW A shadow on the world, and the night guard looked up from their horses to the circling stars and followed the pointers to the North Star, which was their guide to Kansas. Ben Cowan turned restlessly in his blankets easing his wounded leg against the throbbing pain. He stared up at the stars, reflecting again upon the strange destiny that seemed to tie his life to that of Bijah Catlow.

The thought worried him, for Catlow was a reckless man in many ways—never reckless of his life, although to the casual observer he might seem so, but reckless of the law. But in this case Ben Cowan, like many another Texan, believed Catlow was right, and the branding of mavericks was an old custom.

At dawn they were moving north, Ben Cowan riding his own horse, and easing his leg against the pain.

Bijah dropped back beside him. "Ben, I'm holdin' them west of the trail, figurin' we ain't so likely to run up against any trouble, that way."

"You duckin' trouble?"

"The boys have got too much at stake. We worked our tails off to get these steers together. Me, I don't care. Neither does the Old Man or Rio Bray; but Johnny, he's got to get him a stake out of this, now that he's left with only one arm."

They rode along a low hill upwind from the herd to stay free of the dust.

"He figures to start him a restaurant," Bijah went on.

"How about you?"

Catlow shot him a quick look. "You goin' to preach at me again? Damn it, Ben, you know I'm pointed for a hangin' or prison, so don't try to head me off."

"You're too good a man, Bijah. Too good to go that way."

"Maybe ... but I'm a born rebel, Ben. You're the smart one. You'll ride it quiet and come out of it with a sight more than me. I only hope that when the chips are down and they send somebody after me that it won't be you. You wouldn't back up from what you figure is your duty, and I sure wouldn't want you to ... and I'd never back up, either."

"I know it. I've asked for a transfer to another district, anyway. We may never see each other again."

Bijah slapped him on the shoulder. "That's gloomy talk. I figure to whip your socks off four or five times yet." Bijah threw him a quick glance. "Ben, what you figure to do when we hit Abilene? You said you might help."

"First, I'll clear it with Hickok. He's all right. He doesn't give a damn what happened in Texas or anywhere else. All he wants is peace in Abilene."

"You still have to stack your guns when you come into town?"

"That was under Smith. Wild Bill doesn't care whether you wear them or not, as long as you don't do any shooting. If you decided to do any, you'd better start with him, because if you shoot he'll come after you."

"Smith was a good man. I met up with him that time I rode up to Colorado with that Indian beef." Bijah moved downslope to turn a ranging steer back into the drive. "Why are you so willing to front for me with Wild Bill?"

"He'll listen to me. I'm an officer, too. And you might just be cocky enough to try to throw a gun on him and get killed."

"The way I remember it, you fancy yourself with that hogleg you're carryin'. Why, there was a time you claimed you were faster than me!"

Ben chuckled. "Only said it to you, Bijah and you know it, you Irish lunkhead. If anybody shoots you, let's keep it in the family."

Catlow laughed good-humoredly. "When the time comes it'll simply bust my heart to kill you. For a sheriff, you're a pretty good sort."

Ben eased his foot in the stirrup, keeping his face straight against the pain. He had no right to complain, with only a bullet through his calf. Johnny Caxton was riding back there with a stump for an arm; but with one arm or two, Johnny Caxton was a good man, and he drove that team of broncs as though he sat the saddle of a bad horse.

Turning in the saddle, Ben Cowan glanced along the herd. Three thousand head of cattle string out for quite a distance when they are not bunched up, and handling this herd was a good big job for the available men. They had about six horses per man, and it wasn't really enough, short-handed as they were.

Ordinarily a herd of three thousand head would have eleven or twelve riders, and the cost was figured at about a dollar-per-head for the drive from Texas to Kansas. In this case, with the herd owned by the drivers, there would be no outlay for wages, and the men owned their own remuda, so there had been no cost for the purchase of horses.

Dawn to dusk they drove, usually trying to water somewhere late in the afternoon, then pushing on a few miles before bedding down. Cattle watered late had a way of starting off better and traveling better than those allowed to water in the morning.

————

ABILENE IN 1871 was a booming town, but the boom was almost over, although few as yet realized it. There were many in town who detested the cattlemen with their vast herds—600,000 head were driven to Abilene that year—and the men who drove them.

Texas Town was wild and woolly, and it was loud. The more staid citizens looked upon it with extreme distaste, and wanted to be rid of the yelling, whooping cowboys, the dusty, trail-seasoned men who were making the town what it was. Only a few months later they were to issue a bulletin saying they wanted no more of it, and to their discomfiture the cattlemen took them at their word and went west to Newton, to Ellsworth, to Dodge. By 1872 the citizens of Abilene were crying for them to come back, but it was too late.

But in 1871 the town was still booming, and

Marshal Hickok walked the center of the street, a tall, splendidly built man with auburn hair hanging to his shoulders, his clothing immaculate, his gun always ready for action.

He was the first man Ben Cowan saw when he rode into town.

Hickok had paused on a street corner, glancing each way from the Merchants Hotel. He wore a black frock coat, a low-brimmed black hat, and two ivory-butted and silver-mounted pistols thrust behind a red silk sash.

"Mr. Hickok? I'm Ben Cowan."

Hickok's eyes went from Cowan's eyes to the badge he wore. Hickok held out his hand. "How do you do? What can I do for you?"

Briefly, Cowan explained about Bijah Catlow and the herd. "I know the country down there," Cowan said at the end, "and these cattle were mavericks, open to branding by anyone. I have no share in the business, but Bijah pulled me out of a hole down in the Cross Timbers, and he's a good man."

"We've a letter on the cattle," Hickok replied, "but I am not interested in what happened in Texas. You tell Catlow to drive his cattle to the stock pens. He won't be bothered unless he or his men make trouble here."

Hickok thrust out his hand again. "Glad to know you, Marshal. We've heard of you."

Ben Cowan limped back to his horse and rode to the Drover's Cottage, where he took a room, and then sat down to write out his report on the case of the Tonkawa Kid. When he had completed it and left it with the mail at the stage station, he went to the telegraph office and wired Fort Smith.

Back at his room he arranged for a bath, and after he had taken it he changed into new clothing bought at Herman Meyer's Clothing Store alongside of the Merchants Hotel.

Bijah Catlow joined him at supper in the dining room at the Drover's Cottage. "Twenty-five dollars a head," Bijah said with a broad smile on his face, "and we split it ten ways, two shares for Johnny Caxton."

He reached into his shirt pocket. "Here's the tally sheet, stamped by the buyer. We picked up a few head of Tumblin' SS's and Ninety-Fours drivin' through, so here's their money. Will you see they get it?"

Ben accepted the money without comment, but offered a receipt. "You're rawhidin' me," Bijah said. "Money in trust to you is safer than any bank."

He looked at Ben, and slowly he began to grin. As he did so he reached for another bit of paper and pushed it across the table. "Stopped by the telegraph office. This is for you."

Ben Cowan opened the folded paper and glanced at it, then he looked up at Bijah. "Did you see this?"

"Sure! I always was too damn' nosey."

Ben glanced down again.

Office of the U.S. Marshal
Fort Smith, Arkansas.

Consider this a warrant for the arrest of
Abijah Catlow, Rio Bray, and Old Man
Merridew, wanted for murder and cattle theft.
Logan S. Roots
U.S. Marshal

CHAPTER 4

OUTSIDE IN THE street, a drunken cowhand whooped as he raced his horse past the Drover's Cottage. In the dining room, with its tables covered with linen cloths, it was very still.

"It's my duty to take you in."

"I know it is."

"The hell with it!" Ben said. "If you were guilty, I'd take you in, but they'll send you to Texas for trial, with Parkman telling the judge what to do. I'll resign first."

Bijah Catlow leaned back in his chair and glanced around the room. Only a few of the tables were occupied by cattlemen, cattle buyers, or land speculators.

"Ben, you're buying me the best supper this place can offer, with the best wine ... and they tell me these cattle buyers have fancy tastes. After that," he leaned his forearms on the table, "you're going to arrest me and take me to Fort Smith."

"The devil I will!"

"Look, you're the law. You couldn't be anything else if you tried. If you resign now you've lost all you've gained. You go ahead and take me in. It'll be all right."

Ben Cowan started to protest, but he knew it was just what might be expected from a hotheaded, temperamental, impulsive cowhand like Bijah Catlow.

"What about Rio and the Old Man?"

Catlow gave him a saturnine grin. "Now, Ben, you know me better than that. I picked up that telegram about an hour ago, so naturally I stopped by camp first. After all, I had money for them.

"Somehow or other those boys just naturally saw this here telegram and by this time they're far down the trail to somewhere. You can look for 'em if you want to waste time, but you won't find 'em in a coon's age."

"Bijah, don't be a damned fool. You leave out of here now and I'll give you an hour's start. If I know you, you won't need any more than that. You know Parkman has the courts in his pocket. He'll see you hang."

Catlow picked up the chilled wine bottle and filled their glasses. "That waiter's too durned slow." He looked up, his eyes dancing with deviltry. "Sure, you're right as rain. Parkman will sure enough try to string me up, but remember this, Ben, it's a long way from here to Texas!"

Two WEEKS LATER Ben Cowan looked up from his desk where he was making out his final report.

Roots stopped by the desk. "Your transfer came through, Ben. You go to New Mexico." He turned away, then stopped again. "Oh, by the way, that prisoner you brought in ... Catlow, was it? He escaped."

"*Escaped?*"

"Uh-huh ... four or five riders held up the stage and took him off."

"Anybody hurt?"

"Hell, no. From what I hear Catlow had made friends with everybody on the coach, including the driver, and they were glad to see him get away. We did get an identification of one of the men in the bunch that took him, though. The officer escorting Catlow recognized one of the men as Rio Bray."

Bijah Catlow had been right . . . it was a long way to Texas.

———

THE LEGEND OF Bijah Catlow had begun before this, but from this point on, it grew rapidly. The Houston & Texas Central was held up, and Catlow received the credit, whether he was guilty or not. Of one thing men were certain: Bijah Catlow had not forgotten Parkman.

Parkman sent three herds to Kansas the following year, and lost the first one before it was fairly into the Nation. Somebody stampeded the herd, and it vanished.

Nobody could offer more than a guess at what happened to it. Herds of three thousand head are not swallowed by the earth, yet vanish they did.

Meanwhile, it suddenly appeared that Bijah Catlow had registered a brand, the Eight eighty-eight Bar, and around the chuck wagons and in the saloons throughout Texas, men began to chuckle. For three eights and a bar could very neatly swallow Parkman's OP Bar . . . and apparently they had done just that.

Catlow was never at home, but a very tough, very seasoned cowman, Houston Sharkey, was . . . he was not only at home, he was at home with a Winchester and a crew of hard-bitten cowhands who kept strays out of the Eight eighty-eight Bar grazing lands, and allowed no casual visitors.

Several times the law came looking for Catlow, and they were welcomed to look around all they wished.

Parkman came, too, and he came with a couple of tough hands, threatening to butcher a steer and read the hide from the wrong side, where the alteration of the brand would be plain to anyone.

Sharkey levered a shell into the chamber of his Winchester. "You go right ahead, *Colonel* Parkman," he said, "and you better hope that it's an altered brand, because if it isn't I'm going to lay you dead right where the steer lies."

Parkman looked at Houston Sharkey and the Winchester. He looked at the roped steer. He was sure that it was an altered brand... *but suppose it wasn't?*

If it was not, he had called this man a thief, an insult anywhere, and no court in the country would convict Sharkey of murder. Not with the viewpoint of Texans what it was at the time.

Parkman looked, hesitated, and backed down. But he went away boiling mad, determined to catch both Catlow and Sharkey.

Two weeks later a tall, cold-eyed rider headed into the rough country south of the Nueces—a tall man with a Winchester and a tied-down gun.

Bijah Catlow spoke Spanish as well as any Mexican in the country. He spoke it smoothly and easily to the *señoritas,* and he was a popular man about Piedras Negras, across the river from Eagle Pass. He laughed easily, was friendly, and swapped horses and bought drinks. He was so popular that when the tall, cold-eyed man rode into town and asked questions, Catlow was informed within half an hour.

There had been rumors that Parkman had sent a hired killer after him, and the rumors had reached Catlow as well as most of the population of the Mexican village.

Matt Giles was a methodical man. He had begun his killing as a mere boy in the Moderators and Regulators wars of northeast Texas, and had graduated to a sharpshooter in the Confederate Army.

Discharged when the war ended, he drifted back to Texas and the word got around that he was a safe, reliable man for the kind of job he did. Parkman had retained him twice before this.

Matt Giles had never seen Bijah Catlow, but he had listened to all the stories, knew what he looked like, and privately decided that Catlow was a bag of wind. Arrived in Piedras Negras, he had no trouble locating Catlow—he was the talk of the town.

The local law approached Bijah...in fact, they had been drinking and poker-playing companions for some weeks now.

"Our jail," the person of the law suggested, "will hold another prisoner...for years, if necessary. This man—this Señor Giles—I could arrest him."

"Leave him alone," Bijah said. "If he wants me, I'll make it easy for him."

Bijah Catlow, whose entire life had been predicated on the impulsive and the unregulated, suddenly became the most regulated of men. He took to rising at a certain hour, going to the *cantina* at a certain hour, taking a siesta according to Mexican custom, and exercising his horse by a ride each afternoon, and each afternoon he went the same way.

The people of Piedras Negras watched and worried. Bijah Catlow was, indeed, making it easy for the gringo killer.

Giles watched, and studied Catlow's movements. Never having known the man, he could not guess his pattern of living had been altered, and to such a methodical man as Giles, the methodical ways of Catlow seemed right and logical.

Carefully, he studied the route to the *cantina*, but it offered no good cover. By this time Giles knew that Bijah had friends in Piedras Negras, and he knew there might be trouble before he got away. Therefore the killing had to be done where he was offered a good chance of escape, and where he could, preferably, kill with one shot.

Going to or from the *cantina*, Catlow was always surrounded by a group of friends, and it soon became obvious to Giles that the only place where a killing would be safe would be along the road where Catlow exercised his horse. It also became obvious that along this route there was only one place that offered Giles the opportunity he wanted.

There was a pile of boulders and brush about sixty yards from the trail Catlow rode, and a gully behind that pile which offered a hidden approach to the position. It was made to order.

Giles was a painstaking man, but not an imaginative one, and it was his lack of imagination that brought him to the fatal climax. He watched, and he made his choice, and on the seventh day after his arrival in Piedras Negras he slipped out of town and took his position among the rocks. He sighted the exact spot where Catlow's head would be, planned his second and third shots if such were needed—although they never had been.

Then he settled down among the rocks and waited.

Suddenly, some distance off, he saw Catlow coming, riding easily on the handsome black horse. Giles felt a moment of swift envy... *how he would have loved to own that horse!*

He lifted his rifle and waited. Only a few minutes more.

Suddenly the rider on the black horse veered sharply from the trail, and Giles swore. *Now, what the—!*

An instant later a voice behind him said, "Fooled you, didn't we?"

It is given to few men to know the moment of death, but Matt Giles knew it then. With a kind of wild despair he knew he had been trapped, but he was game. He wheeled and fired.

Two bullets tore into him, one going through his shoulder and emerging from the front of his chest, leaving a wound spattered with bone splinters. The second went into his ribs, and for the first and last time he looked directly into the eyes of Bijah Catlow.

His own bullet whistled away into thin, thin air, high above the Mexican landscape.

PARKMAN LAY IN his four-poster bed staring up at the ceiling. He had spent a restless night. In fact, he had spent several restless nights since receiving word from Giles in Eagle Pass that he had found Catlow.

Each day he looked forward to the news of the death of Bijah Catlow.

Finally, he could stand it no longer to stay in bed, and he got up and dressed. As he entered the kitchen he stopped abruptly. The table was littered with dirty dishes . . . his best dishes, brought from Carolina.

Nobody, simply nobody used those dishes but himself, and then only when he entertained guests more distinguished than the usual run.

Also, the cook was not at work, and he should have been up—Parkman glanced at his watch—at least an hour ago.

Parkman was a man who came easily to anger, and he was angry now. He stepped out the door toward the bunkhouse and brought up short.

Something was wrong—radically wrong.

The corral was empty of horses. The bunkhouse was dark and silent, and over each bunkhouse window was a blanket, hung on the outside of the building. From the doorknob to a snubbing post ran a rope, holding the door shut, and against the snubbing post was tied a double-barreled shotgun aimed at the bunkhouse door. It was rigged in such a way that anybody tugging on the doorknob from the inside would fire both barrels of the shotgun. It was obvious that nobody had tried, so those within must have been informed of this.

Parkman went to the post and gingerly unlimbered the shotgun. Then opened the door to the bunkhouse.

"What the hell's going on around here?" he shouted. "By the Lord Harry, I've had enough of these practical jokes, and—"

From the corner of his eye he caught a glimpse of

his front porch, invisible to him until now. There, seated in his own favorite chair on the broad veranda was somebody. . . . Parkman shouted, but there was no reply.

Finally given somebody on whom he could vent his anger, Parkman started for the front porch, almost running. The stranger sat with his hat over his eyes, apparently asleep.

Leaping up on the porch, Parkman jerked the hat away, his mouth opened to roar angry words.

And he looked into the still, cold eyes of Matt Giles.

By nightfall the story was told in every bunkhouse within miles, and within a few days it was riding north with the trail herds.

Parkman had sent a paid killer after Bijah Catlow, and his killer had been returned . . . dead.

Moreover, Bijah had stolen Parkman's corral of fine riding stock, including his own favorite mounts. He had eaten in Parkman's own house, and on his best dishes. Even Parkman's own riders chuckled.

When they buried Matt Giles they noted the position of the wounds, and speculated. Catlow had outsmarted the hired gunman, had come up behind him, given him his chance, and it was quite obvious that Giles had been shot as he turned.

From Piedras Negras the rest of the story was not slow to arrive.

And the legend of Bijah Catlow added another chapter.

CHAPTER 5

DEPUTY UNITED STATES Marshal Ben Cowan rode into New Mexico to conduct a quiet investigation into the reported theft of cattle by Comanches, cattle which were traded to Comancheros and sold in New Mexico or elsewhere. Several Texans had created incidents by riding into New Mexico to recover stolen cattle. Childress had done so, as had Hittson, and they had driven the recovered cattle back to Texas. There had been some shooting, and there was apt to be more.

Cowan heard of the killing of Matt Giles by Catlow before he ever left Fort Smith. He was not surprised. That Parkman had been behind Matt Giles's mission was obvious, although it was impossible to prove. Giles had been the wrong man to send after Catlow. He was too methodical. A man of method himself, Cowan knew that against Catlow method was not enough. Bijah was a man of quick, instinctive imagination, and might on impulse discard all the accepted ways of doing things and do something radically different.

Whatever their former relationship, Cowan and Catlow were now unalterably opposed. There was a line beyond which a man might not go, even in the tolerant West. Cowan had himself been a cowhand, and knew enough of conditions in Texas to feel

Catlow and his friends were right in branding and driving to sale their herd of mavericks. The killing of Giles was obviously self-defense, but when Catlow drove off Parkman's saddle stock he had stepped beyond the pale.

Many were amused, but all recognized it had been a theft. In Laredo, Catlow shot an officer who attempted to arrest him and escaped below the border. It was apparent that Catlow had accepted the role of the outlaw.

As for the train robbery, Ben Cowan was sure that had been done by the Sam Bass gang, but Catlow got the credit—at least in the minds of some.

For three months Ben Cowan rode the lonely trails of New Mexico. He trailed outlaws, dodged Apaches, accepted meals at lonely sheep camps or ranches, and drifted on.

He said he was hunting range and planning to settle, that he was intending to trail a herd from Texas, but would buy cattle in New Mexico to avoid the drive, if the price was right.

This was a feeler—a lead to the Comancheros who might have stolen Texas cattle to sell. He was too wise to push that aspect, and devoted most of his time to scouting range. This he could do in all seriousness, for he really intended to find a ranch for himself.

He scouted along the Pecos and the Rio Grande, talked to ranchers and soldiers, but made no inquiries about cattle. Here and there he did mention returning to Texas to buy cattle, and he talked with those who had made the drive to ask about water holes and grazing.

They were long, grueling rides in the sun and the

wind, but from them Ben Cowan rapidly picked up some knowledge of the New Mexico country, located two stolen herds, and reported to the main office.

A reserved and self-contained man, Ben Cowan was warm-hearted and pleasant by nature, but he was also a hunter. A hunter—not a killer. Yet if need be he could kill, as he had demonstrated against the Tonkawa outlaws and others. Still, by instinct he was a hunter, a man who understood trailing, but even more, a man who understood the mind of the pursued.

A lonely man, he had always envied Bijah his easy friendliness, the casual grace with which he made strangers into friends, and seemed never to offend anyone.

Once, when only a boy, he had heard a man say to his father: "Yes, it is a beautiful country, but it must be made safe for honest people, for women and children. It must become a country to live in, not just a country to loot and leave. Too many," the man had said, "come merely to get rich and get out. I want to stay. For that we need law, we need justice, and we need a place where homes can be built. *Homes,* I say, not just houses."

Somehow from that day on Ben was dedicated. He, too, wanted to see homes. He wanted friends to talk with in the evening, children for his children to play with. And for that there must be peace.

Beyond a daily paper when one was available, he had read little. He was a grave, thoughtful man, but a keen sense of humor was hidden behind his quiet face. No doubt there were those who thought him dull. But he missed nothing, and at heart he was a sympathetic man, understanding even of the outlaws he pursued.

He was happiest on a trail, and the more difficult the trail, the happier he became. He knew wild country, knew it in all the subtle changes of light and shadow, knew the ways of birds and the habits of men and animals. So much was common sense. Men who travel need water, fuel, grass for their horses, and food for themselves. All of these are restricting factors, limiting the areas of escape.

Given a general knowledge of the country, a grasp of a man's nature, and his needs, a trail could often be followed without even seeing anything upon the ground. And a man who knows wild country is never actually a stranger to any wild land.

Landforms fall into patterns, as do the actions of men. The valley, hill, and ridge, the occurrence of springs and the flow of water—these follow patterns of their own. Many a guide or scout in Indian country had never seen the country over which they scouted—but they had lived in the wilds.

Men who live always in cities rarely notice the sky . . . they do not know the stars or the cloud forms, they are skeptical of what a man can read in what is to themselves only a blank page. To Ben Cowan every yard of country he crossed could be read like a page of print. He knew what animals and insects were there, what each tiny trail in the sand might mean. He knew that certain birds never fly a great distance from water; that certain insects need water for their daily existence; and that some birds or animals can go days without any water at all except what they get from the plant growth about them.

So Ben Cowan rode the lonely hills with a mind

alive and alert, noticing everything, adding this thing to that...always aware.

Tucson was baking in a hot July sun when he rode into town. There was little enough to see, but to a man who had not slept in a bed for more than a month and had not seen more than three buildings in a bunch in four times that long, it looked pretty good.

Ben Cowan studied the town thoughtfully from under the brim of his white hat.

Flat-roofed adobes and *jacals* made of mesquite poles and the long wands of the ocotillo plastered with adobe made up more than two-thirds of the town. Main Street was lined with pack trains just in from Sonora, and a long bull train was unloading freight on a side street.

Ben left his roan at a livery stable and walked up the street to the Shoo-Fly Restaurant. It was a long, low-ceilinged room, rather narrow, with a scattering of tables covered with table cloths, red and white checkered. He dropped into a chair with a sigh and looked at the menu.

BREAKFAST
Fried venison and chili
Bread and coffee with milk

DINNER
Roast venison and chili
Chili frijoles
Chili on tortillas
Tea and coffee with milk

SUPPER
Chili, from 4 o'clock on

Ben glanced hastily at the clock on the shelf: 3:45.

"Roast venison," he said, "and quick, before the time runs out."

The Mexican girl flashed him a quick smile. "I see," she said.

A moment later she was back. "No more," she said regretfully. "All gone."

"You tell Mrs. Wallen"—the voice that spoke behind him was familiar—"that I said this man was a friend of mine—or was last time I saw him."

Bijah Catlow...

Ben looked up. "Sit down, Bijah." And then as Bijah dropped into his seat, Ben added, "You're under arrest."

Bijah chuckled. "The .45 I've got trained on your belly under the table says I'm not. Anyway, you'd better eat up. I never like to shoot a man who's hungry."

A slim brown arm came over Ben's shoulder with a plate of roast venison and chili, frijoles, tortillas. In the other hand was a pot of coffee.

CHAPTER 6

BIJAH CATLOW LEANED his forearms on the table, and shoved his hat on the back of his head. He grinned widely at Ben.

"Eat up, *amigo,* and listen to your Uncle Dudley. You're wastin' your time. You throw that badge out the window and come in with me ... you'll make more in a couple of weeks than you'll make on that job in twenty years."

"Can't do it, Bijah. And the word is out on you. You're to be picked up where and when."

"Look." Bijah leaned closer. "I need you. I need a man I can count on, Ben. This here thing I've got lined up is the biggest ... well, nothin' was ever any bigger. One job an' we've got it made ... all of us. But I need you, Ben."

"Sorry."

"Don't be a damn' fool, boy. I know what you make on that job, an' I know you. You like the good things as much as I do. You come along with me, an' after that you can go straight.

"Hell, Ben, after this one I'm goin' to take my end of it an' light out. Goin' to Oregon or somewheres like that an' get myself a place." He flushed suddenly, and looked embarrassed, for the first time that Ben could remember. "Maybe I'll get married."

"Got somebody in mind?"

Bijah looked at him quickly. "Why not? Look, Ben, I'm not the crazy damn' fool you figure me for. I want to marry and have some kids my own self. That Parkman...if it hadn't been for him I'd probably never have got myself mixed up."

"You stole his horses."

Bijah shot him a quick look. "Yeah...that did it, didn't it?"

"And there was that officer."

"He would've killed me, Ben. He was figurin' to take me in, dead meat. It was him or me."

"Maybe...but you were on the wrong side of the law. Odd, you gents never seem to realize that when you cross the law you set yourself up for anybody's gun. And you can't win, Bijah. You just can't."

Ben gulped the scalding black coffee and then he said, "Bijah, give yourself up. Surrender right now, to me. I'll take you in, and I'll do everything I can to see that you get a fair shake. If you don't, I've got to come after you."

Bijah stared gloomily out the window. "There's this girl, Ben. I don't figure she'd wait...or maybe there ain't enough between us to make her want to wait." Suddenly, he grinned. "Damn it, Ben, you nearly had me talked into it. I was forgettin' what I've got lined up." He called for coffee, and then he said, "Ben, how about it?"

"What?"

"You ride with me on this job?" He leaned closer. "Hell, Ben, it ain't even in this country!"

"I wouldn't break anybody's law, Bijah. You know that. Their law's as good as ours. If I respect my own laws, I have to respect theirs."

"Aw, you're crazy!" Bijah stared ruefully into his coffee. "I never figured you would, but damn it, Ben, I wish we was on the same side!"

"I wish we were, too."

Bijah looked up, his eyes dancing with deviltry. "Somebody will have to kill you, Ben. I'm afraid I will."

"I hope you never try. You're a good man, Bijah, but I'll beat you."

"You hardheaded, hard-nosed ol' wolf!" Bijah said. He was suddenly cheerful. "Did you come here after me?"

"How could I? Nobody knew where you were. I'm sorry you're here. Now I'll have to arrest you."

Bijah chuckled. "That head of yours never could see more than one trail at a time. Damn you, Ben, I want you to meet my girl. She lives here in Tucson."

"I'd like to meet her."

Bijah wiped his mouth with the back of his hand and dug out the makings. "She don't know about me, Ben. She thinks I'm a rancher." He looked up quickly. "Well, after this deal I will be!"

Ben was suddenly tired. He ate mechanically while Bijah sat across the table from him. Bijah was the last man he had wanted to see, yet if there was any way, any at all, he meant to take him in. Oddly enough, he knew Catlow expected it of him, and respected him for it.

Nor was there any sense in trying to persuade Catlow. He had tried that, knowing before he began that he was wasting his time. The big Irishman was a stubborn man. Ben looked across the table at him, suddenly realizing he had always known that someday it would come to a showdown between them. They had always respected each other, but had always been on opposite sides of the fence.

What was Catlow planning? It was out of the country, he had said, and that could scarcely mean anywhere but Mexico. And there was already enough strain between the two countries. But Catlow always got along well with the Mexicans—he liked them and they liked him.

Whatever it was Catlow planned, Ben Cowan must stop him. And the simplest way was to get him into jail.

"You said you had a gun under the table. I don't believe it."

Catlow grinned. "Don't make me prove it. It was in the top of my boot, and now it's in my lap. Minute ago I had it up my sleeve, but always in my mitt. Yeah," he added, "I'd never take a chance on you. You're too damn' good with a gun."

"All right, I'll take your word for it, Bijah. But you hand over the gun and I'll take you in—do it now before you go so far there's no turning back."

Catlow was suddenly serious again. "Not a chance, Ben. This deal I've got lined up—I'll never have a chance like this again, and neither will you. The hell of it is...Ben, there isn't a man in that outfit I can count on when the chips are down.

"Oh, there's a couple of them will stick. The Old Man, now. He's one to ride the river with, but he hasn't got the savvy I need. I need somebody who can adjust to a quick change, somebody who can take over if I'm not Johnny-on-the-spot. And you're it."

The Mexican girl refilled their cups and Ben

glanced around the room. It was almost empty, and nobody was within earshot—not the way they had been talking.

Gloomily, he reflected there was no way to stop Bijah from going ahead with this deal, whatever it was. Only jail.

And Bijah was too filled with savvy to be tricked into jail.

Nor was it time for a gun battle. That was the last thing he wanted. In the first place, he liked Bijah, and had no desire to shoot him; and in the second place...It was like Hickok and Hardin...neither wanted a fight, because even if one beat the other he'd probably die in the process. Ben was sure that he was faster and a better shot than Bijah, though with mighty little margin. That would matter, but not much, because Bijah Catlow was game. You might get lead into him, but he'd kill you for it. He would go down shooting.

Ben Cowan knew too much about guns to believe that old argument that a .45 always knocked a man down. Whoever said that knew very little about guns. If a man was killing mad and coming at you, a .45 wouldn't stop him. You had to hit him right through the heart, the brain, or on a large bone to stop him... and there had been cases where even that wouldn't do the job. He knew of dozens of cases where it had not stopped a man, and Bijah Catlow would not stop for it.

Ben recalled a case where two men walked toward each other shooting—starting only thirty feet apart—and each scored four hits out of six shots while getting hit with .45-calibre slugs.

Bijah leaned over the table again. "Look, Ben, while you're in Tucson, why not declare a truce? Then you make your try any time I'm out of town."

"Sorry."

Bijah got up. "Have it your own way, then." The derringer he held in his big hand was masked from the rest of the room by the size of his hand. "You just sit tight."

He stepped to the door, then disappeared through it, but Ben Cowan made no move to follow. The time was not now.

It would come.

———

MEN WHO ARE much alone, when meeting with other people either talk too much or become taciturn. Ben Cowan was of the latter sort. He had a genuine liking for people, finding qualities to appreciate in even the worst of them, but usually he was silent, an onlooker rather than a participant.

People who saw Catlow for the first time knew him immediately for a tough, dangerous man. But with Ben, although people might take a second look at him, it was only the old-timers who sized him up as a man to leave alone. It is a fact that really dangerous men often do not look it.

Strolling to the edge of the boardwalk, Ben looked down the busy street, letting all his senses take in the town. His eyes, his ears, his nose were alert, and something else...that subtle intuitive sense that allows certain men to perceive undercurrents, movements, and changes in atmosphere.

Bijah Catlow had disappeared, but the Mexican

half a block away who was too obviously ignoring Ben Cowan would probably be Catlow's man.

Ben Cowan took a cigar from his pocket and lighted it. He was in no hurry, being a man of deliberation, and he knew that taking Catlow would be quite a trick. And Bijah had obviously made friends in Tucson. Moreover, a substantial portion of the population were something less than law-abiding; and as for the rest, they believed every man should saddle his own broncs. If Cowan wanted Catlow, let him take him.

Vigilante activity in California, and Ranger activity in Texas had contributed to the population of the Territory, but the population had always been a rugged lot, who fought Apaches as a matter of course.

The town was an old one—not so old as Santa Fe, of course, but it had been founded shortly after 1768 on the site of an Indian village, or in its close vicinity. There were Spanish-speaking settlers on the spot as well as Indians when Anza passed by on his way to California.

Ben Cowan had no plans. Catlow had mentioned a girl, but Ben shied from that aspect. Bijah had said he wanted him to meet her, and he was undoubtedly sincere, but Ben was uneasy around women, and he had known few except casual acquaintances around dance halls.

His mother had died in childbirth and he had grown up on a ranch among men, nursed first by a Mexican woman, and after she left, he was free to wander about as he pleased. Moreover, he was going to put the cuffs on Bijah, and he wanted no weepy woman involved.

Actually, he had little time to consider Bijah, for the man he had really come for was somewhere in the area. Ben had trailed him down the Salt River Canyon, through Apache country, and then had lost him somewhere to the north but headed in this direction.

Word had reached him at Fort Apache that a deserter named Miller had ambushed the Army paymaster and escaped with more than nine thousand dollars. He had been heard to refer, sometime before, to a brother in Tucson.

Ben Cowan had picked up the trail and followed his man into the town, where Miller had promptly dropped from sight.

Miller first, Cowan decided, and then Catlow.

Ben turned and strolled on down the street. Evening was coming on and the wagons were beginning to disappear from the street. A few men had already started to drift toward that part of town known as the Barrio Libre—the Free Quarter. Ben glanced that way, and then after a few minutes of thought, turned toward the Quartz Rock Saloon.

The bartender looked up as he entered, noticing the badge but offering no comment.

"Make it a beer," Ben said, and then added, "a friend of mine in Silver City said I should drop in here."

The bartender drew the beer and placed it on the bar before Cowan.

"His name was Sandoval," Ben said.

The bartender picked up the beer and wiped under it with his bar cloth. "What do you want to know?"

"The name is Miller. He may have other names. He rode into town within the last forty-eight hours. He may have a brother here."

The bartender put the mug down. "Are you lookin' for anybody else?"

Ben Cowan did not hesitate. "Not looking. I want Miller."

"It ain't a brother . . . it's a brother-in-law, and he's no friend of Miller's—only there ain't much he can do about it. Miller is a bad one." The bartender leaned his thick forearms on the bar. "Only he'd better walk a straight line this time. Bijah Catlow is courtin' Cord Burton."

"Cord?"

"Short for Cordelia, daughter to Moss Burton, Miller's brother-in-law. From what I hear tell, Catlow is an impatient man."

Ben Cowan took a swallow of his beer. So there was to be no waiting . . . everything seemed to point him toward Bijah Catlow.

He finished his beer and left the change from five dollars lying on the bar. As he turned away he was remembering what he knew about Miller.

The man had ambushed that paymaster. Moreover, every indication offered by his trail west implied that he was a sly, careful man. If such a man thought Catlow was a danger to him he would not say so to his face. He would wait, watch, and if possible kill him.

Bijah was a tough man but a reckless one. Did he know how dangerous Miller could be?

CHAPTER 7

BEN COWAN HAD an uncomfortable feeling that events were building toward a climax that had no place in his planning.

It was true that he wanted to arrest Bijah Catlow and get him out of the way before he got into more trouble. It was also true that it was his duty to arrest him, as Bijah himself well knew. Yet first things came first, and in Ben's plans Miller was first in line. But now the trail to Miller led him right to Catlow.

He made no more inquiries, nor did he manifest any interest in Miller. Tucson was not a large town, and it was easy to find out what he needed to know by listening or by dropping a discreet comment.

He learned that Moss Burton was well thought of locally. He owned a saddle shop, and had some small interest in mining properties, as did almost everyone else in town. Besides his daughter Cordelia, he had two small sons; his wife had taught for a while in the first school organized by the Anglo-Saxon element.

In discussing Burton, it was natural that Miller's name would come up. Miller was a tough man, and Moss Burton was no fighter, so Miller had promptly moved in. Also, he was married to Mrs. Burton's sister.

By the time two days had passed Ben Cowan knew where Miller kept his horse, knew who his friends

were, and which places in the Barrio Libre he preferred to others. He also knew that Miller was involved with a young Mexican woman, a widow, and
trouble was expected, for her brothers disapproved.

Ben was quite sure that Miller did not know he
had been followed to Tucson. Apparently he had
been cautious just because it was his way ... but Ben
Cowan took nothing for granted. He wanted Miller,
but he wanted him alive if possible.

Twice he saw Miller on the street, but each time he
was close to women or children, and in no place to
start anything, and Ben Cowan was not an impatient
man. On his third day in town, Ben Cowan saw the
Mexican.

He came up the street riding a hammer-headed
roan horse that had been doing some running. He
carried a carbine in his hand, wore two belt guns, one
butt forward, one back, and crossed cartridge belts
on his chest. His wide-bottomed buckskin pants had
been slit to reveal fancy cowhide boots, and spurs
with rowels bigger than pesos. The Mexican had a
scar down one cheek and a thick mustache.

The Mexican rode to the Quartz Rock Saloon and
dismounted there. He kept his carbine in his hand
when he went inside. A few moments later, Ben saw a
Mexican boy leave the back of the saloon. Ben drew
back into the doorway of a vacant adobe and lighted
a fresh cigar. Soon the Mexican boy returned.

Ben studied the roan. The brand was unfamiliar,
and looked like a Mexican brand. The horse had
come a long way, by the look of him, as had the man.
But that was a rugged character, that Mexican soldier,

and the ride would not show on him as it would on the horse ... or on several horses.

Soldier? Now, why had he thought *that?* He could put his finger on no reason, yet he must have sensed something about the man—call it a hunch. And Ben was not a man who fought his hunches. Too often they had proved out.

A Mexican soldier here probably meant a deserter—and from just where?

A horse came up the street at a fast walk and Ben drew deeper into the shadows. The rider was Catlow, who dismounted and went inside.

Catlow had come from the direction the boy had taken. It did not follow there had to be a connection, but it seemed likely.

It was strictly by chance that Ben heard the voices.

The doorway in which he stood was set back from the walk by at least two paces. The window of the adjoining building—the side window—was only a couple of paces farther back. What he heard was a girl's voice.

"Kinfolk he may be, but he's none of our blood, Pa, and if you don't tell him to go, I shall."

"Now, now, Cordelia, you can't do that! You can't just throw a man out of the house for nothing."

"He's a thief, Pa, and probably worse. You know it, and I do."

There was silence within, and Ben Cowan waited. He did not like to eavesdrop on private conversations, but in this case it was his business to do so, for without doubt they were talking of Miller.

"Pa, he's afraid of somebody ... or something. He

never steps into the street without looking out the window first."

Her father was silent for several minutes, and then he said, "I know it, Cordelia." A pause. "Cordelia, I can order him from our home, but what if he refuses to go? I was not in the war . . . I've never used a gun but once or twice. I doubt," he added, "whether any other man in Tucson can say that, and living in the country as we do, I am surprised that I can."

"I would not want you to fight him."

"If he refuses to go, what else could I do? I am afraid, Cordelia, that women sometimes make demands on their men without realizing the consequences."

Ben Cowan had lost interest, for the time being, in Bijah Catlow and the Mexican soldier. For a moment he considered going in the shop next door and asking them to invite him to supper . . . then he could leave with Miller and make his arrest. But to do such a thing might endanger the Burtons, and he had no right to bring trouble to innocent people.

Miller was a cross-grained man with a hard, arrogant way about him, a man born to cause trouble wherever he might go. Ben Cowan tried to imagine Miller in the same house with Catlow, and could not; for Miller's attitude was just that calculated to move Bijah to action.

A door closed and Ben Cowan stiffened, glancing swiftly to right and left . . . could it have been the shop door? He heard no voices—only the pound of a hammer on leather. He started to step from the doorway and found himself face to face with Cordelia Burton. He swept off his hat.

"I beg your pardon," he said, greatly embarrassed. "I—"

She glanced from him to the window, then abruptly walked on. He was about to speak, but held his tongue. He remained there, staring after her. She was lovely, undeniably lovely...she was also very definitely a girl who knew her own mind. After a moment of consideration, Ben decided that she was not overmatched in coping with Bijah, for Bijah was basically a gentleman. Miller was another item, another item entirely.

Annoyed with himself, Ben started for the Quartz Rock. He felt a fool, being caught eavesdropping by such a girl, and he had stared at her like a damned fool.

Cordelia Burton walked on down the boardwalk, her heels clicking. The momentary irritation she had felt on seeing the man standing where he could obviously hear all that was said within passed away, but she was puzzled.

The man was a stranger...a tall man with broad shoulders. In the shadow of the building she had seen only his chin, but he had spoken courteously and she had been wrong not to acknowledge it. Who could he be? And why would he be standing there?

The building was empty. There was nothing nearby, unless...unless for some reason he was watching for somebody at the Quartz Rock. Suddenly she had a distinct impression that there had been a badge on his chest.

Badges were not frequent in Tucson, and she had never seen a man who resembled this one wearing a badge. He had been standing in the dark doorway of an abandoned building watching somebody or something. She flushed as she realized how self-centered she must have been to be so sure he had been listening in on her conversation. She paused on the corner.

She knew she had best be getting home. It was late, and a decent woman kept off the streets at this hour. Yet her curiosity made her turn to look back. The man she had seen was crossing the street toward the Quartz Rock Saloon. At the same time she noticed Bijah Catlow's horse tied to the rail.

She would ask Bijah—he would certainly know something about the tall stranger with the badge.

Suddenly, from behind her she heard the quick step of a fast-walking horse, and it loomed darkly beside her. Despite herself, she looked up, and when she did so she recognized the chin.

"Beggin' your pardon, ma'am, it's late for a lady to be out. If you'll permit, I'll just ride along to see you get home safe."

"Thank you."

Oddly enough, she felt shaky inside—an unusual sort of trembling feeling. But she kept on walking, looking straight ahead. After a moment, he spoke again.

"Ma'am, I couldn't help overhearing back there." So he *had* been listening! Her lips tightened. "If you'll allow me to say so, you shouldn't urge your pa to kick Miller out. He might try it."

"And so?"

"You know the answer to that. Miller might kill him. More probably he'd shame him, which would be worse. It's a bad thing for a man to be shamed in front of his womenfolks . . . it's sometimes worse than bein' killed. If he was shamed, he might get a gun and try it on Miller."

Cordelia was appalled. Suddenly, for the first time, she realized what her indignation might mean to her father. Of course, Miller would not go unless he wanted to, and the thought of her father trying to face Miller with a gun touched her with icy fear.

"I—I didn't think of that."

"No, ma'am, and you didn't think about stayin' out this late. Supposing some drunk had come up to you and spoke improper. I'd have to speak to him, and he might resent it. First thing, ma'am, there'd be a man killed—and you'd be to blame."

"It was my only chance to speak to Pa alone."

She had reached the gate at her house, and she turned toward him. "Who are you? What are you?"

"Ben Cowan...Deputy United States Marshal in the Territory."

"You—you came here after somebody?"

"Miller's my man."

Miller? Then why didn't he arrest him? It would solve everything. She started to say as much, but he spoke first.

"I'll thank you to say nothing to anyone, ma'am. I want to do this in my own good time, and where nobody will be hurt—not even him, if I can help it." He turned his horse. "Evening, ma'am."

He rode away up the street, gone before she could thank him. She went through the gate, closing it behind her, then paused in the darkness to look after him. He was briefly seen against the window lights of a saloon.

Bijah Catlow was sitting at the table talking to her

mother as she placed the silver. He looked around at Cordelia. "I near came after you," he said. "It's no time for a decent girl to be out."

"That's what Marshal Cowan said."

Bijah gave a start. "Ben Cowan? You met him?"

When she explained he asked, too quickly, "Did he tell you anything about me?"

"No." She was surprised. "I had no idea you even knew each other."

"Since we were boys. He's a good man, Ben is. One of the best." He looked at her again. "Cord, did he say why he was here?"

She hesitated a moment. "No," she said.

Pa would be coming along soon, and Miller, too. Miller had not met Catlow yet.

Suddenly the door opened and Miller came in—a lean, rangy man with hollow cheeks and sour, suspicious eyes. He shot a quick look at Catlow, and Cordelia introduced them.

Catlow's forearms lay upon the table. He looked up from under his shaggy brows, cataloguing Miller at a glance. "Howdy," he said carelessly.

"Mr. Miller is married to my mother's sister." Cordelia decided she would make it plain at once that there was no blood relationship. "He is visiting us for a few days."

Miller gave her a hard look at the words, "a few days." Then he said, "I got to be around longer'n I figured."

There was a step on the porch outside and Bijah noted the quick way in which Miller turned to face the door. Moss Burton came in.

"I'm driftin' south," Catlow said. He had sensed

the situation quickly, recalling words he had heard dropped before this. "Why don't you ride along with me?" He put his eyes hard on Miller. "Men like you or me, we sleep better outside, anyway."

The stillness that entered the room made Cordelia hold her breath. She hesitated, ever so slightly, before placing the last plate upon the table.

"When I'm ready," Miller said, "I'll go."

Catlow looked up at him and cold amusement flickered in his eyes.

"Get ready," he said.

CHAPTER 8

THOUGH MILLER WAS a cautious man, now fury burst like a bomb in the pit of his stomach. He kept his eyes on his plate, but it was only with an effort that he fought back the urge to lunge across the table at Catlow. He forced himself to take a bite of food and to begin chewing.

"This is your doin'," he said to Cordelia. "I don't like it."

"When you come visiting again," she replied coolly, "we will be glad to see you . . . if you bring Aunt Ellie." Then with an edge to her voice she asked, "By the way, where is Aunt Ellie?"

"She's in Kansas."

"We'd love to see her. She is always welcome here."

Moss Burton had started in from the kitchen, where he had gone to wash his hands. Now, desperately, he wished he had remained there.

Miller saw him and started to accuse him, but Bijah Catlow was nothing if not considerate of the feelings of others. To save Moss the embarrassment of reiterating the request to leave, with all that might follow, Bijah interrupted Miller.

"You ain't goin' to like it around here nohow," he said, grinning cheerfully. "Cordie's got herself a new gentleman friend."

"What's that to me?"

Catlow chuckled, a taunt in his eyes and in his tone. "Figured it might be. It ain't every day a girl has a U.S. Deputy Marshal comin' to set with her."

The hot fury in Miller's belly was gone. Where it had been there was now a cold lump of fear. "I don't believe you," he muttered, and his fingers fumbled with the handle of his coffee cup.

Catlow, who knew what the grapevine was saying, had a sudden hunch and played it. "Army paymaster killed over near Stein's Pass by a deserter. Were you ever in the Army, Miller?"

Miller gulped his coffee to cover his fear. He had seen too much of what United States marshals could do when he had been around Fort Smith. Why had he been such a fool as to ride into Tucson? Too many people knew he had a brother-in-law here.

He would have to get out. To go . . . where? Prescott was out of the question—too many knew him there. Yuma, then? But someone at the Fort might recognize him. The Army was always moving men around . . . and the thought of the Federal pen made him nervous.

"That marshal means nothin' to me, but it's plain enough that I ain't wanted . . . among my own kin." He pushed back his chair and got to his feet, glancing at Bijah, who watched him, amused but alert. "You, I'll see again."

"Right outside the door, if you like," Catlow replied carelessly, "or in front of the Quartz Rock in half an hour."

"I'll pick the time," Miller said, "and the place."

"You an' Matt Giles," Catlow said.

When Miller had gone, Cordelia asked, "What was that about Matt Giles?"

"Man I used to know. Figured Miller might know of him."

Bijah took Cordelia's guitar from its place in the corner and, tuning up, sang "Buffalo Gals," and followed it with "Sweet Betsy from Pike." He sang easily and cheerfully, just as he had sung around many campfires and in bunkhouses. He was a man who did everything well, and he did most things with something of a flair. As he sang, he watched Cordelia.

She was, he thought, a thoroughbred. She had courage, and a cool, quiet strength, but above all she was a lady. Poised, without pretensions, and gracious, she was friendly, yet reserved. What she thought of him, Catlow had no idea. He had met her, asked to call, and had visited the house several times.

Now he was going away, and for the first time he found, with some surprise, that he did not wish to go. He recalled what he had told Cowan about wanting to marry this girl, and he realized he had meant every word of it. Of his life she knew nothing. She assumed he was a cattleman looking for range—a few of them had drifted into Arizona, looking around. Henry C. Hooker had a herd of cattle stampede while driving them through the state for sale to the Army, and when the stampede was over the cattle were grazing around a *cienaga* in the Sulphur Springs Valley, and it was there he established the Sierra Bonita Ranch. Hooker started it; others had followed. All this was known to every child in the street, and Catlow was so obviously a cattleman.

Cordelia would not have been likely to hear any of the stories about him, Bijah decided, nor would her father, for that matter. Moss Burton worked over his saddles, boots, and bridles, paying little attention to gossip; he ate his meals at home, and did not frequent the saloons.

As Bijah played, idly strumming the guitar, his thoughts turned to the venture that lay ahead. There were twelve men in his outfit, and several of them were strangers, but they had been selected with as much care as possible. Bijah knew very well what lay before him. He possessed a sharp, intelligent brain, and he was using it in this.

Every detail had been planned. Not only the move south and the taking of the money, but the escape. This, he felt sure, would be the crux of the whole thing. With any kind of luck, they could reach their destination unseen and, if all went well, take the gold. Their great danger lay in their escape, and to this he had given most of his thinking.

If they were captured during their attempt on the gold they would probably be shot; otherwise they would rot in a Mexican jail. The courts were slow, and nobody would be in a hurry to try a bunch of gringos who had come into Mexico looking for trouble.

His band of men had one thing in common: all spoke Spanish, Mexican-style, and all could pass as Mexicans. This would help during the ride south if they were seen, which Catlow hoped would not happen.

One member of his outfit was a half-breed Tarahumara Indian who knew all the secret water holes and rock tanks, places known only to wild animals and wilder Indians. Catlow and his men would avoid the main trails, avoid the Apaches as well, and reach the heart of Sonora unseen.

Not one of the men he had selected was known for having a loose tongue; nevertheless he had told them only a part of his plan. The escape route he kept to himself, and only the two involved knew about his cattle deal.

Impulsive he might be, but Abijah Catlow had done the most careful planning for this big strike. He was going to make this one and get out . . . and then to Oregon and the cattle business.

It was after ten o'clock when he left the Burton house, and he took the precaution of having Cordelia take the lamp into the kitchen before he left by the front door.

When he reached the house where he was living, Old Man Merridew was loafing at the door. "Marshal's inside . . . wants to talk."

Ben Cowan was sitting in the rocker in the dark, and Bijah removed the chimney from the lamp and touched a match to the wick. He replaced the chimney and looked across the lamp, the light throwing highlights and shadows on his strongly boned face.

"You goin' to pull me in?"

"No," Ben replied. "I just came with a friendly word of advice."

Bijah chuckled. "What else did I ever get from you, Ben? What is it now?"

"Miller . . . you've made an enemy there, and the man's dangerous."

"Him? Small potatoes. I ain't beggin' trouble, but if he wants it he can have it."

"Don't low-rate him. He's worse than Giles."

"*Him?*" Catlow repeated skeptically. "Miller? You're loco."

"I know him. I followed him here from New Mexico. The man's a wolf. He'll wait a year, two years if necessary. He's a hater, Bijah. You and me were never that, and a hater is a tough man to best."

"That all you came for?"

"It's a plenty. Did you ever know me to shy from shadows? I know the man."

Catlow sat down and rolled a smoke. "All right. If you say he's that bad, I'll put my money on it."

"I'm going to take him in, but I want him where nobody will get hurt if there's shooting. I can wait, too."

Bijah sat down on the bed and pulled off first one boot and then the other. He sat there, holding the boot in his hand, wriggling his toes into comfort. Then he dropped the boot and removed his gun-belt, tossing it over the post at the head of the bed where it would hang near his hand as he slept.

The coal-oil lamp threw shadows into the corners and behind the old wardrobe. There was little enough in the room. The bed, a straight-backed chair, and the rocker where Ben sat, the wardrobe, a table, bowl and water pitcher. In the corner near the door was Bijah's saddle and his rifle, saddlebags and a blanket-roll.

Ben took a cigar from his pocket and lit up. His eyes dropped to the gear on the floor. There was a canteen there, too. It had been freshly filled. As Bijah had been out, it must have been filled by one of the others—Merridew probably. They were pulling out, then.

"Like to talk you out of this deal you've got," Ben suggested. "You're asking for it."

"Hell!" Catlow said. "I figured you'd be glad to get me out of town—you walkin' my girl home like you done. You tryin' to cut me out?"

Ben Cowan shook his head. "You know better than that. She was on the street alone . . . besides, she caught me listening to talk between her and her father. It was about this Miller . . . she was fixing to get her pa killed."

He got to his feet. "Bijah . . . this is government business if you cross the line into Mexico. It's up to me to stop you."

Bijah grinned at him, peeling off his shirt. He was a well-muscled man, and the muscle was all power, as Ben Cowan had reason to know. "Stop me, then. But I'd still like to have you in with me. You'd be worth the lot of this crowd."

"You'd have to go far to beat the Old Man," Ben said. "That one's an old wolf from the high country. You turn him loose on Miller and you'd have nothing to worry about."

"I fight my own battles."

Ben put on his hat. "Sorry I can't talk you out of this, Bijah, but I didn't much figure I could." He put out his hand. "We'll meet again."

"You keep your ears pinned back when we do, or I'll notch 'em for you. This is the big one for me, Ben, an' all bets are off."

Ben Cowan stepped out into the night and walked past Merridew, who sat in the darkness near the gate. He went by, and then he came back.

"You know Miller?"

"I know him."

"He's out to get Bijah—sooner or later he'll try."

"Catlow don't need no help."

"I know that. I carry the scars to prove it, but four eyes are better than two."

Cowan walked out into the street and paused there, glancing each way. He had his own back to watch, for Miller would be thinking of him first. But Ben was used to it—in his business the hunter was always the hunted as well.

He thought back to Cordelia Burton, and for a minute he felt a wistful longing, the yearning of a homeless man for a home and all that it can mean. He thought of how it would be to be sitting at a table with her across from him, the soft glow of lamplight on her face.

He shook his head, dismissing the thought. An officer of the law made little enough money...of course, a man could always file a homestead...and there was good range here in Arizona. He'd ridden over a pretty piece of it, time to time.

He had almost reached the Shoo-Fly, where he had left his bedroll, when he saw the shadows of two men on the ground before him. The rising moon had thrown their shadows on the street, otherwise he would have had no warning. Even as he glimpsed them, one shadow vanished and the other drew back close to the building.

Were they waiting for him? Had the other man gone around the building to take him from behind? He hesitated a moment only, then turned on his heel and walked back to the saloon called the Hanging Wall, and went inside.

Several men loafed at the bar in desultory conversation, and there were three or four more around a table where a tired card game continued. One of these men looked around as he entered. It was Rio Bray.

Ben Cowan ordered a beer and waited. A moment passed, and then the door was pushed open and Miller came in. He started for the bar. His step faltered when he saw Ben Cowan, but he put his head down and came on, stopping a little distance away.

Miller leaned on the bar and pushed his hat back. Despite the cool night, he was suddenly perspiring. His eyes avoided Ben's. It was obvious that Miller had not suspected he was in the saloon.

Ben glanced down at his whiskey. Well, he wanted Miller, and there he was.

Why not take him now?

CHAPTER 9

MILLER KNEW HIM, and the instant Ben started for him, Miller would be likely to draw a gun. Ben Cowan turned the idea over in his mind and decided to wait.

They stood not fifteen feet apart, with three other men between. Rio Bray had moved around to the other side of the table where he had been watching the card game, and stood now where he could keep an eye on Cowan.

Moreover, one of the men, sitting alone at a table, was Milton Duffield, an ex-U.S. marshal, now a postal inspector, and a dangerous man with a gun. Duffield was a good man, with many local friends, but temperamental, and there was no certainty as to what he would do if a situation developed into gunplay. And he had been drinking heavily.

Ben Cowan suddenly remembered that his bedroll was back at the Shoo-Fly, and he had best retrieve it before the restaurant closed for the night.

Tucson at that time had no hotel. Those who had no friends in town bedded down wherever they could find a likely spot. There were a couple of abandoned houses used as camping spots by drifters—it was in one of these that Catlow had holed up. Word was passed on by word of mouth, and the houses were continually occupied by somebody. But most travelers bedded down in an empty corral or under a parked wagon.

Rio Bray strolled up and leaned on the bar beside Ben. "Howdy, Marshal! This here's a long way from the Cross Timbers."

Bray glanced down the bar at Miller. "Sure does beat all what a guilty conscience will do for a man, Marshal. Really starts a man sweating."

Miller's quick glance was filled with hatred, but Bray grinned back at him. "Better watch where you sleep, Marshal. Lots of folks around here are mighty careless where they leave their knives."

Miller put down his glass and went to the door. Ben Cowan watched him go, knowing that once outside Miller would dodge for shelter and probably wait for him to emerge.

"He ain't goin' no place tonight, Marshal," Bray said confidentially. "There's Apaches raiding around the country and Tucson's the safest place to be. Anyway, the Fifth Cavalry are going to give another band concert tomorrow night, and that's worth waitin' for."

Obviously Rio Bray had had more than a few drinks and was in a jovial, somewhat taunting mood. Ben was quite sure that Bray did not like him, and he felt no regret over that. Bray was a tough man and a good one, but a man who would have hit the outlaw trail sooner or later, regardless of circumstances.

"Yes, sir . . . a band concert! This town ain't no just ordinary town, Marshal. Why, just t'other day an *hombre* named Mansfield started himself a circulating library . . . got himself a whole stack of books to lend out!"

Rio Bray gulped his beer. "Why, this here's a regular metropolis! Now, I tell you—"

"Excuse me," Ben said abruptly, and turned swiftly to the door at the back.

He went through the short hall, then opened the door and stepped out into the darkness. Instantly, he moved to the right, and held still an instant to let his eyes grow accustomed to the darkness, all the while listening for the front door to close. Grimly, he reflected there was small chance of anybody going out that front door for a few minutes. Not if they suspected, as he did, that Miller was waiting out there.

Ben went around the corner of the building. The night was still. Somewhere, off beyond the town, a coyote yapped. The space next to the saloon was wide enough for a wagon to be standing there, a big freight wagon. He moved past it, his hand close to his gun. When he was half the length of the building he paused and studied what he could see of the street.

Opposite the saloon there was an adobe, the awning in front of it shielding the walk and most of the wall of the building in shadow. As he looked that way, something stirred behind him and he threw himself against the wagon on his left, drawing as he fell against it. He felt the whip of the bullet, then the thunderous roar of the shot between the walls of the two buildings. His answering fire was only an instant later, and he immediately ran toward the back, his pistol ready for a second shot.

All was dark and silent. He waited, listening, but there was no sound; and then, from some distance off, somebody chuckled.

Ben Cowan hesitated, wanting to follow up that shot and find out who thought it was so funny, but his better judgment won and he went out into the street and made his way to the Shoo-Fly. With his bedroll he went through the alleys to the edge of town and bedded down there among some mesquite and cat-claw where he could not be approached without considerable noise.

It was daylight when he awakened.

Returning his bedroll to the Shoo-Fly, he ordered breakfast, and then went down the street to the back of the Hanging Wall.

He had no trouble finding the boot-prints of the man who had tried to kill him, for one of them was superimposed on his own track. Carefully, he worked out the trail.

Whoever had tried to kill him had not come around the building, *but had followed him from the saloon.*

He returned to the Shoo-Fly and his breakfast was brought to him. As he ate, he recalled man by man those who had been inside the Hanging Wall when he left through the back door. His memory for faces was good, but he could find no reason to suspect any particular man. Perhaps Miller had come back into the saloon as Ben left through the back.

He thought of Rio Bray, but dismissed the idea. Rio was close to Catlow, and Catlow would not want him killed . . . or would he?

Bray's random talk might have been simply the beer's effect, but it might have been more. Had Bray been holding him there for a reason?

"The trouble with you," Ben told himself, "is that you're suspicious of everybody."

But in his business a man had to be.

———

CORDELIA BURTON WAS up early, as was her habit. Her father was quiet, and left for his saddle shop earlier than usual. As she worked, her thoughts kept reverting not to Bijah Catlow, but to Ben Cowan.

She had never seen his face clearly, for it had always been shadowed by his hat brim, but she was sure she would know him if she saw him again, and curiously enough, she wanted to.

What sort of man was he? She was accustomed to quiet men, for a great many western men were quiet, not given to unnecessary talk. Was he really as sure of himself as he seemed?

"Mother," she said suddenly, "I'm going uptown."

Her mother glanced at her, mildly amused. "Bijah was here ... before daylight."

"Bijah?"

"He must have been. I found this tucked under the back door."

Cordelia took the note, somehow less interested than she would have been a day earlier. She read:

When I come back, you and me will have a talk.
If you need help, you go to Ben Cowan.

Abijah

He was gone, then. He had told her that he would be going one of these days, that he had some business in Mexico.

She would miss him, for nobody was more gay, more exciting, more full of fun...and yet, she reflected, there was no one to whom she would feel freer to go for help in case of trouble, the kind of trouble Miller could bring to herself and her family.

If she needed help, he said, she was to go to Ben Cowan. She remembered Bijah saying they had been friends since they were boys, and he had referred to Cowan with respect. Well, she needed no help, and she didn't need Ben Cowan. Nonetheless she found herself wondering what he looked like in broad daylight. You could learn little about a man from seeing only his chin and jawline. But there had been strength in that jaw, and a quiet strength in the way he talked.

It was excuse enough to go uptown, but it was not the excuse she used to her mother. Cordelia was nineteen, and at an age when most girls were married, and many already had families, but Cordelia was not to be stampeded into marriage. She had made up her own mind long since; if she did not find the man she wanted, she would settle for nothing less. Bijah had seemed to be the man, but she was not sure, and that was enough to warn her. In spite of all his good qualities, and they were many, there was a curious instability about Bijah Catlow that disturbed her.

Occasionally, he had spoken of owning a ranch, of buying cattle, of building something. He spoke of these things, yet they never seemed real to her coming from him, and she feared they were not real to him either. They represented what his better judgment told him he should do. Now, walking up the dusty street, she suddenly realized that Bijah might do none of the things he planned . . . he would do many things, but not those things . . . unless . . .

There was no sign of Ben Cowan on the street. From under her bonnet she kept her eyes busy as she walked. The usual loafers were along the Calle Real and the other streets she passed. Horses dozed at hitch rails, and here and there a freight wagon was discharging its load.

She stopped to talk to Mr. Kitchen, who ranched south of Tucson, about getting one of his hams. Pete Kitchen had tried large-scale farming in Arizona before anyone else, and was doing well, although occasionally his pigs sprouted so many Apache arrows that they were referred to as "Pete Kitchen's pincushions."

She ordered the ham, talked to Pete about General Allen's venture in bringing honeybees into Arizona, and kept her eyes busy. She would like to try keeping bees herself, she decided. Until General Allen brought his bees to Tucson early in 1872 all their honey had been brought up from Rancho Tia Juana, in Baja California.

She wanted to ask Pete if he had seen Ben Cowan, but she hesitated. Finally, after all her small talk, and just as she was turning away, she said, "Pete, have you seen that new United States Marshal who is around town?"

Pete nodded. "I saw him—he was headed south just after daybreak. He looked to me like a man with something on his mind."

Gone . . . And he might not come back.

Kitchen glanced at her. "You worried about Catlow? That marshal ain't about to catch up to him."

"No . . . it isn't that. I—I had a message for him."

Pete turned away. "If he stops by my place, I'll tell him. I'm goin' back tonight."

Cordelia Burton turned toward home. What had Pete Kitchen meant when he said that the marshal was not going to catch up to Bijah? What would give Pete the idea that it was Bijah the marshal was following?

Obviously, it was a mistake, yet the thought disturbed her.

Ben Cowan had told her that Miller was his man, and Bijah had warned Miller about the marshal. Whatever Bijah knew that she did not, it had obviously frightened Miller into leaving, and for that both men deserved her gratitude.

Mentally, she began to go over that trail to the south. Every mile of it was dangerous, every mile had seen death by Apache warriors, every mile of it was liable to be raided at any time. Of all those who had tried to live to the south, only Pete Kitchen had survived any length of time, and his house and ranch were laid out for defense.

When she reached her own gate she went into the yard where her father had begun to plant grass for a lawn, and then paused as she looked back up the street. It was like her father, she thought, to bring his eastern ideas to Tucson, and to be among the first to plant trees, flowers, and grass with an idea of bringing coolness and beauty to the place.

Would Ben Cowan be like that? So many western men seemed heedless of anything but the present moment. She supposed it was because so few of them planned to stay wherever they were . . . or were too busy fighting Indians, drouth, and disaster to think of beauty.

She was undressing for bed when she heard General Allen come in. He often stopped by to talk with her father, and when she heard his voice she stopped to listen through the door, for he nearly always had news. And it was news he brought now.

"...came in about ten minutes ago. That marshal had irons on Catlow. Threw him in jail."

There was an indistinct mumble, and then she heard the words, "wanted in Texas."

Bijah Catlow *arrested?*

CHAPTER 10

B Y MORNING THE news was all over town—Bijah Catlow had been arrested. And then she discovered what everybody else seemed to know already . . . that Bijah Catlow was an outlaw and a gunfighter, known throughout the West.

Another story got around, too. Miller was wanted for desertion and murder, but he had vanished, dropped from sight as though he had never existed.

Soon everybody in Tucson was talking about the way Ben Cowan had taken Catlow, and it was Catlow himself who told the story, laughing at his own innocence in falling for an obvious trick.

He had been riding south through what seemed to be open country and there, lying in the trail ahead of him was a brand-new white sombrero, obviously expensive. Intrigued, Catlow dismounted and bent over to pick up the hat, and from behind him Ben Cowan ordered him to hold his position.

Bent over as he was, his pistol riding around in front of his hip, his body would impede any attempt at a draw; and to straighten, draw, and turn was too much of a chance against a man as fast as Ben Cowan. Catlow surrendered.

Ben Cowan slipped the cuffs on him. "I don't want to kill you, Bijah," he explained, "and damned if I don't think you'd try to make a break."

"Sure as hell would!" Bijah said ruefully. "I got business below the border."

Ben Cowan did not talk about the capture, but Catlow was full of the story, and it passed from person to person around the stables and the saloons, that Ben Cowan had outsmarted his old friend, lying hidden in a shallow place that apparently would not hide a desert fox, waiting until Catlow bent over to pick up the hat.

It made a good story, and Ben Cowan found himself suddenly a popular man, doubly so as it was obvious that Catlow, who was well-liked, held no grudge.

Cowan was sitting at his desk working over a report when Cordelia Burton appeared with a basket covered with a napkin.

"Marshal Cowan? May I give this to the prisoner?"

He looked at her gravely. "I will have to look it over."

She stiffened indignantly. "You do not trust me?"

"Ma'am, where Bijah is concerned I trust nobody. That man is wily as a snake and trickier than a 'coon."

He rummaged through the basket, his mouth watering as he saw half an apple pie, a large breast of chicken, and other assorted edibles.

Bijah Catlow got up from his cot and came to the bars, his face flushed a deep red. "Ma'am, I sure never calculated to have you see me in such a place."

"Then you shouldn't have done whatever it was you did to get in here. I am sure the marshal had reason for arresting you."

"Oh, sure! He had reason, all right!" He grinned his appreciation. "Where d'you suppose he got the idea for that durned hat trick? I never heard of such a thing! There was that brand-new hat lyin' there in the trail and nobody around, nowhere. Seemed like somebody had lost a good hat. Then just as I bent to pick it up, he had me."

"You like him, don't you?"

Bijah glanced at her quickly. "Ben? Best man I ever did know." He looked at her with a grin. "But you just wait . . . see who has the last laugh."

The town had it the next morning, for Bijah Catlow was gone.

Ben Cowan had stayed on watch until almost daylight, then had unrolled his bed and turned in.

An hour later the jailer shook Ben awake. "He's gone! Catlow's took out!"

The cell was empty.

The jailer's story was simple. He was making coffee when his daughter appeared at the door. He opened it and she came in, followed by three masked men. They had gagged and bound him and his daughter, taken the keys from him, and opened the cell to let Catlow out.

She had not been molested in any way. In fact, aside from threatening her with the gun, they had treated her with utmost politeness.

Knowing Bijah and how well-liked he was among the Spanish-speaking population, Ben Cowan suspected the jailer's daughter had been only too willing to cooperate, and the gun a mere gesture. The jailer himself did not seem very disturbed by the escape.

In disgust, Ben Cowan tore up the report of Catlow's capture and headed for the stable for his horse.

The horse was gone. Tacked to the side of the stall was a note.

You can pick him up at Pete Kitchen's. Sorry to set you afoot, but I got business to attend to.

There was no signature, and no need for one, but within the hour Ben Cowan realized just how many friends Catlow had, and how important they could be, for nobody in town had a horse that was ready to go. Either they had just gone lame, or they had been promised, or they were out at pasture, or somehow indisposed.

By afternoon several people came to him offering horses, but they knew and he knew that by that time Bijah Catlow was gone beyond recapture, and the town of Tucson was chuckling again.

Ben Cowan sat behind the scarred desk in the jail office and considered the situation. Bijah Catlow, and Miller as well—both had eluded him.

Bijah Catlow had undoubtedly gone to Mexico. Ben Cowan considered the probabilities and decided that Miller had gone the same way. He was a deserter, although his time in the Army had been of brief duration, and possibly only for the chance to watch the paymaster. He must avoid places where he might be recognized. His stop in Tucson was probably en route to Mexico, anyway.

Bijah Catlow had spoken of a big strike. Allowing for exaggeration, what were his chances in Sonora or Chihuahua, both within riding distance? Carefully, Ben considered the possibilities, but they were few and none seemed to promise anything like the amount of money Catlow must have had in mind, from the way he talked and planned.

The arrival of the Mexican soldier was obviously tied in with his plan. Had it then, anything to do with the Mexican army? A payroll, perhaps? Or captured loot?

With no idea of what way to take, Ben Cowan began in the only way he knew how: he began by asking questions, by starting a conversation in the direction he wished it to go, and then just listening. What he wanted to know about was Mexico.

The hint that he needed came from Allen. They were talking over lunch at the Palace—the Shoo-Fly's only rival in Tucson—and Allen was commenting on the death of Juarez and the succession of Lerdo to the presidency.

"You know," Allen said, "I have been expecting this would happen, and wondering if when it happened that silver would turn up."

"Silver?"

"Sebastian Lerdo de Tejada was the strong right arm of Juarez during some trying times, and before the French intervention both the Conservatives and the Liberals were in desperate need of money. The simplest way to get it was to confiscate some of the shipments from the mines, and Lerdo moved swiftly. One of those shipments had just been seized when, on June 10th, 1863, General Forey, with 30,000 French soldiers, entered the City of Mexico.

"Juarez fled to San Luis Potosí, and the mule train loaded with two million dollars in silver and gold vanished from sight. Yet in 1867 when Juarez was elected president and Lerdo was in his cabinet, there was already a somewhat reserved feeling between them. Later, Lerdo ran against Juarez for the presidency, was defeated, but became president of the Supreme Court; and on the death of Juarez, Lerdo became president."

"What about the two millions in silver?"

"Some of that two millions was in gold. Well, nobody who knows the whole story will tell it; but Lerdo had ambitions of his own, and apparently kept the knowledge of that treasure to himself, holding it back against such a time as has now come. He is president, and such a treasure would be of enormous use to him—especially with such a formidable rival as Diaz."

Ben Cowan listened as Allen talked on, discussing the involved politics of the land below the border in that year of 1872.

Tucson, in many respects, had closer ties with Mexico than with the United States. Only a few years earlier it had in fact been a part of Mexico, and many of the local population had been citizens of Mexico and had relatives there. Many of the local Anglos had married girls of Spanish descent, and were vitally concerned with Mexican affairs.

Suppose...just suppose...that Lerdo had removed those two millions from their hiding place and was having it transferred to Mexico City?

The possibility was slight, but the chance was there...depending on where that silver actually was...and that Mexican soldier could have been a messenger to Catlow.

"That silver—would it have been somewhere in Sonora when it disappeared?"

"You've heard the story then? Yes, as a matter of fact, it was. And it dropped right out of sight. But you can take it from me that if anyone knows where it was, Lerdo is the man. He's a deep one. Brilliant man," Allen commented; "shrewd, capable, and yet I do not believe he understands the temper of his people. He has lived too far from them, I think."

Later that night Ben Cowan loitered at the bar of the Quartz Rock Saloon. He listened to the talk around him but said nothing himself; when the moment came, he spoke quietly to the bartender. "There was a Mex soldier in here...stranger in town... stopped around here and the Hanging Wall, talked to Bijah Catlow some. I'd be interested to know what they talked about."

The bartender hesitated, then met Ben's gaze with cool, searching eyes. "Bijah is a friend of mine. I'd heard he was a friend of yours...and then you jugged him."

"Look"—Ben spoke softly—"Bijah is a friend of mine, but he's so damned bullheaded he won't listen to a friend, and he's walking himself right into a trap."

Cowan knew he was stretching things a bit, but he felt that what he was saying might be true.

"He's tackled something too big for him, and he's going to get killed unless I can stop him—and I don't even know where he's gone. After all," he added, "I couldn't arrest him in Mexico, anyway."

"Yeah," the bartender agreed, "that's so."

He served a beer down the bar, then came back to

Ben. "I got no idea where they went—only that Mex, I heard him mention Hermosillo a couple of times... and something about a mule train. I think," he went on, "he was trying to sell Bijah on the idea that whatever they did had to be done before that mule train reached Hermosillo."

It was little enough, but Ben Cowan had pieced a trail together on much less. Still, he had no authority in Mexico, and at the moment there was little good feeling between the two countries... although Washington, and the United States Marshal's office in particular, had instructed him to do all he could to promote good feeling with Mexican officials.

If it was true—and he had no evidence at all on which to proceed—that Catlow had gone into Mexico to attempt to steal the two million in treasure long concealed by President Lerdo, then he must be stopped. Such a theft by American bandits, if successful, would deal a serious blow to all future relations with Mexico. Ben Cowan knew what the cooperation of Mexican officials could mean, as did his superiors.

All right, then. The chances were good that Bijah Catlow had gone to Hermosillo. So Ben Cowan would go there too, trying all the way to pick up the trail he wanted. Fortunately, a man as flamboyant as Catlow would not be difficult to follow.

———

FOR DAYS BEFORE Catlow left, Ben had been preparing for a trip. He had bought a pack horse, had purchased supplies and extra ammunition, and while talking with people about the town, he had listened to much discussion of trails into Mexico.

"The Apaches are the danger," somebody had commented, "when they raid they go in small bands so they have no need to hold to the trails where the water holes are. Why, out there in the desert there are seeps and hidden tanks in the rocks with water a-plenty—a-plenty for six or seven men, maybe even a dozen if the water isn't used too often."

Several days had passed since Catlow escaped jail, and Cowan had done nothing. It seemed that he had no plans to do anything. And then, suddenly, he was gone.

Cordelia Burton saw Ben on his last day in town. He was standing on the street nearby when she emerged from her father's shop. She hesitated, and regarded him thoughtfully.

He was a remarkably handsome man, when one took time to look at him, and she liked the easy, casual way he handled his tall, lean body. His face was lean, browned by sun and honed by wind, and there was something about his eyes, something that haunted her, but she could not decide what it was. She should have asked Bijah about him, she thought.

He straightened up when he saw her, and removed his hat. His dark brown hair was curly; now it showed distinct reddish tones that she had not seen before.

He fell into step beside her. "I haven't much excuse to walk you home," he said, "... not in broad daylight."

"Do you need an excuse?"

He smiled slightly, and laugh wrinkles at the corners of his eyes broke the gravity of his expression.

"No, ma'am, I guess I don't." He glanced at her again. "Have you heard from Bijah?"

"No."

"He's going to be a hard man to take." He paused a moment. "You ever lived on a ranch, ma'am?"

"No . . . not exactly. It seems a lonely life."

"Depends . . . there's plenty to do. I take kindly to open lands. I like to look far off. Seems like a man's free, whether he is or not."

"You do not think a man can be free?"

"No, ma'am, not exactly. Maybe . . . some ways. There's always his duty, duty to folks about him, to his country, to the law . . . such-like."

She looked at him thoughtfully, then stood still so she could see his face well. "Ben, you believe in your duty, don't you?"

He shrugged slightly, and squinted his eyes against the sun. It might be that he was embarrassed to speak of such a thing. "Without duty, life don't make any kind of sense, ma'am. If folks are going to live together they have to abide by some kind of rules, and the law is those rules. The law doesn't work against a man, it works for him. Without it, every house would have to be a fortress, and no man or woman would be safe. First time two men got together I expect they started to make laws for living together.

"There's always mavericks who can't or won't ride a straight trail, and the law needs somebody to ride herd on them."

"And you are one of the herders?"

"Sort of." He smiled. "I need some herding myself, time to time."

He looked down at her. "Living on a ranch mightn't be as bad as you think," he said.

At sunup the next morning he was ten miles south of town and riding for the border.

He had a man to take...two of them, as a matter of fact.

CHAPTER 11

BIJAH CATLOW HAD entered Mexico and disappeared.

So far as Ben Cowan could discover there had been only four men in the group. One of these, judging by descriptions, was Old Man Merridew, and a second would surely be Rio Bray. As the fourth man was a Mexican, it was probably the soldier who had met Bijah in Tucson.

Whatever Catlow planned could scarcely be done by so small a group, so Ben Cowan loitered about Nogales on both sides of the border, and bought quite a few drinks, and asked quite a few questions. Had there been any other strange gringos in town that night? Gringos who were no longer around?

There had been—two, at least. They had ridden off on the trail toward Magdalena . . . a very foolish thing to do, for the Apaches made travel along that trail much too dangerous, except for large, well-armed groups.

To the click of castanets, the rattle of glasses, and the somber singing of a Mexican girl, Ben Cowan leaned on the bar and listened. He bought tequila, and he drank it, but most of the time he made idle talk in his fluent cow-country Spanish—and as always, he listened.

Wherever people gather together, they talk, and

often they talk too much. In towns where there is little news and little else but one's surroundings to discuss, they invariably talk too much.

When Ben Cowan rode from Nogales down the Magdalena trail, he rode alone, and soon he picked up the hoofprints left by the horses of Catlow, Bray, and Merridew. He had quickly become familiar with these around Tucson.

Others had left Tucson after them, but he could follow the tracks of Catlow's men with much difficulty. When they seemed to disappear from the trail he turned about and rode back. The trail had been almost obliterated by a herd of goats—undoubtedly not an accident—but soon the goats had turned toward Nogales and the four had ridden on.

Ben Cowan found where they had camped that first night in an arroyo only a few miles southwest of Nogales. Two other riders joined them there, and the party of six rode on.

A half-day's ride farther along, an Indian had joined them, an unmounted Indian. Ben back-trailed that Indian and found where he had waited a couple of hundred yards off the trail, smoking dozens of cigarettes and evidently watching for Catlow. When the party continued on, the Indian trotted beside Catlow's horse.

Now, a man who rides in wild country devotes quite as much time to his back trail as to that ahead, not only because he may be followed, but because he may have to retrace his steps, and the back trail does not look the same to him. Many a traveler has failed to watch his back trail and, turning back, has found nothing familiar in the country over which he has traveled, and becomes lost.

Ben Cowan, who had been holding to low ground for the most part, and riding parallel to the route the others were taking, now discovered that somebody else was following them... or him. A solitary rider and what appeared to be a black horse.

That lone rider raised no dust, so the chances were that Ben himself raised none, yet the rider must know of his presence, for from time to time his own trail had joined that of Catlow's band.

On the fourth day of riding, Cowan came to several decisions. The first was that the other man trailing them must be Miller; and another was that the Indian trotting beside Catlow must be a Tarahumara, one of a tribe noted for their tremendous faculty for endurance. A Tarahumara who could not run a hundred miles was scarcely worthy of belonging to the tribe—though as far as that went, the Apaches were great runners and walkers, men who preferred to fight on their feet, rarely on horseback.

Also, Catlow was looking for something in country with which he was not familiar. That Indian, Ben knew, had been brought along for the purpose of leading them to the little-known seeps, water holes, and rock tanks. There were many of those to be found in the desert, but they were rarely used because they were known only to wild things, including a few wild Indians. They held little water, not enough for any but a small party, sometimes scarcely enough for more than one or two men.

But by following such a route Catlow would be

able to penetrate deep into Sonora without being seen or questioned. It was a shrewd idea, and it indicated that Catlow had planned better than was his usual method. This was something to be remembered... Bijah Catlow was thinking, and Bijah was shrewd, with a brilliant imagination. Knowing all the tricks, he was capable of coming up with a few new ones on the spur of the moment.

The route presented an acute problem for Ben Cowan as well. Most of the water holes the men used would be exhausted before he reached them... in fact, Catlow no doubt depended on that very fact to eliminate pursuit.

That night five more riders joined Catlow. Rather, the five were waiting when Catlow and his men came. This, then, was what he had been looking for, and he had not been exactly sure where their camp would be.

An hour after daybreak Ben Cowan came up to the camp. His canteen had less than a pint of water in it, and his horse was desperate for a drink. And the bottom of the small seep where their camp had been was simply a few feet of drying mud.

There was no question of going on. First, he must have water, for the next water hole might be even worse. With a discarded tin can, Ben dropped to his knees and in a few minutes had scooped out a deep hole in the center of the mud. He worked a little longer, then withdrew to the shade, and settled down to wait.

Water might seep in... if it did not, he would have to strike out for the main trail and hope that he reached it at a point not too far from water.

He thought Catlow was headed for Hermosillo, but he did not know. Their destination might be Altar, not far off now; or, more likely, Magdalena and its rich mines. He could only find out by staying with Catlow and his band.

It was noon before he allowed his horse to drink, and shadows were gathering before he could fill his canteen. There was no possibility of keeping up with their trail in the dark, but a few hours of daylight remained, and there was the man following him to consider.

If he was still back there, he would come up with this seep in the same condition Ben Cowan had found it in, and he would undoubtedly make camp there. During the night Cowan might elude him.

Ben saddled up and rode out of the hollow where the seep lay, holding to low ground as much as possible, and wary of an ambush. But Miller was no longer first in his mind; he hoped above all to prevent Catlow from carrying out whatever it was he had planned.

He picked up the trail and rode away at a canter, making several quick changes of direction in case his follower was taking a sight at him, or circling to head him off. When darkness finally came, he took a last sight along the line of tracks he followed, lining them up with a mountain peak that would be visible for some time after nightfall. The great risk lay in the party he pursued veering off toward another water hole that lay to the east or west, in which case he would lose them, and the water as well.

He slacked off on the reins, trusting to the horse.

The roan was desert- and mountain-bred, accustomed to dry, rocky wastelands, and it would naturally go toward water. Moreover, the horse knew he was following a party of mounted men, and wild horses have been known to follow a scent as well as any hound.

For two hours the roan walked steadily toward the south; when it veered sharply off, he permitted it to go, only pausing from time to time to listen. The slightest noise carries far in the silence of a desert night, and he neither wanted to come on the others unexpectedly, or to betray his own presence by noise.

Suddenly, his horse stopped. Ben gathered the reins, listening into the night. He heard no sound.

They had paused in the deep shadow of a sheer wall of rock that reared up from the desert sand. About him was scattered brush. It was cooler in the shadow of the rock, and he waited, but the roan showed no disposition to move on.

He walked the horse closer to the rock face and dismounted. Judging by the actions of his horse, there was water near, but the roan had not gone up to it, so it was probably beyond reach.

Stripping the rig from the tired animal, he picketed the roan on a small patch of grass, then he dug into his saddlebag for a piece of jerked beef. After a while, when the sky was spangled with stars, he rolled up in his blankets and slept.

Far-off, a coyote howled . . . a quail called its question into the night, and above the horse and man the black cliff leaned, somber and stark against the blue-black sky.

He awakened suddenly in the cool dim light just before the dawn. His first glance was to his horse, for the roan was erect, ears up, nostrils flared. Swiftly, Ben was beside the horse, whispering a warning, putting a hand to its nostrils to stifle a whinny.

After a moment of silence he heard the steps of a walking horse. A horse that walked, paused...then came on again.

Ben Cowan shot a quick glance at his Winchester and gun-belt which lay on his ground-sheet beside the blankets. He wanted those guns desperately, but feared the sounds the move would make, and he did not dare to leave the horse. Something beyond the mere coming of a strange horse seemed to have alarmed the roan.

Suddenly, on a low rise off to his left, he saw the horse. Even as he glimpsed it, the animal let out a questioning whinny. The small breeze was from the strange horse and toward them, but it must have realized the presence of another horse.

The animal came a step nearer...there was something on its back...something more than a saddle. A pack? The shape was wrong.

It was a man, slumped down. A man wounded or in trouble of some kind.

Waiting no longer, Ben Cowan stepped quickly to his gun-belt and slung it about his hips, slipping the thong from his six-shooter as he did so.

Then, leaving his own horse, he walked toward the strange animal, talking in a low, friendly tone. The horse took a step or two nearer, hesitant and anxious, as if wanting the presence of a human.

Ben paused, listening. Never unaware of danger, he

lived always with the possibility of it, and no amount of easy living would ever take this from him. He was born to it, and was glad of it. He listened, but he heard nothing but the breathing of the horse.

He went up to the animal. A man lay slumped upon its back, tied in place crudely but efficiently. Ben led the horse to his camp and, having untied the knots, he lifted the wounded man from the saddle.

He was a Mexican officer in uniform, shot in the body and the leg. Hesitating only briefly at taking the risk, Ben dismissed it as one that must be taken, and put together a small fire. He built it close against the cliff and under a smoke tree where the rising smoke would be spread out and dissipated by even that sparse foliage—if such it could be called.

There was little water in his canteen, but he put a part of it on to boil; then he slipped off the wounded man's coat and split his pants leg. The bullet in the body had gone through flesh above the hip and had bled badly. The bullet hole in the leg seemed to have touched no bone, but the wounded man had lost blood there, too.

When the water was hot, Ben bathed the wounds and bound them up with the matadura herb. He had no powder, nor was it possible to prepare any, but he used the herb just as he had found it.

When he had finished dawn had come, and he sat back on the ground and looked around him.

He had to have water, and water must be close by, for he doubted if the roan would have stopped for any other reason. He glanced up at the rock wall. There could be a rock tank up there, a *tinaja*, as the

Mexicans called it, a natural hollow where water from the scarce rains might be found.

He got to his feet. And then for the first time he had a good look at the horse the man had been riding.

It was Miller's horse.

CHAPTER 12

THE YOUNG OFFICER lay still, but his breathing seemed less ragged and harsh. He was a handsome man, but now, in the early light, he looked pale, drained of blood by his wounds.

Ben knew that the wounded man would awaken to a raging thirst, and there was scarcely a cup of water remaining in Ben's canteen. Under the circumstances, there was nothing to do but leave him and go in search of water.

Taking up his rifle and canteen, he walked northward along the wall of rock. It was a sheer wall for at least forty feet up, then it seemed to break back and rise up farther, jagged and serrated. It was perhaps two hundred feet above the desert floor at its highest, which was to the south of him. If there was any way to get up into those rocks, it must be from the end, or from the other side.

The ridge was all of three hundred yards long. When he reached the end of it, it appeared to be no more than a third of that in width, but there was plenty of room up there for a tank. However, knowing such places as he did, Ben Cowan knew that without some clue he might die of thirst trying to find the water.

He studied the sand for animal tracks, but found none. A bee flew past, pointing away on a straight line of flight into the rocks, and he followed, taking a sight on a pinnacle of rock. He lost the bee, but went on for several yards in the direction of its flight, and then stopped.

The sun would soon be fully up, and the pale light of morning lay all about. Here and there were shadows among the rocks of the ridge. Glancing back toward camp, he could see the horses with their heads turned toward him, watching him. After a moment, they returned to their cropping of the dusty brown grass or brush.

Another bee passed, but he lost it. He walked on up among the rocks and found the track of a coyote or desert fox. . . . It was smudged somewhat and he could not make out which it was. The animal had gone on up into the rocks, and Ben scrambled over the rocks and climbed higher.

By the time he was well up into the rocks the sun was up and already hot. He climbed a shoulder of granite and studied the surroundings with care. He saw nothing green, nothing to indicate water.

The rocks about him were dull red, except off to the left where an upthrust of granite partly blocked his view. Sand had blown into the crevices, but as he climbed there was less of this. Brush grew here and there, sparse gray, unlikely-looking stuff that promised nothing. Here he must depend on chance, on what he knew about rock tanks, and what the wild life, if any, indicated.

He clambered on. Sweat trickled down his face, the empty canteen battered against the rocks. He stopped again, his gaze sweeping the surrounding country. In every direction there was desert . . . greasewood, cactus. His searching eyes found nothing to promise water.

Suddenly a bee went past him, so swiftly that he lost it instantly. He started on again, but where he climbed there was no easy way, no game trail, no way found by Indians. The coyote whose tracks he had seen earlier had not come this way; it must have turned off through some crevice or around some boulder.

He was high above the desert now. Searching for a way to proceed, he saw a flat-topped boulder whose edge he could reach with his fingers. Being a cautious man, he picked up a pebble and flipped it up. If a snake was lying there, it would surely be aroused and rattle. He had no desire to pull himself over that edge and come face to face with a rattler. He flipped another pebble, but nothing happened.

He pulled himself up and looked over a maze of dark rocks, smooth with the varnish of the desert. He got to his feet and looked back down the way he had come.

The picketed horses fed on the brush, but the wounded man was too close to the rock face to be seen from here. Ben climbed a little way over the rocks and suddenly, in a small patch of blown sand, he saw the edge of a track . . . a porcupine track. From the rocks ahead, a bird flew up.

Turning that way, he found himself on a narrow path, scarcely wide enough to place one foot ahead of the other between the rocks. Ahead, a huge boulder blocked the view, but when he rounded it he saw a deep, dark pool of water.

Lifting his eyes, he saw another pool, slightly

higher and just beyond it. Here the runoff from the highest part of the rocks was caught in the natural basins and held there.

The upper pool, which was the easier to reach, was half-shadowed by an overhang of rock. The water was cold, very cold, and sweet. He drank, then drank again and filled his canteen.

He looked down at the lower pool. Bees clustered around it, and he saw at the edge the droppings of a deer or mountain sheep—at this distance he could not make out which.

Following the path back, he found a comparatively easy route, and was quickly down to the desert floor.

The horses whinnied as he approached. The wounded man was conscious, and stared wildly at Ben as he approached.

"What happened?" he asked in Spanish. "Who are you?"

Ben Cowan squatted on his heels, and offered the wounded man a drink. Then he told him, as briefly as possible, what the situation was. "First off," he said finally, "I've got to get those horses to water or they'll break loose and go by themselves."

The wounded Mexican looked up at him. "Have you a gun? If you can spare me one, I'll be all right." He paused. "You know, of course, that this is Apache country?"

"I know."

"Each minute you stay with me you risk your life, señor."

Ben Cowan got his spare Colt from the saddlebag. "Take this," he said, "but don't shoot unless you have to. I'll be keeping a lookout from up above."

When he returned from watering the horses, the Mexican had managed to move and had dragged his bed deeper into the narrowing shadow of the cliff.

"Now you tell me," Cowan said to him, "where you got that horse."

Captain Diego Martinez de Recalde shrugged. "We were riding from Fronteras to Magdalena," he explained, "and as I was going home to Guadalajara, I took with me my very special horse. I was trying his paces some distance from the column when I thought I saw a horse standing alone on the desert.

"I rode closer to see . . . something hit me and I fell, hearing the shot as I struck the ground. A man rode up to me, shot at me again, and I remember nothing more."

"He shot you for your horse," Cowan said. "His own wasn't much good and was about played out."

"You know him, señor?"

"I know him . . . he's one of the reasons I am in Mexico. If I can arrange to take him here, I would like to take him back with me."

Recalde smiled, somewhat grimly. "You shall have every assistance, señor. I promise it. However," he added, "if he rides that horse where any of my command see him, I fear you shall not have much to take back."

After Ben had dressed the wound again, he brought up the subject of travel. Captain Recalde agreed with him at once. Difficult, even dangerous as it might be for Recalde to travel, to remain where he was would be even more dangerous. And by this time his soldiers would be searching for him.

Ben Cowan helped Recalde into the saddle and

mounted up. There was no longer any question of attempting to trail either Miller or Catlow. Now he must get the wounded man to his own column of soldiers, marching southward, and then he could ride with them into Hermosillo, or at least to Magdalena.

Recalde was gripping the pommel with both hands. "It is not a way to ride, señor," he said, "but—"

"You stay in that saddle any way you can," Ben responded, "and don't worry about how."

The desert was like an oven. Above them in the brassy sky there floated an enormous sun, a sun that seemed to encompass the entire heavens. Steadily they rode southward, south by east, hoping to come upon the trail.

Their walking horses plodded through the sand interminably; their slow advance was broken only by the moments when they stopped for Recalde to drink. The sun was high above, and the desert all around them danced with heat waves. Ben's clothes were stiff with dust and sweat, and sweat trickled down his spine and down his chest under his shirt.

His rifle barrel he sheathed, for it became too hot to hold. White dust rose from the desert, a soft white dust that clung and choked. The wounded man rode with head bowed, his fingers clinging to the pommel, his body swaying loosely with the movements of the horse.

The afternoon came; the brassy sun still hung in the sky. The day seemed to go on forever. Once Recalde's horse stumbled, and seemed about to fall. They pushed on . . . and then they came upon the trail. It was empty of life.

Tracks were there, tracks of wagons and of

mounted men, tracks several hours old. They had, evidently, reached the trail some distance behind the column...at this point the Captain's disappearance would not yet have been discovered.

Recalde's horse stumbled again, and had Cowan not thrown out a quick arm, the Captain would have fallen. The horse stood, legs spread, head hanging.

Alone, without a rider, the horse might make it through. Mounted, neither the horse nor the wounded man could make it.

Ben Cowan swung down and helped Recalde, who was no longer aware of his surroundings, into his own saddle. Leaving the other horse behind, he started off, leading his roan.

Slowly, the long day waned. Shadows began to gather behind the shrubs and the rocks here and there along the trail. Ahead of them there seemed to be a small range of mountains, or a ridge of rocks.

Ben Cowan thought no more of time, he thought only of coolness, of shadow, of night, of water. What remained in the canteen, the wounded man would need.

They were stupid with heat and weariness, and they did not hear the hoofbeats muffled by dust. The four riders came upon them suddenly, no less surprised than Cowan; until that moment desert growth had masked their coming.

Four Apaches...not over sixty feet away.

Ben Cowan saw them and drew. He did not think, for he was at that moment beyond thought. This was danger, and his life had been geared to danger. He drew, and the speed of his hand was his margin of safety. The gun cleared his holster and the bullet ripped into the chest of the nearest Indian.

Completely surprised, the others broke for shelter, and Ben Cowan jerked the horse behind the nearby rocks. Reaching up, he took Recalde bodily from the saddle just as a bullet cut a notch in the cantle.

He dropped Recalde and swung the muzzle of his pistol, blasting into the nearest bit of brush. Leaping away from Recalde, he crouched down behind the clustering rocks, and snapped a shot at a brown arm—and missed.

Bullets flaked rock from near his head. One man was there . . . two would be circling him, and he had no defense from behind.

Then a bullet killed the roan. The horse lunged forward and fell, and Ben Cowan swore bitterly, for that had been a good horse, perhaps the best horse he had ever owned.

Ben turned at the shot, and was in time to see the Apache duck to change positions, and this time he did not miss. The Apache stumbled and plunged to his face in the sand, and Ben Cowan put another bullet into him as he hit the ground.

Rock chips stung his face. He glanced toward Recalde. The Mexican had come out of it; feebly he was trying to get at the Colt in his waistband. Dampness stained his coat and shirt . . . he was bleeding again.

There were no more shots. The Apaches knew night was coming, and they knew he wasn't going anywhere without a horse. They could wait . . . and he shot too well.

Ben Cowan crawled to Recalde, got his left arm

under the Mexican's shoulders, and pulled him close behind the rocks. Then he clutched at slabs of rock and took them to build quickly a low, crude barricade around them. He reloaded his pistol, and got his rifle.

When darkness came the Indians might come for him; or more likely—for no Apache liked night-fighting—they would wait until daybreak and take him when he was dead for sleep. They had him, and they knew it.

Diego Recalde looked at him with pain-filled eyes. "I have killed you, señor," he said. "I ask forgiveness, I ask it in the name of God."

"Everybody dies," Ben Cowan said. "If not this way, another. But if it is forgiveness you want, you have it."

He looked up at the sky. The sun was gone. At least, he thought, death would be cool.

CHAPTER 13

H E CHECKED THE action of his rifle, wiping it carefully clean with his bandana. There were at least two Indians out there, and others might have joined them, drawn by the shooting. There could be no thought of sleep, for Recalde was in no shape to take over the guard for even a part of the night.

Cowan not only knew that the Apache does not like to fight during the hours of night, but he knew why. It is the Apache's belief that if a man is killed in darkness his soul must forever wander, homeless and alone; but the love of loot can overcome even superstition, and there might be an unbeliever among these Apaches.

Moving with infinite care, he got several stones and eased them into place among the rocks to make a better barricade. As he slipped the last stone into its notch a bullet smashed against the rock, spattering him with a hail of stinging stone fragments. Then it was quiet again.

The last light faded, stars appeared, and the face of the desert became cool. His canteen with its small bit of water was tied to his saddle, but the dying horse had fallen upon it. For all the good it could be to them, it might have been a mile away.

The long night began. Recalde awoke, and the two

men talked occasionally in whispers. Weariness lay heavily upon Ben Cowan, and he fought to keep his eyes open. He tried to moisten his cracked and bloody lips, but his tongue was like a stick in his mouth, for he had drunk little of the water, saving most of it for the wounded man. It was with an effort that he could make himself heard when he spoke.

Where was Catlow now, he wondered. Far to the south of him, no doubt, and not even aware that Ben was in Mexico.

And what would Cordelia Burton be doing now? He thought of her cool, quiet beauty, of the kind of wistful assurance that was so much a part of her. Bijah Catlow was a fool to be risking his neck in Mexico, with such a girl waiting for him back in Tucson.

Through the night Recalde's muttering became disconnected; he talked of his home, of his father and mother, of his sisters. His head twisted from side to side, and once he cried out in the night.

At last day came with a feeble grayness over the far-off Sierra Madre . . . the fainter stars vanished, and the few bright ones faded—all but one, which hung alone long after the others had gone. His eyes red-rimmed from heat, dust, and exhaustion, Ben Cowan waited for what was to come, staring around him.

Recalde was sleeping . . . well, let him sleep then. If he was lucky, he would never wake.

They came out of the gray dawning like rolling clumps of tumbleweed, so swiftly and silently that at first he thought his eyes deceived him. Their feet made scarcely a whisper in the soft sand, and they ran bent far over to offer little target.

More had come up during the night...how many were there? Six? Eight?

They had not taken a dozen strides before his six-gun shattered the silence with its long, deadly roll of unbroken sound. Slip-shooting, he emptied the gun with no break in the roar of sound, then dropped the gun and caught up his Winchester.

Two Apaches were down...another was dragging a leg, seeking shelter. Cowan dropped the Winchester muzzle on the nearest man's chest and squeezed off his shot; then he turned and fired without lifting the butt to his shoulder, and saw another spin half around.

Recalde came up on one elbow, firing.

An Apache sprang over the rock barrier and Ben Cowan struck with the rifle butt, holding the rifle shoulder high. He heard the bones in the man's face crunch, and then he whipped the rifle around and shot into another—a running Indian.

Running?

With a thunder of hoofs, a cavalry detachment swept by their little fort, guns blasting. Even as the fleeing Apache neared the brush a saber cut him down, chopping through his skull to his eyebrows, so that the soldier had to put a foot on the Apache's shoulder to wrench the blade free.

Recalde caught a rock and pulled himself erect, clinging to its top. "Señor!" he shouted. "I told you they would come! It is my soldier! My *compadres*!"

———

GENERAL JUAN BAUTISTA Armijo smiled tolerantly. "I thank you, my friend, but what you suggest is impossible. No such treasure is known to me, and even if it were, our soldiers would make theft impossible."

Ben Cowan spoke again. "Señor, I do not wish to dispute you, but I have information that two million in silver and gold are to be moved from its hiding place and transferred to Mexico City, by order of the President himself."

The General's expression was unyielding, but his eyes were not unfriendly. "I am sorry, señor. Such is not the case." He paused. "I should be most curious to know the source of such a story."

"It is a rumor, and only that." Briefly, Ben Cowan outlined the story, and coupled it with Catlow's boast and the appearance and disappearance of the Mexican soldier. Yet even as he repeated it, he realized on what a flimsy basis he had constructed his theory. He felt a little ashamed, for there could be no doubt that the basis of the story was weak.

"I am sorry, señor," Armijo repeated, "but I do thank you for your interest. I also wish to extend our thanks for saving the life of my brother-in-law."

"I do, however, have your permission to search for Señor Catlow and those with him? And to arrest them if I find them?"

The General waved his hand. "Of course! We have thieves enough of our own without wishing to keep any of yours. Take him, and welcome! If there is any way in which we can assist you, you have only to call on us."

When they were outside, Recalde shrugged a shoulder. "You see? I was sure he would not believe you, and as for the treasure—"

"He knew about the treasure."

Recalde looked at him skeptically. "Do you think so? He seemed amused by the amount. After all, *amigo,* two million dollars—it is a very great deal."

"He would have been a fool to even hint at it. After all, there are plenty of men in Mexico who would not hesitate to try to steal that much. The fewer who know the better."

"This man, this Catlow...you know him well, then?"

Cowan explained as best he could the strange relationship between himself and Catlow: never quite friends, never quite enemies; always a respect, each for the other.

Recalde listened, his pale face attentive. He nodded at last. "I see...it is, ah—delicate." He glanced at Cowan. "He may kill you, señor. He may, indeed." And then he added, "Or you may kill him."

"I have thought of it," Cowan said. And then he added, "I would like to get him out of this alive."

"It will be most difficult. If he makes the attempt to steal it—always admitting the treasure does exist—he will be killed. The General, my brother-in-law, has small liking for bandits. He is a just man, but stern."

Ben Cowan glanced at the Captain. Recalde had no business even being out of bed. It was exactly a week since they had arrived in Hermosillo, and this was the first time Recalde had been out. Even now he walked slowly, and with a cane.

Day after day and night after night Ben Cowan had searched the town, but he had found no sign of Catlow or any of his men, nor of Miller.

Where was the treasure? Where would the attempt

be made? A dozen men against an army ... Surprise would be needed, and time ... rarely could they be found together.

All the while, Ben Cowan had the uneasy feeling that he himself was being watched, and he thought back to the night someone had taken a shot at him in Tucson—had it been Miller? It might have been Rio Bray, or Old Man Merridew ... except that the Old Man would not have missed.

His mind reverted to the problem of the theft. Surprise, of course; but time ... time to get away with a treasure that could not be easily carried. Gold and silver are heavy, easily noticed, and sure to cause comment. It is easy, perhaps, to imagine gaining possession of a treasure worth millions, but it is something quite different when one actually has to move it.

When Ben Cowan had seen Recalde safely home, he strolled up the street to a cantina he had chosen to frequent, and pondered the problem over a bottle of cold beer.

How could the bandits get away? Burros or mules would be needed, and an escape route that was fool-proof. Of course there was no such thing, but Bijah Catlow would have a plan. Impulsive he might be, but he was cunning as a wolf when cunning was needed.

Ben glanced around the room. It was almost deserted, for the siesta hour was near. Soon even these few would be gone. Catlow might choose to make his strike at such a time, and it was a thought to be remembered. If he could move when most of the town, even the soldiers, were napping, he might have a chance, and it was just the sort of idea to intrigue him.

Despite the insistence of Recalde, Ben Cowan was living at the Hotel Arcadia. Recalde had relatives in the town, and it was with them that he was living and recuperating from his wounds; but Ben Cowan wanted to be in the midst of things where he could see and hear what was going on, and consider his problems without paying attention to the courtesies of a private home.

The last Mexican had now left the cantina, and the proprietor glanced hopefully at Cowan, obviously wishing he would go. Ben finished his beer, decided against suggesting that he be allowed to remain and drink another bottle, and strolled out into the sunlight.

Hermosillo, with a population of less than fifteen thousand, was a pleasant little city on the banks of the Rio Sonora, lying among orange groves and gardens. Outside the town the valley was dotted with grain fields, and all was green and lovely. Now the streets were deserted, and Cowan missed the slender, graceful girls of Sonora, noted for its beautiful women.

He loitered under the shade of the huge old trees in the Plaza, and deep within their shade he must have been invisible to the man who stepped suddenly from a narrow wooden door in a side street off the Plaza.

As the man emerged, he took a swift glance around him, then hurried up the street. His confidence that at this hour he would be unobserved made him miss seeing Ben Cowan standing under the tree only fifty yards away.

The man was Bob Keleher, who had been with Catlow on the trail drive, and who had been with him at the campfire when Catlow killed Mercer.

To attempt to follow Keleher in the empty streets would only betray Cowan's presence in Hermosillo, of which they might not be aware, and to make the man wary of exposing the hiding place chosen by Catlow.

At the building Keleher had left, the shutters were up and the door closed, but Ben Cowan, who had spent his week getting acquainted with Hermosillo, remembered the place as a leather-worker's shop. The man dealt, as Moss Burton did, in fancy bridles, saddles, hand-tooled boots, and such things, doing his work on the premises in full view of the passersby, for the shop's front was open when business was being carried on.

In one back corner there was a curtain of bridle reins hanging down from the thick cluster of bridles hung from hooks on the wall, near the ceiling. Those bridle reins made a perfect screen for whatever might lie behind. In the other corner there was a door leading to the living premises. But now the shutters were up, and aside from the door to the street, the shop front presented a blank wall to the eye.

Was Keleher only visiting in that house? Seeing a girl, perhaps? Or was this the hideout of the gang, or some of its members?

Leaving the shade of his tree, Ben walked slowly to the next street. He glanced along it and saw that except for a large carriage gate there was only a blank wall. Walking up the street, he paused opposite the carriage gate and peered through the crack where the two doors of the gate met. He looked into a paved patio where an old wooden-wheeled cart stood, its tongue resting on the ground. The building just beside the gate was obviously, judging by the smell, a stable. He could see a part of the rear of the house where the leather-worker lived, but it was only a blank wall with one second-story window that was tightly shuttered.

Walking farther on, Cowan satisfied himself that the place had only two entrances, one at the front, and the other through the carriage gate at the back.

He returned to the Plaza and sat down on a bench and smoked a cigar while he considered the situation. From where he sat he could look up the street where the shop was situated, and after a moment he turned his attention to the building across the street from it.

On the second story of that building there were windows from which the leather shop might be observed. He considered briefly the idea of renting a room there, if one was available, and then decided against it. Unless there was a back entrance, his own coming and going could be too easily observed—anyway, he was not yet sure he had discovered anything of importance.

The siesta hour was almost past when Rio Bray came into the street and entered the door by which Keleher had left. Presently people began to appear on the street . . . after a little, shutters were taken down and life resumed its normal movement. Ben Cowan lighted another cigar and loafed in the shade, idly examining a newspaper.

The shutters of the leather shop came down and business, such as it was, resumed. From where he sat Ben could see part of the shop's interior, but nobody else came or left whom he recognized.

He started to fold his newspaper, preparatory to leaving, when someone paused near him. He saw the polished boots, the obviously tailored uniform trousers, and looked up into the face of General Juan Bautista Armijo.

"She is lovely," the General commented, "is she not?"

For a moment Ben Cowan did not realize what he meant, and then he saw the girl.

She was standing, poised and assured, on the street corner near the leather shop. Where she had come from he did not know, but he could see that she was, indeed, very striking-looking.

"I expect the General has seen her closer than this; but yes, I think she is pretty." Cowan got up, and Armijo turned to smile at him.

"You are still with us, señor. We are honored. Have you located your man?"

"No, not yet."

"You still believe he is here?"

"Perhaps not here, but certainly not far away."

Armijo dropped a cigarette into the dust and rubbed it out. "There will be a ball at my regimental headquarters this evening. I have asked the Captain to bring you, señor."

When he was gone, Ben Cowan looked thoughtfully after him. Had his sudden appearance here been an accident? Or was the General having him watched?

Did General Armijo, perhaps, know of what was going on at the leather shop?

There was room enough in that stable for a dozen horses to be hidden.

The girl on the corner had turned suddenly and was coming toward him.

CHAPTER 14

I N THE SHADOWED coolness of the living quarters behind the leather shop, Bijah Catlow made his final plans. The door that led to the cellar where he and his men waited opened from behind the curtain of bridles, as Ben Cowan had half suspected.

There was a hallway of stone . . . the remainder of the house was of adobe, and of later construction. A stone stairway went down into the vast, ancient cellar. Here there were no windows, for the ceiling of the cellar was six feet below ground level, and as a matter of fact, its existence was unknown to the people of Hermosillo.

The builder of the adobe, itself one of the earliest buildings in the town, had utilized what remained of the ruin on this site. It was only after the house was built, when making excavations for repairs, that he had found the vast underground room. Being a wise man, and a discreet one, he had mentioned the find to no one, and he and his sons had finished the work by themselves.

The origin of the ruin was a mystery. This might have been the site of some planned mission, where construction had ceased because of Apache attacks . . . records of many such had vanished from the country with the Jesuits. Or it might have been still older . . .

perhaps an Indian ruin reaching back in time even before the Aztecs.

The owner of the leather shop had himself been a bandit, as his father had been before him, and from time to time, through revolution and change, they had found use for the ancient cellar.

There was an exit, a secret way that opened into the stables...this had been built by the present owner's grandfather on the principle that not even a rat trusts himself to one hole only. In the planning of the present robbery, Pesquiera, the owner of the leather shop, had shared his secret with Bijah Catlow. But now they were of two minds. Pesquiera wanted the gold brought into his cellar and held there until the chase had died down. Bijah Catlow wanted it spirited out of the country quickly. As a matter of fact, Bijah did not entirely trust his Mexican partner nor his nephew, the deserter who had come to him in Tucson.

Pesquiera had known of the treasure for years, but had known only approximately where it was hidden; and Lerdo was shrewd enough to see that living nearby to guard it were loyal members of a family distantly related to his own. There had been no chance until now, when the treasure would be moved, to lay hands upon it.

Bijah had an idea that, once that treasure was hidden in the secret cellar, some accident would happen to destroy his men and himself, or a trap would be laid for them. He preferred to trust himself to the open desert and the risks of flight, no matter how great they might be.

He sat alone now at a table, and stared at the glass

of beer before him, but he was not thinking of the beer. He was thinking of what lay before him.

In a corner, some thirty feet away, several of the men played at cards. In a nearby room, others were asleep. He had been careful to allow none of them to be seen around town, and the men he had on watch at a particular point changed watches only during the time of siesta.

Two things disturbed him. One of these was what he had learned of the character of General Armijo. He was no lackadaisical officeholder, but a competent and experienced soldier and a man of the desert. He had behind him twenty years of war in the field. He had fought in revolutions in his own country, against the French, and against the Apaches. Armijo had only recently been transferred to Sonora, but he knew the country. Bijah Catlow had not reckoned on Armijo.

The other factor that worried him was the whereabouts of Ben Cowan. Bijah had neither seen nor heard of him since that night in Tucson, but he was all the more worried because of that.

He rubbed the stubble on his broad jaw and swore softly. The other men were restless, and he did not blame them, sitting for days in a dark cellar, unable to show their faces on the street of a town known for its beautiful women. And when they did emerge it would only be to make a quick strike and escape.

For a moment he stared gloomily about the room. Catlow was nothing if not a perceptive man, and it came to him suddenly that he had taken a direction that might keep him among such associates, and in such surroundings for the remainder of his years. He might spend his life hiding in abandoned ranch houses, cheap hotel rooms, on the dodge, never sure from one minute to the next when the law might come up to him. He glanced at the table across the room... there was only one man in the lot whom he really liked—Old Man Merridew.

He gulped a swallow of beer and thought again of the two million... with his share of that, a man could live anywhere, do just about anything.

Yet the gloomy thoughts remained with him, brought on in part by the surroundings, the dark and ancient cellar, the foul air, and by the boredom of waiting.

Because he did not trust Pesquiera, he had stalled on making a decision as to where the treasure would be taken. The risks of trying to get it into the cellar were great... if the pack train was seen in the street, that would be an end to it. The plan now called for a midnight strike, for they had learned when the treasure was to reach the town, but Catlow had worked out an alternative plan of which he had said nothing to anyone.

The close confinement was having its effect upon him, too. Even less than the others was he fitted to put up with the restricted quarters, for Bijah Catlow was a man who liked people. He liked gaiety and friendliness, he liked bright lights and music, cheerful talk, and the casual argument and rawhiding that went with any cattle drive or roundup. Yet he must wait in hiding now. He settled down to considering his plans, but his mind kept drifting off at a tangent.

Christina had promised to buy a box of cigars for him, and she should be coming back soon. He got up and wandered over to the poker game, watched gloomily for a few minutes, and then went to the steps.

Bill Joiner looked after him and spoke irritably. "We don't get a chance to move one step out of here, but he goes whenever he's of a mind to."

Rio Bray, too, had been staring after Catlow, but he merely shrugged. "Somebody has to keep in touch, and this is his strike. He laid it out, he brought us in."

Joiner was a border outlaw; some said he had been a scalp hunter. He was a tall, thin man with a mean expression that never left his eyes, even when he smiled, which was rarely enough. Jealousy was a major part of his make-up—that, and distrust.

Catlow had accepted him reluctantly, and he had done so because he was a dead shot with any sort of weapon, could ride all day and all night, and was a man of known courage.

Catlow went up the steps and, avoiding the narrow passage that led to the shop, opened a concealed door and emerged into the living quarters of the family.

Christina was in the kitchen, putting dishes on a tray. She was slender for a Mexican girl, as the Sonora women are apt to be, and her carriage and figure were excellent. He glanced at her with admiration, and she gave him a sidelong glance from her dark, almost almond-shaped eyes.

"You should not be here. My father does not like it."

"Then I wouldn't see you," he said, "and I'd risk trouble with your pa any time for that." He watched her as she put the large bowl of frijoles on the tray, with the tortillas and some large slabs of roast pork.

"You get my cigars?"

"*Si*"—she indicated the box on a side table—"I get them." She paused, then added, "I saw an Americano... a gringo in the Plaza."

Catlow was watching the movements of her body as she worked about the room, and scarcely heard her.

"He was a stranger," she added.

"Who was?"

"The gringo. He looked at me." She glanced at Catlow to see the effect of her words.

"Be a damn' fool if he didn't. A gringo, you say? Maybe a tall man? A quiet-lookin' man? Only smiles with his eyes?"

She shrugged. "He is ver' handsome, this *hombre*. He wears a black suit and talks with the General Armijo. I heard the General invite him to the ball."

"Ball?"

"Oh, *si!* Everybody talk about it. I think everybody will be there...all the officers, the—how you say it?—the important ones...the reech ones."

Catlow considered. According to his information, the treasure was due to arrive in Hermosillo tomorrow. At this moment it was guarded by several hundred soldiers, and any attempt to seize it would be suicidal. He had planned his move to take place at midnight following the arrival in Hermosillo, when the guard was going off duty, eager to get to bed and letting down after the long march and the necessity for keeping watch.

They would be tired and sleepy, and thinking of anything but the treasure they had guarded. It worried him that Armijo was now in charge, for the officer scheduled to be in command had been easygoing and anything but efficient.

Suppose, however, that the treasure train arrived *tonight*?

He had men watching for the train, and he knew about how fast such a pack train could move; but suppose there was added reason to reach Hermosillo tonight?

He glanced at Christina and said, "Do you know the officer in charge of the train?"

"Of course. There are three."

"Old men?"

"*Old*? Very young! And very handsome, too, they are." She gestured toward the tray. "Do you wish to take this? I cannot."

"Sure." He picked up the tray, and then said, "You know about such things—are any of those men in love?"

She laughed. "Mexican men are always in love. When they are not in love with a particular girl they are in love with love. Why not? It is the way for a man to be."

"I won't argue with you. But one of these officers, one of them who is really excited about a girl... Maybe she has not shown him much favor—or maybe she has, and he wants to get back to her in a hurry."

"Rafael Vargas," she said, tossing her head, "he can think of no one but Señorita Calderon... and she—he does not know what she thinks."

Catlow grinned. "Honey," he said, "you get me a

box of the finest stationery you can find! Do you hear?" He placed several silver pesos on the table. "You do that, and I'll—"

The door opened suddenly, and Pesquiera stood there, his features dark with anger.

CHAPTER 15

PESQUIERA'S RIGHT HAND gripped a pistol. "You!" he said to Bijah. "Get out of here! You are not to speak to my daughter, do you understand?"

Catlow smiled. "This is business," he said, "something only she can do. I need some writing paper, the kind a woman would buy, and there was no time to waste. She must go for it now."

Pesquiera's gun did not waver. "Why is this? What do you plan?"

"It is a change in plans if it works, and I think it will work. The robbery tonight instead of tomorrow night."

Slowly the gun lowered. "Tonight?" Pesquiera said stupidly. "But it will not arrive tonight! And there are many soldiers!"

Catlow turned to Christina. "Get that stationery, will you? Get it now!"

When she was gone, Catlow sat down. "I'm sorry you got riled," he said, "but we have to move fast." Briefly, he explained about the man he believed might be Ben Cowan, and his meeting with Armijo. "If that young captain gets this note," he said, "he will come a-running. He will want to meet her at the dance, and the dance is tonight. He'll run the legs off those mules gettin' here . . . and there'll be no guard waitin' to take over."

Pesquiera's expression changed. "You are right, and I am a fool."

"Look"—Catlow leaned toward him confidentially—"not only will there be no guard, but Vargas will be hurryin' to get ready for that dance. He'll be late, anyway . . . everything will be in a mess."

———

BEN COWAN RETURNED to his room in the Arcadia to change his clothes for the ball. He was combing his hair in front of the mirror, thinking about the evening ahead of him. Only once before had he been to such a ball as he expected this to be, and that had been at the Governor's mansion in Austin.

He sat down on the bed and polished his boots as best he could, then swung his cartridge belt around his waist and drew it several notches tighter than he usually wore it, so it would ride higher.

As he was holstering his six-gun Recalde entered. "You are not carrying a gun *tonight?*" he said, amused. "At the General's ball there will scarcely be use for it."

"I wouldn't feel at home without it. And a man never knows what'll happen."

Recalde sat down, easing his wounded leg out before him. He leaned his cane against the side of the chair. "After all, *amigo,* the pack train does not even arrive until tomorrow."

Ben Cowan slid into his black coat and Recalde watched him, smiling. "I can see you will make hearts flutter tonight," the Mexican said. "You have no idea how much interest you have created in Hermosillo.

After all, it is a small town, and we have few strangers here—fewer still who are friends of the General."

"Of yours, you mean."

"Of the General's also. You would be surprised, but he has spoken of you several times. He even asked me to speak to you about joining him in the army. You would be an officer, and the General is close to the President. It might mean a very quick success for you."

"I'm not cut out for a soldier," Cowan replied. "I'm too damned independent. I like to go my own way, figure things out for myself. I think the General has plenty of savvy, and I'd not mind serving with *him* . . . but it might be I'd be serving with some armchair soldier. No, I'm better off as I am."

"He will regret your decision." Recalde used his cane to rise. "Let us go."

A carriage awaited them. Ben Cowan felt odd, riding in the open carriage, but he saw several like it, all polished and bright, hurrying toward the huge old building where the ball was to be held. It was not often such a thing happened in a provincial town like Hermosillo, and the señoritas were in from all the haciendas for miles around.

As their carriage took its turn around the Plaza, which all the carriages seemed to be doing, Ben Cowan glanced up the dark street where the leather shop stood. All was dark and still.

The night was cool after the heat of the day, and it was pleasant riding about the Plaza behind the driver who sat on a high seat in front of them. People bowed and smiled, speaking to Recalde, and glancing curiously at him.

Young Captain Recalde was not only an unusually handsome man, but he had wealth and tradition behind him. Ben Cowan could guess that not a few of those at the ball tonight were going to be looking hopefully in his direction. For young men of family, from the capital, rarely had occasion to visit Hermosillo.

"Vargas will not like to miss this," Recalde commented; "he fancies himself in love. I happen to know he has been writing notes and smuggling them secretly to Rosita Calderon—only it is the worst-kept secret in town."

Ben Cowan smiled in the darkness. It was much the same on both sides of the border. A man would make an unholy fool of himself over a pretty girl—but that was the privilege of any young man, and they all had to do it once or twice.

"He's the man in command?"

"Yes...and a good soldier, but impatient."

They drove at last to the ball, and Ben Cowan decided it was worth it. He had never seen so many really beautiful women...dark, flashing eyes that glanced at him from behind their fans...here and there a redhead or even a blonde among all those with dark hair.

Recalde was looking romantically pale from his recent wounds, and he was very smart in his uniform aglitter with braid and decorations.

Ben sat down beside him and they talked as the people entered and moved about the room. Recalde kept up a running comment. "Now that one"—he indicated with an inclination of his head a tall young girl with large, melting dark eyes—"her father has more cattle on his ranch than there is in your whole state of New Mexico... right at this time, at least. But she is too—shall we say—intelligent. She has nothing to do on that ranch, so she reads... she thinks, also. It is dangerous in a woman."

Ben Cowan glanced at her again. She was not exactly beautiful, but she was very striking. Later, when he danced with her, she said, "You are the friend of Captain Recalde? He is handsome, your friend, but he believes every girl wishes to marry him." She laughed suddenly, with genuine amusement, and looked at Ben, her eyes smiling. "And you know? He is right. They all wish it."

"You too?"

"I scarcely know him, but I do not think he will want a wife like me." She gave Ben a direct, friendly glance that he liked. "I ride the range with my father, you know... sometimes without him. It is not considered the thing to do.

"And I read books. Most young men wish their wives to be beautiful, but complacent—and not too bright, I am afraid."

"I think Recalde should have a wife such as you," Ben said. "I know he wishes for a career in government, and an intelligent wife could help him."

"It is an American viewpoint."

He glanced at her, suddenly embarrassed. "You know, I did not get your name."

"I am Rosita Calderon."

He was startled. This was the girl with whom Captain Vargas was in love—or with whom he fancied himself in love. Suddenly, the thought of Vargas worried him. Did Vargas know about this ball? If so, he must be frustrated at not being present...surely, he would know that Rosita Calderon would be here.

By this time he would not be too many miles from Hermosillo....

"Excuse me," he said suddenly, brusquely, "I must go."

He was almost running when he reached the head of the steps. Recalde called out to him, but he did not stop.

He plunged down the steps and out into the street. The long row of waiting carriages stood on the far side under the trees, and several of the drivers were together in a group, talking. They looked around at him, surprised at his sudden appearance. There was no one else in sight.

Swiftly, he ran to the corner and looked down the street toward the barracks and the courtyard. A sentry stood on guard at the entrance. Ben went toward him.

He spoke quickly in Spanish. "Have you seen the—"

He heard the light, quick step behind him and started to turn. Something crashed down hard across his skull and he slumped forward, fighting to keep on his feet. He fell against the side of the building and tried to turn, but another blow felled him into the street.

He smelled the dust...and there was blood, too. His blood.

A hand grasped his collar and he was dragged around the corner. Somebody was swearing.

A voice said: "Who is it?"

"That damn' marshal friend of Catlow's."

"To hell with him."

There was a momentary silence. Then someone said, "With Catlow, too."

Another silence, and then the first voice spoke again. "Everything in its time, my friend. But we understand each other, no?"

Ben heard, but he could not act. He could not even think. He had no will to act, to think, even to try to move. He simply lay still, and then after a while he was conscious of nothing at all ... nothing.

DIEGO RECALDE STOOD up with an effort. After sitting, his leg became stiff, and it was difficult to handle himself with ease. His doctor had told him emphatically that he must not come out tonight, but Diego Recalde had already been planning which of his dress uniforms he would wear.

Now he glanced toward the door. Ben had left suddenly at least a half hour ago, and he had not come back. It was not like him to do such a thing.

Limping, Recalde crossed the room to Rosita Calderon. She turned to meet him, smiling a little. "You have waited a long time to speak to me, Diego," she said. "Are you still frightened of me?"

"Who is frightened?" She was lovely, he admitted, and there was a frankness about her that he liked. Came from riding around like a boy, or maybe from that American cousin she had—a cousin by marriage, at least. What was his name? Sackett, or something like that. Lived in New Mexico.

"What did you say to my friend? To Benito? He left here as if you had insulted him."

"Do women insult men? I think not until they know them better than I know him. No, he just left suddenly—and rudely."

"You said nothing to him?"

She frowned. "Nothing...unless he does not like my name. When we were introduced he did not hear it, I suppose, and he asked me what it was. I told him, and he ran away."

"I cannot ask you to dance," Recalde said then. "You see I was—"

"I know, and I am sorry."

He frowned, worrying over Ben Cowan's sudden departure.

"You told him your *name*, you say? That would scarcely have meant anything to him. Why, I mentioned you this evening, and he did not seem to have ever heard the name."

Still puzzled, he glanced across the room to where General Armijo was talking casually with a white-haired man, Don Francisco Vargas.

"Vargas!"

He wheeled suddenly, forgetting his leg, and fell flat upon his face as it gave way under him.

"General!" he shouted. *"The pack train!"*

CHAPTER 16

BIJAH CATLOW'S NOTE, written by Christina and signed with the name of Rosita Calderon, reached Rafael Vargas as swiftly as a rider could take it, and Vargas reacted as Catlow had expected.

Excited at the prospect of seeing the girl who had seemed uninterested until now, and of dancing with her, Vargas had driven the pack train at a fast pace over trails where normally they would have plodded. Surely, General Armijo would be pleased to have him arrive sooner than expected.

Up and down the column Vargas rode, urging the muleteers to greater speed. Impatient at the slowness of the exhausted mules, he wished to ride on, leaving the train to follow, but he was wise enough to realize the General would not be pleased at that.

When finally they arrived in Hermosillo the streets were dark and silent. The soldiers, who had been kept alert for a time by their swift ride, now felt its effects, and weariness came over them; they thought of nothing but their barracks, a hot meal, and bed. Sagging in the saddle, half asleep, they rode into the courtyard, and Vargas swung from the saddle, turning to his second in command.

"Lieutenant," he said to Fernandes, "see to the unloading and storage of the cargo, then bring the keys to me. I want a guard posted at once, subject to removal only on orders from General Armijo."

He turned swiftly, and a man stepped from the darkness of a doorway. A gun in the hands of Rio Bray shocked him into his first realization that he had walked into a trap.

Rosita Calderon was forgotten; the distant strains of dance music seemed to come from another world. The courtyard was silent and dark, but he could see clearly enough to make out that his men were being disarmed and backed to the wall.

Everything moved swiftly. The mules were turned toward the gate, the disarmed soldiers marched to the guardhouse.

Captain Rafael Vargas was a brave man. He was also a sensible one—up to a point. With a shock of cold realization, he knew the note for what it was—a trick. Rosita Calderon had not changed, and he had been betrayed. Mexico was about to be robbed.

Somebody stepped up behind him and a hand unsnapped the flap of his holster. Vargas whipped around like a cat, knocking away the grasping hand, and drew his pistol.

A blow staggered him, and then a gun muzzle was thrust under his heart. Something exploded there, and Vargas turned, squeezing off a wild, futile shot that lost itself in the earth at his feet, and then he fell.

Bijah Catlow rushed up, the taste of anger bitter in his mouth. He stared down at the dead man. It was bad—he had hoped to kill no one.

"Get going!" he said to Bray. "There's no time!"

Catlow had no idea that riding the saddle of a captured horse was the one man he did not want anywhere around...Ben Cowan.

Ben Cowan was unconscious. He had fought against the wave of darkness creeping over him, but had lost the fight. Tied now in the saddle, his body bobbed with the movement of the horse. Pesquiera had wanted to knife him, but Rio Bray had ruled against it. "You don't know Catlow," he said. "I'd never want to be the man who killed Ben Cowan."

As the men moved up the dark street, Pesquiera rode in beside Catlow. "The cellar!" he said, sharply.

"No."

"They will never find us there!"

"If they don't find us on the trails they will go through this town like it has never been gone through before. They would find us—and the gold."

But Catlow was not altogether sure of that. He was sure, though, that once that gold got into Pesquiera's secret cellar, it would never get out. He was equally sure that the Mexican had no intention for it ever to get away from Hermosillo.

Nor for them to get away, for that matter. A little poison in their food—and they would have nowhere else to get food—and it would be an end to them. That ancient cellar could conceal bodies as well as gold, as no doubt it had.

Pesquiera gripped his gun butt. "It must be the cellar," he declared, "or—"

Catlow smiled, and Pesquiera did not like what he saw in that smile. "You go ahead, *amigo,*" Catlow said. "You draw that gun."

Pesquiera hesitated, and the moment was past.

"You may be right," he said; "but your friend—it would be wise to leave him here, no?"

It was the first that Bijah Catlow had known of Cowan's presence. There was no more time to be wasted, and Bijah did not want Ben Cowan along. "All right," he said, "leave him here."

BY THE TIME Recalde had explained to General Armijo what he believed was happening, the pack train was leaving the outskirts of Hermosillo.

The first wild rush of cavalry went out the trail toward the border, assuming that Catlow, being an American, would lead his men that way. And they found nothing. Other detachments scattered in several directions, all of them wrong.

Bijah Catlow, with characteristic cunning, had led his pack train down back streets, where they made no sound in the soft dust. Turning from a trail, he took them through an orchard, then opened the gate on the irrigation ditch just enough so it might appear to be an accident but would successfully flood the orchard, wiping out all tracks.

Through country lanes, past orchards and wheatfields, Catlow led his mule train, the animals staggering from weariness. Twice he paused to open corral gates and allow animals to get out that would destroy the trail they had left. Finally, with the mules more dead than alive, he herded them into a pole corral on the edge of a small arroyo. Nearby was a dam. The ranch itself was deserted, and apparently had been for some time.

In another, larger corral, among the trees on the far

side of a low butte, fresh mules awaited him. Swiftly exchanging packsaddles and loads, Catlow led the train off toward the northwest. He had told no one his plans, nor did he intend to.

On the skyline, more than a dozen miles away toward the northwest, was the Cerro Cuevas, a low mountain range that stood out above the comparatively level plain. The trail toward it was a long-unused one. When they came close to the mountains, a Mexican was waiting by the trail to guide them into the caves.

It was midday when they unsaddled inside the caves. Old Man Merridew climbed up among the rocks and settled down to watch. The rest ate, slept, and waited for Catlow to tell them what he planned. But Catlow said nothing.

He had two million dollars in gold and silver and, aside from the Old Man, there was not a one among them he could trust.

If he was unlucky, the mules would be found at the abandoned ranch before the day was out. If he was lucky, they might remain there for several days before some searcher happened upon them. The route he was taking was the least likely of any that could be found. Just as he had done when slipping into Mexico, now in slipping out he intended to use the least-known route and the least-known water holes. But if the men with him had any idea of what they faced he would have mutiny on his hands.

It was a hot, still day. After a while the Tarahumara went up to relieve the Old Man.

Merridew came and squatted near Catlow. "Nothin'

stirrin'," he commented. "Seemed a sight of dust over east, but that might have been anything."

"How'd Cowan happen to stumble on us?" Catlow asked.

The Old Man shrugged. "Durned if I know. Pesky was takin' over the sentry's job so's everythin' would look all right. He says Cowan came up there in a rush and started to ask a question. Rio Bray slugged him."

"Cowan's too smart."

"Well," Merridew replied dryly, "if they got him locked in that there cellar, he'll keep for a time. Lucky if he ever gets out, if that Christina takes after her pa."

Catlow looked from the mouth of the cave toward the north. "Didn't you tell me you'd been down to the Rio Concepcion one time?"

Merridew shot him a startled glance. "Look here, you ain't figurin' on *that* route, are you? There's no water—or so damn' little it don't matter."

"All the more reason. They won't be lookin' for us there, Old Man. Look,"—squatting, he drew a rough diagram in the sand—"there's the border . . . over here is the Gulf of California. The main trail from Hermosillo to Tucson is yonder. Here's where we are. And here"—he indicated a spot on the sand—"is Pozo Arivaipa—'*pozo*' meaning well."

The Old Man looked up. "How far is it between here and that *pozo* you speak of?"

Catlow lowered his voice to a whisper. "Maybe sixty miles—as the crow flies."

"*Sixty miles?* Without water? With mules?"

Catlow lifted a hand. "See here? Right there is the Rio Bacoachi. It's about sixteen miles out. Now, it ain't a reg'lar river. In fact, it flows only part of the time—we might have to dig for water there. But we've had a wet spring...I think it's a good chance."

"You goin' to tell them?"

"No—not until I have to."

Merridew squinted his eyes at the desert. "You're shapin' for trouble, Bijah. I tell you, this lot won't stand for it—not Pesky, nor Rio either, for that matter."

"Rio's been with me as long as you have."

"There's a difference. I'm a *segundo*. I never aimed or figured to be owner or foreman. Rio, he figures he's smarter than you. He goes along, but it chafes him. It really chafes him. Here lately it's been worse, so don't you put faith in Rio Bray."

"What about the others?"

"I'd say Keleher—you can count on him. And the Injun. That Injun likes you, and I don't think he cottons to any of the rest of us. If trouble breaks, it might split fifty-fifty, and it might not break so good for us."

Catlow nodded. "That's about the way I figured, Old Man; but we need them, and once we get far enough into that godforsaken desert, they're going to need me—like it or not."

When the sun went down they moved out, Bijah leading off. He started at a good clip deliberately, to keep them so busy there was no time to ask questions. He pulled his hat low over his eyes and looked north into the desert. He knew what he was going into, and what was likely to happen before he got out—if he ever did.

The last man off the mountain reported no sign of pursuit, and from where he had been watching he could see for miles, with the setting sun making the land bright.

On top of a low rise, Catlow drew up to let the mule train bunch a little and to look over the country. Old Man Merridew had not asked the question Bijah had been fearing; and fortunately, the Tarahumara did not talk. The desert, the lack of water, and the heat . . . they were bad enough, but the country into which they were riding was the land of the Seri Indians.

Usually, the Seris held to the coast except when raiding, or to their stronghold on Tiburon Island, in the Gulf of California. Fierce as the Apaches—Catlow had heard rumors they were cannibals—they had devastated large areas of country, and he was leading the mule train right into the region where they traveled to and from their raids.

But he was gambling on avoiding them, or even defeating them; and as for water, there had been heavy spring rains. Though now it was nearly July, from late July through August and September there were occasional heavy rains in Sonora—rains that fell suddenly upon relatively small areas, then vanished to leave it hotter than before. But for a time they left water in the water holes.

Anyway, there was no other way to get out of Mexico with two million dollars in gold and silver.

Again they pushed on steadily through the warm night.

Two hours passed before the inevitable question was asked, and it was Rio who asked it. "Is there plenty of water where we're going to camp?"

"We're not going to camp. Not until nearly morning, at least."

"Hell, Bijah, everybody's about done in."

"By now," Catlow replied shortly, "Armijo has cavalry scouring the country. Maybe he's found the mules we left behind, maybe not. An' you know how far we've got to go? Maybe two hundred miles."

"We got to rest," Rio said stubbornly.

"You'll rest," Catlow replied, "when we get where we're goin'—not before."

It was rough, broken country. They rode down into arroyos, crossed long stretches of hard-topped mesa, waded through ankle-deep sand. Day was just breaking when they looked down upon a maze of arroyos, the broken watercourses of the Bacoachi... and there was no water in sight.

"Where's the water?" Rio demanded. "I thought there was water."

"Get the shovels," Catlow said.

"*Shovels?*" Rio swore. "I'll be damned if I'll—"

"Give me one of them," Keleher said quietly. "Come on, Old Man. You could always find water."

They found it two feet beneath the surface, and it welled up in quantity wherever they dug. The mules watered; Rio Bray was silent and sullen.

"Fill your canteens and all the kegs," Catlow told them. "It will be forty, fifty miles to the next water."

Nobody said a word—they simply stared at him. Bob Keleher gathered up the shovels and lashed them in place on the pack mules. Now he knew why Bijah had been insistent on loading four mules with two water kegs each.

Loafing and resting in the shadows of the river

bank, Catlow thought ahead. This was going to be the toughest job he'd ever tackled . . . and he figured that by now they had found his trail—or the mules, at least.

They would be coming after him, but he was not worried about their catching him—not that, so much as their heading him off. Would they think of that? Would they leave his trail, gambling on riding ahead along trails where there was plenty of water and where they could travel much faster than he, and then heading him off before he could reach the border?

Or would they think that perhaps he had a boat waiting somewhere along the Gulf coast, ready to pick him up and carry him out of their reach?

Catlow tasted the brackish water and looked at the mules. There were no better mules in the country, and he had prepared them for this. Despite the fast pace, they were in good shape.

Some miles away to the west lay a dark blue range of mountains. There were low hills between, but it was the mountains that were important—more important at that moment than Bijah Catlow knew.

High on a serrated ridge a lone Seri huddled against a pinnacle of rock and looked out toward the east. His sharp eyes picked out a faint thread of smoke . . . a beckoning finger lifting a mute question toward the sky.

The Seri ground some seed between his broken molars, and squinted into the distance. Smoke meant men, men meant horses, and horses were meat. . . . He was hungry for meat.

The hard black eyes watched that finger of smoke and considered. It might be the Army; but the Army rarely came into this land, and then only after some raid by the Seris into settled land—and there had been no such raid.

Rising, he looked eastward once more; then he turned and began to slide down off the rocks. He was several miles from his camp, but he was in no hurry. He knew the country that lay before those marching men.

It would not be hard tomorrow, but the next day it would be easier ... much easier.

CHAPTER 17

BEN COWAN'S FIRST conscious awareness was of a musty odor. He lay for what seemed a long time and could sense only that, and a dull throbbing in his skull. Then he opened his eyes, or he thought he opened them—but it remained dark. He could hear nothing—no sound, no sense of movement anywhere.

He was lying sprawled on a stone floor. . . . And then full awareness returned, and with it full realization. He had rushed from the ballroom to the barrack courtyard, and he had started to ask a question of the sentry. It was at that moment that he had been struck down from behind.

Now he got his palms flat on the floor and pushed himself to a sitting position. His hand went to his holster. His gun was gone.

Feeling for the .44 derringer he habitually carried in his waistband, he found that was gone, too. Of course it would be. Catlow knew of that gun.

Ben stared into the darkness around him. He was in absolute blackness. He put out a hand, but touched nothing. On hands and knees he began to crawl, and brought up against something—a chair leg. He felt the chair and stood up, holding to the back. His head swam, and he clung shakily to the chair back until the confusion in his skull settled down.

There was no smallest ray of light to allow him to see anything. He must be in some sort of an underground place—a dungeon perhaps.

He felt in his pockets for matches and found none...they had been taken from him, too.

If there was a chair, then people sometimes sat here, hence there might be a table. Carefully, he felt around him, but found nothing. Finally, using the chair, he moved about, keeping it with him. If necessary it could be a weapon, or he might break off a chair leg.

Suddenly he paused. He had a faint but distinct impression of heat. Keeping one hand on the chair, he knelt and slowly crawled around it. He was almost all the way around the chair when he felt the heat quite distinctly on his cheek. Moving in that direction, he discovered a hearth and a fireplace.

It was cool down here, but not cool enough to need a fire. Someone must have been cooking, or perhaps making coffee, and there was still warmth there. Feeling around the edge of the fireplace, he found the end of an unburned stick, and he picked it up carefully. Then he moved his hand until he located the place of greatest warmth. Here he poked at the coals with the stick, uncovering some that glowed faintly red. He placed the stick upon them and blew, ever so gently. There was a smell of smoke, but nothing more.

Pulling out his shirttail, he tore a small piece from it and edged it against the coals. There was more smoke, and then a little flame. He saw the ends of more sticks and pushed them into the fire. The flames leaped up, and then he saw a coffeepot on the hearth and several cups at the edge. He rinsed a cup with a little coffee, then filled it and drank.

The coffee was very strong, but it was hot, and after a few gulps he felt better. He found more pieces of wood for fuel and added them to the fire. Then he stood up and looked around.

As well as he could tell, he was in a large, low-roofed room with stone walls and ceiling. No doors were visible, and no windows. There was a table, and several more chairs. On the floor were stubs of cigarettes and cigars, quite a lot of them.

There were also some empty beer bottles. He picked up one of these, hefted it, and placed it close at hand in the shadow. Then he placed others at various points about the room.

In so doing he found the door, but the latch would not give and the door itself was flat with the wall. It was strongly made of heavy oak planks, and he thought it must be reinforced on the other side with iron bars.

Carefully, he paced the room, studying the walls, the ceiling, the floor. He found nothing that offered any chance of escape.

And yet . . . there was something. . . .

The room was musty, as a place long closed might be, or one poorly ventilated. But he had smelled something else, some distance from the fire.

The room was all of sixty feet long and more than half that in width, and he tried pacing back and forth again, pausing at intervals. He had moved several feet before he again detected the faint odor. He hesitated there, then walked slowly back, testing the air.

Nothing. . . .

Or...? He waited, breathing naturally, and suddenly it came to him. The faintest of odors, and yet it was definitely there. What he smelled was a stable—a horse stable.

He went back to the fire and added fuel from a pile nearby, and then, taking a blazing brand, he walked back and held it up toward the ceiling, which was only two feet or so above his head. There, beyond any doubt, was a trapdoor.

Returning his brand to the fire, he was about to make an attempt on the door when he heard the rattle of a bar being removed, and then the outer door opened. Standing in the door, holding a candle in one hand and a pistol in the other, was the girl he had seen from the park when he was talking to the General.

There was no mistaking the menace of the pistol.

"You don't need that," he said quietly. "I am not given to attacking women."

"Try it, if you like," she replied carelessly. "Shooting you might settle a lot of problems."

"The General was very attracted to you. If I were you, I'd develop his acquaintance."

The black eyes stared into his disdainfully. With a gesture, she indicated the doorway. "There is food... get it."

He looked at the food, which was on a tray standing just outside the door. It was an invitation to escape, and yet... he had a sudden realization that she wanted an excuse to kill him. But why?

"I am not hungry."

An odd light seemed to blaze in her eyes, but it might have been his imagination—or some effect of the candlelight.

He looked at her curiously. "You are lovely," he said, "just the sort Bijah might prefer."

"And not you?"

"No...not me." He was watching her closely. Now he turned his back on the door and walked over to the fire. "Will you have some coffee? It's strong, but good."

"No."

She reminded him of a puma or a leopard. She moved in the same way, and there was an odd sense of expectancy about her, as if she awaited some signal from within herself that would tell her it was time to kill.

"Do you think you will ever see Bijah again? Women like Bijah," he added. "I envy him his way with them...he never seems to be anything but at ease, sure of himself."

"And you are not?"

"With women? Never." He added a stick to the fire. "I guess I never saw enough of them for the new to wear off. Or maybe I am simply sort of green."

The pistol muzzle was a black mouth that watched him. She would be a good shot, he decided; instinct and hatred would point that pistol, and nothing was more deadly.

It was women like this one who made fools of the schools of marksmanship. The way to fire a pistol was to draw and point as one pointed a finger. In many cases, the more time taken, the more apt one was to miss. How many times had he known of women, and sometimes men, who had never fired a gun before but who picked one up and scored with the first shot? But this was only in anger or fear. In practice on a target range they probably could hit nothing.

"Is he your father? The man who owns the leather shop?"

"He was my mother's husband, not my father." Her eyes seemed to flicker. "She was too weak for him, too soft."

"And you?"

She laughed suddenly. "I am too hard for him. He listens to Bijah, and would let you live. I shall not. I shall kill you."

She turned suddenly and went up the steps, but she turned at the door and pushed the tray with her foot. It slid to the top step, spilling some beans in the process. She closed the door abruptly, and he heard the bar fall in place.

He glanced toward the tray, then hesitated, and after a while took only the tortillas from it. If she planned to poison him it would be in the more highly seasoned food . . . he hoped.

Sitting by the fire, he ate the tortillas and drank more coffee. Then he took the sturdiest chair—all of them were solidly built—and carried it over under the trapdoor. Standing on the chair, he tried pushing up on the door. But it did not give.

He braced himself well and pushed upward again, with all his strength. He thought he detected just the faintest give. He tried again. Something was piled on top of the door, he decided, something heavy.

Then he brought the table over under the door and got up on it. Being closer to the door now, he could exert more pressure. He tried again, and this time the give was more decided.

He got down then and put the chair on top of the table, and by getting up on the chair he could put his back and shoulder against the door. He heaved, and something up there moved, and the door opened several inches on one side. He heaved again, something rolled off the door, and the door was freed. He pushed it open.

Grain sacks...grain sacks filled probably with corn had been placed over the door to conceal it. Ben straightened up, put his hands on the granary floor, and lifted himself up.

At the moment his heels cleared the opening he heard the rattle of the bar, a muffled cry, and then a shot. Something struck his boot heel and he jerked back from the door and slammed it in place. A swift heave put a grain sack on top of it.

He looked about him quickly. There were horses in the barn, and he was going to need a horse.

How she got there so fast, he never knew, but suddenly, as he hesitated over whether to take a horse or just to go without one, the girl appeared.

Christina's face was white, her eyes deep black, and her breast was heaving with emotion and the running she had done. She lifted the pistol and he felt the heat of its blast as he dove, hitting her with his shoulder and knocking her backwards into the hay.

She fought like a wildcat, writhing away from him, clubbing at him with the gun barrel, and trying to bring the muzzle down on him.

He grasped the gun around the action, gripping the cylinder and forcing her hand back. She tried to sink her teeth into his hand, but he wrenched the gun free and threw it from them.

Twisting, she clawed at his eyes with both hands, raking his face with her nails. He caught her wrists and pinned them down. He had never hit a woman, and did not want to do it now, but this was no ordinary woman; she was an animal, half cat, half devil.

Between gasps he said, "I do not want to hit you!"

She spat in his face.

Her blouse was torn, and quickly he averted his eyes. She laughed at him. "Coward!" she sneered.

He picked her up bodily and threw her down in the hay, then ducked out of the door. The outer gate to the street was locked, so he jumped, caught at the top, and pulled himself up. A bullet clipped the wood near his hand, and he heard the bellow of the pistol. He threw himself over and fell into the street.

A big vaquero was adjusting the stirrup on his saddle. He glanced at the torn shirt, the bloody scratches on Ben's face, and he laughed. "Ah, señor! I have heard of this one! That is a woman, no?"

CHAPTER 18

FROM HIS ROOM in the Arcadia, Ben Cowan went to the offices of General Armijo, only to learn that the General was out. Captain Recalde, despite his wounds, was out also, but he was reported to have gone only as far as the edge of town to interview some peons who had seen some riders. No one remained who had authority to provide Ben Cowan with a horse, and what money he had was insufficient to buy the kind of horse he needed.

His saddle, rifle, and other gear were still at the hotel, and he went back for them now. He settled his bill quickly and carried his gear into the street. The first person he saw as he emerged from the hotel was Rosita Calderon.

She was riding sidesaddle on a magnificent brown gelding, and wore a gray riding habit, her wide skirt spread over the saddle and the flank of the horse. Two vaqueros in buckskin suits and wide sombreros rode with her.

"A horse?" she said. "But of course, señor! You have a horse! Diego bought one for you—a present." She turned and spoke quickly to one of the vaqueros, and the man wheeled his horse and raced away.

"Where will you go now?"

He looked up at her. "I must find those men. They are my responsibility, after all. I must find them and see that the President's treasure is returned, as it should be."

"General Armijo will find them. He is a very good man, the General."

"I know Catlow, and he will do what is not expected of him." Ben Cowan had given a good deal of thought to just what Catlow would do, and he explained as much to Rosita Calderon. Then, seeing her eyes returning to the scratches on his face, he explained that, too.

She laughed. "It is a good explanation. Must I believe it?" Her eyes danced with amusement. "Maybe you were making love to her."

"Do you think a girl I was making love to would scratch that hard?"

She gathered her reins and looked down at him. "I do not know, señor. I know very little of what a girl might do if she were in love, but—I think she would have to love very much, hate very much, or want very much, to scratch like that!"

The vaquero galloped up, leading a brown gelding, the twin of the one Rosita rode—a truly magnificent horse.

"He is yours, Señor Ben. Diego bought him from our ranch as a present to you, who lost your horse in saving his life."

"I was saving my own, too."

"You refuse the horse?"

"Indeed I don't! That's the finest-looking horse I ever did see. No, I'll keep him. I could never refuse an animal as beautiful as that!"

Rosita's eyes sparkled. "It would be safe, I think. Horses do not scratch."

Rosita Calderon looked dashing and lovely on her brown gelding as she smiled at Ben from under the flat brim of her hat. "I think I had better ride along, señor. After all, most of these people you will question know me. Perhaps I can help."

Bijah Catlow, Ben explained, would hit upon the least likely solution; and to escape from Mexico with the treasure, expecting to be pursued, he would be unlikely to take the main trail north toward the border. With a pack train he could not hope to outrun his pursuers.

To go deeper into Mexico to the south would be merely prolonging his task. He might strike for the Sierra Madres and Apache country, or he might strike for the coast. Remembering the Tarahumara Indian, Ben said, "I believe he will try the desert."

Catlow had one great advantage: he knew where he was going. Armijo and Ben Cowan had to discover that... and then Catlow could change his apparent destination.

A quick search of the leather shop and the hidden cellar had revealed nothing that was of help. It was evident that a number of men had been there, but now they were gone. Nobody had seen them either come or go, and nobody had seen them while they were there. Christina was gone, too, and so was a fine black horse known to belong to her.

Riding swiftly, stopping only to ask questions, Ben Cowan rode a semicircle around the northern rim of Hermosillo. He ignored the obvious trails the mule train might have taken, but checked all the minor roads and lanes.

An Indian on the outskirts of town offered the first

clue. He had, he told the vaquero who spoke his language, seen nothing. He had gone early to bed, and today he had been busy . . . somebody had left the gate open and flooded his field.

What did he mean by "somebody"? Ben Cowan's questions soon brought out the fact that when the Indian had gone to bed the night before, his orchard had been dry; when he rose in the morning it was flooded.

Acting on a hunch, Ben Cowan circled the orchard. On the far side he found a mule track, almost obliterated by other tracks, and within an hour he had picked up the trail.

At the desert's edge he drew up. "Thank you," he said to Rosita Calderon. "Now you'd best go back. I'll take it from here."

She held out her slender gloved hand. "*Vaya con dios, señor.*" And then she added in English, "And if you come back to Mexico—come to see me."

He watched her straight, slender back as she rode away, then swore softly and turned his horse into the desert.

Forty mules and a dozen mounted horsemen leave some mark upon the land in their passing; and these did so, despite the efforts of Bijah Catlow to keep the trail hidden. The soft sand of washes, the hard-packed sand of windblown mesas, the shallow streambeds—all these were made use of. But always there was the mule that stepped out of line, that trod on vegetation, or left a hoofprint on the edge of a stream.

Ben was a full day behind them when he reached the Bacoachi and saw where they had dug for water.

He saw the prints left in the sand where the water kegs had stood while being filled, and he studied what tracks he could find, realizing the knowledge might serve him well at a later time. To a western plainsman, a track was as easily read as a road sign.

From Rosita and the vaqueros he had learned about the country that lay ahead of him. He refilled his two canteens, and when he left the Bacoachi it was dusk and he rode swiftly.

There was no need to see the trail here, for the only water ahead lay at Arivaipa Well in the river bottom of the San Ignacio. If there was no water there, eight miles west at Coyote Wells there might be water.

At midnight Ben made a dry camp, watered his horse from his hat, and, after three hours of rest, saddled up and went on. In the graying light of dawn he found a mule. Or what remained of one.

Played out, the mule had obviously been abandoned, and what happened after that was revealed by the tracks and the bones. The mule had been killed, cooked, and eaten.

Ben Cowan studied the moccasin tracks. They were not Apache or Yaqui, and this was the homeland of the dreaded Seri Indians, said to be cannibals, and known to use poisoned arrows. All sorts of fantastic stories were told about them, most of them untrue. It was sometimes said that they were the descendants of the crew of a Swedish or Norwegian whaler or some other ship wrecked on Tiburon a hundred and fifty years before. At any rate, it was clear that the Seris had come upon the mule and eaten it. There had been a dozen or more in the group.

It was mid-morning when Ben cautiously approached the Pozo Arivaipa. The mule train had been there and had watered, and they had left no water in the well. The bottom of it was merely mud.

He hesitated only an instant. Coyote Wells might be dry, too; and to ride there and back would mean sixteen miles with nothing gained in the pursuit. To the north were the Golondrina *tinajas,* where there would surely be water. They were perhaps twenty-four miles away, with other wells fifteen miles or so beyond.

So Ben Cowan rode north, but he rode uneasily, worried by that half-eaten mule. Those moccasin tracks were surely made by the Seris, and they would be somewhere around; if they lived up to the stories about them they would be up ahead, scouting that mule train.

Did Catlow know? The vaquero who told Ben about the Seris had crossed himself when he mentioned them, and that vaquero was a tough man and a brave one. Ben Cowan rode more slowly, studying the country, and taking care to avoid any likely ambush. He could think of a lot of ways to die, but one he particularly did not want was to turn slowly black with a poisoned arrow in his guts.

He had heard many stories about how that poison was made, none of them appealing. Bartlett, who had led the party that surveyed the border between the United States and Mexico along those miles where New Mexico, Arizona, and California adjoin the Mexican states of Chihuahua, Sonora, and Baja California, reported that the Seris obtained the poison by taking the liver from a cow and putting it in a hole with live rattlesnakes, scorpions, tarantulas, and centipedes, then stirring up the whole mass until the creatures exhausted their venom on each other and on the liver. The arrow points are then passed through this and allowed to dry in the shade.

Father Pfefferkorn, who spent many years in Sonora during the earliest times, had a somewhat different story to tell. The poisons, he said, are collected from all those creatures and also from the Mexican beaded lizard, and mixed with the juices of poisonous plants, then sealed in a large earthenware jar so that none of the poison can evaporate. The pot is then placed on a fire under the open sky and cooked until ready for use. The care of this evil concoction was always delegated to the oldest woman, for when the pot was uncovered the vapor invariably killed her.

Thoughts of such tales as these were in Ben Cowan's mind as he rode.

To the north of the route he was following was the Cerro Prieto, the Black Range, so called because it was covered by dark forest. This was a favorite haunt of the Seris, second only to the Isle of Tiburon.

Ben Cowan rode with caution, his eyes continually busy, not only looking for what the desert could tell him in the way of tracks, but searching the horizon, too. In the desert, the careless die...and wherever they are, the reckless die, some sooner, some later. Ben Cowan was neither.

Four miles off to the west, six Seris trotted across the sand. They held to low ground, and they were patient. They knew about Ben Cowan, but they were in no hurry. He was going where they were going, and all in good time they would have him, too. They could afford to wait.

The Seris were of the desert, and the desert can wait.... the buzzard that soars above the desert also knows how to wait. Both desert and buzzard know that sooner or later they will claim most things that walk, creep, or crawl within the desert.

Though the men who drove the mule train were in a great hurry, neither the Seris nor the buzzards were worried. The mule train was marked for death. In fact, death was already among them, and once there, it would not be leaving before its work was done.

Bijah Catlow had seen a mule die...and afterward, another mule.

And now a man was to die...and then more men.

CHAPTER 19

UNDER A HOT and smoky sky the mule train stretched out for half a mile, plodding wearily, heavily, exhausted by the distance, the dust, and the everlasting heat. Contorted by the heat, the air quivered and trembled, turning the low areas into pools of water that beckoned with sly, false fingers of hope.

The sky was blazing with the sun of Sonora; though the sun was masked by the smoke from the fires that burned in the hills, there was no relief from the heat. This was the desert...sand, rock, cactus, greasewood, and ocotillo...and nowhere was there any water.

Bijah Catlow mopped the sweat from his face and blinked at the strung-out train through the sting of the salt sweat in his eyes. He should ride back and make them bunch up; despite all his warnings they did not pay heed to them. It was too far west for Apaches, they claimed, and it was north of Yaqui country; of the Seris, most of them had never heard.

They had watered well at the *tinajas* of Golondrina, but the rock tanks at Del Picu had been bone-dry; so instead of adding another twenty miles to the twelve they had covered, Catlow had turned east toward Pozo del Serna, where there was nearly always water.

Less than an hour ago they had lost the second

mule, and had divided its load between five of the others. At the next camp Bijah planned to bunch the supplies that were left, and so free a mule for packing treasure. Though he had expected to lose mules, he had not expected it so soon.

The Tarahumara trotted up to him as Merridew drew up alongside. The Indian spoke rapidly, using sign talk as well. Merridew glanced from him to Catlow. "What's he say?"

"He says we're bein' followed."

Merridew spat. "Well, why don't he tell us somethin' we don't know?"

"He says it isn't white men—it's Seris. And he's scared."

Merridew looked at the Indian. He did look scared, come to think of it. The Old Man's bleak eyes studied the distance, which revealed nothing—only the dancing heat waves, and faint haze of smoke that hung over everything. But he knew the desert too well to be deceived by the apparent emptiness. If that Indian said there were Seris out there, they were there.

The Old Man's horse, carrying much less weight than Bijah's own, was in better shape. "Ride back and bunch them up, will you?" Bijah said to him. "Tell 'em it's not far to water."

He gestured toward the mountains. "It's up there, maybe three, four miles... Then you come back up here—bring Rio or Bob along and we'll scout those wells."

Catlow watched while the riders bunched the mules, scanning the desert at intervals. He had an odd sense of impending disaster that worried him.

From the slight knoll on which he sat his horse, he watched the Old Man ride up with Rio Bray. The three turned their horses eastward then, and cantered forward toward the dark, looming mountains. The low mountains to the right were bare, but to the left and north the crests were covered with a thick forest of pine.

The springs, when they reached them, lay in the bottom of a branch off a dry wash, surrounded by ironwood and smoke trees. In the trees, birds sang; all else was still.

The Tarahumara came up, drank briefly and then disappeared among the trees.

"If there's anybody around," Catlow said, "he'll find 'em."

Rio Bray stepped down from his saddle and drank, then filled his canteen. "How much farther, d'you reckon?"

"Hundred miles."

Bray indicated the mules. "They ain't gonna make it."

"We'll have to get more."

Bray said nothing, but his expression was sour. Bijah swung down and eased the girth on his saddle, then led his horse to the water. Old Man Merridew was doing the same thing.

Suddenly, Rio swore viciously, and kicked a rock.

Catlow glanced up and spoke mildly. "Somethin' bitin' you, Rio?"

"We were damn' fools to come by the desert! Why, if we'd come up the trail we could have stole fresh animals all the way along! We'd have been nigh to the border by now."

"And have half the country chasin' you? That Calderon ranch has a reg'lar army on it, an' tough vaqueros. Did you ever tangle with a bunch of hand-picked Sonora vaqueros? Take it from me, and don't."

"Halfway to the border and not a shot fired," the Old Man commented. "Don't seem too bad to me."

The mule train streamed into the hollow and the mules lined up eagerly along the trickle of water that spilled down from the springs and then disappeared in the sand.

Rio Bray stalked off, and stopped to talk to Pesquiera. Bijah's eyes followed him. "There's trouble," the Old Man commented.

"Old Man," Bijah said, "if anything happens to me, you take this outfit north to Bisani. There's water there, and the ruins of an old church—good place to fort up if you have to. Caborca's to the east of us, but fight shy of it. You head for La Zorra... about fifteen miles. Less than that distance beyond La Zorra, you come up to the Churupates. There'll be mules waiting there. Follow up the bed of the Rio Seco, then cut for the border and the foot of the Baboquivaris."

"You figured mighty close." Merridew drove the cork into his canteen with a blow of his palm. "Any of the rest of them know that route?"

"No... but stick to it." Catlow took up a twig. "Old Man, there's troops stationed at Magdalena, and we all saw them. By now the troops at Altar have been alerted, too. If we tried to go the way Bray suggested they'd have us in a pocket."

The packs were stripped from the mules, and they were led out and picketed on the grass. Catlow was everywhere, checking their backs for sores, checking their legs and hoofs. Not much farther with this bunch, he realized, but every mile was important now, and every pack.

The Mexican soldier squatted on the sand and put together a small fire. He glanced up at Catlow with an odd expression in his eyes, and Bijah was instantly alert. He raised his eyes and without turning his head or seeming especially interested, he placed every man—all but Pesquiera.

Rio Bray stood up and two of the Tucson crowd were also standing, spread out from Bray.

"I figure," Rio said, "we should go east, up the Pedradas."

"No," Catlow replied quietly, "we'd be walkin' into a trap." His eyes went slowly around the group, pinning each man. *Where the hell was Pesquiera?*

Keleher got to his feet slowly, suddenly aware of a showdown.

"We talked it over," Rio said, "and we've had enough of goin' short on water. We've decided to take off up the Pedradas."

"You've *decided*? Rio, you decide nothing here. What's decided will be decided by me."

Rio's eyes flickered, and Bijah knew where Pesquiera was. On his right, Old Man Merridew held his rifle in his hands. "Go ahead," Catlow said, "you take care of Pesky, Old Man. Rio's my meat."

Rio Bray began to sweat. He looked at Catlow, and suddenly Bijah was smiling. "It's your play, Rio," he said. "You go with us, or you go for that gun."

A few minutes before, Rio Bray had been sure and confident. He had been looking forward to this showdown, and he had Pesquiera for insurance. Now suddenly there was no insurance.

"We're callin' your hand, Catlow," Bray said. "We put it to a vote, and the most of us want to go up the Pedradas."

"Why, now, Rio, you're gettin' mighty democratic about things. You had you a vote, but without me. And I take it, without the Old Man and some others? Well, I want a show of hands. I want the men who want to go by the Pedradas to stand up."

There was a moment of silence and hesitation and then Jake Wilbur stood up. Kentucky and the Greek had already been standing. Nobody else moved.

"All right, Rio. You heard what I said. You go with us, or go for that gun . . . and that goes for all of you." He stood carelessly. "Looks to me like we can almost double our shares right here, Old Man."

Bob Keleher spoke quietly. "Count me with Catlow, boys."

Rio Bray was tense, then slowly he relaxed. "I'll go along, Bijah. No use us shootin' each other to doll rags just when we're all rich."

"What I say," Bijah replied.

Jake Wilbur unrolled his bed and turned in without a word, and after a minute he was followed by the Greek, and then by Kentucky.

Pesquiera's name was not mentioned, and he did not appear.

Afraid to face Catlow after his plan to kill him had failed, Pesquiera drew back in the brush and went to the horses. For a moment he hesitated, wanting to get a muleload of the loot to take with him, but there was no chance of that. Catlow had known he was out in the brush ready to cut him down the moment Rio drew; and when day came, Catlow would certainly call him on it.

Yet there might still be a chance. Ride to General Armijo, claim he had been held a prisoner in his own home, and had escaped. And tell the General where the outlaws were. He might even come out of it with a reward. As for the treasure, he told himself they would have killed him as soon as they reached the border. He believed this because it was what he would have done in their place.

When they saddled up at daybreak, Pesquiera was gone, and no one spoke his name.

Catlow led off before the sun was up, riding due north toward Bisani, which lay twenty-eight water-less miles across the desert. Rio Bray was sullen, and angry with himself. He should have tried for his gun . . . he had been a fool, and this morning his allies of last night held off.

They found Pesquiera's body lying sprawled in the sand less than a mile from camp, with a poisoned arrow through his throat. His face, neck, and the upper part of his body had already turned black with the effects of the poison. He lay there stripped bare. His clothing had been taken away by the Indians.

There was no need to worry about keeping bunched up now. Every man rode with a rifle in hand, and every eye was on the sandhills around them. Bijah Catlow's throat was tight with apprehension. He had never believed the stories he had heard about the Seris. He believed them now.

Mile after mile passed. The Tarahumara ran at Catlow's stirrup now.

They were well clear of the smoke trees and brush when one of the supply mules suddenly reared up, then collapsed in the trail. An arrow projected from its throat.

Keleher started to turn, but Catlow had seen the arrow, and knew that to stop would be fatal. "Keep going!" he shouted, and Keleher swung back to the end of the train.

"Move 'em!" Catlow yelled. "Faster!"

Shouting, and cracking the mules with ropes, they speeded up the train. Catlow and Old Man Merridew galloped back to help Keleher at the drag end of the line.

As they reached the rear of the train, two Indians broke from the sand where they had somehow concealed themselves and ran toward the dying mule, their knives in their hands. Already the nearest mule was a hundred yards from them.

The Old Man raced his horse toward them, and as the Indians leaped up, he fired. The nearest Indian screamed and plunged forward, falling over the dead mule.

Suddenly a dozen Indians broke from the sand within a few yards of the Old Man, and Catlow, slapping spurs to his horse, raced toward them, firing with his Colt. An arrow whipped by his face, and then the Indians were gone, disappearing among the low hills.

Merridew, his face sickly yellow, came up alongside Catlow. "Let's get out of here!" Catlow said.

They had gone less than a mile when Kentucky dropped back from the flank of the mule train.

"Bijah"—he motioned toward the desert to the west—"they're still out there. I just saw one."

Only a few minutes later Bijah saw another, on the other side of the mule train, keeping abreast of it but a good four hundred yards off.

The day grew hot; shadows disappeared. Again the smoke cast a haze across the sun, across the distance where mirage tantalized with its shimmering lakes. The long marches were telling on the horses, and some of the mules were lagging more than ever. The mule train slowed to a walk.

Rio Bray was avoiding Bijah, but he worked as hard as any man to keep the train moving. There was no thought of pausing at noon. They had only one thought now—of reaching Bisani. They had even forgotten General Armijo, and his soldiers who would be riding all the trails, searching for them.

With every mile the danger became greater, but the border drew nearer; and among the weird rocks of the Churupates they would find fresh mules and horses awaiting them, ready for a fast march to the border.

They knew that the Indians were all around them. At times they heard weird calls from the distance, strange singsong sounds from the sandhills. But they saw no one. The Indians never showed themselves, but from time to time their signals to one another sounded across the desert.

Another mule went down, struggled to get up, then stayed down. Ringed by rifles, two of the men stripped the pack and packsaddle from the animal and distributed the load among the others. Then they started on, but only a few minutes later the mule was up and following them on wobbly legs.

Before the first shadow appeared on the eastern flank of a hill, three more mules had gone down—one of them did not rise again.

Now the going was very slow, for all the remaining mules were overloaded.

Catlow rode toward the top of a rise. A coarse stubble of beard covered his face, and his shirt was stiff with sweat and dust. He mounted the ridge, and there, beside the dry bed of Asuncion River, was the ruined church of Bisani. Among the ruins he could see the flickering green leaves of a poplar—almost a sure indication of water.

"Here it is!" he called. "We're safe!"

From behind him came a ragged cheer.

CHAPTER 20

DEPUTY UNITED STATES Marshal Ben Cowan had no need to trace the trail left by the fleeing outlaws and their mule train, for the route was marked by circles of flying buzzards.

From a low ridge crowned with rocks and a clump of elephant trees, Cowan studied the desert before him through his field glasses. He liked the spicy odor of the small trees, and they offered a limited but welcome bit of shade. Nearby the brown gelding cropped at some desert plants.

That the mule train was under attack was obvious. He could hear the distant sound of guns and could see racing horsemen, although where he sat he was too far off for him to identify any individual rider. Nor could he see the attacking Indians.

He watched the fleeing mule train and its accompanying riders. Suddenly a rider went down and others raced to his aid. There was a flurry of shots and white smoke lifting, and then they were racing off again with, he surmised, the rescued man.

The shooting continued, sporadic firing at targets invisible to him. It gave him a strange sensation to sit as at a show and watch men fighting for their lives against a ghostlike enemy. As for the Indians, he had no need to be on the spot to understand their strategy. They were following the mule train like wolves after a crippled animal, attacking, escaping, returning to attack again.

Mounting up, Ben Cowan turned his horse eastward, away from the fight. Obviously, Catlow was pointing toward a destination that could not be far off. Otherwise he would stand and make a fight of it. Topping another rise, Ben saw what they were heading for. Before him opened a wide vista of green fields, long deserted and converted by nature to pasture land. Beyond lay the river, and on higher ground nearby he saw a cluster of ruined walls and arches, and a few trees.

Suddenly, his horse snorted and shied.

Ben looked around swiftly, in time to see a Seri Indian step from the brush and draw his bow. Ben's right hand chopped down and swept up. The gun leaped in his hand and his bullet struck the Indian an instant before the arrow was released. The arrow shot away above Ben's head, and he saw the Indian falling. Abruptly, he leaped his horse between two trees. An Indian rose from the ground in front of him, and Ben saw his face writhe with horror as the forehoofs of the charging horse struck him.

Plunging free of the brush, Ben Cowan saw Indians springing up behind him, and he raced away toward the ruined walls. Even as he rode for sanctuary from the east, Catlow and his mule train came across the abandoned fields from the south. And none of them were prepared for what happened.

Ben Cowan, racing across the fields, caught a glint of sun on a rifle barrel, and with a shock of horror he realized that the fleeing bandits, escaping from the

Indians, were charging into the waiting guns of an ambuscade.

Now he could see them, a dozen Mexicans in wide sombreros crouched behind the walls, rifles ready, and standing over them a woman ... *Christina!*

There was no time to think, no time for a choice. His Colt was in his hand, and lifting it, he fired. The shot struck near one of the waiting Mexicans and he jerked back with an oath just as Ben Cowan leaped his horse over the low outer wall of the enclosure.

The bulk of the ruin was now between him and the outlaws, and he dropped from his horse and, hitting the ground running, dove for shelter among the rocks. But even before he left his horse he had seen the riders from the mule train break stride, and when he hit the ground it was with Catlow's wild yell ringing in his ears.

Someone rushed him and he straightened up suddenly, firing at almost point-blank range into the belly of a charging Mexican.

The man struck him full tilt, and Ben was knocked back off his feet, the Mexican on top of him. All around were roaring guns, stabbing flame, and screams of fear or pain. Above it all he could hear the strident screams of Christina as she urged her men in the fight.

Ben threw off the body of the wounded man and lunged up to grapple with another Mexican. In an instant they were rolling on the ground. Then horses were leaping the walls around him, and the ruins of the ancient mission became a shambles.

Pulling free of his man, Ben saw the fellow grasp the hilt of his knife, and Ben's fist was swinging. The blow caught the Mexican with the knife half drawn, and he hit the ground as if struck with an axe.

And then suddenly the fighting was over. There was the sound of moans, the smell of powder smoke—and Bijah Catlow was grasping him by the hand.

"Man, oh man!" Catlow shouted. "If you hadn't shot to warn us, they'd have mowed us down! You saved our bacon, you old Souwegian, you!"

Old Man Merridew, on one knee behind the wall, fired at a Seri . . . and then there were none in sight.

Cowan looked around him. Christina and four of her hastily recruited Mexican outlaws were prisoners. Three others he saw lying dead on the ground. Two dead mules and a horse lay in the field outside the mission walls, and at least one man—there might be another behind a horse out there. Catlow's force had been cut to seven, including himself. Two horses were standing in the field.

Catlow went to his horse and stepped into the saddle. "Cover me," he said; "I'm going to have a look. Maybe one of the boys is lyin' out there, hurt." And then he added, "While I'm at it, I'll pick up those horses and whatever else."

"I'll ride along," Ben said.

Together they rode out over the field. They walked their horses, and they went warily. There was no cover close by, but the Seris seemed to need none— they could spring from the ground where it seemed no concealment could be.

A man's body was lying half under one of the horses; it was Rio Bray. He had been shot through the skull and through the body.

"He gave me trouble," Catlow said, "but he was a good man to ride with...only bullheaded."

They picked up the guns, gathered the horses and canteens. Beside one of the dead mules Catlow stopped to recover the pack.

"Bijah, why don't you surrender to me? You haven't got a chance, you know."

"What gives you that idea?"

"If Christina could make it here, General Armijo could."

"Nothin' doin'. Anyway, we ain't out of this fix yet. There's no water inside those walls, and there's plenty of Indians outside."

Back within the walls, Catlow dismounted, and glanced around at the loafing men. "All right—get busy. First off, you strip the gear from the horses and mules and give each of them a rubdown. Work on 'em good. We may have to run for it to get out of here."

"How far to the border?" Keleher asked.

"As the crow flies? Eighty miles. Rough miles, if you ask me....Next, you boys clean your guns. Scatter around the walls and keep a sharp eye out. We ain't fresh out of Indians, you can bet."

Bijah took his hat off and wiped the sweatband, and dropped to a seat with his back against the inner wall of the ruined church. Under his breath he whispered to Cowan.

"Ben, if you get shut of this place, I've got a mess of horses waitin' in the Churupates, about thirty miles northwest o' here. Nobody knows but me an' the Old Man. Horses and mules."

They sat there quietly. Nearby were the prisoners,

and three wounded men—one of Catlow's and two of the bandits recruited by Christina.

"I'd watch that one," Ben said, with a slight gesture toward Christina. "She's got no more conscience than a rattler, and she's just as mean."

"Her?" Catlow laughed. "That there's quite a girl. You just seen the wrong side of her."

Then he grew serious. "Damn it, Ben, why didn't I tell Cord the truth? That there's a woman, you know?"

"I think so."

"If I ever get out of this . . ."

"You'd have to go straight."

"Who'd want it any other way? Anyway," he said, "just let me over the border and I'll buy her a piece of Oregon she couldn't ride across in a week."

He got up and delegated some of the men to sleep while others kept watch. There was no cover close to the ruins except on the side of the riverbank, and even then, not much. Then he returned to the place near Cowan and, without another word, stretched out and in a moment was asleep.

Ben Cowan sat beside him for a few minutes, considering the situation. There was no telling how many Indians were out there—there might be few or there might be many. But now the Indians had their chance to bottle them up good.

He glanced at the cottonwoods. There ought to be water here. Had the monks who had lived in this place gone to the river for their water? It did not seem logical. There had been trouble with the Seris in their time, too; and though at first the Seri Indians had yielded many converts, later they had left the fold, perhaps with reason, and had become relentless foes of the Spanish.

Ben got to his feet and slowly scouted the ruins. At one point, in a hollow not far from the wall, he saw a low place where the grass grew thick and green. He went to the packs and got a shovel, and returned to the spot.

Outlining a space about four feet in diameter, he sank the spade in. For several minutes he dug, but the earth was dry. Nobody came near him, and when he had the hole down two feet he put the shovel aside and went back to Catlow. He was still asleep.

Two of the men had started fires, and one was making coffee, the other broiling some mule meat. Nobody spoke to Ben, and he went over to where Christina sat. Her wrists and ankles were tied and she shot him a venomous look, but he merely smiled.

"I should have killed you!" she said.

"You tried," he said. "I'll say that you tried."

He squatted on his heels beside her. "You shouldn't have come," he said. "None of us may get out of this alive. Those Seris, they can wait. They can wait for weeks if they want to—we can't." He paused for a moment, then added, "There isn't food enough—even if we could get water."

Then he left her and returned to the hole and dug again for several minutes. At the end of the time the bottom looked the same.

When he went back to the place by the wall, Catlow had left it. The men had exchanged places, and those who had been on guard slept. Catlow came toward him, a cup of coffee in one hand, and strip of jerked beef in the other.

"Never fancied mule meat. Apaches like it better than beef." He bit off a chunk of the beef and worked at it seriously for several minutes.

"Old Man, he was a mountain man—trapped with Carson, Bridger, and them. He says the best meat of all is puma—mountain lion. Says Coulter told him the Lewis and Clark men preferred it to all other meat. He tried it many a time, swears it's best."

When he had finished eating, Catlow cleaned his rifle and reloaded it, and Cowan did the same. Neither man talked much, and from around the walls the low murmur of conversation was slowly petering out. Not a man but expected an attack. They could not guess whether it would be a screaming rush out of the darkness, or a creeping menace, sliding ever closer to the walls under cover of darkness.

Seated against the wall, Ben Cowan tried to compose himself for sleep, but the face of Rosita as he had last seen her kept coming into his thoughts. And when sleep came Rosita was still in his mind.

Darkness fell, the fires died . . . a sleeping man muttered, and somewhere a coyote howled.

Ben Cowan woke with a start, and for a moment he held himself perfectly still. Never in his life had he awakened as he had now, filled with such a sense of dread.

He lowered his hand for his gun . . . and it was not there.

CHAPTER 21

HE LAY STILL, sorting out the situation in his mind. Carefully, he felt around on the ground, but he was sure the gun had not fallen of itself, but had been taken from his holster. The gun was gone.

He sat up, careful to make no sound. Bijah might have taken it, but that he doubted. Or one of the others might have done it, knowing him for a United States marshal. Yet that, too, he doubted.

The pistol was gone, and his rifle was gone, and whoever had taken them must be incredibly light-fingered. *Christina?*

He got to his feet, and stood listening. The night was still, incredibly still, when one came to think of it.

No one but Bijah had slept near him. Ben's eyes grew accustomed to the night, and he stepped over to where Bijah lay. He bent over him, shaking him gently. Bijah was instantly awake.

Bending down, Ben whispered, "You got your gun?"

Bijah's hand moved, felt. "No! What the—"

"Ssh!" He leaned closer. "Mine's gone, too. Where's Christina?"

Together, they stepped to the break in the wall. All was dark and still. A man turned and muttered in his sleep.

Bijah went quickly to where Christina had been left, Ben Cowan close behind him. *She was gone!*

The other prisoners were gone, too.

Swiftly, silently, the camp was awakened. Every man had been stripped of his guns. The two sentries were dead—they had been strangled. Old Man Merridew had been struck over the head, apparently as he awakened.

Crouching together, every man realized what must have happened. Christina had freed herself, then her men. And then she, moving with the softness of a cat, had gone from one to the other, stripping them of their guns. The Old Man had started to wake up and had been struck; the guards had undoubtedly been strangled without ever realizing what was happening.

"Now what?" Keleher asked.

"The Seris," someone said, "they'll be comin'."

"That's what she figured," Bijah said quietly. "Oh, she's a smart one! When the soldiers found us, we'd all be dead, killed by the Seris . . . the loot gone. And they'd never even look for it again, figuring the Indians had it."

"Look funny, us dead with no guns," one of the men said. "Hell," said another one, "they'd bring those back and scatter them around! And they'd take off with the loot, scot-free!"

"That ain't the question," Bijah interrupted. "Them Seris'll be comin'. We've got to fight."

Ben Cowan spoke up. "Maybe they won't come. Gather all the fuel you can. Get some fires going."

"Huh?" Bijah looked up at him in amazement.

"Indians are puzzled by anything they don't understand—hell, anybody is! So we build fires and we keep them going all night. We make noise around, lots of confusion so they don't know exactly what's happening, and maybe they'll hold off. Meanwhile, we rig any sort of weapons we can find that will help us fight them off."

Bijah went immediately to the remains of the fire, stirred the coals, then put on fuel. Dead branches and brush lay about, and there were two dead trees. All these were gathered. A second fire was started, and in a few minutes the flames were a roaring blaze.

All of the men but one had knives. Bijah had a derringer he had kept as a hideaway gun. Several of the men began making spears whose points they hardened in the fires. Loose bricks and stones were gathered. Some of the men slipped off their socks—a stone in the end of a sock could be used for a club.

Meanwhile they shouted, sang, banged sticks together, and ran back and forth, never stopping where they might offer a target. It was a mad, unbelievable sight, but the men caught the spirit of it and it soon became almost a game. Wild yells rang out, shrill cowboy yells, and Indian warwhoops.

When the stars began to pale, Bijah spoke to the men. "All right—saddle up and load up. We're goin' to ride out of here."

"Them Indians are out there!"

"Sure they are. But have they ever attacked us close up? We'll ride out of here carryin' sticks to look like guns. We'll ride out with our loot and we'll head northwest. We'll ride like hell the first few miles to get ahead of the Indians, then we'll troop along for a ways, then ride hard again. There'll be fresh horses waiting for us when we get there."

"Don't forget," Merridew said, "that woman is out there with her men and our guns."

"How could I forget that?" Bijah said bitterly. "We'll just have to gamble on her."

Their water supply was scanty, and suddenly Ben thought of the hole he had dug. Turning, he went to the corner of the enclosure, and there it was—filled with water! Not enough for them all, but enough to water the horses and some of the mules.

They waited until almost daylight for more water to seep into the hole, and it did come in, but not very rapidly. By the time they were ready to move, there was enough to water the rest of the animals. The men themselves would have to get along on whatever water they had in their canteens, and it was precious little.

They rode out of the walls in a close bunch, down into the streambed and across it. Once on the other side, Bijah gave the word and they rode out at a rapid clip.

They saw nothing, they heard nothing. Morning lay gray upon the landscape. A light breeze drifted across the desert, played fitfully among the cactus, and died out. Carrying their sticks like rifles, the small band kept up the pace.

With Ben Cowan added to Catlow's band, there were eight of them. Catlow's wounded man was able to ride, and to some extent, to fight. There was also one wounded man from Christina's group, the other one having died during the night. Pancho, the Mexican who had brought the news to Catlow in Tucson, had proved one of the best men he had.

After galloping the horses for almost a mile, Bijah

slowed down to a trot. There was no sign of the Indians. The Seris had never shown any indication that they would attack a ready and courageous enemy, but if the least sign of weakness or fear was indicated they would attack like madmen. That they were out there watching them, neither Ben nor Bijah had any doubt.

They kept on, and gradually the ground began to rise. When they reached a comparatively level place, all but the wounded dismounted and walked their horses to rest them.

Ben swore softly at being without a gun. He carried a bowie knife, but that was good only at close quarters. He knew that if once the sharp-eyed Seris detected that the riders were without rifles they would attack. They would not need to come to close quarters; they could stand off fifty or sixty yards and shoot them down with arrows.

"Where d'you suppose that woman got to?" Bijah said suddenly. "How'd she manage to slip out without them catching her?"

But Ben had no answer to this.

The day wore on, the sun climbed higher in the sky, the dreadful Sonora heat came upon them. The last of their water went to the wounded, and miles yet lay before them. The exhausted mules slowed and wanted to stop, but they drove them on ruthlessly. Now they could see, looming above the mirage, a far-off peak. "The Churupates," Bijah said, and they rode with hope.

Ben Cowan's mouth was dry and his head ached from the heat. He loosened his shirt buttons, and squinted his eyes against the salt of the sweat on his face. The good brown gelding went steadily on, but now and then a heavily laden mule staggered.

The wounded Mexican muttered in delirium, and moaned for water, but now there was none to give him. Dust rose in their faces, heat waves shimmered before their eyes. Around them grew creosote bush and cactus, along with the ever-present ocotillo. Otherwise the desert was empty.

Mules stopped and had to be whipped to move them along, for to stop here, whether the Seris attacked or not, meant death. They plodded through a weird hell of cactus and heat, a world in which nothing seemed to exist but themselves.

Suddenly off in the distance toward the east, Ben saw a column of riders. "Look!" he cried.

"Five of them," Bijah said bitterly. "That's Christina."

"We've fooled them, too," Ben said after a moment. "They think we've got rifles. If they didn't, they would move in and shoot us down."

"Maybe you're right."

"I don't think so," the Old Man said wryly. "We're headin' for somewhere, an' she's got an idea what it's for—horses and mules. We're safe until we get there, because she'll need that stock as bad as we do."

The miles unwound behind them. The wounded Mexican raved and screamed hoarsely, crying and begging for water. A mule went down, and they shifted its pack to the others and moved on, leaving it lying there.

Bijah Catlow mopped his chest and swore, turning his eyes toward the distant mountain. The Mexican, Pancho, caught his shoulder and pointed excitedly at a dark loom of cloud beyond the mountain. "*Tiempo de agua!*" he shouted.

"Hell," Bijah said, "he's right! This here's beginnin' the rainy period. Last of July, through August and September, it rains nearly every day. The trouble is, they're just local rains and may not reach us at all. If you've got any influence upstairs, Ben, you'd better pray. We're goin' to need that water before we make the Churupates."

The cloud mounted rapidly, and in the distance thunder rumbled. The far-off cloud was split by a streak of lightning. A faint, cool breeze stirred the desert, and the animals staggered on.

Bijah carried his derringer almost all the time now, ready in his hand so it could be used immediately. Twice Indians had appeared not far off.

Ben was scared, and he admitted it to himself. No gun—only a knife, and the Indians closing in. Once it dawned on the Seris that they were unarmed—and if they got closer they could see that—they would be upon them.

That distant peak of the Churupates seemed no closer. But the wind blew a cooling breath from off the mountains, and the horses perked up, and the mules, too.

Thunder rolled continuously now, lightning flashed, and the wind blew harder. And then the rain came. It came with a rush, the dreaded *culebra de agua*, or water snake, which will flood villages, devastating the countryside. They scrambled across a dry wash and up the other side, and behind them came a rushing turmoil of water that filled the wash.

Holding in a tight bunch, they pushed on. Once

they stopped to allow the animals to drink a little at one of the pools on the desert. The animals seemed to have gained new strength, but the lashing rain and roaring thunder wiped out everything but the storm itself and the driving necessity to go on.

For more than an hour the rain came in a veritable cloudburst. Then it eased off, although it continued for almost two hours more. Finally it eased away, leaving the desert drenched and cool. When the clouds cleared, the Churupates were just ahead.

Bijah Catlow had fallen behind, and Ben lagged behind with him. As the outlaws and their mule train crossed the hill that was the beginning of the Churupates, Ben rode out on one flank to push a mule back into the herd. He heard a clatter of hoofs and looked around to see Catlow disappearing up an arroyo, driving several of the mules ahead of him. He hesitated only a moment then wheeled his horse and rode after him.

He could have gone no more than a hundred yards when the arroyo branched, and the light was too dim to see tracks. Catlow and at least four mules had vanished. Cowan hesitated, chose the wrong arroyo and, after riding a short distance, started back. Bijah was waiting for him in the main arroyo when he reached it.

Only when he was abreast of him could Cowan see that Catlow was grinning. "Fooled, weren't you?" He chuckled. "I believe in a little insurance. The way our luck's been runnin', I don't trust that place up there."

They rode over the hill, then around a bluff. There, in a hollow among the hills of the Churupates was a ruined cabin and a small corral. At pasture in the hollow were the mules and horses awaiting them. But there was something more.

The last light of day showed the scene in the hollow, though against the far wall it was dark. In the center were the outlaws, their hands lifted; around them and all around the hollow there must have been at least two hundred horsemen . . . Mexican soldiers.

Instantly, Ben Cowan whipped the cuffs from his belt, and before Bijah could grasp the situation, snapped one around his wrist, the other around the pommel.

"What the hell!" Bijah burst out in a fury. "You damned Judas, you'd—"

"Shut up, you hotheaded fool!" Ben said quickly. "You're my prisoner—unless you'd rather rot in a Mexican jail, which you justly deserve."

Bijah started to open his mouth to speak again, then he closed it tight. After a minute, he said, "You damned fool," but he said it with affection.

CHAPTER 22

"YOU UNDERSTAND, OF course," General Armijo said coolly, "we need not let you have these prisoners?"

"I understand," Cowan replied. "Of course, they were my prisoners. I was bringing them in—and the treasure."

"So it seems—and, of course, we do have the treasure. Or most of it. You lost several mules, my scouts report."

"There was no opportunity to recover the treasure," Ben Cowan replied, honestly enough. "And not much of it was lost."

Armijo stood up. "We have much to thank you for," he said quietly, "so the prisoners shall be yours. It was your warning that alerted us, and the treasure was recovered by you. Also, there is the matter of Captain Recalde, whose life you saved."

"It was little enough to do."

Armijo thrust out his hand. "Very well, señor. *Vaya con dios!*"

Ben Cowan went down the steps and into the street. His prisoners, roped together, stood waiting for him. The two Mexicans stood to one side, under separate guard.

He went to them. To the Mexican who had ridden with Bijah, he said, "I could do nothing for you, although I tried. Nor for you," he said to the other. "You are Mexican nationals, and I had no claim upon you as prisoners."

Pancho shrugged. "It is nothing, señor. It is the way of fortune. The Army or prison, does it matter?" He smiled. "I think it will be the Army. I am a good soldier, and the General, he knows this. He will say much, there will be the guardhouse, but then I shall be a soldier again. You will see."

Ben Cowan checked his pockets for money. Little enough was left. "I'm taking you boys back on the stage," he said to the men, "but all I can do is pay your fare to Tucson. If you eat, you'll have to feed yourselves."

"I'm wearin' a money belt," Bijah said, "an' you might as well help yourself. What's the fare by stage?"

"Ten dollars per head, from here."

"I'll pay my own way. If I'm headin' for jail I might as well go in style."

They could see the church at Fronteras for some time before they reached the town. The church was built on the very brow of a hill, with the town scattered around it, and the houses—most of them ruined adobes—were built along the side of the hill.

When the stage rolled into town, Ben Cowan stepped down and looked around carefully. The first person he saw was Rosita Calderon.

On this day it was a black horse she rode, an animal as fine as the brown. Her white buckskin skirt was draped over its side. Her yellow silk blouse showed off her olive skin, and her black hair and eyes to striking effect.

"How did you get here?" he asked, startled by her unexpected appearance.

"We have a ranch near Fronteras, and I came north with my father. It is much faster by carriage, and on the main trail."

The cramped prisoners had slowly been unloading from the stagecoach. All wore handcuffs.

"If we can be of assistance, my vaqueros are nearby," Rosita said.

"Thanks, no. All we want to do is eat and keep rolling."

Her eyes were enigmatic. "You leave Mexico, then?"

"I must take them back."

"I—we shall be sorry to see you go. You have many friends in Sonora."

He looked up at her. "It is time for me to go. If I were to remain, I might forget that I am only a man with a horse and a gun."

"My ancestor," she said quietly, "who first came to Mexico, came with Cortez. He was only a man with a horse and a sword . . . he founded a family."

Ben hesitated, for he was a man of few words, and unaccustomed to women. "I am a gringo," he said, "and the badge I wear is all I have."

"In New Mexico," Rosita said gently, "I have a cousin, whose name was Drusilla Alvarado. She married a gringo who wore a badge . . . she is very happy, señor."

Ben Cowan looked down at his boot toes. He looked up the street and down the street, and then he looked up at her, and thought nobody had ever lived who was so beautiful. He said, "I'll come back."

He turned quickly toward the restaurant, then stopped and looked around. "And I won't be gone long!"

He led them all inside and seated them and ordered bull beef for them, with frijoles and tortillas and plenty of coffee. He had no appetite himself. He just sat there staring out of the window.

Bijah Catlow looked at him. "Ben, I swear I never saw the like. The most beautiful girl in Sonora, an' you almost muffed it! I'd a notion to slug you!"

"Shut up," Ben said, politely.

When he had herded them out to the waiting stage he felt for the derringer. That hideaway gun he had taken from Bijah was the only weapon he had . . . but he would need no other for these men as long as he was in Mexico. They all knew what would happen if they escaped in Mexico, and were captured again.

They were handcuffed two by two except for Bijah, and on him Ben had leg irons as well. Bijah was rather proud of them and kept showing them off. "Figures I'm a dangerous man," he would say, grinning. "Either that, or mighty fast afoot."

It might have been the last thing he ever said. He said it to a girl and her mother who were also waiting for the stage, and when he said it he was not looking around. That was why he did not see the man standing on the corner some fifty feet away.

"I told you," the cold voice cut in, "that I'd choose the time."

Bijah turned around and looked at Miller, who was standing there with a gun in his hand, and he was smiling.

If Miller saw the girl on the horse who rode slowly

down the street toward them, he paid no attention. She was a stranger, and he had no reason to think of her.

Ben Cowan stepped out on the street, and Miller had reason to think of him, but Ben wore no gun-belt, and there was no gun tucked into his waistband. Ben thought of the derringer in his pocket, useless at the distance, and for the first time he knew what despair was. He had been frightened in his time, but he had never known despair; but he knew the sort of man he faced, and Bijah was in irons and helpless, and so was he, without a gun.

Miller knew it. "You too, Marshal? Well, why not?"

Rosita Calderon had grown up on a cow ranch, and the horse she rode was a good cutting horse that was a fast starter. She touched him with a spur and he lunged into a dead run from a walking start. His powerful haunches seemed to squat and he was off, charging like a bullet.

Miller saw her, but his attention was concentrated on the men before him. If he thought anything, it was only that she was somebody trying to get out of the way.

"Ben!"

At the cry, Miller's eyes turned briefly. Ben reached up and snared the flying, shining object that came spinning toward him. He caught it in mid-air, as he had caught many a gun doing the border shift, and the .44 Colt struck his palm solidly, his fingers closing around it. He saw the startled fear in Miller's eyes, and saw flame burst from the muzzle of Miller's gun, and then Ben Cowan was walking in firing. He must, at all costs, keep Miller's gun on him. Not a shot must be fired at Catlow, who could not fight back.

Miller was a cornered wolf. He felt a bullet smash his hip and he went down; felt a bullet whiff past his head. He took dead aim and saw dust leap from Ben Cowan's jacket.

Then he felt a violent blow on the skull and he fell back against the porch post, to which he clung, a blazing light in his brain. Squinting his eye, he lifted the gun and felt something smash into his chest, drawing a clear thread of pain through him. His gun hammered into the dust, and he watched the tiny spurts of dust leap from the street in front of him. He kept on clinging to the post with one arm and holding the gun with the other, and he had no idea that he was dead.

Ben Cowan swayed on his feet, and a curious weakness in his knees made them give way. He fell forward, losing his grip on the silver-plated, ivory-handled gun.

For a long moment there was silence in the street, and then Bijah Catlow shuffled forward and, stooping, went into Ben Cowan's pocket for the keys to his irons. First he unfastened the handcuffs, then the leg irons. Then he took up the silver-mounted gun and holstered it.

When he looked up he looked into a Winchester in the hands of Rosita Calderon. It was aimed right between his eyes, and he knew she would shoot.

"Ma'am," he said, "you don't need that. We're goin' to fix this gent up, you an' me, and then we're all goin' over the border so he can turn us in."

He unpinned the badge from Cowan's chest. "I'll just wear this here and appoint myself deputy, so it'll all be official."

———

BEN COWAN WAS looking out of the window for a long time before he realized it. His eyes had opened on a sunlit vista; a lace curtain was stirring gently in the softest of breezes, and he had a feeling of tremendous comfort and complete lassitude such as he had never known before.

The bed was the biggest bed he had ever slept in, and it was the first time he had ever looked out a window with lace curtains.

When he had been lying there for some time watching horses playing on the green field, the oddity of it began to worry him. What could he be doing in such a place? What had happened to him?

Behind him a door opened and when he turned his head he looked into a pair of wide, startled black eyes. He heard an astonished squeal and then the middle-aged Mexican woman was running away, calling to someone.

When he looked around again at the sound of footsteps, he looked into the eyes of Rosita Calderon.

He rolled on his back, clasped his hands behind his head, and smiled up at her. "First time I ever received a lady, lyin' in bed," he said.

A faint flush showed under the olive of her skin. "Maria," Rosita said, "you had better see to him yourself. I think the señor is recovering more rapidly than we expected."

He was sitting up eating a bowl of soup when Bijah Catlow came in. He was wearing the badge.

Cowan looked at it skeptically. "Where'd that come from?"

"It's yours," Catlow said cheerfully. He shoved his hat on the back of his head and hung his thumbs in his belt. "Figured it would look better, me takin' your prisoners over the border to turn them in."

"You took them over?"

"Sure did."

"Who'd you turn them over to?"

"Well"—Bijah's forehead wrinkled with an expression of mock worry—"that there part bothered me some. I didn't rightly know who to turn them over to, so I went to sleep studyin' about it; and you know, when I woke up they were gone! The whole kit an' kaboodle of them!"

Ben ate soup in silence.

After a minute, Bijah said quietly, "So far's I knew, you had nothing on them, anyway. Not in the States. When they got away it was down near Pete Kitchen's place. I figured the only prisoner you really had anything on was me. And here I am."

Ben finished his soup. "Bijah, I'm going to be here a while. You give me that star, and you ride to El Paso and turn yourself in to the office of the U.S. Marshal there. There's a man there temporarily at least, and he'll handle your case. You do that, d'you hear?"

"Sure." Catlow unpinned the badge. "Liable to get myself shot wearin' that, anyway."

Two weeks later, while Ben Cowan was sitting on the porch at the Hacienda Calderon, Rosita placed a letter in his hand.

El Paso

Dear Ben:
I take pen in hand to inform you we are all
pleesed to heer you are comin along fine.
Abijah Catlow, on the Wanted List, showed up
here and said you said he was to turn himself
in. He done it.
He also handed us your report on Miller. He
also handed us a paper from Miller's pocket
locatin the Army payroll stole by Miller. Most
of it recovered.

Yrs. Trly,
Will T. Lasho, Dep.

P.S. Catlow broke jail. Aint seen hide nor
hair of him.

The first came a year later, from Malheur County,
in Oregon.
It said simply: *We named the first one Ben.*
And down Sonora way a boy rides the range whose
name is Abijah.

About Louis L'Amour

*"I think of myself in the oral tradition—
as a troubadour, a village taleteller, the man
in the shadows of the campfire. That's the way
I'd like to be remembered—as a storyteller.
A good storyteller."*

IT IS DOUBTFUL that any author could be as at home in the world re-created in his novels as Louis Dearborn L'Amour. Not only could he physically fill the boots of the rugged characters he wrote about, but he literally "walked the land my characters walk." His personal experiences as well as his lifelong devotion to historical research combined to give Mr. L'Amour the unique knowledge and understanding of people, events, and the challenge of the American frontier that became the hallmarks of his popularity.

Of French-Irish descent, Mr. L'Amour could trace his own family in North America back to the early 1600s and follow their steady progression westward, "always on the frontier." As a boy growing up in Jamestown, North Dakota, he absorbed all he could about his family's frontier heritage, including the story of his great-grandfather who was scalped by Sioux warriors.

Spurred by an eager curiosity and desire to broaden

his horizons, Mr. L'Amour left home at the age of fifteen and enjoyed a wide variety of jobs, including seaman, lumberjack, elephant handler, skinner of dead cattle, miner, and an officer in the transportation corps during World War II. During his "yondering" days he also circled the world on a freighter, sailed a dhow on the Red Sea, was shipwrecked in the West Indies and stranded in the Mojave Desert. He won fifty-one of fifty-nine fights as a professional boxer and worked as a journalist and lecturer. He was a voracious reader and collector of rare books. His personal library contained 17,000 volumes.

Mr. L'Amour "wanted to write almost from the time I could talk." After developing a widespread following for his many frontier and adventure stories written for fiction magazines, Mr. L'Amour published his first full-length novel, *Hondo,* in the United States in 1953. Every one of his more than 120 books is in print; there are more than 300 million copies of his books in print worldwide, making him one of the bestselling authors in modern literary history. His books have been translated into twenty languages, and more than forty-five of his novels and stories have been made into feature films and television movies.

His hardcover bestsellers include *The Lonesome Gods, The Walking Drum* (his twelfth-century historical novel), *Jubal Sackett, Last of the Breed,* and *The Haunted Mesa.* His memoir, *Education of a Wandering Man,* was a leading bestseller in 1989. Audio dramatizations and adaptations of many L'Amour stories are available on cassettes and CDs from Random House Audio publishing.

The recipient of many great honors and awards, in 1983 Mr. L'Amour became the first novelist ever to be awarded the Congressional Gold Medal by the United States Congress in honor of his life's work. In 1984 he was also awarded the Medal of Freedom by President Reagan.

Louis L'Amour died on June 10, 1988. His wife, Kathy, and their two children, Beau and Angelique, carry the L'Amour tradition forward with new books written by the author during his lifetime to be published by Bantam.

The Official

LOUIS L'Amour
Web Site

WWW.LOUISLAMOUR.COM

Visit the Home of America's favorite storyteller

Louis L'Amour Community

Join other Louis L'Amour fans in a dynamic interactive community

Discussion Forum

Guest Book

Biography Project

Frequently Asked Questions

About Louis L'Amour

Exclusive materials and biography written by Louis' son Beau L'Amour

"A Man Called Louis" an exclusive video interview

Photo Galleries

Articles

Great American Tradition

Whether you are new to the thrilling frontier fiction of Louis L'Amour or are one of his millions of die-hard fans, you'll feel right at home at www.louislamour.com!